PENGUIN BOOKS

The Lioness

Katherine Scholes was born in Tanzania, East Africa, the daughter of a missionary doctor and an artist. She has fond memories of travelling with her parents and siblings on long safaris to remote areas where her father operated a clinic from his Land Rover. When she was ten, the family left Tanzania, going first to England and then settling in Tasmania. As an adult, Katherine moved to Melbourne with her film-maker husband. After working there for many years, writing books and making films, they returned with their two sons to live in Tasmania.

Katherine's internationally bestselling novels have been translated into numerous languages. She is especially popular in Germany and France, where she has sold over two million books.

katherinescholes.com

Praise for Katherine Scholes

The Hunter's Wife

'Beautifully written and a crowd-pleaser.' *Herald Sun*

'*Out of Africa* meets *White Mischief* in this classy romance . . .
A bittersweet, entertaining mix of Hollywood, obsessive love and the
unbearable longing for what is not possible.' *Australian Women's Weekly*

'Captures the very essence of East Africa . . . one of Australia's most
respected women's fiction authors.' *Courier-Mail*

The Rain Queen

'. . . a big, sensuous, splendid novel . . .' *Overland*

'Moving and inspiring.' *Australian Good Taste*

'Utterly bewitching.' *The Independent* (France)

'A magnificent portrait of a passionate woman, a superb romantic saga.
The Rain Queen takes us into the spectacular landscape of Africa,
to discover an unknown magical world.' *Elle* (France)

'With the subtlety of Doris Lessing for the depiction of feminine nature
and the vision of Karen Blixen in bringing alive a continent of dark
ancestry and ancient cultures, the author of *The Rain Queen* has given
us an intense vision of grief, solitude and the comfort of strangers.'
L'Express (France)

'Disturbing and enthralling – an authentic African voice, exotic and
magical. An amazing book. Fabulous reading.' *Madam Figaro*

'This most moving book, whose every breath is a love-song for Africa and her people, is a faultlessly woven cloth.' *Le Monde*

'3 out of 3 stars.' *Le Tribune*

'A superb novel . . . wonderful reading.' *Woman* (Germany)

'Beautifully written, lively and sympathetic . . . an adventurous and highly entertaining read.' *Bookshow* (Germany)

The Stone Angel

'Scholes crafts her fiction with such care and subtlety.' *Weekend Australian*

'A truly absorbing book filled with secrets and conflicts.' *Woman's Day*

'A beautifully descriptive read and a soul-searching take on human relationships.' *New Idea*

'Scholes shows a rare ability to understand people in their specific geographical context and find within them the great surging passions of humanity.' *Sunday Tasmanian*

'Full of passion, fine writing and interesting observations about the way potent events that help shape one generation have an impact on the next. Wonderful stuff.' *Australian Women's Weekly* 'Book of the Month'

'Scholes has masterfully captured those fateful moments that can change the course of many lives. *The Stone Angel* touches the senses with its rich descriptions of coastal Tasmania and emerges as a lovingly crafted account of a home we can never run away from.' *Good Reading*

Katherine Scholes

The Lioness

PENGUIN BOOKS

PENGUIN BOOKS

Published by the Penguin Group
Penguin Group (Australia)
250 Camberwell Road, Camberwell, Victoria 3124, Australia
(a division of Pearson Australia Group Pty Ltd)
Penguin Group (USA) Inc.
375 Hudson Street, New York, New York 10014, USA
Penguin Group (Canada)
90 Eglinton Avenue East, Suite 700, Toronto, Canada ON M4P 2Y3
(a division of Pearson Penguin Canada Inc.)
Penguin Books Ltd
80 Strand, London WC2R 0RL, England
Penguin Ireland
25 St Stephen's Green, Dublin 2, Ireland
(a division of Penguin Books Ltd)
Penguin Books India Pvt Ltd
11 Community Centre, Panchsheel Park, New Delhi – 110 017, India
Penguin Group (NZ)
67 Apollo Drive, Rosedale, North Shore 0632, New Zealand
(a division of Pearson New Zealand Ltd)
Penguin Books (South Africa) (Pty) Ltd
24 Sturdee Avenue, Rosebank, Johannesburg 2196, South Africa
Penguin (Beijing) Ltd
7F, Tower B, Jiaming Center, 27 East Third Ring Road North, Chaoyang District, Beijing 100020, China

Penguin Books Ltd, Registered Offices: 80 Strand, London WC2R 0RL, England

First published by Penguin Group (Australia), 2011
This edition published by Penguin Group (Australia), 2012

1 3 5 7 9 10 8 6 4 2

Text copyright © Katherine Scholes 2011

The moral right of the author has been asserted

Cover design by Cathy Larsen © Penguin Group (Australia)
Text design by Debra Billson © Penguin Group (Australia)
Cover photographs: female hiker by Mark Newman/Lonely Planet Images; Mt Kilimanjaro courtesy Shutterstock
Author photograph by Marc Burlace
Typeset in Fairfield by Post Pre-Press Group, Brisbane, Queensland
Printed and bound in Australia by McPherson's Printing Group, Maryborough, Victoria

National Library of Australia
Cataloguing-in-Publication data:

Scholes, Katherine
The lioness / Katherine Scholes
9780143566618 (pbk.)
Lions – Fiction
Missing persons – Fiction
Mothers and daughters – Fiction
Tanzania – Fiction

A823.3

penguin.com.au

In respectful memory of George Adamson

ONE

Northern Tanzania, East Africa

Angel grasped the camel's tether, giving it a sharp pull to check that the knot she'd tied around the tree trunk was still firm. The camel lowered her head and nuzzled gently at the girl's ear. Angel smiled, reaching over to pat the rough-haired neck. She looked across to the shady spot where she'd put down the milking bowl. The sight of the rich frothy milk – so white against the dark wooden rim – reminded her how hungry she was. She went quickly to release the camel's calf, who was straining at his own tether nearby.

As soon as she untied him he rushed over to his mother, nudging impatiently at her udder. The older camel took no notice of him. Nor did she seem bothered by the weight of the bags and blankets loaded onto her packsaddle. She was only concerned with reaching for the tender leaves that grew at the ends of the thorn tree's branches. Closing her thick lips around them, she snapped them off and folded them into her mouth.

'You're a greedy thing, Mama Kitu,' Angel said. She smiled then at the calf, who grunted as he drank. 'And so are you, Matata.'

Turning away from the camels, Angel retrieved the bowl of milk. Grasping it with both hands, she picked her way down a slight slope towards a rocky outcrop. Her feet were bare, but she moved unflinchingly over the scattered sharp stones. Nearing the rocks, she paused, looking down over the desert plains. It was still early and the sun was low on the horizon. Rays of light slanting through dusty air painted the land with colour. The sands were gleaming yellow. The rocks were gold-edged, topped with pink, and the shadows between them made ragged patches of deep mauve and brown.

Lifting her gaze to the distant horizon, Angel traced the shape of the pyramid mountain that stood overlooking the plains. The slopes were a hazy blue, the peak dusted with white lava that looked like a cap of snow. It marked the direction in which they were headed, Angel knew. All day, as they rode, it would be there in front of them, set between Mama Kitu's furry-edged ears.

Ol Doinyo Lengai, the Maasai Mountain of God.

Rounding the last of the rocks, Angel walked over to where her mother sat cross-legged on the ground, beside a large flat stone. The stone looked so much like a table, it seemed almost to have been placed there, inviting travellers to stop and enjoy the view. Laura was dressed in a plain cotton tunic and trousers, like Angel, but she wore a patterned scarf wrapped around her head. She was leaning forward, swishing flies away from some flatbread and dates that had been laid out on the stone.

Angel held out the milk.

'Thank you.' Laura lifted the bowl to her mouth and drank.

When she lowered it, her lips were edged with froth. 'No grit,' she said approvingly.

'I made sure no sand got in.'

'You did well.'

'That's because I'm not little any more,' Angel said. 'And look . . .' She stretched her mouth into a wide grin, waggling a loose front tooth with her tongue.

Laura leaned to examine the tooth. 'You should let me pull that out.'

'No,' Angel shook her head.

'You might swallow it,' Laura warned. 'Then the tooth fairy won't come.'

Angel looked puzzled. 'What's a tooth fairy?'

Laura picked up one of the flatbreads and offered it to Angel, along with the bowl of milk. 'Back in England, parents tell their children that if they put a tooth under their pillow, fairies will take it away in the night and leave money instead.'

'Did you do it?' Angel asked. 'Did they come?'

'Sometimes,' Laura replied. 'Not every time, though.' As she spoke, she dragged off her headscarf. It was a piece of *kitenge* cloth, once brightly coloured but now faded, the edges frayed and torn. Her long hair – the same straw-blonde as her daughter's – reached down past her shoulders. It hung stiffly, laced with dust. After raking it back with her fingers, she retied the scarf, tucking loose strands of hair in under the cloth. Then she glanced at Angel's face. 'What's wrong?'

The child was frowning. 'We don't have any pillows.'

'I wouldn't worry too much – I don't think they have tooth fairies here, anyway.'

Angel narrowed her eyes thoughtfully. 'I think they do.'

Laura smiled. 'Eat up, now. We won't be stopping again for a while.'

As Angel bit into the bread, Laura stood up. She pointed towards the mountain. 'The *manyata* is right at the edge of the plain. We have to get there by nightfall.'

'Maybe they've killed a goat,' Angel said. She spoke through a mouthful of bread, scattering crumbs from her lips. 'We might have meat stew.'

'No, they aren't expecting us,' Laura said.

Angel looked up at her mother, a flicker of anxiety in her blue eyes. 'Maybe they won't let us in.'

'They will. The chief is the brother of Walaita. When we tell him who we are, and show him the gifts she asked us to take to him, he'll be glad to welcome us.'

Angel got to her feet. She followed Laura's gaze, still fixed into the distance. 'Tell me again,' she said. 'Tell me what we're going to do.'

Laura rested her hand on Angel's head as she replied. 'We're going to bring Mama Kitu and Matata safely into the *boma* with all the herds of the tribe. Then we'll put up our tent outside the house of the chief.'

'But we aren't staying there.'

'No, tomorrow we'll leave our camels behind at the *manyata* – then we'll walk to the waterfall. We'll wait there until we can get a ride to the main road.'

'Who will give us a ride?' Angel danced with excitement as she awaited Laura's reply.

'*Wazungu*. Safari people. Women with sunglasses and pink lipstick. Men with big cameras.'

Angel giggled. 'And what else will they have?'

'I really can't remember.'

'And what will we do at the main road?'

'We'll catch the bus to the city,' Laura said.

'The city.' Angel breathed the words softly. 'We're going to the city . . .'

'But if we don't keep moving, we won't be going anywhere.' Gathering up the remains of the food, Laura gestured for Angel to bring the milk bowl. Then she headed up towards the camels.

Angel followed her, swinging the bowl on a piece of sisal string that was looped through a hole in its rim.

She'd only taken a few steps, when she heard a yelp of surprise. Looking up, she saw Laura standing very still, staring at some bushes not far from her feet. Something about the way she just remained there, motionless, made Angel uneasy. She ran towards her, clutching the bowl to her chest.

'Careful,' Laura called. 'There was a snake – but I'm pretty sure it's gone now.' She looked pale, shaken. 'I felt something. I think I've been bitten.'

She pulled up the loose cloth of her trousers, baring her left leg. Halfway up the calf, two tiny red dots could be seen. Angel stared into Laura's face. Her mother's eyes were wide with fear.

'I hardly even saw it,' Laura said. There was a tremble in her voice. 'It was so quick. Then it was gone . . .'

'You have to lie down,' Angel said. 'If you get bitten by a snake you can't walk around.'

Laura dragged in a long breath, then forced it slowly out. 'Yes, that's right.' She lowered herself to the ground, trying not to move her left leg. Snatching off her scarf, she tried to undo the knot, her fingers fumbling uselessly.

After a few seconds, Angel took the scarf from her and worked the knot free before handing it back. Laura began winding the cloth tightly around her leg, starting from below her knee and working down towards the bite marks.

When the scarf was tied in place, Laura and Angel looked at the wounds again. The skin around them was beginning to swell slightly.

'Does it hurt, Mama?'

'Not much,' Laura answered. 'Hardly at all.' She let out another long breath. 'Maybe it wasn't a dangerous snake. I don't know what kinds they have in this area.' She looked down at her leg. 'Maybe it was a dry bite. Sometimes the snake has already used up its venom when it bites. Sometimes they don't get a chance to inject it properly. It was very quick.' She smiled reassuringly at Angel. 'I think we should just keep moving. I can put my leg up along the saddle and hold it still.'

Angel nodded. 'We should get to the *manyata*.'

'Yes,' Laura said. 'That's what we have to do.'

Angel ran up the slope to the camels. She was glad they'd only stopped here for a quick rest break – if she'd had to pack up camp and load all the bags on her own, it would have been a long time before they could leave. Instead, it took only a few minutes to untie Mama Kitu and lead her down towards Laura. Angel drew comfort from the rhythmic plodding of the camel's feet. Mama Kitu was a good camel – the kind you could trust. Even when she was in season,

she never kicked or bit her owners. She could
being hobbled, and she was always easy to ca
reached the place where Laura was lying f
Mama Kitu instantly obeyed Angel's signal for her

Matata, unsettled by the tension in the air, skittered restlessly around his mother. Angel tried to shoo him away, afraid that he would step on Laura.

'Go away,' she called to him, waving her arms. He took no notice. 'Go away. Get out!' she shouted again. Her voice echoed in the stillness. She began to breathe quickly, panic rising.

'It's all right, Angel. It's going to be okay. I need you to stay calm, now. You have to help me.'

Angel recognised the tone in Laura's voice. This was how her mother spoke when she was working. Her voice was so steady and firm that the person who heard it felt stronger. Angel nodded, willing herself to become brave.

After Laura had eased herself into position on the folded blankets that made a pad over the saddle, Angel climbed up in front of her, holding the rope that was tied to Mama Kitu's halter. Laura held on to Angel as the camel rose, grunting, to her feet. Then she leaned back on one of the bags, her leg stuck forward and resting on the wooden frame. Angel had to keep one leg raised a bit to leave her room, but was still able to keep her balance.

As they moved off down the slope, Laura gasped in pain. Angel looked back over her shoulder.

Laura gave her a small smile. 'It'll be easier when we're on flat land.'

ıama Kitu made her way down the hillside, then they travelled over sandy ground that was flatter, but still scattered with rocks and dotted here and there by stunted trees. Angel stared ahead, towards the edge of the plains. Each step they took was a step closer to the *manyata*. She imagined arriving at the village. There would be people there to help – but what would they do? It all depended, Angel knew, on how dangerous the snake was, and how much poison it had put into its bite. She remembered the herder from the village by the river, who had been bitten by a viper. He'd lain in his hut for days, moaning with pain. He'd survived, in the end. But plenty of people had died from snakebite. Everyone knew that. It was why people made sure they killed any snakes that came to live near their homes.

Angel felt a surge of anger at this thought. Why hadn't Laura been more careful? Ever since Angel could remember, her mother had nagged her about things like tucking in mosquito nets properly, not paddling in water unless you could see that it was flowing, and checking where you were about to put your feet, especially if you weren't wearing sandals.

'What do you want to do in the city?' Laura's voice broke into her thoughts.

Angel swallowed, her gaze fixed on the distant mountain. 'I don't know.'

'Come on,' Laura said. 'Think of something.'

Her voice sounded normal, now, and Angel began to relax. 'I want to . . . see a roundabout. A big one with flowers growing in the middle and a statue.'

Laura laughed softly. 'And what else?'

'I want to buy an *aiskrimu* from a man with a cart.'

'Me, too. I want an ice-cream and . . . a new dress.'

Angel smiled, recognising the shopping game. 'I want to buy an ice-cream, a new dress . . . and a school uniform.'

'But you don't go to school,' Laura protested. 'You do lessons with me.' Her voice sounded thin, but carried clearly over the soft thudding of the camel's feet.

'I still want one. Then I'd look the same as the other children,' Angel argued. 'Anyway, that's what I've chosen.'

She waited for Laura to continue. In the quiet, small sounds seemed large – the squeak of leather rubbing against leather, the water gourds clinking together, the fluting song of the weaver birds. Angel turned to look over her shoulder. With a jolt of panic she saw that Laura was gasping for breath. She had fallen further back against the bags. As Angel watched, she began to slip sideways.

Angel yanked at the halter rope and yelled at Mama Kitu to sit down. She tried to hold Laura in place as the camel lurched to her knees, then dropped her haunches. But her mother's body was heavy, and limp. As the camel settled on the ground, Laura slid down onto the sand.

She lay there, still struggling to breathe. Beads of sweat appeared on her forehead and upper lip.

Angel stared at her, rigid with fear. 'It did bite you! It poisoned you!'

Laura licked her lips. 'Angel. Listen. You have to leave me here and go to the *manyata*. The healer will have the black stone. They will send someone back to help me.'

'I don't want to,' Angel said. She knew she sounded like a younger child – the kind that still asked to be carried on someone's back.

'You have to do what I say,' Laura said gently. 'But first, get my bag.'

Angel untied a well-worn leather satchel from Mama Kitu's saddle and carried it round to her mother's side. As she crouched there, unbuckling the straps that held the top closed, she felt a flash of hope. Many times she had seen Laura reach into this bag and produce whatever was needed to solve a problem. Maybe there was some medicine in here that would help. Inside the satchel, Angel's hand hovered over a big plastic bag of white tablets. 'What do you want?'

'Get my money pouch. I want my passport.'

Angel searched her mother's face, wondering if she was speaking with the madness of a fever.

'Please,' Laura murmured.

Reaching into the bottom of the satchel, Angel found the money pouch. Feeling inside it, she located the hard edges of the passport and pulled it out.

Laura moaned. Her eyes were half-closed and squinting, as if she were struggling to focus. 'Put it in your pocket. Don't lose it. Ask the chief to take you to the game warden in the national park. Show him this, and tell him I am your mother. Then people will know who you are.'

Laura closed her eyes. Angel watched her for a while, waving away the flies as they landed on her skin. She was breathing more easily – but she still looked tired and pale. Perhaps she just needed to rest, Angel thought. Then she would feel better, and they could continue on their way.

Angel looked at the passport, lying in her lap. She didn't understand why Laura wanted her to keep it in her pocket, and not in the satchel. Or why she'd told Angel to show it to the game warden. He would be an important man, like all the government officials – but why would he be interested in the passport? As she sat there, frowning in confusion, the last thing Laura had said came back to her.

Then people will know who you are.

Angel stared at the motionless figure on the ground, as the real meaning of the words slowly dawned on her.

Laura was not hoping to be rescued.

She wanted Angel to ride on to the *manyata* – and she did not expect to see her daughter again.

Angel's mouth felt dry and her stomach twisted inside her. Another thought came to her, then – the memory of something Laura had said one day, to some friends from the fig-tree village. Angel prodded Laura's shoulder, then shook it. Laura's eyes opened, meeting her gaze.

'The black stone doesn't work,' Angel stated. 'You don't believe in it.'

Laura's eyes grew shiny with tears. 'No.'

'Are you going to die?' Angel asked quietly.

A small sob broke from Laura's lips. She opened her mouth, but gave no answer.

Angel just sat there, looking into Laura's eyes. In that moment, their shared gaze, locked together, was the only reality. Angel felt it could go on forever, if only she didn't move. Then a spasm of pain came over Laura's face. Angel wished there were something – anything – she could do to help. She grabbed the hem of her tunic and used it to wipe the sweat from Laura's clammy brow. Then she dabbed at the beads of moisture on her upper lip. The small gestures made her feel calmer. And as she brushed Laura's skin, trying to be as gentle as a butterfly landing on a flower, she was reminded of the way Laura had cared for Walaita, the sister of the chief. Only a few weeks ago, Angel and her mother had been sitting at the woman's bedside in her dim, smoky hut. Everyone knew she was soon going to die. Cancer had spread through her body.

'I can promise you this,' Laura had said, taking Walaita's hand in hers. 'I will be with you until the very end.'

Even in the faint light of the hut, Angel had seen the relief that had swept over Walaita's face.

Angel lifted Laura's hand and held it gently.

'Don't be afraid, Mama,' she said. 'I will be with you until the very end. There will always be a lamp kept burning. The night will never be completely dark.'

Laura smiled. Tears, leaking from the corners of her eyes, ran back over her temples into her tangled hair. 'I love you, my Angel. You are so . . . brave. But you can't stay here. You must go.' Her words came in bursts, between gasping breaths. 'I'm not afraid of death. You know that. I'm afraid for you. Being left alone out here. You have to take Mama Kitu and Matata—'

'No!' Angel broke in. 'I won't go.'

Laura shook her head helplessly. 'Don't be stubborn. Please. Not now . . .'

Matata chose that moment to approach. He circled Mama Kitu, trying to get her to stand up so that he could feed. Then he began nudging Laura's face and body.

Angel pushed his head away. She would have to move the two camels, she realised, if Laura was not to be disturbed. After taking down the water gourd from its place on the saddle, she called Mama Kitu back to her feet, and led her – with Matata following, as he always did – across to a thorn tree. After tying the lead rope to one of its limbs, Angel returned to Laura. Bending over her, she poured water between her lips. Laura managed to swallow.

'Good.' Angel nodded to herself. It was important for a sick person to drink. It was always important to have enough water.

Angel could feel the heat of the sun as it rose in the sky. There were several spindly thorn trees growing nearby, but she knew that it would not be possible for her to drag Laura into the shade of even the closest of them. But not far from Laura's head, there was a big rock, about as high as Angel was tall. Opening the leather bag, Angel pulled out a *kitenge* printed with pink and brown birds on an ivory background. It was the one Laura always used cover her head when they entered a Muslem village. Angel managed to secure one end to the rock, by piling stones on top of it. Then she draped the rest of the cloth over Laura's body. It was like a badly hung mosquito net, offering no protection to her legs and feet. But at least Laura's face and body were now shielded from the sun.

Angel stood back to view the canopy with a sense of pride. Laura often told her how capable and useful she was. She said it was because Angel spent so much time helping Laura with her work. And also because Angel had grown up living in villages where young children took care of the herds instead of going to school, and if their parents were sick, or dead, they were responsible for looking after babies and toddlers as well. 'You're like an African child,' Laura had told her daughter. Angel liked to think of herself this way, and it made her try even harder to be strong and sensible.

Before climbing in under the canopy, Angel pulled up Laura's trouser leg. The knee was now swollen and red. The taut flesh bulged out where it met the tightly wrapped scarf. Angel bit her lip, wondering if she should undo the cloth. It looked so uncomfortable. But Laura had tied the bandage so carefully that Angel decided it should stay.

Angel sat by Laura's head. Light filtered through the canopy, throwing a rosy hue over her mother's face. She looked almost healthy, except for the greyish saliva that leaked from the corner of her mouth. Angel kept wiping it away, but it soon reappeared.

Time seemed elastic, moving slowly in one moment, but then speeding up. It felt like only a short while since she and Laura had been riding towards the *manyata*, talking about the things they wanted to buy in the city. But then, Angel discovered that her periodic sips of water – one for her, and one dribbled into Laura's mouth – had almost drained the gourd. Soon, Angel would have to get another water bottle from the collection tied to Mama Kitu's saddle.

She looked out over the hot, dry land. The pastel-toned light of the early morning had given way to a harsh glare. The sand and the rocks had returned to their real colour – shades of grey. Even the green of the trees and bushes was lost beneath grey dust. The only spots of colour were the bright pink desert roses that sprouted from strange-looking bushes with no leaves.

Angel was gazing blankly over the ashen land, when Laura suddenly stirred. The girl swung round, fixing her eyes on her mother's face. Laura was frowning. Her lips were moving. She looked like someone struggling to swim up from the depths of a murky pool – straining towards the light. 'Angel?'

Her voice was urgent. Angel leaned over to reply. 'I'm here, Mama.' She waited for Laura to speak again, but no words came. She began to stroke Laura's hair, taking care to avoid snagging her fingers in the tangles. Laura had often done this for her, when she'd been ill with a fever. There was a song that followed the movement of the hand. As the tune and the words came back to Angel, she began to sing, softly.

Lala salama mtoto. Sleep now my little one. When you awake you will see . . .

There were lots of verses – each one describing the animals, the birds and the people that would be a part of the baby's life. Angel sang through all the verses, then started again at the beginning. As Laura's breath became hoarse and ragged she just kept on stroking, singing.

Tears ran down Angel's face, salt creeping into her mouth. Soon she was sobbing and singing at the same time, but she did not stop. If she kept singing, she told herself, Laura would keep breathing.

But even as she sang, she could hear the breath becoming shallow. The gasping giving way to a whisper. Then just the faintest of sighs.

Angel froze, her fingers still buried in Laura's hair, the thick strands damp with sweat and gritty. Holding her own breath, she waited. But all she heard was the stirring of wind in the bushes, and the distant call of a raven.

Slowly she lowered her face, resting her cheek on her mother's chest. Closing her eyes, she strained to hear a heartbeat. But there was only silence. Stillness. Nothing.

A gust of wind tugged at the canopy, rippling the cloth. Before long, the end of the *kitenge* pulled free of the stones that had anchored it to the boulder. Angel grabbed it, just as it was about to be swept away. She hugged the cloth to herself, seeking the faint perfume that lingered there. Frankincense – Laura's smell. She knew she had to get Mama Kitu and Matata and head for the *manyata* while there was still enough daylight for the journey. But she didn't want to move. She had the sense, again, that if she just stayed still, time would be frozen. The world that she knew would remain.

Reaching into the pocket of her tunic, she took out the passport. She knew what was inside the little book – she'd been allowed to look at it from time to time, as long as she put it away afterwards. Usually she turned straight to the page with the small photograph of Laura – it was interesting to see her looking so different, with tidy hair, cut short, and wearing lipstick and a necklace like one of the safari women. Now, Angel barely glanced at the picture, or at the collection of pretty inkpad stamps with their mix of colours and patterns. She flipped to the very last page of the passport. Leaning over it, she read the words that Laura had written there by hand.

James Kelly, 26 Brading Ave, Southsea, Hampshire, England.

James was Laura's brother, Angel knew. He had never been to Africa, so Angel had never met him. He sent a present to her once, though – a doll that was beautiful, but so fragile no one could play with her. Laura had suddenly started talking about him one day. Angel had been younger, then, but she remembered the conversation clearly. They'd been sitting on the concrete floor of the verandah at the Sisters of Mercy, waiting for some supplies.

'He's not married and has no children,' Laura said. 'He lives in a beautiful big house near the sea.'

There was a serious expression on her face. Angel began to feel uneasy. 'Why are you talking about him?' she asked.

'If anything ever happens to me, James is the one who will look after you. I asked him to make a promise that he would – because you have no *Baba*, and no *Bibi*; no father and no grandmother.'

Angel sat quietly, painful thoughts and images filling her head. 'If something happens to you,' she said eventually, 'I'll look after myself. I'll be like Zuri.'

'It's not the same for white children,' Laura said. Her voice was gentle but firm. She opened her mouth to say more, but Angel stood up and turned her back on her. She felt sick inside, and afraid – but angry as well. She didn't want to hear Laura talking like this; she didn't want to imagine something bad happening to her mother, or to picture what would then happen to her. She'd taken just a few steps away when some words came into her head. It was a saying she'd learned in the village. She went back and quoted it to Laura. 'Misfortune has sharp ears. If you call his name, he will come.'

Laura had never mentioned the subject again.

Angel gripped the passport tightly in her hands as she looked down at Laura's handwriting – her eyes fixed on the last of the words, shaped in thick black ink. *England*. Angel had heard stories about England from Laura. It was a place where everyone had lots of money and children spent their time playing inside with toys. People lived in cities with good hospitals, but there were many more strangers than friends. There were cars instead of camels . . .

Angel let the stiff covers of the booklet fall shut. She rested the passport on the palm of her outstretched hand, as though trying to judge its weight. Then she hurled it away, watching as it flew through the air and landed between two rocks, a small dark red shape resting on the grey sand.

Folding her legs, she hugged her knees to her chest. She let her head fall, resting her forehead on her bony kneecaps. She felt tired and empty, as if her own life had been drained from her body.

She imagined staying here forever. Just her and Matata and Mama Kitu. Her family . . .

Suddenly, from nearby, came the sound of flapping wings. Then the faint rustling of a large bird shaking out its feathers. Even as Angel lifted her head, a second bird glided to the ground.

Angel stared at the vultures. They were ugly birds, with hooked beaks and hooded eyes. Their scrawny plumage always made them look sick, as though a lifetime of feeding on carrion had left the whole species diseased.

Jumping to her feet, she ran towards them. '*Nendeni! Nendeni mbali!* Go! Go far!'

Both birds spread their huge wings and rose into the air. But then they settled again, only a short distance away.

Angel looked back to where Laura lay on the ground. More vultures would gather, she knew. And it would be impossible, in the end, to scare them away. Angel looked across to the camels. If she could somehow manoeuvre Laura up onto Mama Kitu, she could take her to the *manyata*. But the vultures would not be deterred, Angel knew. They'd swoop down onto the camel. Even Mama Kitu would panic and bolt.

As Angel watched, a third bird came and landed on Laura's chest. Angel ran at it, waving her arms. But like the other vultures, it only retreated a little way, taking up a position on the rock.

Quickly, Angel spread out the *kitenge*, wrapping one end over Laura's feet and pulling it up towards her head. She faltered, for a moment, as she drew the cloth towards the face. With one hand, she brushed back a strand of hair that clung to Laura's cheek. A tear fell from her eye, splashing the pale skin. She covered the face, smoothing the cloth over its contours. Then she began to gather stones and pile them onto the shrouded shape.

The heat of the day had begun to wane, and there were plenty of stones to be found – but still, the work was hard. The rough volcanic rock felt like sandpaper against Angel's skin. As she reached towards each stone she had to check for scorpions and snakes. And the birds kept clamouring around her, sidling towards the makeshift grave. But eventually there was no more cloth to be seen. The last remnant of Laura's favourite cloth was gone. Angel piled on even more stones to make sure the grave was secure.

The vultures unleashed a frenzy of flapping and screeching, as if this final step had caused an outbreak of fury. Angel froze, still crouched over the mound. Vultures sometimes attacked people, she knew. Maybe not an adult, fit and strong. But a small child, unable to defend itself . . .

You are not small, a stubborn voice whispered in her head. *You are older than Zuri, who goes out to the cattle posts on his own. And you are stronger than him, too. You always beat him in a fight.*

Grasping one of the rocks in her hand, Angel got to her feet, and turned to face the vultures.

They were not looking at her. The hooked beaks were all pointing in the same direction – away to her right. She followed their gaze, a new fear rising in her as she saw what it was that had disturbed them.

Fisi. Hyena.

There was a whole pack of them. They were still some way off, but were coming quickly towards her with their strange loping gait. The one at the front let out a long whoop that sounded like a crazed laugh.

Over by the thorn tree, Matata bleated in alarm. Mama Kitu's head rose up, high and anxious. Angel looked from the hyenas to the camels, wondering whether to leave the shelter of the rock and run across to them. Mama Kitu would soon kick them away.

She wasted precious moments trying to decide whether she

could make it in time; she didn't want to be caught out in the open between the rock and the camels. Then the hyenas were at the grave, growling and coughing as they sniffed at the rocks. Angel watched them in horror. The biggest one must have been injured in a fight. Something pink dangled from a wound in its neck. Slowly, it turned its mangy head towards her. The laugh came again, an eerie sound that rose high at the end – a vicious sneer, with a question in its tail.

Angel grabbed Laura's satchel and swung it towards the animal's head. There was a dull thud as the solid leather connected with a furry skull. The hyena recoiled, but then pushed forward again, baring its teeth.

The other hyenas closed in upon her, their rank smell tainting the air. Angel was mute with fear. She swung the bag again and again. The animals howled in anger, but only backed off a few steps before creeping forward once more. Finally Angel cried out, her voice wrenched from her throat.

'Mama! Mama!' The words came instinctively to her lips, even though she knew there was no one to answer her call. 'Mama. Mama . . .' Her voice broke into a sob. 'Please. Help me.'

She was dimly aware of the camels bellowing, their voices sharp with panic. The air was thick with noise. There were the close-up sounds of breathing and sniffing coming from the hyenas. The excited squawks of the vultures watching on. And a high, thin wail – like the cry of a newborn baby – that seemed to be coming from her own mouth.

Without warning, another sound broke into the melee. A loud deep roar. It rolled out over the land like a wave, sweeping aside all in its path. The hyenas pricked up their ears, turning their blunt-nosed faces towards the plains.

A lioness was approaching, bounding over the sands. She moved with a long stride, her hide rippling in the afternoon sun. Soon, she was drawing close. When she reached the flat stone where Laura and Angel had eaten breakfast, she paused. Tipping back her head, she roared again, showing off huge teeth and a long pink tongue.

Angel stared at her. At the edges of her vision she saw the hyenas slinking away. The big one stood its ground for a while, scraping the ground with its back feet and snarling. But as the lioness drew closer, it turned its head and crept away.

A cracking sound made Angel look up towards the camels. Mama Kitu was rearing in terror, the limb of the tree to which she'd been tied now swinging from the lead rope and hitting against her legs. As Angel watched, the camel lunged away up the slope, Matata following behind.

Angel pushed herself back against the rock as the lioness walked towards her. She knew nothing could save her now. She pictured the bloody carcasses the butcher hung from the tree outside his village shop, the white fat and red flesh all spotty with flies. Her heart raced with terror, her breath snagged in her lungs. But then, a thought came to her. She would die here, like Laura. She would not have to live on. With a sense of calm, she closed her eyes and waited for the lioness to come.

A dense quiet closed in around her. She listened for the sound of the animal's feet, padding towards her, but heard nothing beyond the usual chatter of birds and humming of insects. She began to wonder if the lioness was going to leave her alone. But then a dank musky smell entered her nostrils. Seconds later, warm breath brushed her face. She opened her eyes. The lioness was standing right in front of her. The pale brown chin and muzzle were already stained with fresh blood. Angel watched, numb with fear, as the jaws parted, exposing black gums, sharp teeth, a curled pink tongue. A low noise began deep in the lioness's throat. But instead of erupting into a roar, it rose into a soft high call that lingered in the air like a note from a song. Angel's lips parted in surprise. Raising her eyes, she met the lion's gaze. For a long moment she was held by a clear golden stare. But then, from somewhere in her memory came Zuri's voice. 'Never look into the eyes of a wild animal unless you want to start a fight.' She bowed her head and turned it to the side. Watching the lioness from the corner of her eye, she saw the mouth opening again. Next, she felt the dry rasp of the long tongue, licking her cheek.

The song-call came again – this time it was even softer, almost a murmur. As Angel stood, her limbs clamped rigid with tension, she sensed movement behind the lioness. Cautiously shifting her gaze, she saw a fluffy spotted cub. It looked up at her with round yellow eyes, the lids neatly lined with black. A second cub appeared; then a third. The lioness ignored them. She took a step away from Angel. She seemed to be waiting for her to react. When Angel remained unmoving, the lioness lowered her tawny head and nudged her with her nose. When this had no effect, she pushed at Angel again.

Angel side-stepped along the rock. When she was standing in open space, the lioness moved in behind her. In fear and confusion, the child stumbled forward. The lioness followed her up the slope, past the broken tree where Mama Kitu had been tied up, and on. The three cubs milled around her feet, touching wet noses to her toes.

When they reached the brow of the hill, the lioness came up next to Angel. The two walked side by side. Angel lifted her head, watching her step. Instinctively, she sensed that she had to be careful not to trip over. She must not fall down like someone weak and useless. She must look brave and strong. She swung her arms, and forced her shaky legs into a steady walk. The late-afternoon sun shone from behind her, casting the shadow of her slender body over the earth. Shadow cubs played around her feet and the shadow lioness was next to her, strolling, strong and fearless, over the land.

TWO

Emma leaned forward in her seat, searching the dusty track that stretched away into the distance. It was bordered on both sides by low-growing bushes, mounds of rock and yellow clumps of dried-out grass. Here and there a thorn tree rose up, spreading a canopy of patchy shade. It was not yet nine in the morning, but the day was already hot. Emma's damp shirt clung to her skin.

'I think we should be there by now,' she said to the driver.

'We will find it very soon,' Mosi replied. 'Do not worry.'

He braked without warning as they came to a deep pothole. The Land Cruiser slid sideways in a patch of sand and Emma grasped the metal dashboard. Mosi turned the steering wheel hard, bringing the vehicle back onto the gravel.

They entered a stand of candelabras. The giant cactus trees clustered in close, towering over them. Emma looked up at the fluted blue-green limbs, each lined with rows of sharp spikes. They were beautiful, in a way – but it was a tough, harsh beauty, in keeping with the rest of the sun-ravaged landscape. She turned her gaze back to the narrow track, winding ahead. Gradually the cactus trees became more widely spaced. Then they petered out, the country becoming open again.

Suddenly, Mosi pointed to a large sign on the left-hand side of the track. The bushes had grown up, partly obscuring the writing, and the paint had almost completely peeled away. But Emma was just able to pick out the words. *Olambo Fever Research Project.*

She stared at the sign until it disappeared behind her. Then she shifted in her seat, tucking her shirt back into her jeans. She released her dusty hair from its band, did her best to smooth it back, and retied it into a ponytail. Finally she took her lip salve from her pocket and ran it over her lips.

The track led them round the side of a small hill. Emma searched the countryside on either side. She felt a surge of excitement, mixed with apprehension. After all these years, she was nearly there. Then at last she saw it: a small building with a flaking whitewashed façade, standing out starkly against the grey earth speckled with yellow grass.

'It is good that we are about to arrive,' Mosi said. He pointed at the instrument panel. 'The engine is becoming hot.'

Emma leaned to see the temperature gauge. The needle had risen almost into the red area. Mosi tapped the small circle of glass with his finger, but the needle didn't move.

When they came to a standstill, dust enveloped the Land Cruiser. Emma waited for it to settle before climbing out, bringing her green leather shoulder bag with her. Puffs of fine grey sand rose up as she planted her feet on the ground. She felt grit collecting on her face, sticking to the film of sweat and sunscreen. Catching sight of her reflection in the wing mirror she bent down to check her appearance. In the dust-clouded glass, her dark hair and eyes contrasted starkly with her fair complexion. She wiped a smudge of dirt from her cheek and adjusted her collar. Straightening up, she pulled her shirt away from her back. There was moment of coolness as air washed over the damp skin.

Mosi stood at the front of the vehicle, opening the catch to the bonnet. 'I must check the radiator straight away.'

'I'll go and see if anyone's there,' Emma said. She had a tense frown on her face. She'd received no reply to her letter. Judging by the state of the sign, the place could well be locked up, abandoned. But still, she told herself, even if she could not go inside, she would be able to look in through the windows.

As she set off along the track, she heard the squeak of the Land Cruiser's bonnet being raised, then a hiss of steam escaping from the radiator.

She looked ahead at the building. It seemed out of place, standing there all alone, as if it belonged in another setting. Only the high wire fence that protected the yard behind it seemed to anchor the structure to the land. Beyond the tin rooftop, the sparse grasslands continued, dotted with stones and the occasional thorn tree. There were anthills as well – strange lumpy towers made of red earth. Emma's step slowed as her eyes were drawn to the horizon. A mountain rose up there – a perfect triangle of vivid purple, set against the hazy blue sky. She traced its outline. It looked like a volcano. She thought, suddenly, that if Simon were here he'd be able to tell her the whole story of this land, explaining how every detail of its long lifetime could be read in rock, stone and sand. But he was about as far away from Emma right now as it was possible to be.

She walked quickly on. As she came closer, she took in a set of concrete steps leading up to a deep verandah. There was a green painted door, with a single barred window on either side. The whitewashed walls were badly stained and the tin roof was patterned with orange rust.

'Hello?' Emma called out. The only sounds were the buzzing of insects and the thin wail of a bird as it wheeled overhead.

She headed down the side of the building to the back and peered through the wire mesh fencing. The rear wall of the building was shielded from view by a water tank. She looked around the yard – a large square of grey earth. There were a few makeshift outbuildings made from corrugated iron. A sagging washing line ran between the roof and a leaning pole, but there was no laundry drying there. A garden plot, marked out by painted stones, had long been abandoned; even the weeds had died. Parked near the gate was a Land Rover that looked so ancient it seemed unlikely it would ever move again.

Returning to the front door, Emma walked up the steps and knocked. The solid timber swallowed the sound. She tried the handle. With a gentle grating sound, the door swung open.

She jumped back as a chicken ran out between her legs and flapped away along the verandah. Then she stepped inside. She was in a narrow hallway, breathing air that smelled of wood-smoke and cooking. At the far end, light entered from the open back door. A person was sitting on the step, facing out to the yard. At first, the figure was just a silhouette, but as her eyes adjusted to the light Emma caught an impression of black hair and skin; broad shoulders;

strong muscles moulding the sleeves of a white T-shirt. She hesitated for a second, then called out again. 'Hello? Excuse me?'

In a single fluid movement the man got to his feet and turned around. He had bare feet and was wearing long khaki trousers. Against his chest he held a small animal – a lamb with a red, curly coat. Freeing one hand, he pulled a set of iPod headphones from his ears.

For a moment, the two just looked at one another. Emma registered the man's even features, a purple scar high on his forehead, eyes that were almost black in the dim light of the hallway; he was not a teenager, and not yet middle-aged, she guessed, but somewhere in between. Then she looked at the lamb resting in his arms: four spindly legs and a broad flat tail hung down over his T-shirt; the fuzzy-topped head nestled in the crook of his elbow.

'This little one has been sick,' the man said. 'But now she is ready to go back to her mother.' He nodded towards a brown beer bottle with a baby's feeding teat attached. 'She has drunk a lot of milk.'

Emma smiled. 'She's beautiful.' In response to her voice, the lamb opened her eyes. They were bright and clear.

'Can I help you?' the man asked. 'Are you lost?' He spoke English easily, with a light African accent.

'No, I'm not lost. I'm looking for the person in charge here.'

'There are only two of us working here – my assistant and me. I am the veterinary surgeon in charge of the research project. My name is Daniel Oldeani.' He shifted the weight of the lamb to free his right hand, which he held out to her, palm up.

Emma shook his hand – it felt awkward, as though they were

each miming a slightly different gesture. 'I'm Dr Lindberg – Emma Lindberg. I wrote a letter, saying I'd like to visit the station.'

Daniel looked puzzled. 'I did not receive any letter. Maybe it was lost. It can happen.' He ran his eyes over Emma, as if seeking clues to who she might be. She guessed he would be thinking she looked too young to be a doctor; visitors to the Institute were always mistaking her for one of the undergraduates. Then he smiled, his teeth showing up white against his dark lips and skin. 'Are you are coming to work here? I have also sent letters – many of them – asking the aid organisations for some help.'

'No, I'm sorry.' Emma shook her head. 'It's just a personal visit. My mother came here a long time ago – in the early eighties. She was a field investigator from the Centre for Disease Control in America.' She glanced behind her at the two rooms she'd passed. 'I'd just like to see where she worked.'

Daniel was silent for a few seconds. When he spoke his voice was soft. 'I am sorry for the sadness that has brought you here.'

Emma stared at him in surprise. 'You know about her?'

'I was only a child. I do not remember for myself. But she has not been forgotten. You are the daughter of Dr Susan Lindberg.' He nodded slowly. 'You have come to honour her. You are very welcome here.'

Emma's throat tightened with emotion. Of all the people she'd told about this journey, Daniel Oldeani was the first who'd understood straight away why she'd had to come here. That this trip was not just a matter of curiosity, or an excuse to visit Africa. It was more like a pilgrimage.

'How long will you stay?' Daniel asked. 'There is no guest room here, but something can be arranged.'

'It's okay,' Emma said quickly. 'I wasn't planning to stay long. I'm with a driver from a safari company. He's taking me to join a tour at Ngorongoro Crater. We have to be there by tonight.'

'You are in a big hurry!' Daniel smiled again. He gestured towards the front of the building. 'Let me show you.'

Emma was about to turn away, when she saw Mosi approaching the back door. 'This is my driver,' she told Daniel.

The two men greeted one another and then held a conversation in what Emma assumed was Swahili. After several minutes, Daniel turned to her. 'Your driver must find the man who can help him mend his radiator. I will have to guide him to the village. At the same time, I shall return this lamb.' He pointed along the hallway towards the door on her right. 'The lab is in there. Please begin looking. Unfortunately my assistant is away in Arusha, so you will be on your own. But I will return soon.' As he spoke, he lifted the lamb above his head and draped her body gently around his shoulders. He closed his hands around the pairs of hooves – front and back – holding her safely in place.

As the two men disappeared outside, Emma headed towards the laboratory, her footsteps slow and steady on the concrete floor. As she pushed the door open, bright sunlight spilled into the hallway. The familiar smell of chemicals wafted in the air.

Standing in the doorway she shrugged off her shoulder bag, letting it slide to the ground. She ran her gaze over the room. The light came from two windows, one in the front of the building and another on the side. A workbench near the door held a field isolator: an airtight glass tank with two holes in the front that had yellow washing-up gloves fitted to them. Along from the bench was a large porcelain sink with a mirror hanging above it. Beyond that, one whole corner of the room was stacked with wire cages of various sizes. In another corner was an odd structure with a curtained front, which might have been for storage. Over by the side window, there was a second long workbench and a battered wooden chair.

Emma crossed the room to stand by the bench. There was a collection of small boxes containing swabs, slides, specimen vials, disposable gloves – all the standard supplies. In their midst was a jar of unusual pink flowers growing from thick succulent stems with no leaves.

Emma rested her hands on the back of the empty chair. She'd seen photographs of her mother working in the field – she knew what Susan wore, how she looked. Emma was glad she was alone. There was nothing to interrupt her, now, as she concentrated on evoking the image of her mother sitting here, at this desk, all those years ago.

She saw Susan dressed in a green lab coat and shiny plastic apron. There were white gumboots on her feet. Her long dark hair was tied back, revealing her face – the dark shadows under her eyes, the frown of tension on her forehead. An array of slides and vials were spread out on the work surface around her. It was late in the day, the sun slanting in towards her through the window. She was holding a syringe in one hand, the chamber filled with dark blood. In her other hand was the cap she'd use to cover the needle so it could be safely removed.

Carefully, Susan brought her two hands together, the needle angled towards the cap. It was a routine action, carried out dozens of times a day. Only this time, the light was in her eyes, or she was too tired to focus properly, or something happened to break her concentration . . .

She gasped at the sting of the needle piercing her thumb. Tearing off her glove, she held it to the light, stretching the rubber, searching for a pinprick hole – hoping the needle had not actually penetrated, then feeling a wave of terror as she saw that it had. The frantic washing came next, dabbing of bleach, squeezing of blood from the tiny wound. It was futile, Susan knew. The only way she could protect herself now would be to slice off her thumb, straight away. But the blood in the syringe had not yet been tested. It might not be infected with the virus. Susan's colleague was in the village, collecting samples. She was alone with her agony. She reached for the scalpel, using the very hand she was about to maim.

Then she changed her mind. She decided instead just to wait, and hope for the best.

For four harrowing days Susan worked on, dreading the first sign of illness. Then came the faint tickle of a sore throat. Within hours, she knew, she'd be dangerously ill. There was no treatment for the disease, and less than twenty per cent of infected people survived it – within days she would most likely suffer the same agonising death that she'd witnessed so many others enduring.

She would not be leaving this place. She was never going to see her husband or child again.

Emma closed her eyes. She'd relived this story countless times

ed the details of Susan's death, several years
this room, it was much more real. A cold sweat
legs felt weak. Going to the sink, she turned
t over the basin to splash water over her face.

When she lifted her head, she looked at herself in the mirror, water dripping from her nose and eyebrows. She drew in a deep breath. Susan had been dead for twenty-five years. Emma had been only seven when it happened and had only a handful of clear memories of her. Yet she'd clung to the idea of her mother, adding dreams and speculations to the real images in her head. Over the years she'd drawn comfort from knowing that Susan had gone ahead of her – that she knew what it was like to turn twelve, or leave school, get her first boyfriend or her first job. Her mother's wise, strong presence, always there in spirit, had made Emma feel less alone.

But that was about to change. Today was Emma's thirty-second birthday. She was the same age Susan had been when she'd died. The footprints that had always led the way stopped here. They had reached the edge of the map. It was time for Emma to move on by herself.

The thought sent a twist of tension to her stomach. She simply did not know how she would manage without the sense of Susan always being there. But at the same time, she clung to a hope that if she could somehow draw a line under the past she would finally be able to be happy. She knew she had a lot to be grateful for. Standing there, facing her reflection, she checked off the list in her head. A fulfilling and successful career, with a job in Australia's top medical research institute. A partner who shared her passion for science and supported her in her work. Their brand new apartment with its stylish Swedish decor. A wardrobe full of designer clothes. A cleaner who came twice a week, bringing fresh flowers for the table. Fine dining at the top restaurants in Melbourne, without even the need for a special occasion. It was a lifestyle anyone would envy. Yet, with all that she had, Emma still felt incomplete – as if, when she'd lost her mother all those years ago, she'd lost some vital part of herself.

Emma gazed steadily into her own eyes. Now that she'd reached this day, and come to this place, she wanted some feeling of achievement – a recognition that the end of a cycle had been reached. But all she experienced was a sense of being left in limbo. She had felt the same way, all those years ago, when her father had led her into his study and told her the terrible news. For a long time, she'd not really believed in Susan's death. She'd imagined her mother was living a secret life somewhere in Africa, and would one day come back home. After all, no one had offered any proof that Susan Lindberg was dead. There had been no coffin to send home to the family. A body that was host to an unidentified deadly virus could not be transported. It had been burned right here at the station, apparently – along with all Susan's clothes, even the mattress she had lain on. Everything. Burnt away into nothing.

Emma turned back towards the window, picturing the ashes blowing in the wind, merging with the grey dust of the land . . .

She jerked back her head in surprise. Almost filling the window frame was the brown hairy face of a camel.

Emma stared at it, motionless. The bars over the glass made it look as though the camel were in a zoo – except that the animal was on the outside, peering in at Emma. The camel's eyes were huge and dark, fringed by long curved lashes. As Emma watched, it pushed its pale nose between the bars and butted the glass.

Leaning close to the window, Emma craned her neck to look up at rest of the camel's body. Strapped to its back was a wooden frame with blankets folded over it to form a kind of saddle; bulging bags made of coarse fabric woven in colourful stripes were tied on either side. But there was no sign of the owner.

Emma opened the front door. She found that the camel she'd seen at the window was accompanied by a young calf. Walking down the steps, she noticed that the older camel had one foot slightly raised from the ground. The hair around the toes was stained with dried blood. Then she saw a broken tree limb hanging from the rope attached to the camel's halter.

Lifting her hand to shield her eyes against the sun, Emma searched the bush in all directions, her gaze jumping from tree to anthill to pile of rocks. There was still no sign of anyone. She checked the sandy path that led from the track to the building. The only footprints there were her own.

The adult camel came towards her, then, limping on the injured leg. As it drew near, Emma backed away. This camel was much taller than a large horse – and the biggest animal Emma was used to encountering was her friend's golden retriever. The camel kept coming. Emma forced herself to hold her ground. The animal walked right up to her, looming over her for a moment, before bending its head to sniff her hair. Emma flinched, but thought it was best to remain still. A bony chin came to rest on her shoulder, a hairy muzzle tickling her cheek.

Emma stood there, rigid, wanting to escape but afraid to disturb the camel. She wondered how long it was going to remain like this – its head pressing heavily on her shoulder – and what it would decide to do next. From the corner of her eye, she saw the calf wandering off towards a bush, where a couple of chickens were resting in the shade. To her relief, the other camel limped away in the same direction. Emma wiped a spot of saliva from her shoulder. Having scattered the chickens, the young camel began feeding from the bigger camel, butting at her udder with its head. The mother stood there, patiently. She looked hot and tired. Emma remembered the water tank she'd seen at the back of the building, and the bucket that was sitting under the tap.

She hurried round the outside of the building, heading for the yard. Soon, she realised the camels were following her. She ran ahead, dragging open the gate. Crossing to the water tank, she squatted to fill the bucket from a low tap, keeping a wary eye on the approaching camels. There was another bucket near the back door, so she filled that too. She placed the two buckets well apart and stood back. The mother camel snorted warily, but seemed drawn by the sight of the water. She limped up to one of the buckets, plunging her head into it and beginning to drink noisily. As the calf followed her example, Emma crept away and closed the gates.

Standing at a safe distance, she watched the camels drinking. As the female turned side-on, she noticed that one of the saddlebags was torn, revealing some of its contents. Moving cautiously closer, she saw a piece of mosquito netting, some patterned fabric, and a rounded black jar with a red lid and a label that was immediately familiar. Emma stepped closer, peering up. Marmite. One of the post-doctorate researchers at the Institute was from England and he always kept a jar of it in the lunch room, insisting that Vegemite, the Australia version, was too thick and not salty enough. Emma frowned. A jar of Marmite was not the kind of thing an African camel driver would be likely to carry on his journey.

The mother camel finished drinking and kicked the bucket away with her foot. Emma hoped she was going to sit down, as she'd seen camels do in films. But the animal remained on her feet, head held high, eyes half closed against the sun.

Emma wiped the sweat from her face with her arm. Then she went inside and brought out a chair. Placing it by the camel's side, she climbed onto it – making slow, careful movements – then reached up and opened the saddlebag. Standing on tiptoes, she pulled out whatever she could grasp. There was a woman's tie-dyed cheesecloth shirt, followed by a silk sleeping-bag liner. Then her hand closed over an object she could not identify by touch. As she pulled it out, she saw that it was a bundle of knitting. The needles poking from each end were fat and the wool thick. Using a plain stitch, someone was halfway through making a simple red scarf.

Emma was still standing there on the chair when Daniel appeared at the gate. He paused for a few seconds, his mouth dropping open in surprise. Then he hurried across the yard.

'They just turned up,' Emma told him. 'There's no one with them.'

She climbed down from the chair and showed him the things from the saddlebag.

'These are the possessions of a European,' he stated. He touched the pastel shirt. 'A lady.'

Emma chewed tensely at her lip. 'Something's happened to her. We have to contact the police. I've got a mobile in my bag.'

'There is no signal here. We are too far away.'

'Do you have a radio?'

'It is in the Land Rover that Ndugu – my assistant – has taken to Arusha.'

Daniel removed the chair from its place beside the camel, then bent down next to her, examining the wounded leg. 'Keep away,' he warned Emma. 'They can kick you very hard.' He ran his fingers over the bloodied patch of hair. Then he grasped the foot with both hands and somehow persuaded the camel to lift it up. He brushed off the underside of the foot, exposing a deep gash in the pad. 'Can you give me that knife?' he asked Emma, nodding his head towards the back door. In a washing-up bowl, lay an old dinner knife. Daniel took it from Emma and used it to dig into the wound. The camel shuddered, but then remained still, as though she understood he was trying to help her. Daniel removed a couple of small stones, dropping them on the ground. He whistled through his teeth, shaking his head.

'The leg is okay. But this is a bad injury. Infection is spreading. She will need treatment. I can help her. But first, we must make a search for her owner.'

Emma eyed him uneasily. 'What do you mean?'

'Perhaps there has been an accident. Someone may need our help.'

'You can't be suggesting . . .' She shook her head. 'I'm sorry, I can't get involved in this. I'm just a visitor. You should go and get someone from the village.'

'But you are a doctor. If someone has been hurt I will need you to help me.'

'I'm only a medical researcher,' Emma protested. In truth, she'd only recently updated her first aid certificate to meet the requirements of the Institute's workplace health and safety policy. But it was absurd to think she could just drive off into the wilderness with this man she'd barely met. On the other hand, she knew that if the owner of the camels was found injured, Daniel could not manage alone; on the return journey he'd need to concentrate on driving.

'Surely it's a job for the police?' Emma argued. 'Anyway, we don't even have a vehicle – unless Mosi's fixed the Land Cruiser.'

Daniel grunted dismissively. 'I would not trust that vehicle.' He pointed across the yard towards the old Land Rover.

Emma looked at it in disbelief. It appeared no more roadworthy at a second glance.

'Well,' she said, 'I think the best plan is for you to drive to the police station. They really are the ones to handle this.'

Daniel strode to the back door before answering. Picking up a plastic jerry can, he went to fill it from the tap. 'It will take two hours to get to the town.' He raised his voice over the sound of running water. 'Then the police must drive back here. We can save time.'

'But how will we know where to look?' Emma regretted her words as soon as they'd left her lips. If Simon were in her position, she knew, he would not even have discussed the situation.

'I can follow the camel tracks,' Daniel answered. 'But I know where the camels have come from.'

'How could you?'

'I know this area very well. Our work involves trapping animals. Ndugu and I have walked everywhere together, even the places where the Maasai herders do not go. You saw the stones I took from her foot? They come from only one place,' Daniel explained. 'It is in the desert.'

He pointed beyond the crisscross of wire mesh at the boundary of the yard. Following the direction of his arm, Emma gazed across the plains, looking into the far distance, to the purple-blue pyramid of the mountain.

'Do not worry,' Daniel said. 'You will be safe.'

Emma felt torn with indecision. She weighed up all the reasons why she should refuse to go with him, and all the reasons she should offer her help. She turned back to Daniel. It was then that she noticed a strand of fine red lamb's wool clinging to his T-shirt. There were grubby marks there as well – left behind by the hooves. It reminded her of how gently yet confidently he'd handled the little lamb.

Meeting his gaze, she nodded slowly. 'Okay. Let's go.'

THREE

The terrain was flat and open, and Daniel had no difficulty picking a path across the plain, though the old Land Rover seemed to be full of loose parts that rattled with each bump.

'Keep looking everywhere,' he said to Emma. His eyes were fixed on the ground ahead, where vague indents could be seen, marking out the route taken by the camels. 'If you see anything that is not usual, tell me.'

Emma studied the landscape, searching for some sign of the camel's owner: a flash of colour; the shape of a person; something moving in the stillness. But there was no hint that any human had ever been in this area. There were no roads or trails, and no huts or wells or cattle enclosures like the ones she'd seen on the journey to the station. She was very aware that this would not be a good place to break down. She peered ahead through the windscreen. Spider-webs draped the inside of the glass and the exterior was crusted with dust. It must have been years, she guessed, since the wiper on her side had worked. She glanced across to the line of gauges on the crude metal dashboard – then looked away. It was better not even to think about petrol, oil levels, engine temperature . . .

She looked down at her green bag, lodged beside her feet. When she'd made the decision to go with Daniel, she'd run inside to get it, while he wrote a note for Mosi. Tucked away in the many pockets and zipped sections of the bag were all the things she'd thought she might need in Africa – including sunscreen, tropical strength insect repellent, antibacterial gel, a packet of moist wipes, bandaids, iodised antiseptic, rehydration sachets, and a collection of medicines. She'd packed with a luxury safari in mind – not a rescue mission – but still, she found the presence of the bulging shoulder bag reassuring.

They reached an area of bare, sun-hardened earth. Daniel slowed down. 'I have lost the tracks.' Half standing, he leaned his head and shoulders out through the window to get a better look. After a few minutes he sat back again, and accelerated. Emma relaxed, guessing he'd picked up the trail again. She stole a close look at him as he drove, his attention focused ahead. He was very different from Mosi. The safari driver had a round face to go with his plump figure. Daniel's face matched his body as well: it was lean and finely sculpted. The sun gleamed on his skin, highlighting his cheekbones, the curve of his lips and the shape of his nose. Emma noticed there were faint lines in his cheeks, close to his mouth. He must be a man who smiled a lot, she thought. Yet she detected something serious, almost solemn about him as well. Not wanting to be caught staring, she looked quickly away as he turned to speak to her.

'We are in the desert now.' He waved one hand to take in their surroundings. There were hardly any trees; the few that were growing here were low and stunted. The air was hot. The ground was made of grey sand scattered with small stones. The larger rocks were rough black chunks, pitted with holes. 'You can see,' Daniel added, 'it is not really desert. That is the English word that people use. In Swahili it is called *nyika* – "the wild land where nobody lives". You know Tanzania was once called Tanganyika. It means "the wild country behind the town of Tanga".'

Emma wasn't sure she'd ever heard of the old name for this country, but nodded as if she did. They were driving directly towards the mountain. It was still a long way off, but the dust haze was thinner and she could see it more clearly. She was surprised to discover that the upper slopes of the mountain were white.

'There's snow on the mountain!'

'That is white lava,' Daniel said. 'It is an unusual volcano. To the Maasai it is a very special place – the Mountain of God.'

Emma gazed into the distance. There was an air of unreality about the whole setting – the black rocks, the grey plains, the white slopes of the mountain: she felt like someone viewing black-and-white film of a scene that was meant to be in colour.

She checked her watch. They'd been driving for over two hours and it was now well past midday. She thought of telling Daniel she didn't think they should keep going; that it was time to turn back. But then, she imagined a woman – a foreigner, like herself – all alone in this desert, injured and in need of help. She kept on searching, raking her eyes left to right over the land.

As the journey lengthened, neither she nor Daniel spoke; the air became dense, weighed down by a sense of futility. Emma was aware of the early afternoon sun beating in through the large V-shaped tear in the canvas roof right above her head. She reached down to her bag, pulling out her tube of sunscreen. Squeezing a generous dollop onto her hand, she smeared the cream over her face.

Daniel glanced sideways, a curious look in his eyes.

'I try to avoid getting sunburned,' Emma said.

Daniel smiled. 'Your skin is the wrong colour for Africa. We had a Dutch visitor once. He let his face and arms become burned. His skin came off in pieces. It looked like the skin left behind on the ground by a snake.'

Emma wrinkled her nose. She could just imagine how white, peeling skin must appear to Daniel – his own smooth and flawless skin looked like burnished bronze in the sun.

Now that the silence between them had been broken, Emma felt an impulse to keep talking.

'Where did you study to become a vet?' she asked. Daniel spoke such good English that she was half expecting him to name an English or American college.

'Here in Tanzania. First, at the Sokoine University of Agriculture in Morogoro and then at the campus in Dar es Salaam.' He broke off as he swerved to avoid a large rock. 'After I graduated, I got a job in Arusha.'

'And how long have you been working at the Olambo Fever Research Station?'

'Three years – nearly four.'

'What made you take on the project?'

Daniel didn't answer straight away. His features became suddenly still, as if a mask had fallen over his face. 'I knew people who had died from the disease.' He looked across to Emma. 'Now it is your turn. Where do you come from?'

Emma hesitated. She couldn't decide whether to give the simple version – not mentioning that Rebecca was her stepmother, or that Emma herself was only half-Australian – or to say more, and risk opening the way for a whole series of personal questions. But then she remembered that Daniel already knew about Susan. For once, she could answer freely. 'I was born in America, but Dad's Australian. After Mum died we moved back to where he came from. We moved straight away. He couldn't bear to be reminded of her.'

'So you lost your home as well as your mother,' Daniel said.

'I lost everything. I even had to give my kitten away – there are very strict quarantine laws in Australia. I didn't speak to anyone for days after they took Fifi from me. Then I had to say goodbye to Mrs McDonald as well. She used to look after me when Susan was away. I missed her terribly. She was like a grandmother to me.' Emma smiled at the memory. 'She told me my mother was still alive in heaven, that I could talk to her. My father was annoyed with her for telling me that. But it didn't matter to me if it wasn't true – it was a huge comfort.' She paused, amazed at how easily she was confiding in Daniel. She thought perhaps it was because he was so different – in the way he spoke, the words he chose. Or maybe it was because they were out here together in the middle of nowhere. Her usual habit of being reserved with strangers just didn't seem relevant. 'So I've lived in Australia ever since. I studied at Melbourne University.'

Daniel nodded. 'And you are married?'

'Yes,' Emma replied. It was the simplest answer: she'd been living with Simon for five years now.

'How many children do you have?'

'None.'

Daniel was quiet for a few moments. When he spoke, his voice was heavy with sympathy. 'I am sorry.'

Emma looked at him in confusion, then smiled. 'No, it's all right. Simon and I have chosen not to have children.'

'Not yet,' Daniel suggested.

Emma shook her head. 'We're both very busy. I work full time at a research institute and Simon is a scientist as well. Our lives are very full. We just don't feel the need to have children.'

Daniel drew his brows together. He was about to speak, when suddenly he jerked up his head and braked violently, sending a stack of wire cages in the back crashing forward.

Emma searched the ground for whatever it was that had caught his attention. Before she had any success, Daniel jumped out of the vehicle, leaving the engine running. He bent down and picked up something yellow. It was tube-shaped and about the size of his hand. Hurrying back to his seat, he handed a plastic torch to Emma.

'The camel tracks were there next to it. There were no human footmarks. I think it must have fallen from the saddlebag.' Daniel let out the clutch and the Land Rover lurched ahead. He drove faster, now, spurred on by the discovery of the torch. Emma held on to the door with one hand and braced herself against the dashboard with the other.

She noticed the tree first – the raw white strip on its trunk where a limb had been ripped away. 'Look over there!'

Daniel brought the Land Rover to a halt. This time he turned off the engine and wrenched up the hand brake.

'That is where the camels were tied,' he said, pointing out through the window. 'You can see from the prints that they panicked.'

Emma followed his gaze as he scanned the area. Not far away was a long narrow pile of stones. It was exactly the right width and length for a grave. The large boulder at one end even looked like a headstone. Emma felt a knot of apprehension inside her.

'Stay behind me,' Daniel said as they climbed out of the Land Rover. 'I want to study the ground before we walk over it.'

He spent a long time stepping cautiously towards the mound, crouched over, turning his head from side to side. His feet were still bare, the black skin coated with pale dust. Emma watched the way he moved, like a dancer in slow motion. In spite of his modern clothing he looked like a figure who belonged to the past.

Emma kept behind him, following in his footsteps, looking ahead over his shoulder. The ground was largely stony, with no tracks visible, but where it was sandy, the surface was almost covered in small dents and mounds.

'Hyenas have been here,' Daniel said without turning round. 'A pack of them.'

Emma glanced nervously around her, but said nothing. As she walked on, she fixed her eyes on Daniel's back; on the white T-shirt stretched over his shoulders. When they were close to the mound, he stopped, suddenly, and reached down behind a flat-topped boulder.

He picked up a leather satchel, swinging it by one of its straps, then placing it on top of the rock.

Emma looked at it for a moment, taking in the battered yet sturdy leather. It was a bag made to last, and had been well used. She lifted the leather flap and peered inside. The bag was deep, and it wasn't possible to see everything that was inside it. After glancing quickly at Daniel, she tipped the bag upside down, scattering its contents over the pitted surface of the stone. There was a tube of insect repellent. A paperback copy of the second Harry Potter book. Batteries. A sun hat. Then there was a large plastic bag full of white pills. Emma bent to look at them more closely. A simple M was stamped on each one.

'It is morphine,' Daniel said. 'The cheap brand that is sold in Africa.'

'It's a big supply. Too much for one person – even if they were very ill.'

She was about to scoop the contents back into the bag when a black wallet tumbled from a side pocket. She picked it up, feeling the softness of worn leather resting against her palm. Flipping it open, she saw a photograph displayed behind a square of clear plastic. It showed a fair-haired woman and child, standing side by side, arm in arm.

'They look like mother and daughter.' She held it out to show Daniel. 'They've got the same hair and eyes.'

They were both dressed in African clothes – they had matching traditional cloths tied over their shoulders and wore beaded bangles on their sun-tanned arms. It was the kind of photograph tourists took of themselves pretending to be locals. The mother even wore sandals made from old car tyres, like the ones Emma had seen piled up for sale in some of the villages Mosi had driven through. The girl wore no shoes at all. Emma looked from the photograph to the mound of stones, a sick feeling growing inside her. She took a step towards it, then remembered to let Daniel go ahead, checking for tracks.

When he reached the end of the mound closest to the boulder, he bent down and began removing the stones. Emma came up next to him, dodging as he tossed them aside. She glimpsed a flash of colour beneath one of the rocks. Squatting down beside him, she helped clear more of the stones. Flies buzzed around her face, but she barely noticed them. Soon they uncovered an area of fabric – bright African cotton, printed with a pattern of birds. They worked on, moving stones quickly but carefully. Gradually, the shape of a human face became apparent through the cloth shroud – first the curve of the forehead. Then the nose pushing up. The chin jutting forward.

Daniel turned to Emma. 'You can go back to the Land Rover if you want.'

'No,' Emma said. 'I'm okay.'

When the end of the cloth was exposed, she watched while Daniel peeled it slowly back, exposing a clump of white-blonde hair half-covering a wide smooth forehead. Next she saw finely arched eyebrows, closed eyelids with long lashes resting against the skin that was – somehow – tanned, yet pale. Nose, cheeks, chin – the shapes Emma had seen through the cloth now appeared moulded in flesh. Emma caught her breath. The woman was beautiful. Her bone structure had been accentuated by the relaxation of all the fine muscles. Her lips, gently closed, were a perfect bow shape.

Emma closed her eyes for a moment. There was no doubt that it was the woman in the photograph. The mother . . .

She looked sideways at Daniel. He was sitting back on his heels, gazing down at the body. His eyes were screwed up, his lips twisted, almost as if he were in pain. He seemed lost in his emotions.

Emma turned back to the body. 'It doesn't look as if she's been here very long. And there's no smell.'

Daniel stared at her blankly, but then gathered himself. 'The air is very dry here – so it is hard to tell. We need to find out if the body is stiff.' He was quiet for a few seconds. 'Could you examine her?'

Emma gave him a questioning frown. Until now, he'd taken the lead.

'According to the tradition of my people, I should not touch a dead person of the opposite sex,' he explained. 'So it would be difficult for me.' There was no sign of distress in him now. He spoke as though simply stating a fact.

Emma nodded, hiding her surprise that a man who'd spent years studying at university was still ruled by traditional taboos. She was uneasy about her new role and as she bent over the grave she had to remind herself that at the Institute she was a team leader, the one others turned to for direction. Leaning closer, she studied the body, trying to remember what she knew about post-mortem symptoms. She checked the back of the dead woman's neck. The colour of the skin deepened suddenly to purple, almost black: the classic stain of pooled blood. Emma felt in her jeans pocket for the pair of dispos-able gloves she'd taken from the kit in her green bag. She pulled them on, the latex snapping tight around her wrists. Pointing one gloved finger towards a section of the dark skin, she pushed into the flesh. After a short time she took her finger away. There was no blanched patch, which meant the blood had not moved under pressure. And there was no warmth coming from the flesh, but no smell either. Cupping the head with both hands, Emma tried turn-ing it to one side; it moved freely, as if the person lying here were deeply asleep.

'I'd say she's been dead for between two and three days.' Emma spoke without lifting her eyes.

When Daniel did not respond, she looked round to find him crouched on hands and knees, examining the ground.

'The child was here, with her!'

His eyes were wide with alarm. Emma locked her gaze to his, as the meaning of his words sank in.

'Look!' He pointed towards a patch of grey sand, where a small footmark could be clearly seen. The print was a perfectly formed. Emma could even see the deeper indent made by the ball of the foot as the child had moved on.

Daniel gestured towards another mark nearby. He opened his mouth, but then seemed reluctant to speak.

'What? What is it?' Emma demanded.

'There was a lion as well. No wonder the camels were afraid.'

'A lion!'

'It is not surprising. This place is the home of lions – not people.'

Emma stared at him. 'Would the lion kill the child?'

'Not usually.' His face was drawn into a worried frown. 'But this lion is injured. An injured animal can be very dangerous.'

He pointed to a single clear print, on a small swathe of sand. It looked to Emma just like the foot of a domestic cat, except that it was as large as her hand – and there was something about its shape that didn't look quite right.

'You can see, one of its pads is damaged. That is a bad injury for a wild animal because it cannot heal well. Like the mother camel, this lion needs treatment.' He gazed down at the ground. 'I think there might be other animal prints here – small ones – but they are very faint.'

Emma swallowed a lump in her throat. 'So . . . where's the child?' She looked around at the open countryside, the tracts of sand and gravel broken only by piles of stones and jagged boulders. She pictured a small body abandoned somewhere here. Or perhaps just a pool of dried blood on the ground, a scrap of cloth . . .

Turning back to Daniel she saw her fears mirrored on his face. 'What are we going to do?'

Daniel narrowed his eyes as he searched into the distance. Then he cupped his hands around his mouth. 'Hello! Is someone there?'

His words carried over the land. There was a tense waiting hush, but no reply came back.

He turned to Emma. 'You go that way and look for her. I will go in the other direction. Do not go so far that you cannot see the grave. Keep looking out for danger as well. Watch where you put your feet.'

Emma checked the ground close to her. She noticed her new

canvas walking shoes were coated with dust, the colourful logos embroidered on the sides completely hidden. The cuffs of her trousers were grey as well, and on one there was a smear of what looked like engine grease. She had the impression, for a moment, that she was looking down at the feet of a stranger.

She began walking in the opposite direction to Daniel, calling out as loudly as she could. 'Hello! Is anyone there?'

From behind her came Daniel's voice, forming the same words, like a distorted echo of her own.

Reaching an area of sand, she bent down to search for footprints, but there was only a trail of star shapes left behind by a large bird. She wiped her sweaty face with the sleeve of her shirt, thinking longingly of her bottles of water in the Land Rover. It was so hot, here, and so dry. Two or three days without food would not kill anyone, she knew. But three days with no water in this heat would be difficult to survive. Though children were more resilient than adults. Slower to die . . .

She walked, shouted, walked again, all the time searching the land around her. She'd lost track of time when, suddenly, she heard Daniel call her name. She saw that he was beckoning her back to the grave.

'Did you see something?' she asked hopefully as she reached him.

'Nothing.'

'Maybe someone's rescued her?'

'It is rare for people to be in this area. There is a village closer to the mountain where it is not so dry. But there is nothing for cows to eat here.'

'She could have wandered a long way in two days.'

'Yes,' agreed Daniel. 'A proper search is needed. We must inform the police. When we have put the stones back, we should leave.'

Before moving, the two stood in silence for a few moments, looking down at the woman's face. She seemed so peaceful, lying there – as if she really were just asleep.

'I wonder what happened to her,' Emma said.

'She has died from a sickness or there was an accident,' Daniel replied. 'If a crime was involved, she would have been hidden. Instead, her body was protected with stones.'

Emma frowned. 'Who did that? Her husband maybe? A guide?'

'No, I have seen footprints of a woman and a child only. The small foot is the right size for the child in the photograph.'

'She looked about seven years old to me.' Emma could nearly always pick a child of that age – she held frozen inside her the image of herself at that time, when her life had so suddenly changed. Whenever she met seven year olds – there were two among the offspring of her colleagues at the Institute – she found herself seeking some link with them. But they always seemed younger than she remembered herself to have been, more dependent on adults, more easily upset.

Emma shook her head. 'I just can't imagine such a young child burying someone – let alone her own mother.'

'It would be a terrible thing for any child. And I agree it would be unusual for a European child to be strong enough. They grow up very slowly. But I cannot think of another explanation.'

'If she can bury her mother like that, perhaps she can look

after herself as well. We have to get the search started as soon as possible.'

Bending over, she replaced the shroud, gently covering the face. Then, with Daniel working alongside her, she piled the stones back. The little printed birds disappeared one by one as they repaired the hole in the mound. When they were finished Emma quickly picked a posy of flowers – the same pink, leafless ones she'd seen in the laboratory – and placed them at the foot of the grave. While Daniel went to gather up the contents of the satchel, she stood there alone, looking down at the curled petals resting on the hard dark rock. A faint breeze brushed her face. The smell of sap rose from the broken stems. Away in the distance, a bird cried out in a high, strained voice.

Emma pictured the woman lying there hidden beneath the stones. It was hard to imagine what agony she must have suffered as she faced her death. When Susan had died, she'd at least known that Emma was safely at home with her father and Mrs McDonald. But to die, leaving your child all alone, and in terrible danger. It was unbearable. Emma bit down hard on her lip, wanting to feel the pain. She wrapped her arms around her body, staring down at the mound of stones. The quiet air seemed taut, as though a breath had been drawn in, and held. She had a strange sense that the dead woman's presence remained here. And that she was looking to Emma to do what she could not – to make sure that her little girl was found and brought safely home.

Emma rubbed her hand over her face. She felt disoriented. She was probably in shock, she told herself. Anyone would be upset by the experiences she'd had today. But as she turned away, heading towards the Land Rover, the thoughts that had come to her only grew more solid. They drove her on, pushing the pace of her footsteps.

'Which direction is the police station?' she asked Daniel as she reached him.

'Malangu is over there.' Daniel swung his arm well to the right of the Land Rover. The desert continued in that direction: the same stony ground, the same rock – the same grey wilderness.

'So can we go straight there?'

Daniel shook his head. 'We have to go back the way we came, to get onto the road. Anyway I thought you would want to return to the station? I could leave you there. Mosi would be back from the village by now.'

'No. I'm coming with you.'

Daniel looked surprised, but then nodded as though he understood that her priorities had changed. He seemed to look at her with a new respect. 'We can try to drive from here to Malangu. But I have never done it before.'

'Well, is there a map in the Land Rover?'

'I do not use maps,' Daniel said. He looked intently into the distance in the direction of Malangu. 'I have not walked in that area for a long time, but some of it I knew when I was a boy herding cattle. We might find that we cannot get through. But I think it is a risk worth taking. We would get to Malangu much more quickly.'

'Let's go, then.'

At the Land Rover, Daniel took a jerry can from the back seat and poured petrol into the vehicle's fuel tank. The smell wafted in the air. Emma waited impatiently, eyeing her watch.

Then, at last, they were driving away. Emma looked back. She could see the spot of pink standing out against the dark grey. It grew smaller and smaller – then it was gone.

FOUR

Emma leaned her elbow on the door and rested her head in her hand. The steady bumping of the Land Rover and the constant drone of its engine would have lulled her to sleep, if not for the vivid images of the day's events that kept appearing – sharp and fractured – in her mind.

They had to make several detours around deep gullies, and were forced to backtrack at one stage, but by late afternoon the country-side began to change from the flat stony desert to scrubby bushland. Daniel drove towards a Maasai village: a collection of grey mud huts set in a circle surrounded by a ring of grey thorn thicket and match-ing groups of donkeys. As they came nearer, Emma saw cattle and goats as well, and red woolly sheep with broad flat tails – grown-up versions of Daniel's lamb. The herders, dressed in red plaid cloths, stood out against the colourless backdrop. Daniel saluted them as he passed and they raised spears or herding sticks in reply.

'How can anyone live here?' Emma asked as they left the village behind them. There seemed to be no feed for livestock, no gardens, no water.

'We know how to do it,' Daniel said, a note of pride in his voice.

'We can find hidden water, and places where the grass grows. Even in the *nyika* we can do this. We learned it from our brothers.'

'You're a Maasai . . .' Emma tried to picture Daniel dressed in a plaid blanket, wearing beads and carrying a spear like the men they'd just passed. It was easy and difficult, both at the same time. He looked comfortable in his Western clothes, the iPod cord dangling from his pocket. And, of course, he was a university graduate running a scientific research project. But he was tall, like the Maasai men they'd passed, and held himself in the same way – upright, yet graceful. And then there was the skill he'd shown in following the tracks; the way he'd placed his bare feet almost lovingly on the earth.

Daniel turned to her with a smile, the lines around his mouth deepening. 'My *manyata* is not so far from here. If we went there you would see my brothers, my cousins, my uncles and aunts – many people. You would meet my father, and also my mother.' As he spoke about his family, there was warmth in his voice and his eyes. 'But we cannot make a visit today. If you go to a *manyata* you must have time to enjoy a welcome feast.'

Emma smiled back politely. She hadn't eaten since breakfast and her stomach felt hollow, but she was glad they had no time to partake in a feast. She didn't want to have to choose between refusing to eat, and risking getting brucellosis from drinking unboiled milk. She thought back fondly to the breakfast that she'd eaten in the hotel where she'd stayed overnight, on the way from Arusha. She'd had soft-boiled eggs, toast, warm croissants and pawpaw jam. Along with the starched white tablecloths, the air laden with the smell of freshly brewed local coffee, the vases of tropical flowers, the meal was part of a completely different world.

'I hope we can get some food in Malangu,' Emma said. 'I'm pretty hungry.'

'We will eat,' Daniel assured her. 'But first we will go to the police. The day will be nearly over by the time we get there. For now, you must have one of these.' He reached into a storage pocket on the inside of his door and pulled out a bag of butterscotch sweets. 'This is my secret supply, for emergencies only. I have to hide them from Ndugu.' His face was serious, but there was the hint of mischief in his voice.

Emma took one, her mouth watering as she removed the wrapper. Sucking it eagerly, she could almost feel the sugar entering her bloodstream, bringing fresh energy.

'Soon we should find a road,' Daniel said. 'Near the top of that hill.'

When they reached the place he was pointing at, the pale band of a dirt road was visible, running between the bushes. Daniel had to accelerate so that the Land Rover mounted the ridge of earth along its edge. As he turned left onto the comparatively smooth surface, he rested back in his seat, steering with one hand on the wheel. After a few kilometres they reached a river, a silver strand of water set between barren banks. Daniel barely slowed the Land Rover as he drove straight through it, water cresting in waves to each side of the wheels. It occurred to Emma that if she found herself in a vehicle being driven this way by Simon, she'd be clutching the seat and pressing her feet into the floor. But Daniel drove with a confidence that she could feel herself absorbing. He treated the vehicle as if it were an extension of his body, as much at home in the land as he was.

Soon they were passing dusty gardens with maize standing in rows. There were straggly banana palms, pawpaw trees, and square mud huts with rusty tin roofs. People looked up as the vehicle passed. Daniel lifted his hand again and again to wave.

'Do you know them all?' Emma asked.

'No, but if my eyes meet those of another, I must greet them.'

The space between the dwellings became smaller, the settlement more dense. There were lines of tiny shops with painted facades and barred glassless windows. There were lots of people, now, and sparse traffic made up of old cars, trucks and the occasional well-worn mini-van. Emma waited for something more elaborate to come into view – two-storey government buildings, offices, hotels. But then the narrow dirt road ended abruptly in an open square of bare earth. The shops continued around its perimeter. At the far end was a small church, marked by a cross, and a mosque topped with a green dome. Between them was an outdoor podium decorated with banners of coloured cloth. On one side of the square stood a long mud brick building, the space in front of it cordoned off with white painted stones and featuring a flagpole. The Tanzanian flag hung there, limp in the still air.

Daniel drove the Land Rover in between two larger rocks that marked the entrance to the enclosure and swung round to park near the front door. Then he turned off the engine.

'We are here.'

He reached over to the back seat and picked up a pair of leather boots. When he'd pulled them on, he climbed out, bringing with him the satchel and the yellow torch.

Emma joined him outside the front of the Land Rover, carrying her own bag. Daniel stood on one foot and rubbed the toes of his boots clean, in turn, on his trouser legs. He smoothed down his T-shirt.

'I should have a proper shirt,' he said to Emma.

'At least brush off the dirt from the lamb's hooves.' She reached towards his chest, careful not to touch him as she pointed out the marks. 'And the bits of hair.'

She watched him do as she'd suggested. Then she nodded her approval. 'That's better.'

While they'd been talking a boy had climbed onto the bonnet of the Land Rover and now sat in the spare tyre mounted there.

'He will look after our things,' Daniel said. He nodded towards the green bag. 'You can leave that behind if you like.'

Emma shook her head, tightening her hand on the strap. In the bottom of the bag was a plastic folder containing her passport, credit cards, air ticket, vaccination booklet and travel itinerary. She had no intention of entrusting them to the care of a young boy.

Daniel led the way towards the entrance to the police station. 'I will tell you everything that has been discussed, afterwards,' he said over his shoulder. 'The police officer will understand English, but it will be easier to explain everything in Swahili.'

Emma wanted to protest that she needed to know what was being said, but she understood that the situation was too urgent to risk any miscommunication. She stood behind Daniel as he pushed open a door that was pitted with holes left by drawing pins. The remnants of a notice still hung there, the writing bleached away by the sun.

The police officer was sitting on the other side of a wooden desk, his head bent over a large, lined notebook. Beside him a collection of mismatched documents spilled from a fat manila folder. As Emma and Daniel approached him, he put down his pen and looked up, his eyes moving back and forth between them. After a few moments, he spread his hands on the desktop, and levered himself to his feet. He was a huge man, tall and heavy. His dark skin blended in with the dark green of his uniform and the deep red of his beret to create an aura of sombre authority.

'How can I assist you?' he asked, addressing them both. He glanced at his watch as if to point out that it was late in the day.

Daniel placed the satchel and torch on the table, and began talking in a calm, deliberate tone. Emma listened intently, driven by an irrational thought that if she tried hard enough she might be able to understand the conversation. Suddenly, both men began to speak more loudly, firing off quick exchanges. Emma felt a shiver of anxiety, seeing how the whole story might look to the policeman. She and Daniel had disturbed the scene of a burial. They'd moved evidence that could still turn out to be related to a crime. The fact was, they had no idea what they'd become involved in. Over the officer's shoulder Emma could see into a dim corridor lined on either side with floor-to-ceiling bars. The scene reminded her of news images of tourists, accused of trafficking drugs, locked up in foreign jails. Remembering the bag of morphine tablets, she looked quickly away. There was a window to her right, overlooking the square. She occupied herself by watching two men taking down the cloths from the podium and folding them into neat bundles. Some kind of public event must have taken place today, she thought, and now it was all over.

When the policeman disappeared into another room, Daniel smiled reassuringly at Emma. The officer returned with a folded map in his hand. He spread it out over the desk, turning it round to face Daniel.

Daniel studied it for a time, frowning, his finger hovering over the paper. The police officer was at a loss as well.

'We both come from this area,' Daniel said. 'He knows the place I am speaking about. But we must find it on this map, so he can show other people.'

Emma peered over his shoulder. It was a survey map, with a lot of detail that would be confusing to someone unfamiliar with reading such things. She could see the dense contour lines of the volcano, and the flat unbroken beige of the desert plains. It didn't take her long to work out the route they'd taken and then to find the site of the makeshift grave. 'It is right here.' She planted her finger on the map.

'You are an expert,' Daniel said. He sounded impressed by her, again. Emma wondered for a second how many other white women he had encountered, and what they had been like.

'I live with a geologist,' she told him. 'We have maps on the sitting room wall instead of paintings.'

Daniel placed his hand on the map, his palm covering the

location of the grave, and then said something to the police officer. Emma guessed he was indicating the area that had to be searched.

'Does he understand that it's urgent?' she asked.

The officer turned to her with a stern look. 'It is very urgent. I will telephone the police station in Arusha straight away.' He spoke perfect English, though with a strong African accent. 'A ground and air search will begin tomorrow as soon as it is light. Do not worry. I will make sure that everything is done the best way. As soon as we know the nationality of the deceased person, their embassy will become involved as well. They will inform the next of kin: the woman's husband; the father of the child.'

Emma looked at him in surprise. 'Have you organised a search like this before?'

'There was an emergency two years ago. An American became lost. He was planning to walk across Africa.' The man shook his head disapprovingly. 'He was found easily.' He refolded the map and carried it away.

Emma spoke to Daniel in a low voice. 'Have you told him about the camels?'

'Yes, I have told him,' he replied. 'He said the police truck will be needed for the search. Afterwards they will come and take the camels away.'

Emma felt a wave of relief. Everything was being sorted out. She had confidence in this police officer and had no doubt that a proper search would soon be underway. From the vantage point of a light aircraft, the desert would be spread out like an open book. If the child were still out there, alive – she would be found. Emma pictured the grave, far away in the desert. She knew she had now done what she'd felt was expected of her.

'You can leave now,' the policeman said as he returned to his place at the desk. 'But you must both return the day after tomorrow. Friday.'

Emma frowned. 'I'm sorry? I don't understand.'

'The Inspector will come from Arusha tomorrow. He will be very busy with the search. The next day, he will have time to take your statements. You must come after lunchtime. Three o'clock.'

Emma opened her mouth to protest that she couldn't possibly do that: she was due in Ngorongoro and if she didn't arrive in time the safari tour would leave without her. But one look at the officer's face discouraged her from doing anything other than nodding her agreement.

She followed Daniel back outside. As soon as she was away from the door she turned to him.

'Do we really have to come back?'

'Yes, we do,' he said firmly. 'You cannot argue with the police. If they think you are showing disrespect, they will inconvenience you further.'

As they walked towards the Land Rover, he pointed diagonally across the square. Emma lifted her head. Rising above the buildings was a tall red and white mobile phone tower. She'd been too preoccupied to notice it when she'd arrived earlier. The structure looked bizarrely out of place.

'You will have a good signal here. You can make some phone calls,' Daniel said.

Emma looked at him blankly for a second, then nodded. 'Yes, I'll have to contact the tour company.'

'And your husband,' Daniel suggested.

Emma considered whether it was now time she explained that she and Simon were partners, not spouses – but it still didn't seem important. 'There's no need to bother him. He's away on a field trip. He won't know there's been a change of plan.'

Daniel nodded, but looked puzzled. As they reached the Land Rover, the boy waved his hand in greeting. He remained where he was, idly swinging his skinny legs. As Daniel reached into his pockets for change, Emma looked past him over the square. The sun was low in the sky and dusty shafts of light reached across the barren ground. Children in blue school uniforms, their feet bare, played with a homemade soccer ball. A man on a bicycle wove an erratic path between them, a large dog loping along behind him. Around the edges of the square, women in bright cloths, babies tied to their backs, strolled between the shops. The sound of their light-hearted chatter floated on the air. No one was hurrying; there was an atmosphere of peace and order. It was not the kind of place, Emma realised, where the loss of a day or two of someone's time would matter very much. She thought of the bumper sticker on Mosi's Land Cruiser. *No hurry in Africa*, it read. When she'd first seen it, she'd wondered if it was meant as a kind of advance warning to his safari clients not to expect punctuality. Now she could see that it might be a more general comment on life here. She sighed, raking her fingers through her hair. Daniel had made it clear she had no choice but to adjust her plans. She would have to make the best of the situation. At least she would be able to learn first-hand the results of tomorrow's search. She pictured returning to the police station and finding the child, safely in the care of the officer, awaiting the arrival of her father or some other relative who would be able to comfort her.

Daniel drove across the square, and parked again outside a building that had walls only waist high, with no glass above them, just broad open gaps. The door was painted bright yellow and green. Above it hung a handwritten sign bearing the words *Salaam Cafe*.

'We will eat here,' Daniel said. 'And afterwards we will drive back to the station for the night.'

Emma looked at him in silence – shocked by the idea of having to sleep in that place where Susan had died. She glanced around the square. There was nothing remotely like a hotel in sight. Her only hope was that there was some more developed area of the town she had not yet seen. Even a basic guest house would be preferable to the station.

'Is there somewhere I could stay in Malangu?'

Daniel shook his head. 'There is no place where a foreigner could stay. I am afraid there is no choice. You must come back to the station.' He had a look of sympathy in his eyes, as if he understood that it was a daunting prospect for her.

Emma pressed her lips together. The station was just a building, she reminded herself, a place made from brick and wood. She could stay there. Of course she could. All she needed to do that was put mind over matter, fact over feelings – the way she did when she was working at the Institute. The laboratory leader had drummed it into her: emotions had to be set aside, or good judgement suffered. She forced a smile.

Daniel smiled back. 'I will be glad of your help with the camels. They must be fed tonight.'

'Yes, of course.' Emma tried to sound as though she hadn't forgotten all about them. She wasn't used to having to think about the needs of animals. After losing her kitten, she'd not wanted another pet as a child. And she and Simon had never contemplated having one. They wanted to be free.

Daniel climbed out of the Land Rover, gesturing for Emma to follow him. As she closed her door, the boy who'd minded the vehicle before arrived – out of breath from sprinting across the square – and took up his position on the bonnet.

Daniel led the way in through the yellow and green doorway, steering Emma towards one of the high stools drawn up to a bar made of white-painted wood.

'Please wait here,' he said. 'I will be back soon.' Then he disappeared into a doorway to the left of the bar.

Emma sat on the stool, her bag by her side, the strap looped over her arm for safekeeping. Resting her elbow on the table and propping up her head, she looked around her. There was a fridge containing bottles of beer and Coke and soft drink, but the only items of food on offer were some pieces of cooked chicken and a few samosas stored in an unrefrigerated glass cabinet. They looked as if they had been there all day. They might as well have been placed in a bacteria incubator. She tried to decide what she would say if Daniel suggested eating them.

She slapped at a mosquito whining near her left ear. Taking her insect repellent from her bag she covered her eyes with her hand and sprayed her face and hair. Then she rolled down the sleeves of her shirt and turned up her collar. She looked out across the square to the police station, picturing the officer at his desk, already at work making phone calls, writing lists in his notebook.

Emma checked her phone. There were no messages – she'd bought a sim card for a local company, Vodacom, and only texted the number to her lab assistant. She felt far away from her world. For a moment, she pictured phoning Simon – as Daniel had expected her to – but she knew that she couldn't. Simon was in his own separate world: Antarctica. A place Emma could only visualise as white and cold and empty. The very end of the earth. Emails could be sent to and fro, and phone calls made by satellite. But the times Emma had phoned Simon he'd sounded preoccupied, as if her words were dragging him from a private place where he wanted to stay. She understood how it was to be completely absorbed in your work, so she'd never tried to talk for long – but still, she could tell he pre-ferred her to stick to email. She smiled wryly as she looked down at her mobile. She imagined what Simon would say if she did call and tell him where she was, and how she came to be there. He'd be stunned that she'd allowed herself to get caught up like this. He was a great believer in people sticking to their own affairs. It kept things simple, he'd often said to Emma. If you start blurring the lines, everything gets messy. In the lab, as well as in life.

Leaving thoughts of Simon aside, Emma flipped through her travel itinerary until she found the phone number for Seronera

Lodge. When her call was answered, she explained that she'd been unavoidably delayed.

'Don't worry, madam,' the receptionist said. 'You can join the safari at Ngorongoro. I will arrange everything.'

As Emma slipped her phone back into her bag, Daniel reappeared. A young boy wearing a torn singlet accompanied him, carrying two plates heaped with rice. The load looked heavy for the child's thin arms, but he carried the plates with steady hands.

Emma followed the two over to a table and sat down. The boy placed one plate in front of her and the other by Daniel, then sauntered away towards the bar.

The rice dish was cooked in the Indian style with whole spices and pieces of meat and vegetable mixed through it. The food looked freshly made and the steam that rose from it was fragrant with spices. The plate and cutlery were shiny clean. Emma felt a surge of hunger.

'It is not from this cafe,' Daniel said. 'The owner's wife has prepared this food for her own family. I asked her if we could have some of it. I explained to her that you must be careful what you eat.'

'Thank you. That's very thoughtful,' Emma said gratefully. It occurred to her that she hadn't experienced a man looking after her like this for a long time. It wasn't because Simon had been away for so many months: it was more that their relationship was based firmly on being an equal partnership. They were each presumed to be capable of looking after themselves. It was the same with her male colleagues at the Institute.

'What would you like to drink?' Daniel asked her. 'Coke? Beer?'

'I'd like beer,' Emma answered. 'I'm going to pay for us both, by the way.'

Daniel accepted her offer with a nod of his head. 'Would you like Tusker, Kilimanjaro or Safari?'

Emma smiled. 'You sound like an expert. You choose.'

Daniel attracted the attention of the boy. '*Kilimanjaro mbili!*' He turned back to Emma. 'It is Tanzanian beer. Some people like Tusker but it is made in Kenya.'

The boy brought over two bottles, slung between the fingers of one hand. Setting them on the table, he expertly flipped off the lids with an opener that hung from a string around his neck. He looked too young to be so confident and efficient.

'How old are you?' Emma asked.

'*Una miaka mingapi?*' Daniel translated for her.

The boy held up six fingers.

'You are doing a good job,' Emma said.

Daniel passed on the compliment, but with a shake of his head. 'He will expect a big tip now.' He was about to shoo the boy away, but then started talking to him instead. The boy spoke animatedly, as Daniel leaned round to look across the square to the podium.

When the interchange was finished, and the boy had wandered off, Daniel turned to Emma. 'I asked him what special event has taken place here. He told me there was a visit by a very important man – Joshua Lelendola, the Minister for Home Affairs.'

Emma tried to look impressed. The way Daniel had named the politician suggested he held deep respect for him. And someone had gone to a lot of effort decorating the podium. She guessed that politicians might be of more interest to people here than in Australia.

'I went to school with Joshua,' Daniel said. 'He is a Maasai as well. We were best friends.' A note of disappointment entered his voice. 'Unfortunately he is no longer here. He has returned to Dar es Salaam.' He seemed to remember the food, then, and motioned for Emma to eat.

As she tasted the first mouthful, he leaned forward, waiting for her response. She could see the beginnings of a smile on his face – he had a way, she'd noticed, of holding back his smile, keeping his lips closed, then suddenly setting it free. In that moment, his face was transformed.

'It's delicious!' she announced. As his smile broke through she took a second mouthful, closing her eyes in enjoyment. The pilau tasted of cardamom and cloves; the small pieces of meat dotted through it had a rich chicken flavour.

Emma ate steadily, pausing only to take long gulps of beer straight from the bottle. She didn't stop eating until the plate was empty, the beer almost gone.

When she looked up, she was surprised at how much time had passed. The square was now in shadow; the sun had sunk behind the buildings. The day was nearly over.

Her thirty-second birthday.

'It's my birthday,' she found herself saying to Daniel.

'This very day?'

'Yes.'

He lifted his bottle of beer towards her. 'Happy birthday to you.' He half-sang the words to the traditional tune. He grinned, looking relaxed and carefree. Emma smiled back. Right then, it was easy to picture him as a university student, enjoying life in Dar es Salaam. Though he looked so different from the men she knew at home, he seemed suddenly familiar. She felt at ease with him and she sensed that he felt the same. The experiences they'd shared today – more potent that many close friends shared in a lifetime – had drawn them together. She lifted her bottle in reply.

'Cheers.'

'This will be a birthday to remember,' Daniel added. 'Dinner at the Salaam Cafe . . . I must apologise that there is no cake!'

Emma laughed. 'That's okay. I don't eat cake, anyway.'

Daniel raised his eyebrows. 'I have never heard of someone who does not like cake.'

Emma thought of explaining that she did like it, but that she avoided getting into a habit of eating sweet things. Instead, she just took a long gulp of beer. She found she wanted to tell Daniel more about why she was here.

'I always promised myself that the year I turned thirty-two I would travel to Tanzania and find the research station. You see, that was the age Susan was, when she died.' Now that she'd begun, the words kept pouring out. 'I thought seeing the station might help me forget her, somehow. Bring it all to an end. Then I could stop missing her. Stop thinking about her. I know I should be able to.'

She broke off, watching Daniel's face. She waited to see a look of confusion appear there, or pity. After all, it was such a long time since Susan had died. How could she still be talking about missing her?

But Daniel just shook his head. 'She was your mother. She gave you life. You should never stop thinking about her.'

Emma looked down at the table, tracing the round shapes of the stains left by glasses and bottles on its once-varnished surface. He made it sound so simple. She should not even try to forget Susan. His words brought her a feeling of relief, as if she'd been told she could abandon an almost impossible task. But then, Simon's face swam into her mind. She knew he wouldn't agree with Daniel. He'd discouraged Emma from seeing a psychologist to talk about her mother – he felt there was nothing to be gained by going back over the past. He'd even tried to make Emma get rid of the bag of Susan's possessions that she still treasured. Once, when he'd found Emma trying on Susan's old wedding dress he'd become almost angry. His response to his own unhappy past – a childhood torn between two warring parents, each as bitter as the other – had been to walk away from it. He had almost nothing to do with his family; he claimed he was free of them at last. He wanted Emma to be free as well – he believed that was the whole point of her making this journey. The thought made Emma feel guilty, like someone who was reneging on an agreement. And anyway, she was still not sure that Simon's approach was wrong. As long as Emma could not forget Susan, she would continue to carry with her the aching feeling of loss, a heavy weight inside her. She felt hopelessly caught between needing to remember and wanting to forget.

'You admire your mother.' Emma lifted her eyes as Daniel continued speaking. He sounded matter-of-fact, as if what he were saying was obvious. 'You have given your life to follow her. You said you are a medical researcher, just as she was.'

'Yes, I am, but I'm nothing like her. I could never go out into the field at short notice, and work in such remote places. She was so brave.' She looked closely at Daniel. 'You are brave, too, working in that lab at the station. At the Institute, we only deal with Level Four virus samples in a PC4 lab. We have an air-locked chamber with negative pressure. I wear a breathing suit with an air-tank. Before leaving the chamber I scrub off under a hot shower.'

Daniel smiled ruefully. 'Being afraid of Olambo fever is not our big problem. We would be pleased to encounter it!'

'What do you mean?'

'Our goal is to find out where the virus hides between outbreaks. There must be a host animal or insect that sustains the virus reservoir but is unaffected by the virus itself. We trap wild animals and collect blood samples. We test domestic animals as well. Rats. Fleas. Everything.' He spread his hands. 'We can't find the virus. Not yet.'

'And until you do, there's no way to prevent an outbreak.'

'That is right. The last one was in 2007 – the same year as Ol Doinyo Lengai erupted. Lots of people died of the fever.' Daniel's voice died away, momentarily, and Emma recognised the look of distress that she'd seen on his face at the graveside. 'Children and old people became victims. So did strong, healthy adults. Anyone.' He looked straight into Emma's eyes. 'I don't know how much you know about Olambo fever. It is a very hard way to die.'

'Well, I've studied all the cases documented by the CDC. I know the first symptoms are sore throat and eyes, fever, muscle pain and headache, soon followed by a rash. The throat becomes so sore that it looks like a raw wound. Then the bleeding begins.' Emma had read the CDC fact sheet on Olambo fever so many times she was almost reciting it word for word. 'Blood may ooze from injection sites, or the patient's gums; a woman can bleed heavily from the uterus. Eventually patients slide into a coma as organs begin to fail. Mortality is around eighty per cent. Basically, the patient bleeds to death from the inside. As you've said, the original source of the virus is unknown, but it can be passed on through exchange of blood, saliva, vomit, etc.'

Daniel was silent for a few seconds, then he nodded. 'It is exactly as you have said. In an outbreak everyone is very frightened of catching the fever. Olambo is a clever virus to create so much bleeding. Sometimes, when a member of a family becomes ill, others will even run away and abandon them to die on their own. That is a terrible thing.'

Emma looked down. 'That's what happened to my mother. I got the reports from the archive at the CDC. Her colleague left the area to try to arrange for her to be evacuated. Her local assistant ran away. She had no one to give her painkillers or even a drink of water. She was all alone when she died.' Emma lifted her gaze. 'Her body was found in the bedroom of the station.'

'I have heard this,' Daniel said sadly, a look of sympathy in his eyes. 'But I can tell you something – she was not completely alone.'

Emma stared at him. 'What do you mean?'

'When I came to the station to start my research project, I found a photograph on the wall in the bedroom. It was hung beside the bed where someone could see it without lifting their head from the pillow. The picture is of a little girl.' His voice softened. 'I think it is you.'

Emma swallowed. Her mother had always carried a framed photograph of her daughter on field trips. She normally kept it under her pillow.

'What did you do with the picture?' Her voice came out in a whisper.

'The people who used the building before me did not touch it – and neither did I. It looks as if it belongs there. When we get back, I will show it to you.'

Emma nodded, unable to speak. She felt she'd been given an unexpected gift. She would be able to see the photograph, and touch it – this proof that she had, in some way, been with Susan when she died. If nothing else came out of the journey to Tanzania, it would all have been worthwhile.

'The room where it hangs is the one where Ndugu sleeps,' Daniel said. 'My room is on the outside of the building. It is just a shed, really.'

Emma looked at him in surprise. From her memory of the station, there were only two main rooms – the laboratory and the one opposite; the rest of the facility was made up of outbuildings. She assumed the only proper bedroom would be used by the senior researcher, not his assistant. Scientists were normally very careful about their status.

'I like to sleep in a small room,' Daniel added, as though he'd read her thoughts on her face. 'I feel more at home.' He looked searchingly at Emma. 'Ndugu's room has been cleaned and the bed made up, ready for his return from Arusha. It is the most suitable place for you to stay. But if you prefer, we can swap.'

Emma's lips parted as the reason for his offer dawned on her. She tried to imagine what it would be like to lie down in the very room where Susan had died. To try to sleep there. She recoiled from the idea: it was almost macabre. She was about to ask to have Daniel's room – she didn't care what kind of place it was. But then, something inside her stirred against that choice. What would it really be like, she asked herself, to stretch out her limbs in the space that had once been occupied by Susan? To look up at the ceiling and see what she had seen. To hear the same noises in the night, breathe the same smells . . .

Emma struggled to reach a decision. She scanned Daniel's face – his calm features, patient demeanour. She remembered the look of respect he'd given her, after she'd said they should drive straight to Malangu. She wanted to see that expression again. She knew it would make her feel stronger.

'I would like to sleep in my mother's room,' she told him.

Daniel nodded slowly as if he understood the battle she'd just fought. Then he got to his feet and called the boy to take away the dishes.

The main road out of Malangu was wide and smooth compared with the terrain they had crossed during the day. The darkness seemed to wrap itself around the Land Rover, parting only grudgingly to let the beams of the headlights break through. Emma and

Daniel sat in silence, their bodies jolted now and then by corruga-
tions in the road. The movement of the lights ahead of them was
mesmerising. Emma was beginning to feel drowsy when she heard
Daniel's voice.

'Do you mind if I listen to music? It will help me stay awake.'

Emma remembered the iPod lead protruding from his pocket.
'Go ahead. But I could drive if you like.' It occurred to her that he
would be tired by now, after all the driving he had done. But as she
made the offer she looked doubtfully at the unlit dashboard and
the gear stick with its diagram worn off.

'It is too dangerous to practise driving this Land Rover in the
dark. I will listen to music and you can go to sleep.' Daniel dragged
out his earphones, along with a silver iPod. Shaking the leads until
they were untangled, he placed the earpieces in his ears. Immediately a new energy entered his body and he moved his head faintly
to a beat Emma could not hear.

After a few minutes, Emma leaned across. 'What's the music?'
She wasn't sure what answer she was expecting – Swahili pop, like
she'd heard in the taxi on the way into Arusha from the airport,
or classical music, perhaps, that Daniel might have discovered at
university.

Daniel took one of his earpieces out and offered it to Emma.
She slid across onto the middle seat, so that the cord would reach
her own ear. Her shoulders were close to Daniel's, but not touching. Holding the earpiece against her ear, she listened intently. The
music was unlike anything she had heard before – a mix of American
rap and reggae, combined with what sounded like tribal chanting.

There was a single vocalist who was half-talking, half-singing, in what she guessed was Swahili.

'It's Tanzanian hip-hop,' Daniel said. He grinned, his teeth showing up in the darkness.

Emma raised her eyebrows. 'Really?'

'Tanzania is the home of African hip-hop,' Daniel added. 'I used to go to the clubs in Dar es Salaam and listen to it. This man – he is called Nasango – he comes from this area. You can hear Maasai men singing with him.'

'What is he singing about?' Emma asked.

'He is singing about the problems of the poor and the lost, and how they look to the strength of Ol Doinyo Lengai, the Mountain of God.'

The Mountain of God.

Emma could no longer see the volcano, but she remembered how it had looked, rising up on the horizon. It did have a grand, otherworldly presence that she knew would never be acknowledged, let alone explained, by one of Simon's geologist's talks.

Emma closed her eyes. She let the music enter her, the beat overriding the erratic movement of the Land Rover. Across the small gap between their shoulders, she sensed the same beat running through Daniel's body.

After a time, the lead vocalist fell quiet, and the chants rose into the space left behind. She imagined the blend of voices – bold and strong – spreading through the darkness, way out across the land.

*

Daniel steered confidently along the track to the station. When he turned off the headlights, Emma's eyes adjusted gradually to the gloom. In the faint light of a half-moon she could see the dark shape of the Land Cruiser.

'Mosi has probably gone to the village to sleep,' Daniel said. 'We will see him in the morning.'

He took a torch from the storage pocket in the front door, and switched it on. A single, narrow beam lit the way as Emma followed him round to the back of the Land Rover. There they each picked up an armful of cut grasses and wild plants. They had bought the load of fodder from a farmer who'd been carrying it home on a handcart. Emma had paid for the whole bundle, so that the camels could be fed for at least a couple of days.

She stumbled along the path in the darkness, her bag swinging from her shoulder and both hands buried in dry grass that scratched her wrists. As they neared the wire gate the camels called out to them – loud bellows coming from the shadows. Whether they were upset or frightened or just hungry, Emma couldn't tell.

Daniel opened the gate, letting them both into the compound. He immediately began speaking to the camels in a reassuring voice. There was a rustling sound as he dropped his load of feed. Then a door squeaked open, and banged shut. A short time later, Emma heard a diesel generator shuddering into life, and a light came on outside the back door. The bare bulb was mounted high up on the eaves so that it shed a wide circle of light.

Emma crossed to where the camels stood. She saw that Daniel had dropped his armful into a wheelbarrow.

'Give them your load,' Daniel said. 'We will keep the rest for later on.'

Emma scattered the grass on the ground, then stepped back as the mother began to eat, thrusting her nose almost desperately into the pile of grass and leaves, while keeping her injured foot slightly raised. The calf pushed the grass around playfully with its nose.

Daniel came to stand beside Emma. After a few minutes, the mother stopped eating and limped up to them. She ignored Daniel, turning her head towards Emma, sniffing her hair, then brushing her cheek with plump velvety lips.

'She likes you,' Daniel said. 'Because you are a woman and you are white, she thinks she belongs to you.'

Emma smiled. There was something flattering about being admired by this huge animal. 'What will the police do with them?'

'They should be kept for the owners to reclaim. However, that could take time and someone would have to care for them. So I think they will be sold straight away. The calf is old enough to be taken from his mother. He will be sent to a camel merchant. The injured one will go to the lion man.'

'The lion man?'

Daniel hesitated. When he spoke, his voice was guarded. 'He is an old man – an Englishman – who has a camp in this area. He looks after lion cubs that have no mothers. When the lions are grown up he lets them go back into the bush.'

'So . . . why would he want this camel?'

'He has to feed the cubs. Also, the adult lions return to visit him and he likes to give them meat. He buys all the old camels and the injured ones.'

Emma jerked her head up in shock. 'You mean – she's going to be killed?'

'I am afraid it will happen,' Daniel said. 'This is Africa. Only the tough can survive.'

Emma turned to the mother camel. The animal held her head high, her eyes closed contentedly as she chewed at a clump of grass. Green saliva dribbled down her chin. 'Can't we do something for her foot?'

Daniel nodded. 'I am going to put antiseptic on it now. Tomorrow, I will do a proper examination.'

He moved the wheelbarrow of feed into a small enclosure, out of reach of the camels, then crossed to a small shed where Emma heard him searching for something. She refilled the buckets from the tank, being careful not to waste any water, and carried them over to the camels. As the female drank, Daniel lifted her foot and squeezed ointment onto the cut, rubbing it in with his thumb.

'That will help for now,' he said. He yawned, covering his mouth with his forearm. 'I am very tired. You must be, as well.'

Emma thought back over the long day – the many hours of driving, all the things that had happened. 'I am.'

He led the way across to the back door. From inside his shirt he pulled out a key hanging on a leather cord. After jiggling the key in the lock for a few seconds he managed to turn it. Emma followed him into the hallway. She recognised the smells of kerosene and wood smoke, blended with the insect repellent that still clung to her hair. Daniel switched on a single light – a bare bulb dangling from the ceiling in the middle of the hallway. Then he headed towards the two doors that stood opposite one another. Opening the one that led to the bedroom, he turned on a light and disappeared inside.

Emma faltered, then walked in after him. She found herself in a large room that mirrored the laboratory in size and shape. She went straight to the single bed. The patch of wall near the pillow was half-obscured by a mosquito net that hung down over the mattress from a wooden frame. But she could just see the edges of a picture frame. Kneeling on the bed, she pulled the netting aside.

Emma caught her breath. The print was faded – the colours bleached to pastels – but she knew the picture well. There was another copy of it in her father's photograph album. The shot had been taken only days before her seventh birthday – just before Susan left for Tanzania. Emma looked into her own, child's eyes. They looked so bright and open and warm.

'It is you?' Daniel asked quietly.

She nodded, a lump rising in her throat. She thought of Susan, lying here, looking at the little face. It would have been some comfort to her – but surely, that emotion would have been outweighed by the terrible pain of loss and regret. Emma felt herself being swept up in a wave of darkness.

'There is water here.' Daniel's voice came to her – gentle but insistent – pulling her attention away from the picture. He pointed at a bedside table covered with an African cloth, on which stood a bottle of water and a tumbler draped with a circle of muslin edged with coloured beads. 'You can drink it safely; it has been boiled and filtered.' He spoke in a calm, almost soothing voice. 'When Mosi returns tomorrow and opens the Land Cruiser you will have your suitcase.' He turned towards an old laboratory bench to one side of the doorway. 'Put it there. White ants will eat anything you leave on the ground.' He crossed to a series of wooden pegs along one wall. Removing several garments, he layered them one on top of another, leaving two hooks free. 'Hang up your clothes.' Next, he pointed to an enamel basin set on a wooden crate. On the floor beside it was an old fuel drum with the top cut off, filled with water. 'You can wash here. Do not use the outside toilet after dark – there is a pot under the bed.' Emma nodded. She sensed that all this practical information was intended to reassure her. 'In a little while I will turn off the generator. The lights will go out.' As he handed Emma the torch he gave her a searching look. 'Are you sure you will be all right?'

Emma managed a smile. 'I'll be fine.'

'Then I wish you goodnight.'

Emma stood there as Daniel left the room, closing the door behind him.

She was still for a few seconds, her hand clamped around the handle of the torch. Then she pushed herself into action. She hung up her backpack, and washed her hands and face in rusty-coloured water. She stripped off her shirt and trousers. Standing in her under-wear, she hesitated. She eyed a blue T-shirt hanging from one of the pegs. Normally she wouldn't dream of wearing something that belonged to a stranger; she didn't even know if it was clean. But she didn't want to sleep naked – not here. She already felt too vulner-able. She pulled the T-shirt over her head. It smelled of washing powder, with a hint of wood smoke. The soft cloth hung loosely on her body making her feel small, like a child.

She looked across at the bed. She told herself she had to walk over and climb in straight away, before the generator was turned off. But her feet refused to move. Her arms stiffened at her sides, her hands balled into fists. Her breath caught in her chest. Spinning round, she grabbed the torch from where she'd left it by the washbowl, and switched it on so that she would not be left in darkness – even for an instant – when the light went out. She took two steps back towards the bed, but then froze again. She made herself breathe out slowly, focusing on the yellow beam of torchlight.

At that moment, the light bulb hanging from the ceiling flickered and died. The distant hum of the generator stopped. Into the quiet came sounds from outside – two birds calling to one another; the flutter of moths against the window; something on the roof, making small pattering footsteps.

Emma searched the wall by the bed with her torch, jerking the thin shaft of light along until she found the photograph. The light bounced off the glass, but it was still possible to see the pale oval face behind it. Emma trained her eyes on it as she moved – step by step – to the bed. Without faltering she climbed onto the mattress. Then she untied the mosquito net and pulled it into place, carefully tucking the end in under the mattress, all around.

Emma lay down, resting the torch beside her. The beam shone through the gauzy netting onto the photograph, like a small yellow sun. She let her eyes travel over the image, taking in the details of the face, the hair, the rounded cheeks. She focused on her breathing again – felt the air entering her lungs, the rhythm gradually slowing. She kept her hand on the torch. She would not turn it off, she decided. The light would stay on until the batteries ran out – she had spare ones to replace them in her bag. She would lie still, watching and waiting for the circle of light to fade and finally die.

She stared into the little girl's eyes – her own eyes, framed in a young face. They conveyed such innocence and happiness. Emma searched them for some hint of darkness, a foreshadow of the damage that what was to come. But there was none. As she lay there, under the child's clear gaze, Emma felt her panic ease. As the fear left her body, exhaustion took over. Within moments, she slipped into sleep.

FIVE

Dawn light seeped in through gaps between the rocks, painting the floor of the den a deep golden pink. As the light played over her face, Angel stirred, yawning, and opened her eyes. A spider hung by a silver thread from the stony roof above her. She watched it turn slowly, its eyes glinting like tiny jewels. Carefully, she eased herself from amongst the sleeping cubs. Warmth spread from their bodies and her skin – sticky with sweat – clung to their fur. The lioness had not yet returned from the night's hunting; the place where she had lain earlier was still empty. Angel stretched her cramped legs into the vacant space.

Closing her eyes, she braced herself for the wave of grief that was already building inside her. She knew what came next – the nightmare images of Laura's lifeless face. The body half-covered with stones. Vultures hovering with their eager stares . . . It was like this each time she awoke. There was the short interlude of peace before the reality of Laura's death returned, shocking and raw. Angel had survived three mornings so far – maybe four, she'd lost track of time – but repetition did nothing to dilute the horror. If anything, the haunting visions only became more potent. Angel struggled to shake them off. She couldn't risk letting herself think about what had happened. She would begin to cry. Once she began, she knew she would never be able to stop. The sobs would break her into pieces – tiny jagged pieces like the shards of a broken cooking pot.

She focused all her attention on the sounds of the morning. Outside, the birds were waking. She recognised the warble of the sunbirds. She pictured them poking tiny curved beaks deep into the throats of the desert roses, hunting for their breakfast. There were weavers out there as well, chattering brightly. Then she heard the call of the Maasai sparrow and the faint cry of a goshawk. The chorus grew as new birds joined in, adding their own layers to the song.

But there was another sound outside, as well – a low buzzing drone, like a swarm of bees in the distance. Angel sat up, her head brushing the stone above, sending the spider scurrying away. The sound became steadily louder. She gazed into the shadows at the back of the den, her body stiffening in surprise as she worked out what it was. An airplane approaching. It sounded like a small one, the kind the Flying Doctor Service used. The doctors never came to the villages to help people like Walaita, but Angel had seen them land at the airstrip near the Sisters of Mercy hospital, the pilots climbing out, their smart white uniforms proving they had begun their day far from the bush. Tourists and people who studied wildlife used the little planes as well; sometimes they were painted with stripes like a zebra.

Angel crawled out through the entrance hole and stared in the direction of the plane. There it was – hovering above the horizon, like a bird of prey approaching.

Angel felt a jolt of alarm. Suddenly she realised it was coming for her. She saw it swooping down, lowering the huge taloned feet that would grasp hold of her and carry her away. She'd be like a baby gazelle, lost to a desert eagle.

She backed in through the entrance, taking refuge in the shadowy den. The cubs were awake. They seemed to have picked up on her fear and were mewing anxiously, turning their ears towards the noise. Angel gathered them close to her. She put her arm around Girl, keeping a good grip on her – she was the inquisitive one, who was always first to taste the kill or bury her nose in a stream.

'No,' Angel said to her firmly, as she wriggled and spat. 'You can't go out.' Then she turned her attention to Mdogo, the smallest of the litter, the least brave. She laid her cheek on his head. 'It's all right. We're safe in here.'

Her voice sounded calm, but she felt a lurch of fear. It would be easy for a pilot to land the plane in the desert – it was like one big airstrip. And if someone looked around outside the den, they'd soon find the tracks of a girl.

Angel closed her eyes. Was it possible that someone had found Laura? That they'd worked out her little girl was missing? She pictured the dark red rectangle of the passport flying through the air, landing behind a bush. Had someone found it? If she were caught, Angel knew, she'd be sent away to the uncle in England. She would never be able to find Mama Kitu and Matata.

'You won't get me,' she said aloud.

She looked at the flattened grass where the lioness had stretched out, so strong and reassuring beside her. Even if Angel had wanted to be found, she would never have led the cubs out into the open. She'd seen how carefully the lioness searched for safe shelters where the cubs, and Angel, could stay hidden while she was not there to protect them.

As the plane passed low overhead the cubs grasped at Angel with their forelegs and struggled with one another to push their heads under her arms. Even Girl was subdued with fear.

Angel sat still, her ears trained on the sound of the engine. She tried to work out if it was slowing down, preparing to land. But then, with a surge of relief she realised the noise was diminishing – the plane was flying away.

She smiled at her fear. The plane was nothing to do with her. No one could know she was lost. To reassure herself, she played out the facts in her mind. The chances of some cattle herder just happening to be in the part of the desert where she'd left Laura were tiny. The chances of other travellers passing through were even smaller. The only people who might worry about the camel lady and her daughter were the nuns at the Sisters of Mercy, or the village people – like Zuri – who lived nearby at the fig-tree *manyata*. But Angel and Laura had only left there a few days before and everyone had known they were going on a trip to the city. Angel breathed out calmly. But then she thought of the camels. If they'd been found, questions would be asked. She felt torn between hoping they'd found someone to care for them – and hoping they were managing to look after themselves.

She was about to release the cubs when the engine noise grew louder again. They were coming back.

Angel stared blankly for a moment, rigid with tension. Then she glanced around urgently, trying to work out if she could move some of the smaller stones to block the entrance. But they looked too heavy and it would take too long. She heard the plane circling, swooping low – but then – with a burst of engine noise – it accelerated off again.

Angel slowly relaxed. She pictured the plane tilting as it wheeled away, getting smaller and smaller, until it was speck in the dawn sky. She bent to kiss the three furry heads.

'It's really gone, now,' she said in a soothing voice. 'We're okay.'

The cubs looked at her with wide, trusting eyes. Angel smiled down at them. She imagined the lioness watching her with approval. Pride welled up inside her. She knew she'd played her part in keeping the cubs safe, as if she were a real member of the family. It was hard to picture, now, how afraid of the lions she'd been at first – of the mother lioness, mainly; but of the cubs as well. As she sat there, breathing the smell of sleep-warm fur, the memory returned to her, vivid and strong. She felt, again, how shaky her legs had been as she'd stumbled away from the place where Laura's body was hidden under the stones. Caught between the sturdy bulk of the lioness and the rambling trio of cubs, she'd concentrated on placing her feet. She feared stepping on one of the cubs, or doing something else to attract the anger of the lioness. She knew the lioness could strike her down with one flick of her huge paws.

Finally, when Angel had barely been able walk any longer, the lioness had stopped by a thorn tree. After circling and sniffing the ground, she flopped down. The cubs ran to her and began suckling, thrusting their heads against her pale belly. Angel squatted at the edge of the group. While the cubs suckled from their mother, she hunched over her own belly, aching with hunger. She felt faint and sick. Her throat was swollen half-shut, the inside of her mouth was sticky, her lips dry. She gazed at the cubs and longed to be one of them. Flies clustered around her nostrils and eyes, but she was barely aware of them. She hardly noticed the ache in her head. The only part of her that seemed real was her belly. Roiling in pain, it felt like an unquenchable fury inside her.

When the lioness stood up and began leading the cubs on again Angel could hardly manage to force herself to her feet. She clutched at the thorn tree, spiking her fingers.

'I can't.'

She looked at the ground as she spoke. She would lie there, she thought, just lie there and wait for the hyenas to find her again. She could already feel ants walking over her toes. It would not be hard to stop, let go. It would be easy.

But then, the lioness was there, behind her again – prodding her, refusing to let her stop.

Angel stumbled on. With some part of her mind she wondered why the lioness didn't just leave her behind. The idea came to her, then, that the animal had her own reasons for making Angel walk. She was marching her prey to the place where it suited her to dine. A special place for a special meal.

The girl began to laugh, a strange, high sound she did not recognise. It was a relief to think that it would be over soon. All she had to do was put one foot down after the other and the end would be reached.

Her dry lips were stuck together, the skin fused. Forcing them apart, she gasped the hot air. She felt moisture on her lips, and the salt taste of blood. When she looked ahead of her she saw only a spiralling haze of heat.

Then she picked out the shimmer of water. And a pile of dark stones that looked like a miniature city made of toy blocks – something she might have built herself, if she'd not grown out of little children's toys.

She stumbled on, half-closing her eyes to shake off the mirage. But then, suddenly, there was the sound of running water. The lioness was stopping, the tawny head bending to the ground. And there, bubbling out from under a ledge of rock, was a stream.

It appeared to arise out of nowhere, flowing away between sandy banks that were bare and grey. Angel crouched beside the lioness, gulping mouthfuls of water, each swallow sounding loud inside her head, and mirrored by the noisy lapping close to her ear. She scooped water over her face and hair. She buried her hands to the wrists.

When finally she stood up, her stomach was so full she could hear water sloshing as she moved.

The lioness went to lie down beneath a nearby acacia tree, and the cubs fed from her again, suckling greedily. Angel crouched in the shade of another tree close by. As she watched the cubs, she forgot the relief of no longer being thirsty. Hunger returned like an inescapable nightmare. A thought stirred in some distant part of her mind. She turned to the trunk of the tree behind her. Tearing off a piece of bark, she peeled away a strip of the light-coloured inner skin. She chewed it slowly, as Zuri had taught her.

'The hunters eat this,' he'd said. 'It can cure hunger.' He'd fallen quiet, after telling her. Angel had known it was because he was thinking of his father and his older brother. They were both famed hunters, admired by all for their skill. But they'd died from the bleeding sickness, along with Zuri's mother. If he'd not been away at the cattle camp when the outbreak occurred he would probably have died as well.

As Angel sat there chewing, she was aware of the lioness watching, her head tilted as though she were trying to make sense of what she could see. Angel sucked the last of the sap from the bark and tossed the fibres away. The hunger was still there, the sweet bark only slightly dulling its edge.

One of the cubs came over to her, its face splashed with milk. It nudged her hands, leaving wetness behind. As a drop ran across Angel's fingers, her hand seemed to move of its own accord, carrying the bead of milk to her lips.

Even from this tiny taste she could tell that the milk was sweet and rich. It reminded her of Mama Kitu.

At the thought of the mother camel another kind of hunger swept over her. Alongside the desperate need to eat, she longed for the touch of the camel's fur against her skin. She wanted to feel the velvet lips nibbling her shoulder. She craved the impression of safety that came from being close to an animal that was big and strong. Before she could stop it, another memory came to her – Laura's body on the saddle behind hers, her own small shape resting, sheltered against her mother's chest. She pushed the image quickly away. She would think only of the camels. And Zuri.

She closed her eyes tightly and whispered the names. 'Mama Kitu. Matata.' One day she would find them, she told herself. Or they would find her. She would ride them to the fig-tree village. Zuri would be there. He would welcome her into his hut – a home without adults. They'd be two orphans, alone together . . .

But to do that, she had to survive. She had to eat.

Just then, the lioness made a soft calling sound, as if she sensed Angel's thoughts. The child crawled towards her, keeping her eyes turned away. She edged close, moving slowly, giving the lioness every chance to warn her off. But the lioness swung her head round and brushed Angel's face with her muzzle – a gentle touch. The three cubs fed side by side. Angel pushed her way in between two of them, where she could see the fourth teat. Lowering her face against the tickly fur, she began to suck. Along with her mouth, she used her hand with the same movement by which she'd learned to draw down the milk from Mama Kitu's udder. Warm sweetness entered her mouth, running over her tongue, down her throat. As she drank and drank, she felt strength and fullness returning.

When at last she lifted her head, she looked into the face of the mother. Big golden eyes blinked at her, once – then the lioness sighed deeply and settled down to rest.

SIX

Emma watched the first of the morning light creep into the room. She felt strangely calm and well rested after a long unbroken sleep. She waited until the outlines of the furniture, the washstand, and her shoulder bag hanging from its hook all became clear, and the shadows in the corners of the room had disappeared, chased away by the rising sun. Only then did she decide it was time to let herself picture Susan lying here, where Emma herself now lay. She tried to bring images and emotions to life. But she was unable to focus. Susan remained vague and distant. It was because of the photograph, Emma realised. The child was a distracting presence that kept demanding her attention.

Emma tried to ignore her. She turned deliberately away, looking around the room, taking in the crooked shape of a stack of dusty boxes with names of pharmaceutical suppliers printed on their sides. She skimmed her gaze over a crude bookcase which held a pile of faded journals and a collection of empty jars. She noticed that there were hardly any of Ndugu's possessions in evidence. She thought perhaps he owned only a few sets of clothes and other personal effects and had taken most of them away with him. It was a stark contrast to the bedroom she shared with Simon. They had so many clothes between them that even though they'd both packed up to go away, there was no obvious gap in the contents of their walk-in wardrobe.

Glancing back at the photograph, Emma found herself instantly caught up again. There was such a lively, friendly look on the girl's face, as if she were welcoming Emma to a day that should not be wasted. A restless energy sparked inside her. Climbing out of bed, she quickly changed the blue T-shirt for yesterday's clothes. She wrinkled her nose at the smell of sweat and dust. She wondered if Mosi had returned from the village yet – she was keen to get her suitcase from the Land Cruiser and unpack some clean clothes before having a proper wash. She put on her boots – shaking them upside down to check for scorpions, as advised by her book on travellers' health – then stepped out into the hallway.

She paused then, re-tucking her shirt into her jeans. She eyed the back door. It was closed, but the morning light spiked in through gaps between the planks and around the edge of the doorframe. She could hear Daniel talking to someone outside in the yard. She guessed it was Mosi. But even with that in mind, she didn't hurry on along the hallway. She felt suddenly unsure about encountering Daniel. She expected that the closeness they'd shared yesterday would no longer be there – and in its place would be an awkward feeling of unfamiliarity. She half-smiled. It reminded her of facing someone on the morning after a one-night stand, when – in the cold light of day – she found it impossible even to want to get dressed in front of the stranger she had slept with. She told herself that postponing the moment of meeting would not achieve anything – and at least she and Daniel would not be alone. She made herself walk towards the door. But halfway along the hall, her step slowed. There was a sharp tone in Daniel's voice that she'd never heard before. He seemed to be telling someone off in no uncertain terms. The source of his voice kept moving, as if he were striding around the area near the back door.

Reluctantly, Emma pushed open the door, deliberately making a noise to announce her presence. Stepping outside, she stared in surprise. This end of the yard was strewn with clothes. There were books as well. And a down sleeping bag, half-pulled from its cover. Some unravelled bandages lay coiled like white snakes in the dust. Emma recognised the tie-dyed shirt, lying on the ground amid the chaos. Then she saw the two saddlebags, resting flat and empty on the ground. The young camel stood next to them. As Emma watched, he pushed his nose under a pair of cotton trousers and tossed them into the air.

Daniel was moving from one spot to another, bending down to gather the scattered items. He looked up at Emma, his face grim. 'That young camel has done this! He is very bad.'

Emma covered her mouth with her hand, dismayed by the sight of these things that belonged to the woman and her daughter, spread out in the dirt. She looked across the yard to where the mother camel was watching on, calmly chewing the cud. Then she turned back to Daniel. He yelled at the young camel, pushing it away. In response, the calf picked up a book and began nibbling at the cover. Daniel looked up at Emma with an expression of such outrage that she felt an urge to smile. She tried to keep a straight face, but a laugh escaped her. Daniel looked shocked. Then a grin broke over his face. They both began to laugh. The calf dropped the book and screwed up his face – twisting his lips sideways, closing one nostril – looking confused and annoyed. It only made them laugh more. Several moments passed before Emma was able to compose herself enough to join Daniel in gathering up the clothes. She didn't try to put them back into the bags. No damage had been done, but everything would have to be shaken or dusted before being packed away.

'I am going to put these saddlebags in the hallway,' Daniel said as he carried a couple of books over to the growing pile of objects they had retrieved.

Emma picked up a round, flat shape wrapped in cloth. She felt it with her hands, curious about what was inside. Ignoring the thought that she should not invade the privacy of the owner, she untied the cloth and looked inside. She recognised one of the wide, disc-like beadwork necklaces the Maasai women wore. It was an intricate piece, with a striking pattern. She held it up for Daniel to see. He came over for a closer look. He took it from Emma and turned it over, cradling it reverently in his hands.

'It is very old,' he said, 'very precious. It has been given by a mother to her daughter for many generations.'

'I wonder why foreigners have got it,' Emma said.

'I do not know. Something like this would never be sold. It has to stay in the family.'

Emma wrapped the necklace back up, tying the cloth in place, and added it to the pile, resting it carefully on top of some folded clothes.

'Should we take the saddlebags in with us to the police station tomorrow?' she asked.

Daniel hesitated, frowning. 'I forgot to mention the bags to the police officer. It was just a mistake, but I am afraid he will think I did it on purpose. And now, when he examines the bags I think he may be able to see that they have been unpacked here. He might think I have stolen things. So I prefer not to say anything for now. When his boss, the inspector, has gone back to Arusha and everything is normal again – then I will take them.'

'That sounds sensible,' Emma said. She, too, was keen to avoid any trouble.

There were only a few more things to collect from around the yard when Emma noticed a book lying half-hidden under a spiky plant. Reaching gingerly past the sharp-edged, dusty leaves, she pulled out a school exercise book. On a printed line marked 'name', was the word *Angel*, written in round, childish script. Emma stared at the word. Angel. That was the little girl's name. It suited her, with her fair hair and blue eyes. She showed the book to Daniel, pointing to the name.

'It is a common name in Africa,' he said. 'In Swahili it is *Malaika*.'

Emma opened the cover, revealing a full-page drawing done in coloured pencils. It showed a woman and a girl, both with long fair hair, holding hands. On either side of the pair were two camels, one big and one small. Names were written under each of the figures. *Mama Kitu. Mummy. Me. Matata*. The images were finely drawn, with a child's confidence and eye for detail: Emma recognised immediately the look of mischief on the face of the young camel, Matata, and the way in which Mama Kitu watched him with fond disapproval. The girl's mother stood tall, looking strong and reliable. The girl was the centre of the picture. She had a proud smile on her face. The page had a heading, written in big bold letters: *MY FAMILY*.

Emma looked over at Matata and then Mama Kitu. The names suited the two camels as much as Angel's suited her. She fixed her gaze on Mama Kitu's lame foot. She chewed tensely at her lip, remembering what Daniel had said about the mother camel being sold to the lion man. When she turned back to him she found that he, too, was looking across at Mama Kitu.

'I examined her foot this morning,' he said. 'The cut needs to be opened and cleaned properly. She needs a course of antibiotic injections. Then she will heal quickly. If I had some time – a couple of weeks – I could make her well again.'

Emma knew it was likely the police would be here much sooner than that. She studied the picture again. 'It looks like there's no husband or father in this family,' she said. 'And no brothers or sisters either. If Angel is rescued she'll have only the camels to comfort her.'

Daniel nodded. 'If she is still alive, they should find her today or tomorrow. There will be enough time for me to find a way to speak to her or her relatives and warn them to claim the camels straight away.'

'I wonder what will happen – who's going to look after her.'

Daniel spread his hands. 'Maybe she has a father who does not live with the family, but is still around. And she must have some aunties, or a grandmother.'

'I really hope they live in Africa, or some other place where the camels could go.'

'Yes,' Daniel agreed. 'But even if they do not – if Angel has to leave Africa – at least she will see them before she goes, and know they are safe and well.'

'Would you keep them for her, if she has to go away?' Emma knew that it was a big favour she was asking of Daniel. She'd already seen that caring for camels was a lot of work. But she felt, again, that sense of being responsible for Angel – as if this role had been passed on to her as she'd stood by the mother's grave.

'I don't need two camels,' Daniel responded. 'But I could arrange for my oldest brother to take them. He is a kind man and he could make use of them. They would be well cared for, I promise.'

'Thank you.' Emma smiled with relief. She felt sure Daniel would keep his word, whatever it took. He, too, had been swept up in Angel's plight.

Daniel was watching the calf nudging an empty bucket along the ground. He began to chuckle. 'That young one is well named,' he said. '*Matata* is the Swahili word for trouble.'

As Daniel went to pick up the last garment Emma closed the book and sat on the back step, resting it on her knees. She looked down at the name written on the cover, tracing the round letters with her eyes.

'Angel.' She said the name aloud. An orange hen that was stalking past her feet looked up at the sound of her voice and scuttled away. It was followed by a bird of similar shape but with grey feathers spotted with white. Its bare neck looked as if it had been daubed with blue paint. Emma recognised it as a guinea fowl. As far as she knew, they were wild birds, but this one was as tame as the chickens. The strangeness of it seemed to match the rest of this place: the station that looked abandoned even though it was not; the pink flowers that grew on bushes with no leaves; the fine grey sand of the plains; and the mountain, a perfect triangle like something from a child's drawing.

Emma rested her head on her elbows. Feeling the warm touch of the early sun on the back of her neck, she closed her eyes.

She did not notice the sound at first, the distant buzzing as faint as a bee in a garden. But as it grew steadily louder, she lifted her head. After a few minutes a dark shape appeared in the sky. A small plane.

'There they are,' she called to Daniel. The plane was heading into the desert. Flying low. Searching.

When Daniel came to stand next to her, Emma turned to him, frowning. 'I feel like we should be doing something to find her, not just waiting here.'

'To search on the ground in an area like the *nyika* is pointless once the tracks are lost,' Daniel said. 'There are so many gullies and rocks that could hide her. She could be too weak to cry out even if someone is searching nearby. The only chance of finding her is to see her from the air.'

Emma nodded. She would have felt much better if she'd been

able to do something herself, but she understood that what he was saying was true.

They stood there, staring up, squinting against the crystal blue of the sky until the plane was just a small black dot in the distance.

A small free-standing hut made of corrugated iron stood just a short distance away from the back doorstep. Daniel was inside, squatting on a three-legged wooden stool beside an open-topped wood stove, cooking breakfast. Emma watched from the doorway. She was trying hard not to betray her reaction to the bare earth floor, the spots of bird droppings on the ground, the primitive stove that sent smoke rising to a hole in the roof. There was no sign of a sink or tap – the water supply seemed to consist of an earthen pot full of water. Emma peered around the room, looking for signs of built-up dirt. There was the blackness of soot, the smell of charcoal, spiderwebs hanging from the corners of the tin roof. But when she looked closely she saw that the surfaces Daniel was using – a wooden tray with short legs, a chopping board, a small table – were perfectly clean. The insides of the enamel cooking pots gleamed silver in the firelight. The part of the floor where they sat was well away from Daniel's feet. And the smoke was keeping the flies at bay.

Daniel looked relaxed and organised as he leaned over the fire, using a stick to rearrange pieces of charcoal. Reaching behind him, he picked up a bowl of what looked like dough and carried it to the fire. He must have made the dough, Emma realised, while she was feeding the camels and refilling their buckets with water. She'd been proud of how smoothly that task had gone. It was as if she'd slipped into a well-worn morning routine.

Emma found herself watching Daniel, his actions so fluid and confident they might have been choreographed. She wasn't used to seeing a man cooking, unless you counted male chefs on TV, or the glimpses of them you sometimes got in restaurants. She had vague memories of her father cooking when they'd first moved to Melbourne – where there was no Mrs McDonald – but that had stopped when he'd remarried. As for Simon, the only cooking he did was on the barbecue that stood outside on the balcony. He always had a large array of implements on hand, and all the ingredients laid out in separate plastic containers on a special folding table. He wouldn't have contemplated cooking over a fire. His barbecue was made of stainless steel and fuelled by gas. After using it, he'd spend the best part of an hour making sure it was spotless. The food looked and tasted as clean as the equipment on which it was cooked. When Emma cooked, she tried to make sure her meals met that same standard. She always followed recipes to the letter and never experimented. Since she was usually in a hurry she used mainly pre-packaged ingredients, but she always made sure they were low in sugar, salt and fat.

She looked round at the sound of the gate scraping over the earth. Recognising Mosi, she hurried over to meet him.

'You did not come back last night!' he said as she reached him, his face a mixture of relief and concern. 'I was very worried!'

Emma gave him a brief account of what had happened to prevent their return. As she reached the end of her story, he turned away from her, frowning as he looked out past the end of the yard, towards the desert.

'God willing they will find her today,' he said.

Turning back to Emma, he held out a length of black rubber hose; it was curved at each end and looked like a piece of a snake. 'I can mend the radiator now.' He glanced around the yard. 'Where is Daniel?'

'He's cooking breakfast.'

Mosi smiled. 'Good! I am hungry.'

He walked with Emma back to the hut. After exchanging greetings with Daniel he sat down on an upturned fuel drum next to the fire. The men launched into a discussion, conducted in Swahili. Mosi appeared to be asking lots of questions. Emma guessed from the shocked tone of some of his responses that he was being told in detail about their experiences in the desert. As she listened to their voices, Emma ran through the sequence of events in her mind. So many things had happened. It had been only one day, but it seemed to have gone on for much longer than that.

Finally the two fell quiet, as though the story were complete. Daniel cracked eggs into a frying pan shiny with melted butter. When the whites began to set he scooped the fat up over the yolks until they, too, were cooked. Then he shifted the pan off the heat.

'Everything is ready, now.' He passed Emma two enamel plates and signalled for her to hold them out in front of him. He piled one of the plates with fried eggs; on the other he placed a damper, its crust dusted with grey ash. The whites of the eggs and the pale mound of the bread stood out in the dingy light. Mosi held out a bowl carved from wood, the inside stained dark with use. Daniel filled it with pieces of baked sweet potato, then he picked up a metal teapot that was keeping warm at the edge of the fire.

He led the way across to another room, which had been built on to the outside of the house. Like the Salaam Cafe it had walls that were only waist high, but there was wire mosquito mesh above it. Mosi held open a screen door while Emma and Daniel hurried inside, careful not to let flies follow them. The only furniture was a wooden table and a pair of long benches. A square of red and white oilcloth had been spread on the tabletop; in the middle stood a bottle of Tabasco, a jar of honey and some faded plastic salt and pepper shakers. Places had been set for three, with plates, mugs and cutlery.

The two men sat on one side of the table and Emma faced them. Daniel began filling the three plates with food.

'Don't give me too much,' Emma protested. With the portion sizes he was serving, she estimated breakfast would contain twice her daily energy requirement.

He looked at her in surprise, a spoon loaded with a hunk of sweet potato hovering over her plate. 'I am sorry,' he said after a moment. 'We are not used to having a woman here.'

He poured the tea. Emma looked on as Daniel and Mosi each added several spoonfuls of honey to their mugs. As Mosi stirred his tea, something floated to the surface. He scooped it out, dropping it onto the table.

'A dead bee!' Emma exclaimed. Then she smiled, not wanting to be rude.

'Sometimes there are bits of bark or stick as well,' Daniel said. 'It is wild honey from the desert. You can see how dark it is.'

'It is the best honey,' Mosi said.

Daniel nodded agreement. 'It is a gift from my mother.'

Emma sipped her tea, almost scalding her lips on the rim of the enamel mug. The strong, smoky brew aroused her hunger. She forgot about the primitive state of the kitchen, and just began to eat. The eggs were perfectly cooked: crispy around the edges with runny yolks of rich deep yellow. The damper was light and moist and the white flesh of the sweet potato was soft and buttery.

'It is very good,' she said to Daniel. 'Thank you.'

As she ate, she looked past Mosi's shoulder to where another room had been built up against the mud walls of the station. Through the open door she glimpsed a narrow bed with a plain white cover, a row of hooks that held a collection of khaki clothes, a basket woven from undyed sisal string and a green plastic shopping bag. It was Daniel's room, she realised.

Outside the door, a rope was strung between a post and a spindly tree. Pegged to the rope was a pair of trousers and a white singlet. Next to them was one of the plaid cloths that the Maasai men wore. Daniel's was woven from purple and red threads. It fluttered in a faint breeze.

'That is called a *shuka*,' Daniel said.

Emma snatched her gaze away, feeling as if she'd been caught invading his privacy.

'You have learned your first word of Maa.' He began stacking the plates. As he picked up Emma's he smiled. 'You have left nothing!'

Then he stood up. 'Now, I have to operate on Mama Kitu's foot. She will need to be thrown and tied before I can begin. I would like you both to help me.'

Before tackling the camel, Daniel and Mosi took off their shirts and hung them over the washing line. Emma wasn't sure why, at first, but then guessed they didn't want to get them dirty – it was easier to wash skin than cloth. For her part, she had plenty of changes of clothes in her suitcase, and as soon as she reached Ngorongoro she planned to send everything she'd worn so far straight to the hotel's laundry. As she stood beside the men, her sleeves rolled up exposing her bare white arms, she felt like a pale shadow next to the two big, dark figures. Mosi eyed Mama Kitu nervously. It was clear that he was more at home with his Land Cruiser than a camel. He looked unfit, from spending his days behind a steering wheel. Emma tried not to look too overtly at Daniel, but when she did snatch a glance, she felt she could see every muscle in his body laid out beneath his skin.

Mama Kitu backed away from Daniel when he approached her, as though already aware she was about to undergo some painful treatment. Emma and Mosi kept their distance until Daniel had convinced her to sink to her knees. After a short hesitation, her back legs folded as well. Daniel asked Emma to hold the rope attached to her halter, while he and Mosi lashed her legs into the bent position, so that she couldn't struggle to her feet. When she was securely tied, the two men pushed and pulled at her bulky frame, both becoming bathed in dust. Finally they managed to roll her onto her side. Her belly was a huge mound, cloaked in fine smooth hair that was creamy white.

Mama Kitu's face lay on the sand. She protested briefly, then resigned herself to the situation, adopting the same patient manner she used with Matata. Emma knelt beside her.

'Talk to her,' Daniel said to Emma. He was positioning a short-bladed knife over the camel's damaged pad. 'Make her feel calm.'

Emma looked at him as she smoothed Mama Kitu's neck, running her fingers down the sparse mane made of short curly tufts. 'What should I say?'

'Make your voice strong and kind. Speak as if you are her mother.'

Daniel made the first cut. Mama Kitu shuddered, rolling her eyes towards Emma.

'It's all right. It's okay,' Emma said. 'Just stay calm. There's a good girl.' She could see the camel responding to her voice. The eyelids lowered a bit. The neck relaxed. 'You're a good girl.'

Emma kept talking, crooning nonsense that would have made her self-conscious, except that the camel seemed to drink it in. She kept stroking the rough-haired neck. Mama Kitu gazed gratefully up at her. When Emma stopped talking, the camel swivelled her hairy-tipped ear as though searching for something.

Emma peered over Mama Kitu's shoulder to where Daniel was crouched, his head bent close to the injured foot. He frowned with concentration as he pushed the blade hard into the sole. There was a film of sweat over his face and chest and shoulders. On a wooden tray beside him she could see a bottle of disinfectant, a jar labelled 'Stockholm Tar' and a wad of dressings. Nearby was a dish containing a huge hypodermic needle and a couple of equally oversized syringes.

'There,' Daniel breathed out. 'I have opened it now.' He dabbed at the foot with the dressing. When he lifted it away Emma saw that the gauze was yellow with pus. Daniel poured the disinfectant freely over the wound. He kept working, scraping out the hole, and drenching it again. Then he opened the jar of tar and painted it over the raw flesh.

Finally, he sat back on his heels. He wiped his brow with his forearm. 'She is probably feeling better already. The pressure has gone.' He signalled for Mosi to hand him the needle. With a fierce jab he pushed it into the camel's shoulder. Then he attached a syringe, pressing in the plunger. As soon as it was empty, he replaced it with a second syringe. There was a bump like an egg beneath the camel's hide. 'Tetanus and Terramycin.' He sat back, looking pleased. 'I am finished.'

Emma looked down into Mama Kitu's shiny brown eye. The lids looked as if they'd been painted with an Arabian dancer's kohl. The eyelashes were long and lush.

'You are a beautiful girl. You were so good. So good . . .'

Daniel laughed. 'You sound just like a mother.'

Emma went to change her clothes, which had somehow picked up spots of tar, and smelled of disinfectant. On her way back outside, she paused in the hallway where Daniel had stored the two saddlebags and the four rough piles of their contents along the wall. As well as the various items of clothing, there was a thick tuft of animal hair, set into a handle covered in coloured beads. It looked like another Maasai artefact. Emma was about to examine it when her eye was diverted by a splash of red – it was the knitting, wound into a bundle, perched on a heap of clothes. Even in the dim light she could see that it was covered in bits of hay. She picked the knitting up and carried it to the back step. Sitting there – her body in the shade, her legs stuck out into the sun – she unrolled the knitting and began pulling out the seeds, husks and broken stalks one by one. She could hear the distant voices of Daniel and Mosi, who were working on the Land Cruiser. There was an easy companionable sound to their words. Emma suspected Daniel was the kind of person who got on well with anyone from the minute they first met. Simon was the opposite. He could be very brusque with people he didn't know well, and he chose his friends carefully. Nearly all of them were scientists – people who were capable of having conversations that would hold his interest.

As she picked out the last few grass seeds, Emma studied the finished section of the scarf. She guessed the knitting belonged to Angel: the stitches were even, but the needles were large, the wool thick. The needles had been pushed into the ball of wool so that the loose one would not get lost. Emma pulled them both free and unwound a length of yarn. Tentatively, she balanced the needles in her hands. Then she poked one point into a stitch. Wound the wool around. Picked up the new stitch. Looped it over and let the old one go. As the pattern came back to her, she remembered the feeling of Susan's bigger hands moving over hers – the gentle pressure guiding her fingers, the touch of older, harder skin against her own. She heard again the peaceful clicking of the needles, and smelled Susan's powdery perfume. But just as she was savouring these memories, another moved in, pushing it aside. Instead of Susan, there was Rebecca – Emma's stepmother – sitting in her favourite cane chair near the window, working away at her own knitting. Her hands rested on her huge belly. She was making two of everything – little jackets and bunny rugs – for the twins that were on their way.

'Why don't you do some knitting, too?' she asked Emma.

Emma just shook her head.

'Come on, I'll show you.' Rebecca tried to coax her.

'No, thank you.' Emma was aware that her voice was a touch too loud, verging on rude. 'You don't do it like my mummy did. You hold the needles the wrong way.'

Rebecca looked for a long moment, her lips pushed together. When she finally spoke, her tone was gentle and sad. 'I understand.'

Emma had walked off to her room, aware that she'd hurt her stepmother's feelings once again. She'd felt satisfied, and guilty. It had not been the first time she'd rejected Rebecca's overtures – Emma's stepmother had tried to engage her in cooking, craftwork and gardening projects. But it turned out that the invitation to share in some knitting had been the last one Emma had the chance to decline. Not long after that day, the twins had been born premature and Rebecca had become totally absorbed by their needs. Nick and Stevie swamped everything, everyone. Emma was left to herself. She felt gratified, as if she'd won a battle. But underneath was a cold feeling of loneliness, made worse by the knowledge that Rebecca had tried to be like a mother to her. Emma had pushed her away and now the opportunity was gone.

Emma closed her hands over the knitting, squashing the wool into a lump. The thought came to her – new and unexpected – that the damage caused by losing Susan had not been inevitable. It did not need to have been so deep and lasting. Perhaps if there had been one baby instead of two. If they had not been born early. If Emma had been introduced to her stepmother-to-be earlier on instead of meeting her after she was already pregnant. If Emma's father had been less busy at work. So many ifs . . .

Emma rolled up the knitting, putting it down on the step. She stared out across the yard, but she could still see the redness at the periphery of her vision. She closed her eyes, wishing it away. The memory of the scene with Rebecca had taken her by surprise. It seemed that by coming here she'd opened up the past and now she wasn't able to control what came to the surface, or how it spoke to her. A knot of anxiety formed in her stomach. Perhaps Simon was right, it was better not to look back.

Opening her eyes, she gazed at the two camels standing idly in the sun. The only movements they made were the flicking of their ears, dislodging flies, and the endless chewing of the cud. That was the problem, she realised – like the camels, she had too much spare time on her hands. She and Simon always carried their laptops with them so that they could edit a paper or read an online journal if they found themselves with some unoccupied moments.

Emma thought, suddenly, of Daniel's laboratory. With all that had happened, she hadn't even looked at it properly. And she'd barely spoken to Daniel about this research. Maybe she could help him in some way. After all, he was virtually working alone here, and he'd made it clear things were not going well. Emma got to her feet. Already, she could feel her mind settling, focusing. It would be a good use of her time. Not only that, she admitted to herself, she welcomed the chance to impress Daniel with her professional knowledge and insights. She wanted to see, again, that look of respect in his eyes.

Emma stood in the middle of the laboratory, turning slowly round, taking in the contents of the room – seeing lots of things she'd not noticed on her first brief visit. She was waiting for Daniel to finish helping Mosi fit the new radiator hose. She glanced over the small workbench again, noticing the crude construction of the isolator. Then she crossed to have a look at the freestanding structure that had been erected in the far corner. It looked like a fortune-teller's booth, hung with curtains made from a set of child's sheets decorated with red and blue trains. Pulling them apart she peered into the shadowy interior, taking in the matte black shape of a fluorescence microscope. It was an outdated model that in Australia would only be used by students. She pictured Daniel sitting here, day after day, studying the samples he'd collected – searching for evidence of the virus, and finding nothing. Susan may have sat in there, too, but she would've had no shortage of positive results. She was in the middle of an outbreak. It must have been a harrowing experience for her, reading the patient's names on the vials, one after another, then discovering that they were almost certainly going to die. It occurred to Emma again how brave Susan must have been to keep putting herself through such trauma. No wonder her university had created a scholarship in her honour – the Lindberg Award for Excellence, given to a graduating medical science student. Susan had been utterly dedicated as well as fearless. When she was called to the field, she never said no.

Emma had been watching television when Susan received the phone call summoning her on what would turn out to be her final mission. Sometimes the calls from the CDC came at night, but this time Susan had just arrived home from the laboratory. Soon, Emma's father would return from work as well, and they'd all sit down to the meal Mrs McDonald had left for them. Emma knew straight away who was calling. She recognised the look on Susan's face, as if everything around her had suddenly grown small and unimportant. There were the usual urgent questions from Susan. Then the brief stillness after she'd replaced the receiver, followed by intense activity. Emma trailed behind her, watching the travel-worn suitcase being pulled down from the top of the bedroom cupboard. Work clothes being dragged from drawers. Toilet bag packed. Passport wallet placed on the bed.

'What about my party?' Emma asked.

'I'll be back soon,' Susan said. 'Three or four weeks, maybe less. We'll have your birthday then.'

'But we've sent the invitations.' Emma had made them herself, decorating each one with a big number seven cut out from pieces of old wrapping paper.

'I'm sorry, honey,' Susan said. 'You know I have to go. Mrs McDonald will help Daddy with the party. She'll enjoy doing that. I'll bring you back something special.'

'No,' Emma protested. 'I want you to be here for my birthday. Tell them you can't – just this once. Please.'

She willed her mother to step back towards the phone. But Susan just continued with her packing. She didn't need to go over it all again: how the job of a field investigator was to respond to emergencies. How outbreaks of disease didn't follow any schedule.

When the car arrived, Emma was sitting in the driveway, scooping gravel into dusty piles. The side panel of the station wagon came to a halt right beside her. The words printed there loomed large, only an arm's length away from her face. United States Centre for Disease Control. When the driver went into the house to help Susan with her bags, Emma stood up, a handful of gravel in each hand. She hurled them at the car, one after the other, then bent down and filled her hands again.

That was what she remembered most vividly. Not the goodbyes that followed, Emma pressing her face into her mother's hair, breathing the chemical smell that always followed her home from work. Not the final kiss, or the last promises. Just the sound of the little stones hitting the gleaming duco, then pattering onto the ground.

Emma stared into the interior of the booth, still clutching the curtains. When she'd been told Susan was dead, she'd carefully preserved these last memories in her mind. But all her other memories of her mother were just splinters – bits of songs, the feel of a kiss on her forehead, a hand holding hers as she walked in the park. Emma knew Susan had gone away regularly ever since her baby was only a few months old, but she had only vague impressions of her mother's presence and absence over the years. Now, as she stood there in the quiet room, she tried to reach for more pictures, more details of the many farewells there must have been. What came to her, instead, was the image of Simon's back as he walked away, his duffel bag slung over his shoulder. Simon heading across the tarmac to a small plane. Simon on the deck of a ship, waving goodbye. Before him, it had been Jason, the pilot, who kept leaving her behind. And before him, the actor who could not afford to miss any chance he got to further his career.

She gazed into the shadows as the usual thoughts began to unwind in her head. She told herself there was something wrong with her. She was not interesting enough, or attractive enough, for people to want to stay with her. Maybe there was something about herself that she needed to change. But then, her thoughts turned in a new direction. What if was less to do with who she was – and more that she'd always chosen to live with people who would keep abandoning her? That the pattern set in place by her mother had followed her down the years like a curse.

Emma dropped the curtain. She pushed the thought away, shocked at the sacrilege, especially here in this place where Susan had been. She walked over to examine a couple of faded posters pinned on the wall near the door. One was a dosage chart for a veterinary drug. The other was from a health campaign promoting vaccinations. It used a drawing of a small child sheltering from a collection of spears, behind a traditional Maasai shield. The spears were labelled in English and Swahili: 'polio', 'tetanus' and 'typhoid'.

'It is our dream that one day we will see Olambo fever written there.'

Emma jumped at the sound of Daniel's voice; she hadn't heard him approaching on his bare feet. He came to stand beside her. She could smell engine grease backed by something that reminded her of honey.

Emma nodded. A vaccination was the dream solution to a virus. Anti-viral drugs were rarely fully effective, even if someone went to the expense of developing them.

'But it is too expensive,' Daniel continued.

Emma just nodded again. She didn't want to put into words the fact that it would be impossible to attract the necessary funds to develop a genetically engineered vaccine for a disease that had so far only appeared in a few small parts of East Africa. If a lethal virus was threatening people in New York or Sydney it would be a very different matter. 'All you can do,' she suggested, 'is focus on controlling transmission and minimising outbreaks.'

'That is our plan,' Daniel agreed. 'But as I told you before, we cannot find where the virus hides itself. We look and look and there is just no sign of it.' He spoke as if he were describing some kind of exotic animal that was difficult to track down.

'How are you going about collecting and processing your samples?' Emma asked.

'I will show you.' Daniel walked with her around the laboratory, showing her the traps he and Ndugu used and describing how they took blood from the animals and then tested them for antibodies to Olambo. He showed her the old hand-cranked separator that he and Ndugu had used before they'd managed to acquire a kerosene refrigerator. 'Now we just leave the vials upright in the fridge over-night,' Daniel told Emma. 'The blood cells clot and sink – in the morning we can just pour off the serum.'

Emma felt humbled by his appreciation of something as basic as a fridge. She couldn't help thinking of the facilities at the Institute. Without the best equipment and the desired level of support staff, researchers like herself would not be prepared even to begin work.

'Can you see something wrong?' Daniel asked. 'Is there some-thing we should be doing differently?'

Emma shook her head. 'I can't fault your methods.'

Daniel looked despondent, as though he would have been pleased to learn he'd been doing something incorrectly, rather than having to face the fact that his research was failing to find a result.

Emma searched for something to say to comfort him. 'They've never found the reservoir for Lassa fever. And a lot of work's been done on that by whole teams of people. So it's not surprising you haven't succeeded with Olambo.'

'But I am not planning to give up,' Daniel said firmly. 'There is one thing left to try. We have not tested all the big mammals – buffalo, wild dogs, lions, elephants. The only way to take blood from them is to shoot them, either with tranquilisers or bullets. We have no tranquiliser guns. Also, these wild animals react unpredictably to the drugs. It is dangerous for them. I would not like to kill animals just to collect a sample of their blood. I could not do that. So I am trying to find some way to proceed. Meanwhile, we will continue our rodent work.'

Emma felt rush of sympathy for him. He was so uncomplaining about the lack of resources, and so committed to his work. She wished there was something she could do to help. 'When I get back to Melbourne in ten days' time,' she said, 'I'll see if I can find some organisation that might be able to support you.'

'Thank you,' Daniel said. 'I would be very grateful.'

'I can't promise anything,' she said. 'But I'll do what I can.' She looked away from him, shamed by his open gratitude when, really, she was offering so little.

Her eye was caught by a splash of pink – the cut flowers in the jar of water, that she'd noticed the first time she'd come in here. They were same as the ones she'd picked out in the desert and placed on the grave. She touched the petals lightly with her finger. She wondered who'd put them there. It was a woman's touch, surely. She was shocked to feel a twinge of dismay at the thought of this unknown woman. It was as if – after the intense experiences they'd shared – she felt some kind of ownership of Daniel, which was clearly absurd. But still, she couldn't help replaying in her mind the words Daniel had said at the breakfast table.

We are not used to having a woman here.

'Where did the flowers come from?' she found herself asking.

'I picked them,' he said. 'I like to have flowers in here. It reminds me that even though terrible things happen in the world, it is still a beautiful place.'

For a moment there was a look of deep sadness on his face, but he chased it away with a smile.

'It must be time for morning tea,' he said. 'Let us go and find Mosi.'

Emma knelt in the grey earth, leaning forward to pull out clumps of yellowed, straggly plants. Daniel was beside her, digging up the ground with a small hoe.

'I was planning to do this while Ndugu was away,' Daniel said. 'I cannot do field work without him, so I decided this would be a good chance for me.' He looked up at Emma, smiling. 'But I was not expecting help.'

'It's not the holiday I was expecting either,' Emma smiled back. 'But I don't mind,' she added quickly. 'It's something new for me. I live in a third-floor apartment.' She reached for another dead plant, enjoying the satisfying feeling of the roots relinquishing their hold on the soil. At first, she'd been taken aback by Daniel's suggestion that she join him in the task of weeding the abandoned garden plot next to the kitchen, but now she was enjoying the work. She'd begun by wearing a pair of her silicone gloves – aware that tuberculosis was probably endemic here – but they hadn't lasted long before tearing. Within minutes of taking them off, her hands had become grey with dirt. Once she'd accepted that she had to give up worrying about insect bites and disease, she'd come to enjoy the free movement of her hands, the soft feel of the sandy earth against her skin. Now, as she worked, she looked from her hands to Daniel's. They were an odd contrast. The soil was a grey coating on her skin, but showed up pale against his darkness.

'How did anything ever grow here?' Even in the layers well below the surface the earth was bone dry.

'We have rain in the wet season,' Daniel replied. 'And the plants used to be kept alive the rest of the year with water from the wash-basins. Then I became too busy to remember about it. I let them die.' There was note of self-reproach in his voice.

'Well, I hope you aren't going to let that happen again,' Emma teased. 'After all my hard work!'

Daniel smiled. 'If I see the plants looking thirsty, I will think of you sitting right here and I will hurry to give them water.'

Emma's hand stilled, poised over a small tussock of grass. She dropped her gaze, in case Daniel saw how warmed she felt by the thought of being remembered. She'd been spending too much time alone, she told herself. She was becoming desperate for attention.

They returned to their work, moving with separate rhythms as they pulled out plants and tossed them into the barrow. Now and then, they looked up and their eyes met. Emma saw on Daniel's face an expression of faint surprise, as though he could not get used to seeing this white woman in his yard. But it was good surprise, she could tell. He was glad to have her here.

'My father would shake his head if he could see me,' Daniel commented. 'He is an old-fashioned man. The traditional belief of the Maasai is that they are God's chosen people and that Lengai gave them the gift of cows to provide for all their needs – meat, blood, milk, hides. A traditional Maasai does not kill wild animals to eat. And they truly despise people who dig in the ground and grow plants.'

'But you don't,' Emma said.

He looked up with a grin. 'I am a modern Maasai.'

'Does your father accept you being different from him?'

'Oh yes. My father is very proud of me.'

'And your mother?' Emma went on weeding as she asked the questions and she kept her tone light. She didn't want to appear too inquisitive, but she was curious about Daniel. He came from such a completely different world than hers.

'Of course, my mother loves me with her whole heart. I am her first-born son. When she sees me, she looks back to the time before I became a *moran* – a warrior – when I was a boy, still living in her home, even sleeping in her bed.'

Emma felt a thread of envy. He spoke so confidently of his mother's love – as if it were something that he could feel every day, like sunlight on his face. As she watched him digging with the hoe, she was struck by the matter-of-fact way he'd referred to himself as a warrior. She tried to picture him with his face and hair daubed with red mud, like images of young Maasai men prepared for initiation she'd seen on television. Something came to her, then, the one fact that was most often mentioned in connection with the Maasai.

'Did you have to spear a lion to become a warrior?' She bit her lip. Put baldly like that, the very idea of a ritual killing of lions sounded so primitive and cruel that she wondered if Daniel would be offended.

But he didn't seem perturbed. 'These days there are not enough lions, so it is discouraged by the elders. In my age group, I am glad to say, we did not kill lions. But my father did. And my grandfather was known by everyone as "Two Lions" – of course it is said in Maa – because he killed two lions.'

Emma kept her hands busy, pulling out plants. She felt she could sit here all day asking Daniel questions. She loved his lyrical African accent, and the way he never abbreviated words – instead giving each its full place in a sentence – made the things he said sound new and special. She eyed him surreptitiously. With his body so well proportioned, his skin gleaming in the sun, he looked like a god carved in ebony. The features of his face were perfectly symmetrical. Emma could feel warmth building inside her. She wanted to know what it would feel like to smooth her hand over those strong shoulders. She lowered her gaze, unnerved by her response. But it was natural, she told herself. She was drawn to him because he was – physically – the opposite of her. And as any genetics student knew, symmetrical features were attractive between the sexes. In Darwinian terms, he was a desirable mate.

When she looked up, she found Daniel watching her. She felt her cheeks flush.

'Should I pick out the stones as well?' she asked him. She was immediately aware that it was a stupid question. Who'd want stones in their garden bed?

'That would be good,' Daniel replied. 'It will be easier to plant.'

She tried to think of something more sensible to say that would lead them back to the relaxed conversation they'd been having. She thought of asking him how he got the scar on his forehead. But she knew what she really wanted to ask was whether he was married, or if he had a girlfriend, perhaps. He'd spoken openly about his extended family, yet made no mention of a wife or children. And it was clear that he lived alone here with Ndugu. Emma knew it wasn't uncommon for African men to leave their families behind in their home villages when they moved away to work. But wouldn't someone like Daniel at least bring his wife and kids to live in the nearby village where he could see them? Emma thought of asking him about it, straight out – after all, he'd asked her if she was married not long after they'd met. But she wasn't sure how he might interpret her interest. And she feared she might blush even more. She bent her head over the garden bed, concentrating on picking out the small stones, gathering them into a heap.

In the late afternoon, Daniel and Emma sat with Mosi sharing a pot of tea. The men were perched on the back step and Emma had a low, three-legged stool. It had been carved expertly from a single piece of wood; the seat was a shallow bowl worn smooth with use. As she looked idly towards the distant volcano, Emma sipped her tea. She'd followed the example of the others this time and stirred in a spoonful of honey – she felt she needed the energy, working in the heat. The smoky sweetness tasted foreign at first, but she was coming to enjoy it. She shifted her gaze, seeking out the camels. The two of them stood side by side, staring balefully across from the temporary corral that Daniel and Mosi had just constructed in the back corner of the yard. Earlier, Mama Kitu and Matata had seemed offended by being tied up; now they looked equally unhappy about being in an enclosure. Emma had the feeling they were more used to mixing at close quarters with their human companions. She looked over to the garden bed. She'd kept working on it without the men, and it now was clear of debris.

'What will you plant?' Emma asked Daniel.

'Maize, tomatoes and beans, to begin with.'

Emma tried to picture green plants taking over the greyness. There would be a trench, Daniel had explained to her, to catch any water that ran off the bed. Every drop had to be well used. As she studied the plot, she became aware of some uneasiness in the air. Glancing at Daniel, she saw that he and Mosi were exchanging a look, as if something was passing, unspoken, between them. She got the impression that each of them was waiting for the other to speak.

Finally, Daniel put down his mug. 'Mosi has offered to stay here tonight instead of returning to the village. It is possible to make a bed for him in the lab.'

Emma couldn't see why they were discussing it with her. 'If that is what he prefers . . .'

'He would rather return to the village,' Daniel said. 'He has made some friends there. But we are concerned about your reputation.'

Emma's eyes widened. She wondered if she'd understood him correctly.

'Last night was an emergency,' Daniel explained. 'No one would criticise us for being here alone, in the same place. But tonight, it would look like something we have chosen.'

'Daniel is right,' Mosi confirmed.

'I am not concerned from my own point of view,' Daniel said. 'I am thinking of you.'

Emma took a gulp of tea to conceal her surprise. It seemed so old-fashioned, even quaint, to worry about something like this. She wondered what Daniel and Mosi would think if they knew that she and Simon often travelled to conferences or meetings with members of the opposite sex, sometimes in groups, sometimes with just one other colleague. Plenty of the delegates shared not just rooms but beds, and no one raised an eyebrow. Emma had never slept with a colleague, and she didn't think Simon had either – but she did not know for sure. He was a very private person and he certainly didn't expect to have to answer invasive questions. Emma felt a sudden stab of jealousy as she pictured the woman who was, right now, living and working at close quarters with him – Dr Frida Erikssen, the glaciologist from Finland. Simon had mentioned that a woman was joining the expedition, but it had only been at the pre-departure drinks party that Emma had seen her. She was a classic Nordic blonde, aged thirty-something, with perfect honey-coloured skin. Every man in the room, including Simon, had been unable to stop looking at her.

Emma forced a relaxed smile. 'Thank you, but it really doesn't worry me what people think. After all, I don't know anyone here. And I'll be leaving tomorrow anyway.'

'Then there is no problem.' Mosi looked pleased. 'I will return to the village. I have been invited to join a wedding party.'

Emma stole a glance at Daniel. She thought he looked pleased as well. Perhaps he felt, like her, that after all they'd experienced over the last two days, it was right that they should be alone together for this one last evening.

The plane flew over once more, just as the daylight was fading. Daniel was already preparing food in the kitchen, and Emma was sitting nearby on the wooden stool, shelling peanuts. As soon as she heard the distant buzz of the engine, Emma jumped to her feet, searching the sky until she saw the dark shape of the plane. Daniel came to stand beside her, his gaze following her own. The plane was coming from the direction of the desert, flying back towards Malangu. Emma stared up at it. She visualised Angel sitting safely inside the cabin, her ordeal over at last. Daniel had told her the pilot could easily land in the desert. If someone in the search party saw the child from the air, it would be possible to simply swoop down and land – to pick her up and carry her away.

The plane flew low over the station, disturbing the camels. Emma turned to Daniel, meeting his gaze. No words were needed between them. She knew they were both thinking the same thing – hoping for the same miracle. They stood watching as the plane flew on, the silver underbelly flashing as it caught the late sun.

SEVEN

As the shadows lengthened over the sand, Angel began watching the lioness, waiting for some sign that she was searching for a den. The sun was almost at the horizon; soon it would be getting dark.

Angel glanced anxiously away to her left, where the Mountain of God could be seen in the distance. Until mid-afternoon today, the volcano had been directly behind her, as it had ever since she'd begun following the lioness. She wondered why they'd changed from such a firm course. She had thought the lioness might have some particular shelter in mind. But the detour had been long. And the lioness seemed uneasy; she walked with her head held low, her tail moving from side to side. The cubs had picked up on her mood, and were walking close on their mother's heels. Angel made sure she kept up with them as well.

The only landmark ahead was a tree. It stood out on the plain, unusually tall, with broad-spreading limbs, suggesting its roots had found some source of water underground. The lioness was walking directly towards it. Angel frowned. It didn't look like a suitable place to spend the night: the ground was too open. There were a few large rocks sticking up out of the yellow grass, but they were spread out, rather than being grouped into a shelter.

Still some way from the tree, the lioness stopped. Lifting her head, she let out a long high calling sound. It was like the dove-song Angel had heard before except there was a different quality to it now. It seemed lost and mournful.

The lioness called again, turning her head, as if hoping to hear a reply. But the air was heavy with silence. There were no birds even, chattering in the branches of the tree. No hum of insects. The lioness began shivering – great rhythmic shudders travelled through her body. Angel's stomach tightened. She wrapped her arms across her chest as she looked around her, searching for the cause of the tension. Everything appeared normal.

The lioness moved off again, towards the tree and the rocks. She sniffed the ground ahead as she walked. A low growl rumbled in her throat.

Angel followed her, picking her way cautiously through the long grass. Dry and brittle, it rustled against her calves. As she came closer to one of the large rocks, her step faltered. Then she stopped. The shape was not solid. There were stripes of darkness, separated by pale curved lines. Ribs. Angel raised her hand, pressing her fingers against her lips.

No smell came from the carcass. The bones had been picked bare, but for a few shreds of meat, dried hard and black. Along with the ribcage, which was almost intact, there were various single bones. Big, solid bones, that had once worn strong muscles. They lay here and there, at mismatched angles. There was no skin, Angel saw – not a single remnant of hair or hide. She searched amongst the bones. There was no skull.

More carcasses were dotted through the grass. The lioness was moving from one pile of bones to another, the cubs trailing close to her feet. The low growl merged into a desolate moan as she stood still by each, looking down, before walking on.

There were four bodies ranged around the tree. Each one of them had been stripped of its hide and was missing its skull. No animal would leave a kill in this state, Angel realised. Someone had skinned them, taking care to include the head.

She remembered a ranch she and Laura had once visited to get water for the camels. The owner's wife had invited them inside for a cold drink. There had been a rug on the floor, made from a lion's skin. It still had its head, stuffed back into shape, the mouth propped open to show off fierce ivory-yellow teeth and the tip of a dusky pink tongue. There were glass eyes, staring blindly out over the room. Angel could still picture the woman walking around with her tray of clinking glasses, her high heels making dents in the tawny fur.

Each of the mounds was about the same size, the girth of the ribcages matching that of the lioness. The fifth body was much smaller. The ribcage had been crushed into a crisscross of fine bones. The skull was there, still clinging to the top of the spine. It lay on one side, showing half of the teeth – the same perfect little spikes and the long canine that Angel saw whenever the cubs yawned. Angel felt anger rising inside her. No one would want the skin of a cub to put on their wall, yet this little lion had been killed as well. Then she felt a sense of relief that it had not been left to wander off on its own, to die of hunger or at the teeth of some other animal.

When the lioness had visited all of the piles of bones, and her agonised patrol was done, she stood staring into the lowering sun. Lifting her head, she opened her mouth. Now, the moan grew into a roar. Her black lips pulled back from her teeth. Her throat was a dark cavern.

The sound erupted from inside her, rolling out through the air. She moved her great head in a slow circle. As the roar died away she shook it slightly. Then she filled her lungs – her own ribcage showing beneath her hide – and roared again. This time, the sound was even louder. The cubs backed away, their ears flattened. Mdogo sat on Angel's feet, pressing his body against her legs. She could feel his heart racing.

The lioness was oblivious to the presence of her cubs, or Angel. She stood roaring over and over, the fury in her voice mixed with despair. Angel could almost hear the word, the plea, held within the roar.

No! No! No . . .

Angel wanted to go to the lioness and touch her, to break the spell of pain. But she didn't dare. Whoever had done this – professional hunters, or poachers, Europeans or Africans – they were humans, like her. She wouldn't blame the lioness for holding it against her. But, Angel reminded herself, when the lioness had chosen to help her, she had already known about this awful scene. The way she'd approached the place had been like someone visiting a grave. There was the initial moment of hope that the nightmare was not real – but after that, she'd shown no sign of shock, only grief and pain and anger.

Angel crouched with the cubs. Had they been to this place

before, she wondered? She could not guess how long ago the kill-
ings had taken place; whether it was before the cubs were born,
or after. Either way, she wanted to hide their little eyes and cover
their ears. She hoped they did not understand.

As the sun neared the horizon, it reached out across the land.
Angel caught her breath. The lioness was standing, still and tall,
backlit by the golden rays. She looked like a creature made of fire.

EIGHT

The dawn light was thin and dull. In the yard two roosters strut-
ted around, crowing loudly, each trying to outdo the other. Emma
stood near the back door, reaching behind her head to weave her
hair into a single plait – she wanted to look as neat as possible when
she faced the inspector from Arusha. She was about to join Daniel
at the breakfast table when Mosi appeared at the gate, back from
the village.

She waited to greet him. As he came towards her, he seemed
to be studying her, as if he were trying to gauge whether anything
scandalous had taken place while he was gone.

Emma waved brightly at him. 'Good morning, Mosi.'

'Good morning,' he replied, looking slightly awkward.

As he headed on towards the kitchen, Emma smiled to herself,
thinking back over the evening she'd spent with Daniel. At first,
after Mosi had left them alone, they'd been self-conscious with one
another. Each look, each gesture was suddenly overloaded with
meaning. But when they sat at the table and shared a tall bottle
of Kilimanjaro beer, they both became more relaxed. Daniel had
turned off the generator to save fuel, and also so that they would

not be disturbed by the noise. The table was lit by the glow of a
kerosene lantern hung from a hook on the ceiling. The lantern's soft
flickery light cast dancing shadows. Daniel served out his spinach
and peanut stew. Emma let him fill up her bowl. They'd only had
bananas at lunchtime and she'd spent nearly the whole day outside;
she'd built up a healthy appetite.

They chatted easily as they ate. Emma no longer wanted to ask
about Daniel's private life; nor did she want to talk about hers. She
could tell Daniel felt the same. They talked about politics first,
comparing their two countries. Emma was struck by how little she
knew about Tanzania, in contrast to Daniel, who knew which party
was in power in Australia. She asked Daniel how he came to speak
English so well. He explained that his high school and university
studies were all carried out in English and that while he was living
in Dar-es-Salaam and Arusha, he'd spent a lot of time watching television news and current affairs. Then they turned to books. Emma
was surprised to learn that Daniel's taste in authors ranged from
Salman Rushdie to Agatha Christie. He didn't have a lot of choice
in what he read, he explained; his books came from a second-hand
dealer in Arusha, who resold the paperbacks tourists left behind.
Emma thought of how – when Simon was away and she allowed
herself to abandon her professional reading in favour of a novel – she
would wander the aisles of the local bookshop overwhelmed by the
thousands of titles on offer. Daniel's world was so much simpler.
Life here was not easier – in fact, there was terrible hardship – but
there was more time and space in which to move.

As the evening lengthened, they had spoken less. They'd sat

companionably in the screened dining room, listening to the camels mooching around in their corral, the moths fluttering against the mosquito wire, the hiss of the kerosene lantern. When it was time to pack up the dishes and carry them to the kitchen, Daniel started up the generator, electric light banishing the mellow glow of the moon and the lamp. He washed up in a basin and Emma wiped the bowls and cups dry. Then Daniel walked with Emma to Ndugu's room, as he had the night before. This time Emma had felt no apprehension. Her thoughts didn't turn to Susan, or to the child in the photograph. All her senses were focused on Daniel as he walked just a step ahead of her, leading the way.

He had stopped at the door, handing her the torch.

'*Goodnight*, Emma,' he'd said.

Emma had felt a tremor of pleasure at the way he said her name, emphasising both syllables. Em-mah. It sounded new and different, as if he had his own special way of addressing her.

'In Swahili we say *Lala salama*,' he'd added. 'It means, "may you sleep in peace and safety".'

'*Lala salama*,' Emma had repeated. The words had the song-like feel of a lullaby, a blessing.

She looked up into Daniel's eyes, holding his gaze. The moment stretched out, the air between them taut. Then, almost at the same time, they'd each turned away.

Emma had moved into the bedroom, switching on the light. She'd stood still, staring blankly at the stacked boxes, listening to the sound of Daniel's footsteps fading as he moved along the hall.

*

Emma took her place at the dining table, sitting next to Mosi and opposite Daniel. She looked down at the breakfast that had been set out for her. It was even bigger than the serve she'd been given the previous morning. She sliced through an egg, letting the yolk ooze over a hunk of sweet potato. It looked good, but she wasn't hungry. Her stomach was knotted with tension. She kept thinking about the fact that very soon she would learn whether Angel had been found – whether she was alive or dead, or still missing. And also that very soon, she would be setting off for Malangu with Mosi. Daniel would follow behind in his Land Rover. Emma and Daniel would meet at the police station and give their statements to the inspector. Then they would go their separate ways.

'Today you must eat a lot,' Daniel said. 'As you know, the Salaam Cafe does not offer much. And it is a long drive to the Serengeti.'

Emma made herself take a mouthful. She thought his light tone sounded forced and guessed he was feeling the same way she was. As she chewed slowly, she looked over the low walls, across the yard to the camels. Matata was sniffing at a pair of tame guinea fowl as they pecked in the remains of the morning's fodder. Mama Kitu was lying down, her legs folded under her. She had her neck laid along the ground, her chin resting on the sand. She was looking directly towards the screened room where the three were eating. Emma had to smile. The camel's whole posture conveyed an attitude of deep reproach.

'Mama Kitu has not forgiven us for what we did to her yesterday,' Emma said, turning back to Daniel.

Daniel shook his head. 'It is not that. She knows you are going away. She is sad.'

Emma eyed the mother camel. 'But she doesn't know I'm going today. How could she?'

'A camel is a travelling animal. They are used to watching people prepare for a journey. Mama Kitu has seen your suitcase, standing by the gate. She has noticed small changes in the way you move, the tone of your voice, the clothes you are wearing. Maybe she can even feel your emotions. Some camel drivers believe the camel can feel everything they feel. They can tell if you are excited about the journey to come, or if you are sad to leave.'

Emma chewed at her lip. She wanted to say out loud that she was not excited at all about going on the safari, that she was very sad to be leaving the station, saying goodbye to Daniel. She wanted to promise that she'd be back here some day – but she knew she never would.

They ate in silence for a time. The rattle of cutlery on the enamel plates, and even the tearing of the damper into pieces, sounded loud. Mosi poured more tea into the mugs, stirring honey into all of them, the teaspoon clinking against the metal.

'Emma, I must ask you something,' Daniel said suddenly. 'Do you wish to take the photograph? It should be yours.'

Emma was quiet for a few seconds before replying. 'No, I think it should stay there, where it's been for so long. It seems wrong to remove it now.' As she spoke, she was conscious that her feelings about the photograph were not connected with Susan so much as they were with Daniel. She wanted to know that when she was back in Melbourne some small part of her would remain here in this place where he lived.

Daniel met her gaze, nodding. 'It will stay here.'

*

Emma stood by Mama Kitu, stroking the rough hair of her neck. She felt the warmth of the camel's body and breathed her damp-wool smell. The camel looked down at her with liquid dark eyes.

'You're a beautiful girl,' Emma murmured. She smiled at herself, realising she'd slipped back into her pretend-mother's voice.

Matata appeared at her side, pushing his head into her face, seeking his share of attention. Mama Kitu grunted at him, then bent her head and butted him away. Turning her focus back on Emma, she rested her chin on the woman's shoulder. She gave a long sigh, wafting out the smell of freshly chewed grass. Emma stood still, watching saliva drip onto the shoulder of her clean shirt. Only a short time ago she'd been stiff with fear when the camel had done this; now, Emma wished she did not have to move.

'Goodbye, Mama Kitu.' She rubbed her cheek against the velvety muzzle. Then she looked down at the injured foot. 'Get well. You have to get well quickly.'

'It is time to go!' Mosi called to her from the gate. He'd brought the Land Cruiser round and parked outside the yard. Emma could see her suitcase stowed on the back seat. Beside Mosi's vehicle was the Land Rover. Daniel was sitting at the wheel, dressed in a freshly ironed shirt, ready to leave.

Emma glanced back at the station, taking in the main building, the extra rooms built on in haphazard style, the scruffy yard. It looked so familiar to her it was hard to believe she'd only arrived here two days ago. As she headed for the gate she avoided looking towards the camels, but from the corner of her eyes she saw the two heads held high, turning to watch her leave.

Soon they were on the road to Malangu, leaving the station behind. Sitting in the passenger seat of the Land Cruiser, Emma was struck by how clean and modern Mosi's vehicle now seemed. In the rear-vision mirror she could see the old Land Rover with its torn canvas roof, bouncing along the track. It was already falling behind, but she could still pick out Daniel's face. She tried to see if his head was bobbing in time with his music, but the dirty windscreen clouded her view.

In a small room behind the bar at the Salaam Cafe, Emma sat in front of an old desktop computer. The letters on the keyboard were almost illegible, coated with a build-up of grime, and the screen was hazy with dust. The teenager who had taken her payment and led her in was lingering at her shoulder.

'It is slow,' he said. 'But it is coming. Shall I bring you lunch?'

'Just a cup of tea, thank you,' Emma said. As she waited for her email site to load she peered out through the open doorway. She could see Mosi sitting at the bar sipping a Coke and eating a samosa while keeping an eye on the police station across the square so they would know when Daniel arrived. There was already a large truck standing in the parking area. Emma wondered if this was the one that would be sent to collect the camels.

She typed in her user name and password. When the inbox finally showed up she looked quickly down the long list of unread emails, stopping only when she saw Simon's name. While she waited for the message to open she chewed nervously at the side of her finger. When the text appeared she leaned forward eagerly. It was a long message: a whole page. There was no opening greeting, as was typical of Simon – he just launched into writing. As she read, a frown tightened her face. Before long, she was skipping down the lines, just picking up phrases: 'core samples', 'week-long traverse over the ice', 'fortunate to have access to the chopper for half a day', 'promising samples', 'cute penguins'. There was a lengthy account of a visit to the Russian base, and some complaints about not being able to sleep well when it was dark twenty-three hours a day.

Reaching the end of the email, Emma stared at the screen. Simon had finished off with some kisses and a smile icon, but he'd made no mention of her trip, no mention of the fever research station, no mention of her birthday. She shook her head. The fact was, Simon probably didn't even know what day it was. He was like an addict getting a fix – as he liked to tell people, Antarctica was in his blood. It was his first love. Since he and Emma had been together he'd only gone there for short summer trips and now he had the chance to spend a full winter there. Eight whole months. Emma replayed in her mind the day he told her he'd managed to secure a place in the expedition. They'd been sitting in a wine bar after work. Simon had come from a meeting and was dressed smartly. He'd opened the top button on his shirt and pulled his tie loose. The contrast between his weathered, handsome face and the businessman's clothes, casually worn, was very attractive. While he'd been at the bar ordering drinks, Emma had seen a group of young women watching him.

'It may not work out with the trip to Tanzania,' he'd said. He spoke casually, but his posture betrayed his unease.

'What do you mean?'

'I've got the chance to winter over at McMurdo Station this year.'

Emma was too surprised to speak. Simon let a moment of quiet pass, then began laying out the details of the research he would be doing. It was an international-level project, based in the dry valleys. He was hoping to get some serious results, now that he had the right amount of time.

It was clear to Emma that the plan had been developing for some time and was now set firmly in place. She bent her head over her glass, fixing her eyes on the filmy surface of the red wine. She knew there was no point in trying to change his mind.

'Anyway it would be better for you to go on your own,' Simon suggested. 'After all, it's about your mother – your past.'

Emma nodded mutely. He had a point. She knew he wasn't interested in her mother, or the place where she'd worked. For him, the purpose of the trip was the simple matter of Emma saying goodbye, moving on. Maybe it *was* better that she went on her own – she'd be free to respond however she wanted to. But set against that was the fact that she had wanted to share such an important experience with Simon. And she had been looking forward to the time spent together – unbroken by work – that the trip would entail.

'Perhaps you're right,' Emma said finally.

He smiled. 'I knew I could count on your support.' His arm

crept around her waist, and he leaned to kiss her cheek. She could smell the beer he was drinking, mixed with traces of his citrus body shampoo. His lips moved towards her ear, leaving a trail of kisses on her skin. 'I love you, Em – you know that,' he whispered.

Emma resisted for a moment, then leaned into his embrace. She told herself she should not be surprised. She had always known that Simon was not the kind of man you could own. If she tried to hold him too closely, he would pull away. And then she would be left alone. She felt a chill fall over her as she pictured how it would be. A single toothbrush in the bathroom, the sheets on one half of the bed always remaining crisp and unwrinkled, the laundry basket containing only her own clothes. And the pages of her diary stretching ahead over the year, with no date circled in red and marked 'Simon coming home'.

Emma gazed at the computer screen for a while, then wrote a brief reply to the email saying that she was safe and well and enjoying herself. As she pressed 'send', a bleak hopelessness ran through her. She set the feeling quickly aside, focusing instead on the only other email she was interested in reading. It was from her lab assistant, Moira. As she clicked to open it, Emma felt an instant sense of relief as she was once again connected to the organised world of the Institute – the one place where she always knew exactly who she was and what she was doing and why.

Moira's email was a brief note letting Emma know that the MS4 mice had been delivered by caesarean and successfully transferred to a foster mother.

'That's good,' Emma murmured to herself. The mice had been

bred with the specific genetic mutation she needed for her current work. The natural mothers of this strain were not good at raising their young, so it was important to transfer them at birth to a surrogate. The re-bonding could be a risky process and she was glad to hear it had been successful. It meant that when she returned, she would be able to begin her new project without delay.

After signing out, she left the computer and went to sit with Mosi.

'You were very quick,' Mosi said. 'Usually tourists sit in the internet cafe for a very long time.'

'I just had to check my work emails.' Emma gave him a brief smile. 'You know how it is – you can never escape from work!'

Another vehicle entered the square, heading for the police station. It was a four-wheel drive, covered in the distinctive grey dust of the desert. Emma watched it steer into the area marked off with white stones.

'It looks like one of the search vehicles,' Emma said, pointing towards it. Her worries about Angel rose again to the surface.

'God willing they have found her,' Mosi said.

Emma took a deep breath, trying to ease her tension. She turned her attention to a large tabby cat that was sitting nearby on one of the benches. The animal looked half-wild; it had a scarred face, bare patches in its fur and a torn ear. As she watched, it lifted a muscle-bound back leg and began licking its pockmarked fur. Suddenly a rubber sandal flew through the air, hitting the cat on its head. In a flash, the animal had jumped from the bench and disappeared. Leaning round, Emma saw the young boy who had been here on her previous visit. He grinned, pleased with himself, and came to reclaim his sandal.

Mosi got to his feet. 'I can see Daniel's Land Rover.'

Daniel stood waiting for them on the steps to the police station. He looked nervous, Emma thought. He re-tucked his shirt into his trousers and checked that his collar was sitting neatly. Mosi had remained in his Land Cruiser, glad that he was not involved.

When they entered the office, little had changed since their previous visit. There were some more folders and papers spread out over the bench and several crates of Pepsi had been stacked along the wall, but that was all. The police officer was in his place behind the bench.

He greeted Emma briefly in English, then changed to Swahili for a lengthier interchange with Daniel. Emma listened impatiently for the moment when it sounded as though the exchange of courtesies was over, then she broke into the conversation.

'Have you found the little girl?'

The officer shook his head. 'Unfortunately we have not been successful.'

Emma's lips parted. She pressed her hands onto the bench as the meaning of his bald statement sank in. 'You found no sign of her?'

'We found signs of her. The police tracker followed her footprints quite a long way from the grave. But he did not see her.' He shook his head again. 'It is bad news. From the prints he could tell there was a lioness with her. And cubs.'

'That makes sense,' Daniel said. 'I thought some smaller animal was there, too. But the tracks I found were very faint.'

'It is definite,' the police officer said. 'The tracker found very good prints.' He turned to direct his comments at Emma. 'A lioness with young is always dangerous. She has to protect them. And she has to look for weak prey because she does not want to leave her cubs alone for a long time.'

'But there was no sign that the lion had attacked her?'

The police officer paused before replying. 'I am sorry to say this, but she is only small. If the lion ate her, there would not be much left over. And after the hyenas and vultures, there would be nothing.'

His words seemed to linger in the quiet.

'But we did find something.' The officer opened a drawer at his side and took out a small dark red booklet with gold writing on the front. Emma glanced over the cover, taking in the words *European Union . . . United Kingdom . . .*

The officer opened the passport to the page with the photograph and name. Emma studied the picture. She instantly recognised the dead woman's face – but here, her blonde hair was cut short and she wore make-up. She was dressed in a white shirt and had a silver necklace. She looked like an ordinary English tourist. Though there was, Emma noticed, a bold expression in her eyes, and the hint of a smile on her lips that could have been clues to the free spirit she must have had.

'Her name was Laura Jane Kelly,' the police officer said. 'She was a British citizen. She had a tourist visa when she entered Tanzania, but that was nearly ten years ago. No work permit has been issued to her. It seems she was living outside the law.'

He frowned disapprovingly. His last words stuck in Emma's head. She imagined the life of an outlaw – one of freedom and danger, bravery and recklessness – something she knew she would never remotely be brave enough to choose for herself.

'We have notified the British High Commission,' the officer added, 'and they have located the next of kin.'

Emma's thoughts turned to Angel. If she was found – and there was still hope that she would be – the next of kin would presumably be the person who would look after her. 'Who is it?' she asked. 'Are they here in Africa?'

'I cannot give you that information,' the officer said. 'But I can tell you that we know how Laura Kelly died.'

Emma raised her eyebrows. Surely it was too soon for an autopsy to have been carried out.

'The body was removed and examined. It is very clear that she died from snakebite.'

'Snakebite!' Emma repeated. A shiver ran over her skin. It seemed too bizarre, too primitive that an Englishwoman could suffer such a death. But this was Africa. It was a beautiful continent, but it was also a place where life could be snatched away at short warning, whether by a virus like Olambo fever, or in the jaws of a wild animal or by the venom of a deadly snake.

'So there are no suspicious circumstances,' the officer added.

As he spoke, the door opened and a man strode in. He was as tall as the police officer but lean, like Daniel. He wore a green beret and dark green shirt and matching trousers. His eyes skimmed over Daniel and Emma, barely acknowledging their presence. He had broad cheekbones, below which there were lines of purple scarring. They had been cut deep and straight and were evenly spaced.

'This is Mr Magoma, head ranger of Tanzania National Parks, Northern Region.' The police officer waved his hand from the newcomer to Emma and Daniel. 'These are the people who discovered the English woman.'

Magoma looked at them as though for the first time. 'It is a terrible tragedy that the child has been killed.'

Emma frowned. 'But she's only missing. You don't know she is dead.'

'She is dead, I am afraid,' Magoma said. 'The lioness has eaten her. It is the only answer. The tracker saw that the lioness is injured and she has cubs. These two things mean she is dangerous. But that is not the main point.' He paused.

'What is the main point?' Emma bit her lip. Half of her didn't want to hear the answer. There was a hard tone in the ranger's voice.

'This is the area where the lion man takes his lions. The lioness who has eaten the child is most likely one of his.' His mouth curled with distaste. 'They are not normal lions. They are unpredictable. We have had problems with them before. I myself have tried to close the lion camp. Perhaps now the government will listen to me.'

Emma glanced at Daniel. His eyes narrowed, but he did not respond to the man's words.

'So . . .' The police officer rested his hands on the desk. 'Now we are not investigating a crime, we do not need your statements. The inspector has returned to Arusha. You are free to leave.' He seemed about to send them away, then paused, as if some new thought had come to mind. He said something to Magoma in Swahili.

Emma saw Daniel lift his head in alarm. She turned to the police officer. 'What are you talking about?' She smiled politely to help smooth over her rude interruption.

'I am asking Mr Magoma if he can help us collect the camels tomorrow. Our truck has broken down. It is outside at this moment.'

Emma took in a sharp breath. 'The camels?' She threw a sideways glance at Daniel. 'Well, there is a problem. I'm really sorry. It was my fault. You mustn't blame anyone else.'

The officer looked confused. 'What are you saying? Has something happened to them?'

'They ran away,' Emma said. She was aware of Daniel becoming very still beside her. She felt a flash of panic, but knew she could not retract the lie she'd just told. She forced another smile. 'I'm just not used to being in the country. I left the gate open.'

The officer turned to Daniel, his eyes wide with disbelief. Daniel said something in Swahili, and then gave an exaggerated sigh, spreading his hands. The three men swapped veiled smiles. 'If the camels return,' Daniel addressed the police officer, switching back to English. 'I will tell you straight away.'

To Emma's surprise, both the police officer and the head ranger looked relieved by Daniel's words.

'So you can go,' the police officer said.

'But what about the search?' Emma asked him. 'It is too soon to give up. Much too soon.'

'The area has been completely examined from the air. This afternoon some sections will be searched again. But after today, we will not be continuing. Nobody is hopeful any more. Now, you must excuse me,' the police officer nodded towards Magoma, 'we have to attend a meeting.'

He spoke quickly to the ranger. Amid the stream of meaningless Swahili, Emma heard the words Salaam Cafe.

Daniel offered a polite farewell, then steered Emma towards the door.

Outside, he stood still for a moment, looking unsure what to do next. Then he led the way towards the Land Cruiser. Mosi was sitting in the driver's seat with the door open, his head bent over a newspaper.

Emma waited until they were a little distance away from the police building, then stopped. 'Daniel, I'm really sorry I said the camels were lost. I just had to. We can't let them go until we know for sure about Angel. And I couldn't bear the thought of that lion man getting hold of Mama Kitu—'

'No, it was good,' Daniel broke in. 'Now she can recover in peace.'

'But what if they come out to the station and find them there? You could get arrested.'

'They will not come,' Daniel said confidently. 'No one likes to visit Olambo Fever Research Station. Even hearing the name, they are scared. For once, it is a good thing.' He smiled at Emma. 'You are a good liar!'

Emma opened her mouth to protest that she almost never told

lies. But instead, she just grinned back at him, feeling a wave of relief. 'So, the camels are safe?'

'Yes, I will take good care of them. You do not have to worry.'

They walked on a few steps, then Emma stopped again. 'By the way, what did you say about me to those two, that made them smile?'

'I said you had caused a lot of trouble for me. I said you were like a thorn sticking in my foot. I would only smile again when you were gone.'

Emma just looked at him for a second, then she began to laugh. Daniel joined in. But soon they both became serious again.

'What can we do about the search?' Emma asked. 'We have to make them keep looking.'

Daniel frowned. 'I am suspicious about the attitude of the police officer. I think he may have been influenced by that ranger, Magoma. That man sounds as if he has some personal dislike of the lion man.'

'There must be something we can do,' Emma said. As she was speaking an idea came to her. 'Maybe the lion man could help? He might know something about a lioness with a wounded foot.'

'I was thinking that as well,' Daniel said. 'People say he knows every one of his lions as if they were his children. The prides visit him at his camp, and he goes into the *nyika* to visit them. If that is true, he will know where that lioness is likely to be. He can give us his opinion about whether she would have killed the child. It is true that a lioness with cubs can be dangerous, but humans are not their natural prey.' He paused, looking thoughtful, then seemed to come to a decision. 'I will go there.'

Emma looked down at the ground. With the toe of her boot she kicked the dusty earth. Words formed in her head, pushing their way to her lips. They felt at once clear and true, and completely crazy. She was silent for a long moment; when she spoke, her voice was quiet but firm. 'I want to come with you.'

Surprise and wonder flashed over Daniel's face. He looked into her eyes. 'I would like you to come with me, Emma. There are no words to say how much I would wish to have your company, to keep you at my side.'

Emma stared at him. She knew he didn't need her help with going to the lion camp – she had nothing special to offer. But he wanted it. He wanted her. His manner was so honest, his tone so gentle, it brought an ache to her eyes.

'But you do not understand what will be involved,' Daniel continued. 'The lion camp is very far from the station. It will be necessary to stay there overnight, and maybe longer than that. It is a camp. There will be no proper buildings.'

'I don't mind about those things. They're not important.'

Even as she argued against Daniel's objections, Emma felt a twist of panic. If she sent Mosi on to the Serengeti without her, she would not be able to change her mind. Simon's face rose before her. He would be shocked that she was even considering driving off again with Daniel. He wouldn't be jealous – that was an emotion he despised – but he would be furious that she was going to waste the safari tour he'd paid for. These thoughts fluttered like moths in Emma's mind, but she brushed them aside, her resolve hardening. She knew she had to do this one last thing to try to find Angel, and she knew she wanted to go on this journey with Daniel.

'And I have never met this lion man,' Daniel was saying. 'Who knows what he is like . . .'

When he fell quiet, Emma lifted her head and squared her shoulders, facing him with a level gaze.

'I still want to come with you.'

Daniel nodded slowly, a smile warming his face.

NINE

Angel sat cross-legged in the entrance to the rock shelter, looking out between the boulders over a strip of moonlit landscape. There was a wedge of grey-black sky, faintly dotted with stars, and a wider patch of silvery ground. Close by, blades of grass threw wispy shadows on the sand; further away, there were fan-shaped patterns made by the fronds of a native palm. Behind her, deep inside the den, she could hear the slow breath of the lioness and the quiet snuffling of the cubs. They were all asleep, the lioness having abandoned her usual night-time hunt. She'd already made a kill that day. Near sundown, they had surprised a gazelle drinking from a stream. As the lioness dropped to her belly, stalking, the cubs and Angel had stayed well back. The gazelle barely had time to lift its head when she pounced. Angel and the cubs watched as the lioness tore the hide open, beginning at the soft inner part of the hind legs. She'd dragged out the insides, sucking at the intestines. Then she'd paused to bury the inedible parts of the entrails under the sand. Angel guessed that the lioness – like people living in villages or even in temporary camps – wanted to avoid attracting scavengers. When the lioness had settled down to gnaw at the exposed meat, Angel and the cubs joined her. The cubs hardly knew how to eat meat, but they followed the example of their mother, licking at the flesh with their rasping tongues.

Taking her penknife from the pouch on her belt, Angel had prised out the blade, locking it safely into place. Careful to avoid the hairy hide, she'd then sliced off a piece of dark red meat, close to the white bones of the gazelle's haunch. As she'd picked away loose hairs, then lifted the fillet to her lips, she'd heard Laura's voice in her head.

'Don't eat raw meat in the village. You'll get tapeworms. And you hate the taste of the tablets, remember?'

Now, sitting in the den, Angel shook off the memory with a flash of anger. Who was Laura to be offering advice, when she was not here any more? When she'd left her daughter to manage all alone?

Angel rested her head against the cool stone of the shelter. She focused on prodding her loose front tooth with her tongue. It wiggled freely, ready to come out. She remembered Laura's warning about the danger of swallowing it. Then the story about the tooth fairy came back to her. With another burst of anger, Angel grabbed the tooth and yanked it out, welcoming the quick pain followed by the release of salty blood. She flung the tooth into the corner of the den.

Closing her eyes she pressed her fingers against her eyelids. They felt hot and scratchy. All she wanted to do was curl up with the others and sleep. But her mind was alert; her thoughts refused to slow down. She was worried about whether she'd able to keep up, when they set off the next morning. She wished she knew why the lioness kept them all moving, relentlessly, as though they were running away from something. Maybe the lioness knew that poachers were on their trail, but Angel had seen no sign of people, no fireplaces or tracks. She'd heard no unusual noises. The soles of her feet were sore and a cut on her toe was not healing well, even though the lioness kept licking it clean. The heat soaked up any energy she had, and no matter how much water she drank she was always thirsty. The cubs were worn out as well: by mid-afternoon each day, Mdogo started whining at her ankles, until she picked him up and carried him for a while. And as she trudged over the sand, there was one thought always uppermost in her mind. Each step she took led her further and further from Mama Kitu and Matata. She pictured them wandering lost, or worse – being found by strangers. Not everyone was kind to camels. At the markets she'd seen camels scarred from beatings, staggering under loads that were too heavy. She'd seen them so underfed that their ribs stuck out through their hides. When she thought of her camels meeting with such a fate, she felt like escaping from the lioness and turning back towards the Mountain of God. But she knew that if she did that, she would simply die of hunger in the desert.

Angel pulled her knees up and hugged them to her chest. She told herself she should join the cubs, nestling around the lioness. There would be comfort, there. Closeness. When Mdogo woke up he'd lick her arm, giving her one of his baby kisses. But she didn't move. She wanted more than this. She needed someone to talk to. It was as if all the words she'd left unspoken were building up inside her, making a heavy hard lump. Of course, she talked to the cubs, and sometimes to the lioness, but there were only certain things she sensed they would understand. She listened in on their conversations, picking up all the different sounds; learning which ones went with which actions. But she was like a traveller struggling to interpret a foreign language; sometimes she succeeded, but often she was at a loss. Sometimes she knew she even offended the lioness with her ignorance. Or she caused trouble between the cubs.

It was tiring, and lonely.

Angel rested her head on her knees and closed her eyes. She felt frail and empty, like the husks peeled from an ear of corn. She was not tough like Zuri, after all. She was just a white girl. She wasn't strong enough to keep walking. She wasn't strong enough to keep being brave. She felt a sob building in her chest, squashing out her breath.

'Angel.'

Her eyes flew open. Lifting her head, she listened into the night. She thought she must have imagined the familiar voice. But then it came again, softer this time, no more than a sigh. 'Angel . . .'

The lioness stirred. Angel looked around to see the tawny head raised, the eyes open wide.

You heard her, too, Angel thought. You heard Laura call my name.

The lioness sprang to her feet. Cubs tumbled against one another, but didn't wake. Angel stared out into the desert, frozen with shock. The lioness pushed past her, padding into the moonlight.

Angel followed, ducking her head to squeeze through the low opening. She looked around her, hunting the landscape with hungry eyes.

'Laura! Mama!' she cried out, her voice loud and harsh in the still night. Her heart pounded inside her.

The lioness stood still, her tail swishing from side to side. Her gaze was focused on an area of open ground just a short distance away. But there was no one – nothing – there. Moving close to her, Angel bent over, looking along the lioness's line of sight. There was a small rock, a broken stick, a cluster of desert roses clinging to the leafless fingers of a low bush.

A prickle of fear ran up Angel's spine. She pressed herself against the lioness. She could feel the muscles clenched tight beneath the hide. The lioness was alert, poised. Tension emanated from her like heat from a fire.

Angel listened as hard as she could, as if by force of will she could recreate the voice she'd heard. But there was only the panting of the lioness and the beat of her own heart echoing in her ears.

The lioness made a low, gruff noise – a questioning sound. Then, after a few moments, she let out her high singing call. She pawed the ground as if she wanted to get closer to what she could see, but knew she should hold back. As Angel watched her – the way she moved, the intent look in her eyes – she was reminded of something she'd seen before. In Walaita's village she and Laura had come across the holy man sitting outside his hut, talking away to someone neither of them could see.

'He's in a trance,' Laura had whispered as they retreated to a respectful distance. 'They say that sometimes the *laibon* can see spirits of people who have died.'

Angel had watched the old man, fascinated and afraid. He'd not just talked; he'd used gestures as well. She hadn't doubted for an instant that his unseen companion was real.

She stared, now, towards the nothingness that held the animal's gaze. She felt sure the lioness could see someone there. And Angel had heard her mother's voice.

Laura was there.

'Mama,' she whispered. 'You found us.'

She willed herself to see her mother's tall, slim figure. Or at least some hint of her. A shadow or a smudge of light, like the final glimpse of a face as the last glow of dusk is sucked away by the night.

All she could see was a rustling amongst the blooms of the desert rose. It was like a breeze, except that the air was still. It could have been a disturbance made by an insect, a lizard, a small snake. Or by the brush of a trouser leg . . .

Then the flowers were still again, the leafless branches steady.

Suddenly, Angel felt the lioness relax. The animal shook her head, grunting out a long breath.

Angel kept staring ahead. Her hands were fists at her sides. She was poised on the balls of her feet.

'Don't go,' she whispered.

The lioness made a low murmuring sound, the same one that she used to soothe Mdogo when he was afraid. She looked into Angel's eyes.

Angel nodded slowly. The lioness had seen Laura. Laura had seen the lioness. Something important had happened. The knowledge brought Angel a sense that she need not worry any more. The camels would be safe. She would be reunited with them. She would find the strength to do whatever she had to do.

The lioness turned, brushing whiskers along Angel's arm – then she led the way back to the safety of the den.

TEN

Emma stepped out into the yard, dressed and ready to leave, but rubbing her eyes and yawning. It was still almost dark, and the air was eerily quiet. Insects had stopped their night-time chatter, and the restless animals that had pattered over the roof and rustled in the bushes were now gone, but the noises of the morning had not yet begun.

'Mama Kitu. Matata.' She called softly to the camels penned in their enclosure. They were just blurry shapes in the shadows – both lying down, their legs folded under the bulk of their bodies, heads raised up like sentinels. Mama Kitu bleated in reply. Emma felt uneasy about leaving them, but she knew Daniel had arranged for a farmer from the village to feed them and to bathe Mama Kitu's foot every day until he and Emma returned.

Emma headed for the gate. Her green bag, stuffed full with a change of clothes, was slung from her shoulder. In her hand she carried a basket. Daniel had given it to her so that she could pack provisions for them to eat breakfast on the road. Just before leaving the building she'd added a few of Angel's things as well, laying them on top: the bundle of red knitting, the drawing book, some clothes and a pair of sandals.

Daniel was waiting by the Land Rover. There was a jerry can on the ground near his feet and the smell of petrol tainted the air. He looked into the basket, his gaze lingering on Angel's possessions. Emma wondered if he thought it was wrong of her to have brought them. She'd been unsure herself, and had dithered over the saddle-bags in the hallway – a superstitious person would have said it was tempting fate. But Daniel made no comment, so she opened the back door and stowed the basket on the seat beside two sleeping bags and some rolled-up mosquito nets.

She climbed into her seat. It felt familiar to her, now – the broken spring that tipped her slightly to the left, the tear in the vinyl upholstery that snagged against her jeans. And the smell of engine oil, dust and hessian sacking.

Daniel drove with the headlights on, the beams weak and pale in the thinning dark. They set off along the track that connected to the Malangu road, but after just a short while, took a turn-off that led in the opposite direction. They were doubling back, passing behind the station, and heading on.

'Will we be driving towards the mountain?' Emma asked.

'No, Malangu, the station and the lion camp are almost in a line, but it is a curved line.' Daniel moved his hand in an arc to illustrate his words. 'Inside the circle lies the desert – and Ol Doinyo Lengai. But the road to the lion camp is not straight, it has to go right around that long hill.' He pointed at a rounded shape in the distance. That's why it takes such a long time.'

'Do you know exactly how to get there?' Emma could not get used to the way Daniel never needed a map.

'I have driven along this track with Ndugu. We have set rodent traps in the area. But we have not visited the camp.'

'Aren't you curious about this lion man?'

'There is a problem,' Daniel said carefully. 'That ranger, Magoma, is not the only one who does not like him. Many people speak against him.'

Emma lifted her eyebrows. 'What's he done?'

'He has not done anything. But they are afraid of him. They believe that a man who lives with lions is not really a man. Or he is a man with special powers, given to him by the lions.'

'What kind of powers?'

'I will give you an example. People say the Africans who work for the lion man never become ill.'

'Do you believe that?' Emma remembered how he'd not wanted to touch the body in the grave.

Daniel paused, thinking about his answer. 'As an educated man,' he said finally, 'I do not believe he could protect his workers in that way. But as a Maasai, I am not so sure. I have seen healthy people die from a curse. And I have seen sick people recover when they are blessed by the *Laibon*. So I am in two minds.' He pointed across the cabin, past Emma, towards the mountain. 'When Ol Doinyo Lengai erupted, I saw the tower of smoke with the flashes of lightning shooting up. I heard roaring coming from inside. I felt the earth shaking under my feet. I understood the scientific reasons for it all. But at the same time, I believed my relatives when they said they could feel the power of Engai.'

Emma looked in the direction of the mountain. In the half-light all she could see of it was a faint plume of white hovering ghost-like above the horizon. A shiver ran through her.

'So, are you afraid of the lion man?'

Daniel shook his head. 'The reason Ndugu and I have not visited the lion camp is not because of our own feelings – it is because of our work. People find it hard to understand what a virus is. They cannot see one, they cannot touch one. So when lots of strong, healthy people die quickly – and in such a terrible way – they believe something evil is involved.'

Emma nodded. Even scientists like her, who knew all about Level 4 viruses – and had peered down at samples of Lassa, Ebola and Olambo infected blood through the eyepieces of microscopes – struggled to hold on to a rational perspective. When you thought of the devastation they could inflict, the fine-featured little organisms looked deeply sinister. It didn't help that the specimens were viewed in the dark, stained with fluorescent dye so their shapes were always seen glowing in a sea of blackness.

'It has taken many years,' Daniel continued, 'for us to change people's ideas so they can understand how the virus is spread. If we had been friends with the lion man, they would not have trusted us.'

'But now you are going to the camp,' Emma said. 'Can you keep it a secret?'

'It will soon be known by everyone. But we can explain the reason. A child is lost. I hope it will not damage our work.'

Emma looked ahead. The horizon was broken by low hills. Behind one of them was the sun – a brimming glow only just held back. Above it the grey sky was turning a pale shimmering green.

'You're very dedicated to your work.' Emma did not look at Daniel as she spoke. 'It doesn't seem as if you have much time for anything else.'

'I do not need time for anything else.'

The bleak words made her falter, but she continued. 'You don't have a wife, a family?' Glancing sideways she saw his hands tightening on the steering wheel.

'I had a wife, Lela, but she died three and a half years ago.'

Emma was about to ask what had happened, but then made the connection. 'Oh, no. During the last outbreak . . .'

Daniel kept his eyes on the road. 'She was just over six months pregnant when she became ill. I knew she would almost certainly die, along with the baby.' His words came out slowly but steadily. 'I also knew there was more chance of saving her if labour was induced. I did not know what to do. But in the end I made the decision to take this path. I did this even though in Africa a baby born at twenty-eight weeks cannot be kept alive.' He took a deep breath. When he spoke again, his voice was ragged with pain. 'Lela was in a coma when she gave birth. The baby was a little girl. She was perfectly formed. She was beautiful. But she was grey and had no strength at all. She soon died. Lela died also.'

Emma stared at him mutely as she imagined the nightmare. 'Where did all this happen?'

'In my mother's hut, in my village. We passed near it when we drove from the grave to Malangu. Lela and I were living in Arusha but we had travelled back to the village for a wedding. When the outbreak was identified the area was closed off and we had to stay there.'

'You didn't take her to hospital?'

'That only helps spread the disease,' Daniel answered. 'And, as you know, there is no medicine to cure it. I could not leave Lela, so my uncle went to the hospital and asked for the things I needed. Everything was in chaos there. Most of the staff had run away. So when he said I was a vet, they agreed to give him the drip to induce labour, and a few morphine tablets. Lela could not swallow them, so I ground them up and mixed them with water. When they were finished I made a strong drink from opium pods. But she was always in pain.'

'You nursed her yourself?'

'Others were too afraid to help.' His eyes were haunted by the memory of despair and exhaustion. His voice cracked and became hoarse. 'She was ill for four days. The baby was born on the third day. It all felt like a dream. It happened quickly, and at the same time it felt as if it was going on forever.'

'Daniel, I am so sorry.' Emma thought of how compassionately he'd responded to her grief – so old and distant – while all the time bearing his own tragedy. She recalled the advice he'd given her about continuing to remember Susan. 'Do you think of them all the time?' she asked gently. 'Lela and the baby?'

Daniel nodded. 'At first, my thoughts were full of pain. But now I can see memories that make me happy as well.'

'What was she like? Was she a Maasai?'

'No, we met when I was studying in Dar-es-Salaam. She came from Zanzibar. Her family was from one of the Swahili tribes who live there on the coast.' He smiled. 'When she agreed to marry me,

I was so happy. We did not care about the rules of our families. We went out alone before we were married. We even lived together while we were saving up for our wedding. We could not bear to be apart. When she died I felt as if I was losing half of my self. My heart was gone. I did not think I would remain alive.'

Emma watched his face. He looked torn between memories of warmth and pain. 'All that time, when I was talking about Susan, you said nothing of this.'

'It is not the Maasai way to talk of such things,' Daniel said. 'If someone dies young, or in a tragic way, the old people will not even mention that person's name. So I have always kept my feelings about Lela and our baby to myself.' He looked at Emma. 'But you are an outsider. I can talk freely to you.'

Emma could see relief in his eyes, as though sharing his story with her had allowed him to shed some of its weight.

'I'm so glad you told me,' she said.

Daniel drove with one hand, resting back in his seat. Emma looked out through her side window at the unchanging landscape. The steady drone of the Land Rover had lulled her into a daze. It took her a few moments to notice when Daniel began to slow down and she looked up in surprise as he veered off the track to park beside a tree.

He reached down to turn off the ignition. 'Let us eat now.'

Emma nodded approvingly, suddenly aware of her hunger.

'What did you find in the kitchen?' Daniel asked her.

'There was some left-over flatbread, and some of those fried sweet things.'

'*Mandazi.*'

'*Man-da-zi,*' Emma repeated. 'Then, I packed a pawpaw and the jar of honey, some hard-boiled eggs. Some bananas. And Mosi left behind a bottle of lemonade.'

Daniel grinned. 'It is a feast!' He looked suddenly younger, and light-hearted, fuelled by a new energy.

Emma climbed out, lifting her arms over her head and twisting to ease her stiff back. Daniel appeared beside her, holding the basket, along with a folded *kitenge*. He ushered her towards the shade of the tree and spread the cloth out on the ground. The bold black and yellow design stood out against the muted tones of the surroundings.

Emma checked the ground for thorns or insects, then sat down cross-legged. Lifting Angel's things from the top of the basket, she set them down next to her. Then she unpacked the breakfast, laying out all the food. She unwrapped the parcel of *mandazi*, spreading open the torn square of newspaper, spotted with oil and frosted with sugar.

Daniel sat opposite her, his long legs stretched out sideways. Angel's possessions rested between them. The little heap of bright colour kept catching Emma's eye. It was as if it marked the place reserved for a third guest who was yet to arrive.

Daniel watched Emma arranging the food. He seemed to be taking in each action, as though she were some rare specimen of wildlife whose habits were new to him. When everything was ready, they began to eat. They didn't speak. It was enough to savour the tastes and textures of the food, and the view of the land around them. It was Daniel who finally broke the quiet.

'You would be nearly halfway to the Serengeti by now if you had gone with Mosi.' He studied her face. 'Do you mind missing your safari?'

Emma shook her head. 'It wasn't my idea. Simon arranged it for me as a birthday present. It was going to be very rushed – five national parks in seven days . . .' As she spoke, she relived the moment when Simon had handed her the brochure. She'd tried to be pleased, but had been unable to escape the knowledge that his gesture was motivated by guilt.

'Why did he not come with you? It is a long way for you to travel on your own.'

'He got a job in Antarctica. He left back in March. It's not the kind of place you can come and go from.'

'Antarctica! That is even further away than Africa.'

'He'll be down there all winter. He has another three months to go.'

Daniel looked shocked. 'It is a long time for a husband and wife to be apart.'

'We're used to it,' Emma said. 'We don't find it hard any more – in fact, it's probably good for us. We don't take one another for granted.' She broke off. These familiar lines came easily to her. She always reeled them out when people expressed surprise at the way she and Simon lived. But here – talking to Daniel – they sounded more hollow than usual. And he'd spoken so openly and honestly to her.

She began again. 'Simon is not my husband. I just said that when you asked me, to keep my answer simple. He's my partner. We've been together five years. Simon will never marry me, because he wants to stay free. I don't think he minds not being with me. He says he loves me, but . . .' Her voice wavered. 'Sometimes I don't think I know him at all.'

She hung her head. She felt ashamed, but whether she was ashamed of herself for not being able to inspire a deeper love in Simon, or of Simon for not being able to give it, she could not tell. She picked up a grass stem and shredded with her fingers.

There was a brief silence, then Daniel spoke. 'Emma, I have only known you for a short while but I can already see that I agree with Mama Kitu. She admired you straight away, and animals are usually right in their judgements of people.' Emma looked up, her lips parting in surprise. He smiled at her, his eyes travelling over her face. 'And you are beautiful as well.' He shook his head. 'I do not understand this life you have described – having a partner, and spending months apart. I cannot see why any man would want to leave you behind, even for one day.'

Emma smiled back at him. His words were like a fine shawl coming to rest over her shoulders, enfolding her in softness, making her feel cared for and safe.

The two sat quietly for a time, content to let the birdsong fill the air. Then Daniel stirred.

'We still have a long way to go. We must keep driving.'

He began to pack up the leftover food. Emma helped him fill the basket, then she carefully replaced Angel's things. Daniel stood up, his tall figure towering over her. Emma was about to lever herself to her feet when she saw his hand reaching down towards her. His fingers wrapped around hers, strong and firm. Effortlessly, he pulled her up next to him. They stood there, face to face, eye to eye. Their hands lingered together, skin against skin, sharing warmth – then they eased their grip, and broke apart.

ELEVEN

A hand-painted sign mounted on the trunk of a tree was the first proof that they were finally nearing the camp. It bore a picture of a standing lion, with the words 'KAMPI YA SIMBA' drawn in large black letters underneath. Daniel slowed the Land Rover as it drew level with the sign. The lion image was pocked with bullet holes. Emma glanced at Daniel, meeting his gaze, but neither of them commented as he drove on.

Before long, a line of fence posts appeared in the distance: tall, solid poles rising up from the flat earth. As the Land Rover came nearer, Emma could see a tracery of wire mesh running between them. The fence was high and topped with lines of barbed wire. Inside, a few spindly trees and one large one offered shade to a collection of huts with thatched roofs.

'Do you think the fence is there to keep lions in, or out?' Emma checked the land around them for large tawny-yellow shapes.

'Maybe both.'

The track led towards two high gates – crude wooden frames covered in wire mesh. They stood wide open. Daniel drove up to them and stopped. To one side of the entrance was a collection of sun-bleached bones, huge skulls and vertebrae Emma guessed must have come from elephants or rhinos. There was a heap of old truck tyres worn completely smooth.

The dust settled into stillness. A pair of long-beaked storks eyed them from the compound. The Land Rover exhaust creaked as it began to cool.

When minutes passed with no one coming out to meet them, Daniel looked puzzled. 'Maybe he is not here. But the gates would not be left open. And I can see a Land Rover.' He nodded towards a vehicle parked near a collection of large gas cylinders. It looked almost as old as the one Daniel was driving, but bigger, with an open tray back and solid roof.

Daniel turned to Emma. 'I will have a look around.'

'*Hodi!*' he called loudly as he approached the entrance. 'Hello?'

A few steps into the compound he stopped, clearly reluctant to proceed until he'd had some response. He held his arms slightly away from his sides, his hands outstretched. Emma recognised the alert posture from watching him tracking in the desert; it was as if he were looking and listening with his whole body. For a long moment, nothing happened.

Then a figure emerged from behind a hut – a white-haired man, wearing only a pair of khaki shorts. He was holding a rifle, the barrel raised, ready to aim.

Daniel lifted his hands a little, baring open palms. The old man looked him up and down, then shifted his attention to the Land Rover, peering in through the dust-scoured windscreen. Emma stared back at him, taking in his half-naked body, weathered and aged, and his long white hair combed back from his face, the ends hanging almost to his shoulders. She opened the door and swung her legs to the ground.

As she came to stand beside Daniel, the old man lowered the barrel of his rifle, pointing it at the ground just ahead of his feet. His face relaxed and he smiled apologetically.

'You must forgive me for greeting you like this.' He spoke with a refined English accent. It was at odds with his scruffy shorts and sun-toughened chest and arms, but suited his neat moustache and matching beard, trimmed to keep most of his jawline bare. 'We've had trouble with poachers. My assistants are not here at the moment, so I have to be careful.' He looked from Daniel to Emma and back, raising his white bushy eyebrows. 'What is it that you want?'

Emma moistened her lips. 'We've come to see you.'

'You can't come in, I'm afraid. I can't have people just turning up here. I'm sorry, but this is a lion rehabilitation project, not a tourist attraction.'

'We're not tourists,' Emma said. 'We're looking for a missing child. We think she might be with one of your lions.'

The man frowned with concern as he absorbed her words. 'You'd better come inside.' Shouldering the rifle, he held out his hand to Daniel. 'George Lawrence.'

Daniel shook his hand, smiling politely. 'Daniel Oldeani. I am a vet. I work at the Olambo Fever Research Station. This is Emma Lindberg, who is visiting the station from Australia.'

When George took her hand, Emma could feel the bones

beneath his loose skin, but his grasp was firm. He picked up his rifle and walked off, yellow rubber thongs slapping against the soles of his feet.

George stopped outside one of the huts. It was bigger than the other buildings in the compound and had a thatched verandah held up by posts made from tree trunks. As Emma came closer she saw that the whole front was open, so that the interior space blended with the outdoors. George ducked his head under the leafy eave without breaking his stride.

Emma followed him in towards a long dining table with carved legs, its top scarred and stained. Her gaze flicked past some camping chairs, a row of milk churns with lids, a bulbous old-style fridge – then stopped on an antique sideboard. Set out on its polished mahogany top was a cut crystal whisky decanter and an ornate silver ice bucket. Next to the sideboard was a red leather armchair, its back speckled with bird droppings. A Persian rug lay on the bare sand floor.

Emma glanced at Daniel. He was turning on the spot, scanning the walls and looking up at the angled ceilings. There were photographs everywhere. Some were framed, but most were just prints pinned up in rows, their edges curled by the heat. They were all pictures of lions. Emma glimpsed full-grown males with thick manes, furry cubs with big ears, and females with wide smooth brows. There were solo portraits as well as shots of couples and whole families. Some had handwritten dates and captions on them – 'Toto 1986', 'Simian's pride', 'Louisa and her first litter 2004'.

'Sit down, please.' George waved towards the dining table.

Emma pulled out an old captain's chair with a leather cushion and sat down. In front of her, on the table, was a scattering of peanut shells. She was about to brush them away when she noticed brown droppings amongst the debris. She folded her hands in her lap instead.

George took the chair at the head of the table. Moving aside a soda siphon and an empty glass he spread his hands on the tablecloth. 'Tell me what's happened.'

Daniel told him how he and Emma had tracked the camels to the gravesite and found the footprints of a child and a lion. He added that the police tracker had reported spoors of cubs as well.

George listened without interrupting, his eyes fixed on Daniel's face.

'There has been a search, from the air as well as the ground,' Daniel concluded. 'But there has been no success.'

'The poor child. What a terrible tragedy.' George pulled at his beard, then touched his tongue to his top lip. Emma could see he was not only upset by the story, but also anxious and uneasy. 'But what makes you think one of my lions is involved?' he asked. 'There are several wild prides in this area.'

There was a thread of defensiveness – almost anger – in his voice.

'We aren't the ones who are suggesting that,' Emma said quickly. 'But we met the head ranger at the police station. He was pretty sure it would be one of your lions.'

George grunted. 'It would suit Magoma very well if it were true. He wants me gone from here. I refused to pay him a bribe and he's been trying to punish me ever since.' His grey eyes turned from

Emma to Daniel. 'I know the territory of each of my prides. Can you describe to me where they say it happened?'

Daniel nodded. 'Yes, we can. But first, there is something special about this lioness whose tracks were found. She has a damaged pad. A part of it is missing.'

'Left front foot?'

Daniel nodded.

George let out a slow breath. 'Moyo.' He shook his head wonderingly. 'I've been worried about her. Last time I drove out to visit her I couldn't find her. I haven't seen her for months. So she has given birth. She has cubs!'

Emma leaned towards him. 'Please tell us the truth. Would she have attacked Angel?' The question was blunt, she knew, but she couldn't wait any longer. 'Would she have killed her?'

'No. No. No!' George said vehemently. 'Never. She is not like other lions. I have reared nineteen lions and set them free. They are like my children. I love them and they love me. But with most lions there is always the danger of a moment in which something can go wrong. I have wounds to prove it.' He lifted his hair, revealing a pair of deep red scars – puncture wounds – on the back of his neck. Daniel flinched from the sight. George smiled wryly. 'One of my boys. He was terribly sorry later on. But with Moyo it is different. I would trust her in any situation. Absolutely.' George pointed across the table. 'If this missing child was with Moyo, then she is alive. I would stake my life upon it.'

Emma looked into the lion man's grey-blue eyes. She felt a burst of renewed hope that Angel would be found.

'Could the injury to her foot have changed her?' Daniel asked.

'No, it is an old wound. She had it when she came here. It was treated by a vet. It healed well and it's never given her any trouble.'

Daniel was still for a moment, then he pushed back his chair, standing up. 'Do you have a map?'

'Of course.' From the top of the fridge George took down a folded map, spreading it open. 'Show me where you saw their prints.'

Emma reached across the table to point out the site of the grave. She jabbed her finger urgently against the paper. She could feel a tense hollow in her stomach.

George eyed her for a second, then gave her a reassuring smile. 'Don't worry. We'll find Moyo. And we'll find the girl.'

'Angel,' Emma said. 'Her name's Angel.' She felt, somehow, that it was important he know her name.

George nodded as if he understood, then bent over to study the map. He stroked his beard thoughtfully. 'It's not where I'd expect her to be. But since she has cubs to feed, she might have been forced deeper into the desert. It happens at this time of the year.' He looked up, turning from Emma to Daniel. 'Let's get going then. We'll take my Land Rover. I have to get the battery from the solar charger. Wait for me by the gate.'

Emma glanced at Daniel to gauge whether he was going to be happy to leave his trusted vehicle behind but he was already nodding his agreement. She wondered if he'd cast his eye over George's Land Rover as he'd entered the compound, or if he just took it for granted that the lion man should be in charge.

*

They sat in a row of three across the front of George's Land Rover. Emma was in the middle, her legs wedged in beside Daniel's to avoid the gearbox. As the vehicle jolted along, she was conscious of the hard muscles of his calves rubbing against hers, and the touch of his shoulders. Whenever he turned to look at her, she felt her skin warming. She found herself replaying the moment they had clasped hands as they stood near the remains of their picnic.

George studied the land as he drove, now and then commenting on a tree that had been struck by lightning, or pointing to a bird, giving its name. They passed a family of gazelles.

'See that old male,' he said, gesturing towards an animal that was trailing the herd. 'He was badly injured a few months back, but he's looking pretty good, now.'

Further on, he showed them deep tyre tracks left in the ground. 'That was me, six months ago. I was well and truly bogged. I was afraid I'd never get the vehicle out. It's surprisingly wet here in the rainy season, but not much grows on this kind of ground. It's just ash, really, from the volcano. It hasn't been here long enough to break down into fertile soil.' He looked across at his companions. 'It's hard to imagine that one day – long after the time of humans, I suspect – this could be a rich grassland, like Serengeti.'

Within an hour they were back in the desert. The landscape felt familiar to Emma, yet different. There seemed to be more trees and bushes. The grass grew longer and thicker, like yellow hair sprouting from the land. Even the stones were more varied in colour: they were not just grey, but tinged with blue in the shadows and shining, silver and gold, where flat planes met the midday sun.

'The desert doesn't look the same as where we went before,' she said to Daniel. 'It's not so grey and monotonous.'

He eyed her for a second, before shaking his head. 'It is the same. It is you who have changed.' He sounded pleased, as if her clearer recognition of the place was linked in some way to him.

Emma looked back out over the plain. Daniel was right – the landscape was becoming more real to her. She could see it in more detail. She'd had this experience before, while travelling. Any new city – Paris, Madrid, Houston – was just a confusion of cafes, shops, highways, tall buildings and parks, until events and people became linked with it. Then the place slowly came alive. She gazed out of her side window, across the desert, towards the volcano. Even the Mountain of God looked different. The sides seemed steeper, the unusual white lava dripping further down from the peak.

The area around the gravesite was cordoned off with fluorescent yellow police tape. Emma stepped over it, approaching the mess of scattered stones. Laura's body was gone. The pink flowers Emma had placed at her feet were dry husks strewn across the sand. There was an empty Coke can nearby. Cigarette butts made white and tan spots on the ground.

Emma stared down at the place where Laura had been, trying to recall the pale, beautiful face. She hoped that in some way the essence of Laura might still be here. Then she would know Emma and Daniel had returned – that they had not abandoned Angel.

George came to stand beside her, pausing for a moment as

though to pay his respects. Then he moved round to the large stone that overlooked the site. Placing his hands high up the rock he began to scale it. He moved awkwardly, the sleeveless safari vest he'd put on flapping open, his hair falling forward over his face, binoculars swinging from a strap round his neck. He used one hand to support himself; in the other he held an old megaphone painted bright orange. Daniel stepped forward, offering his hand, but George politely waved him away. When he had his feet planted on the top of the rock, George lifted the megaphone to his lips.

A strange call – half-song, half-words – carried over the land. Emma tried to recognise some word or phrase, but failed. She couldn't tell if this was due only to the crackling of the megaphone distorting George's voice, or if he was speaking in another language. After calling out several times, facing in different directions, George lowered the megaphone, using his binoculars to search the landscape. Then he called again.

Everything was still. A large black bird moved restlessly in a tree. A twig cracked under Emma's feet as she shifted her weight. George called again. Nothing.

'Well, she's not around here,' George said eventually. He jumped down from the rock, setting off back towards the Land Rover.

Daniel and Emma followed him. When George reached the Land Rover, he stood still, staring at the ground. 'She might have headed back to her old territory. But then – I don't know. What would she do? That's the question . . .' He smoothed his beard thoughtfully. Then he looked up, his face clearing. 'We'll go to the old camp! It's worth a try. She could have taken the girl there, hoping to find me.'

Emma raised her eyebrows, but said nothing. She was afraid her voice might betray her disappointment and a growing feeling of doubt. She saw, now, how easily she'd been swept up in the lion man's confidence. She climbed into the Land Rover and sat there, looking silently ahead.

Emma followed George across to a large thorn tree with low-stooping limbs. As she stepped in under the canopy she noticed that the foliage was surprisingly dense and green. Near the base of its trunk stood a small structure, like a cupboard with no sides or top, made of branches crudely nailed together.

'The washstand,' George said. 'And there's the fireplace.' He pointed to a triangle of blackened stones. 'That's all there is, now. I took down the hut before I left. No sense in providing accommodation for poachers.'

He gazed around him, the megaphone swinging gently on a strap looped around his bony wrist.

'I stayed here for three months, trying to persuade Moyo that she had to become a wild lion. She desperately didn't want to go off on her own. In the end I shot a gazelle for her and then drove off quickly while she was on the kill. I felt terrible, leaving her behind like that . . .' He seemed lost in the painful memory.

'Where else could she be?' Emma tried to keep her voice neutral, hiding her frustration. It had taken a long time to reach the camp. At several points along the way George had stopped to call to Moyo, with no success. When they'd finally arrived here at the old camp, he'd tried once more. But still there was no sign of Moyo. As George stood talking to Emma, Daniel was walking around the camp searching the ground for tracks.

'She must be further away,' George said, 'somewhere she can't hear me.'

'So what are we going to do now?' Emma sighed, picturing the long drive back to the camp, with a failed journey behind them, and nothing to hope for ahead.

George didn't answer. He went across to the Land Rover and leaned in over the open tray, reaching towards a large metal trunk. There was the harsh creak of corroded hinges as he pulled up the lid. Moments later, he returned to the tree, holding a cardboard tube about half the length of his forearm, with a point at one end. It looked like a giant firework, except that the casing was plain khaki. The words 'HOLD WHILE IGNITING HERE,' were printed at one end.

'Get ready for a loud bang,' George said. He removed a cap from the top of the tube, before ripping away a piece of tape. With a sharp striking movement he scraped the cap over the exposed point. A fuse began to fizz like a sparkler. Emma stepped back as George held the tube high above his head, then hurled it away.

The tube glided through the air in an arc, then fell onto open ground. A few seconds later it exploded and a boom rang out over the plains. There was a flash of white light and thick grey smoke poured from the tube. Birds broke from the treetops, squawking in alarm, and bushes shook as hidden occupants rushed away. A deer blundered through the clearing, almost colliding with the Land

Rover, before fleeing in terror. Then everything was still and quiet again. The acrid smell of cordite drifted in the air.

George looked from Emma to Daniel with a satisfied smile. 'That should reach her!'

Emma stared at him for a few seconds, then turned towards Daniel. He was looking in the direction of the explosion. He seemed shocked, like Emma, but there was also a look of admiration in his eyes. Following his gaze, Emma saw smoke still streaming from the tube. It rose in the breathless air, forming a pillar of cloud.

Emma looked back at George. 'Wouldn't that noise make a lion run the other way?'

'Normally it would. But I've trained my lions to associate it with me.' He wiped his hands on his shorts. 'Let's have a cup of tea while we wait. She must be quite some distance from here.'

'If she's there at all,' Emma said. She bit her lip, immediately regretting her words.

George looked at her calmly, then walked away.

After another visit to the metal trunk, he produced three enamel mugs, a plaid-patterned thermos and a bunch of bananas. Brushing off the flat surface of one of the firestones, he knelt on one knee, setting out the mugs and pouring black tea from the thermos.

Emma sat down on the sandy ground, crossing her legs. She took a sip from her mug. The tea had been sweetened with smoky honey and had a spicy tang as well. 'That tastes good.'

'I add fresh ginger,' said George, straightening up. As he drank his tea, Emma watched his face, searching for some sign of hope or despondency. But she saw neither. He just looked serenely over the plain. When he'd finished his tea, he began to wander, seemingly aimlessly, around the camp. He came to a halt by a large patch of darker ground. The surface, Emma noticed, was cracked, as if it had once been wet mud.

'There used to be a soak here,' George said. 'There's water underground.' He kicked at the darkened earth with his boot, barely denting the sunbaked crust. 'But the animals can't get to it.'

He unclipped a spade that was mounted on the back of the Land Rover's cabin. He began to dig, stabbing the spade deep into the ground. The effort showed on his face; his mouth was pressed into a thin line, his eyes screwed up. The muscles in his arms tightened visibly beneath his wrinkled skin. Emma could see Daniel hovering, unsure whether he should offer to take over. Soon, George was panting and sweat was beading on his face. But only when a damp patch appeared in the bottom of the hole did he hand the spade to Daniel.

As Daniel began digging, Emma gathered up the thermos, mugs and banana skins. She wondered if she should insist on taking a turn herself. Simon would certainly have expected her to – she was an able-bodied person, after all. But it didn't feel necessary, here. Daniel seemed almost to be enjoying the digging; he stood with his legs braced apart, swinging the spade with an easy rhythm.

George pulled a pipe from his pocket. After packing in some tobacco with his thumb, he lit it with a match. He stayed by the hole, puffing steadily, as he watched Daniel work. Now and then he pointed out where the spade should be planted next, and nodded his approval as his instructions were followed. Emma stood watching.

Something was going on between the two men, she realised. They were taking part in a ritual whose meaning they both understood – a dance played out between a young man and his elder.

Eventually, water began to seep into the base of the hole, milky brown and topped with foam. When George gestured with his pipe, Daniel stopped digging and climbed out. Emma stood between him and George as they all looked down at the spring. Sun sparkled off the surface of the water. It seemed miraculous. Emma looked up at Daniel, then turned to George. A smile travelled between them.

'The elephants used to do this with their tusks, each dry season,' George said. 'Now the poachers have all but driven them out. Rhinos as well. The lions will be next.' He gazed down into the spring as he spoke, his hair falling forward. It was yellowed on the ends, Emma noticed – the same colour as the dried grass. 'I thought I'd live to see this whole area declared a national park. Then we'd have a proper base out here, and full-time rangers on patrol.' He shook his head. 'I've put in an application, supported by two wildlife trust funds, backed by plenty of experts. But nothing has happened. Having Magoma against me doesn't help, but I think it's more than that.' A note of frustration entered his voice. 'The problem is that people see national parks in terms of tourism and they believe the only Africa visitors want to see is the savannah or the rainforests – not this kind of country. And they don't see the point in protecting wild animals just for their own sake. They don't understand that having a magnificent creature like the lion out there in the bush – wild and free – makes something more of us all.'

He fell silent, staring down into the gathering puddle of water.

Emma walked away. She looked out over the plain, searching for some sign of the lioness – a patch of yellow-brown, or something moving amongst the rocks and bushes. But she didn't hold out any real hope. Despair of ever finding Angel settled inside her, cold and heavy. She shifted her gaze to the sky, wanting the relief of the wide clear blueness. Then she jerked her eyes back to the land. She'd just caught an impression of something – an image so fleeting she could not even name what she'd seen. She swept her gaze left to right and back. Then a slow shiver ran through her body, touching every nerve.

On the brow of a low hill stood a lioness – a cut out shape set dark against the sky.

'Moyo,' she breathed. She spun round, barely containing a shout of excitement. 'She's come!'

George strode across, shading his eyes with his hand. 'It might not be her,' he cautioned. 'I've seen Simian's pride in these parts.'

The lioness began walking down towards the campsite, a gold-tan shape moving against the grey hillside. Her head was raised, eyes searching ahead.

George watched her intently. A few moments passed, then a smile spread across his face. 'It's her.' Stepping out from the shade of the tree he marched towards her over the open plain. He moved like a young man now, his body upright, head held high.

Emma followed, keeping a good distance back, but shadowing him step by step. A voice inside her warned that the situation was dangerous – it had to be. But she was drawn on, mesmerised by the sight of the big, powerful animal coming nearer and nearer. She was dimly aware of Daniel's footsteps, close behind her.

Moyo kept strolling along with an unhurried gait, moving foot-sure between the stones. When she reached flat ground, her steps became more purposeful. Now Emma could see her toned muscles moving beneath her smooth hide. The fierce strength and the sheer weight of the lioness were almost tangible.

Moyo broke into a jog, heading straight for George. Then she was bounding towards him. Emma tensed with alarm. George's wiry body suddenly seemed thin and vulnerable. The lioness looked as if she were about to attack. But George kept walking towards her, showing no sign of fear. When Moyo was only a few metres away, he spread his arms wide. She reared on her hind legs and launched herself at the old man. As she planted her two paws on his shoulders, George staggered back. Emma gasped – it looked as if he would fall, with the lioness on top of him. But he regained his footing, propping one leg behind him, bracing against the weight. The lioness wrapped her front legs around his shoulders, holding him close. George's arms came up under hers, mirroring the gesture. The two heads rubbed together, Moyo opening her mouth, nuzzling his neck, his face, his shoulders. George buried his face in her fur, his white hair mingling with the tawny brown.

Eventually, the lioness broke away. Back on four legs, she stood facing George, as though wanting to take a good look at her old friend. Her back was level with his waist, her dark-edged ears matched the height of his shoulders. George bent forward, taking her face between his hands, and leaned to kiss her forehead. Then he patted her sides while she wrapped herself around his legs. Before long, Moyo rose on her hind legs again, pulling George back into her embrace. Now they appeared to be wrestling, testing one another's strength, but with no hint of aggression – only affection and joy.

The two finally drew apart. Emma took in the lioness's perfect, symmetrical features, her wide brow, the white fur under her chin. Moyo was all gold and cream, adorned with lines and smudges of deep brown and black. It was as if a painter had been at work on her, using dark brushstrokes to define the shape of her eyes, her ears, the upturned curve of her mouth, her triangle nose.

George began moving towards Emma and Daniel. Moyo followed him, her head lowered cautiously. As she walked, she sniffed the air, her ears constantly moving, seeking sounds from all directions.

She came to a halt right in front of Emma and Daniel and hovered there, looking almost uncertain.

'Just stay still,' George said quietly. 'Don't look into her eyes. Let her make a move in her own time.'

Emma held her arms stiffly at her sides, and kept her chin up. Her heart was pounding. She could hear Moyo's breath moving in and out between her open jaws. Then she felt its warmth on her skin, and caught the salty smell of fresh raw meat.

Moyo sniffed at her body, the huge head moving over her torso and limbs, whiskers brushing the bare skin of her forearms, neck, face. A vision of the livid scar lines on George's neck swam into Emma's mind. She reminded herself that this was Moyo: the lioness who could always be trusted. She fought to believe it.

After what felt like a long time, Moyo shifted her attention to Daniel, pushing her nose against his bare chest.

Emma could look at her close up, now – at the tan-yellow coat, whorled with sweat; the milky hide of her face, marred by small scars. Flies made black dots around her eyes. There was a tear in one of her ears. Looking down, Emma found the left front foot. The tips of three sheathed claws rested on the ground; the fourth claw was missing.

She looked at Daniel. His eyes were wide with amazement and awe. He seemed spellbound. When Moyo finally backed away, he took a step after her as though pulled by an invisible cord.

Moyo padded across to stand beside George. She looked intently into his eyes. A low grumble rose from her throat.

The lioness stalked away a few steps then began prowling restlessly, turning her head in the direction of the hilltop from where she'd approached. Turning back to George, she made a short gruff sound. Then she took two purposeful steps away, heading back out to the plain. She stopped and looked behind her, then set off again.

George nodded his head. 'Good girl, Moyo.' He turned to Emma and Daniel, a gleam of pride in his eyes. 'She's taking us to her den.' He waved a hand towards Daniel. 'I'll walk with her for a bit. You two follow in the Land Rover. When she knows we're coming along, I'll hop in. It might be a fair way.'

Moyo jogged at an even pace, leading the Land Rover across the stony plain. Heat shimmered like a halo in the air around her and dust rose in small puffs as her paws met the earth. Daniel drove right behind her as George had instructed, only a couple of metres from the dark-tufted end of her tail.

'She is not afraid of the Land Rover,' Daniel said, glancing past Emma to where George now sat by the passenger window.

'She *loves* the Land Rover,' George replied. 'If she wasn't on guide duty she'd be riding up here.' He tapped the roof of the cabin above his head. 'I had to get the roof reinforced to carry her weight.' He chuckled. 'She could always tell when I was planning to go to town. She hated being left behind. She'd get up there and nothing would induce her to come down.'

'So what would happen then?' Emma asked.

'She'd come with me. It always caused a stir, but there were no problems unless she caught sight of a chicken. She'd jump down, grab the bird and bring it back up with her.' He laughed. 'I spent a fair bit of money on chickens.'

Emma leaned forward, watching as Moyo picked a path between the boulders and skirted rocky outcrops. The lioness did not look back. She kept on at a regular speed, confident that she would be followed. Emma shook her head, feeling a sense of unreality about what was happening.

George's voice came to her. 'I should prepare you. There's a good chance we're about to meet up with some wild lions. Moyo's pride.'

Emma turned to him. 'You mean Angel hasn't been only with Moyo and the cubs?'

'It sounds as if they were on their own at the grave, but a lioness will usually bring her cubs into the pride by the time they're six or eight weeks old. Moyo's cubs must be older than that, or they wouldn't have been able to make it this far in – what – four or five days? It's a long journey.' He pulled at his beard again. 'She's moved on each day.'

Emma could tell from his tone that this was unusual. 'Why would she do that?'

'I think she's been working her way back to the lion camp.' George's voice was soft with admiration. 'She was bringing that lost child to me!'

'Do you really think that's what she was doing?' Emma asked.

'Without a doubt. Lionesses move their dens to stop a build-up of smells that would attract predators, but they don't shift camp each day. She had a purpose in mind.'

Emma stared ahead again at Moyo. She pressed her hands together, clamping them between her knees. She felt shaky with excitement and anxiety. The end of the search was now so close. She refused to consider the possibility that Angel would not be at the den. The alternative was daunting enough. Emma warned herself they were about to encounter a child who would be deeply traumatised, hungry, exhausted, afraid. She'd have dirty skin, infected cuts, sunburn, matted hair, torn clothes . . .

'These are the rules about mixing with lions.' George's words broke into her thoughts. 'Don't make sudden movements. Never crouch or circle – they'll think you're about to attack. And never walk ahead. Stay at the side, or behind, because if you stumble, you suddenly look like prey. Don't touch a cub unless you are invited to by its mother – it's very obvious when that's happening. Never run from a lion. Hold your ground. As a last resort, lift up your arms like the horns of a bull.' He rested a lean hand on Emma's shoulder. 'Don't worry, though, lions are very rarely dangerous.'

They drove on in silence, all looking ahead, as if urging the lioness on. She seemed tireless, jogging along. Then she picked up speed, almost breaking into a run. She was aiming for a small rocky hill. At its base was a collection of large boulders shaded by native palms.

Moyo ran up to the rocks, coming to a standstill a few metres away, her tail swishing from side to side. In front of her was a gap like a doorway between the two largest stones.

Daniel stopped the Land Rover well back from the rocks. As the engine noise cut out, they could hear Moyo making a low crooning sound. She was gazing fixedly into the gap.

'It's only a small den,' George whispered. 'She must be on her own with the cubs.' He opened his door, making slow movements to avoid unnecessary noise. Climbing out, he motioned for Daniel and Emma to follow. 'Act as if we belong together.'

The three approached Moyo, who was still watching the gap in the rocks. The black tuft of her tail darted through the air like a creature with a life of its own. The lioness stepped forward as though she were about to enter the den. But just then, the small furry face of a cub appeared in the shadows. Moyo raised her head, making her low calling sound. The cub ran out to her, rubbing its head against her legs. The lioness licked the little face with a big pink tongue.

After a few moments, a second face came into view – head

cocked, bright eyes turning from the Land Rover to the group of people, and then to Moyo. When the lioness called again, this second cub trotted out. Then a third cub rushed out of the shadows as though afraid of being left behind. It ran to Moyo, sheltering between her front legs.

The lioness was still eyeing the shelter.

Emma bit her lower lip so hard that she tasted blood. There was no movement from the den. Nothing. She kept watching the darkness, willing another face to appear.

Then Moyo let out an abrupt commanding sound, almost like a bark.

Something moved in the shadows: a pale smudge of a shape. Emma trained her eyes into the gloom. Her breath caught in her throat. She could see a child's face.

Without thinking, Emma stepped forward. There was a flick of long fair hair, and the face vanished.

She stared at the blank darkness. A single thought ran through her mind. It was her – Angel. She was there! After a few seconds, she looked back at George and Daniel.

'Call to her,' George whispered.

'Maybe you should,' Emma whispered back. 'She'll trust you because of Moyo.'

'No, you're a woman,' George argued. 'She'll be less frightened of you.'

Emma swallowed nervously, afraid of saying the wrong thing. 'Angel?' She pushed herself to continue. 'Angel? Angel, I can see you there. Don't be afraid.'

'*Nendeni! Mbali!*' A high clear voice carried across from the den. '*Sasa hivi.*'

Emma turned to Daniel with questioning eyes.

'She's saying, "Go away. Go far away. Go now".'

The three exchanged glances. Emma spread her hands helplessly.

George walked slowly across to stand beside Moyo. She greeted him affectionately again, then watched on as he knelt amongst her cubs, patting them and rubbing his face against theirs.

Emma felt a surge of impatience. He seemed completely absorbed in the encounter, as if he'd forgotten why they were here. She had an irrational fear that Angel would somehow disappear from the den and never be seen again.

Just as she was beginning to think that she, or perhaps Daniel, should go over to the den, she saw the child's face in the shadows again. Angel was following George's every movement, and watching the way Moyo responded to him. Her eyes were wide, her mouth hanging open.

George stood up next to Moyo, resting one hand casually on her shoulder. Then he addressed Angel. 'We want to talk to you. Don't be afraid of us.'

As Angel called out a reply, Emma looked to Daniel again for a translation.

'She says, "Leave me alone. I just want to stay here with the lions".'

George spoke again, this time using what Emma took to be Swahili. But when Angel replied, he looked mystified.

Daniel stifled a smile. 'Now she is speaking Maa. She wants to confuse us. She thinks we will not understand her. Then we might give up and go away.'

'What's she saying?' Emma asked.

'The same thing. "Go away. Leave me behind here".'

Emma was torn between frustration, and relief that Angel seemed so strong and alert. 'Tell her we have to see if she is all right.'

Daniel moved closer to the den and spoke in a voice that was clear but gentle. There was an interchange of several sentences. Then Daniel turned to Emma. 'She wants to know who you are and why you are here.'

Emma nodded. It sounded like a step forward. She tried to decide how to answer the question. She was not a relative, after all, or a friend of the family – or even someone from the embassy, or the Red Cross. She was . . . no one. She decided to make do with the simple truth. 'Tell her the camels found me. That's why I'm here. Because of Mama Kitu and Matata.'

The moment Emma named the camels, Angel stepped out of the shadows. She stood still for a few seconds, blinking in the bright sun. Her brown tunic and trousers were rumpled and dusty and her blonde hair was a tangle around her shoulders. But her smooth, suntanned skin was clean. Her eyes looked bright, her lips rosy.

'Where are they? Are they all right?' She spoke with an English accent similar to George's.

Emma took a couple of steps towards her, but stopped as Angel retreated until she was half lost again in the shadows. 'Yes, they're fine. Mama Kitu had an injured foot but she's going to be okay.' She pointed at Daniel. 'Daniel's a vet. He operated on it. Someone is still nursing her now, while we're here.'

Angel crept forwards, away from the den. 'What about Matata?'

'He's fine, too.' Emma smiled reassuringly. She wanted to run up to Angel and touch her, hold her – make sure she could not vanish again. But she was careful not to move. 'He's been very naughty. He pulled all the things out of your saddlebags and made a big mess.'

A smile crossed Angel's face. Then she looked confused. 'How do you know their names?' She folded her arms over her chest and lifted her head boldly. 'How do you know my name?'

'I found your drawing book. I saw the picture of your family. The names were written underneath. Angel, Mama Kitu, Matata and . . . your mother.'

'She's dead,' Angel said. 'A snake bit her.'

The bald words seemed to cut the air. Angel pressed her lips together as if she regretted having spoken.

'I know,' Emma said. 'I'm . . . so sorry.' A lump rose in her throat, stifling her voice.

'How do you know about her?' Angel let her arms fall to her sides. She looked suddenly vulnerable.

Emma took a breath. 'We followed the camel tracks to the grave and saw your footprints. We found her bag and saw a photo of you both in her wallet. We drove straight to Malangu and told the police. They mounted a big search for you.'

As Emma spoke, Angel moved slowly towards the lioness. George backed away to give her space. When she reached Mayo, her shoulders were almost level with the lioness's back. She was a slight figure, her arms and legs stick-thin and knobbly at the elbows and knees. However there was a confidence in her movements that suggested strength. Emma could picture her lifting all those stones, piling them up over her mother's dead body. But the sight of her standing there so calmly brought a stab of pain to her chest. Angel was too young, too small – surely – to be so brave.

Moyo turned her smooth-browed face towards Angel, and began licking her cheek – the pink tongue making long strokes across her fair skin. The cubs pawed at Angel's thighs, standing up on their hind legs, competing for her attention. She patted them in turn, and bent to pick one of them up. The cub looked big, in her arms, yet it settled there comfortably. She rubbed her nose into its fur. Her manner was casual, the gestures intimate. With her brown clothes, milky-blonde hair and tanned skin she looked as if she belonged amongst the lions – more than she belonged with the people watching her.

She looked at Emma, George and Daniel in turn. She seemed to be weighing them up. 'Why did she bring you here?' she asked eventually, gesturing towards the lioness.

As if in reply, George walked back up to Moyo and placed his hand on her solid shoulder. Angel took a step away, poised for flight. She threw a look at Moyo as though seeking an example of how to react.

Moyo rested her head against George's chest.

'She came to get me because she wanted me to help you,' George said.

Angel raised her eyebrows, but said nothing.

'Let me tell you about her.' George smiled at Moyo as he spoke. 'She came to me when she was just a tiny cub. Her mother had been killed by poachers. I found her in the bush, all alone, nearly dead from hunger.' He shifted his gaze to Angel. 'I brought her home and looked after her until she was big enough to return to the wild. I named her Moyo.'

'Moyo,' Angel repeated the name. 'That means "heart".'

George nodded. 'She was always a very kind-hearted lioness, even when she was only small.'

A flicker of emotion crossed the child's face. She turned to bury her face against Moyo's shoulder. George waited for a moment, then bent over, bringing his head to her level. 'You know, Angel, when Moyo was a cub, there was one thing she really loved to be given as a treat.'

Angel lifted her face. Strands of blonde hair clung to her cheek.

'I'll show you.' George went to the metal trunk and came back with a sapphire-blue glass bottle with a cork stopper, and a large enamel bowl.

Moyo immediately rushed up to him, sniffing at the bottle. He had to push her head away while he poured a golden liquid into the bowl. A faint fishy smell, combined with something softer, almost honey-like, rose into the air.

'Cod liver oil.' He stood back, giving Moyo access to the bowl. 'I give it to all my lions when they're growing up. They love it. They never forget the taste.'

Moyo lapped up the oil without pausing, then pushed the bowl across the ground as she scrubbed it clean with her tongue. The cubs trailed her, sniffing and licking at her whiskers. Angel put down the cub she was holding so that it could join the others.

Emma moved to stand near her. 'You must be hungry, as well,' she said, trying to sound relaxed. 'Or thirsty.'

'I'm fine, thank you,' Angel said politely, 'but I think the cubs might like to have some of that.' She pointed at the bottle.

George picked up the enamel bowl, but didn't refill it. He just looked distractedly at the lioness. 'Angel, can you tell me – while you were with Moyo, did you see any other lions? I'm worried about where her pride is.'

Angel turned away from Moyo to hide her reply. 'I think they're dead. She took me to a place where there were lots of bones.'

George stared at her. 'All dead? How many?'

'Four. And there was a cub as well.' Angel's voice was muted with distress. 'They had no skin, no heads.'

George flinched, screwing up his eyes. He looked grimly into the distance. After a long moment, he seemed to reach a decision. He straightened his shoulders and lifted his chin. 'I'm taking them home.'

Angel looked alarmed. 'Where to?'

'The camp where I live.'

'What if she – Moyo – doesn't want to go there?' Angel went to stand in front of the lioness and the cubs as if preparing to defend them. Though she was small, beside Moyo, she looked surprisingly fierce.

Emma glanced uneasily at Daniel. George had been handling the situation well, but now she feared his concern for the lions might be clouding his focus.

'Moyo's been taking you all to a new den each night, hasn't she?' George said to Angel.

She nodded. 'We've been walking and walking. We're all tired.'

There was a faint tremble in her voice. A bird flapped past, swooping low overhead, but she barely glanced up.

'She was bringing you to me at the camp,' George said calmly. 'It would have taken you several more days, but now we can drive there.'

Angel watched his face, still wary. 'Will Moyo like it at the camp?'

'It was her first home,' George said. 'There will be lots of fresh meat and water and shade. And she will be safe from poachers. Not only that, I have some new friends for the cubs to meet. A pair of orphans – two male cubs – just a few weeks old.'

Angel smiled, showing a gap in a row of baby teeth. For a moment, she was like the happy child in the photograph Emma had found in Laura's wallet. Then she frowned anxiously.

'What about me?'

'You'll come too.'

Angel chewed tensely at the side of her thumb. She looked towards Moyo, again, as if seeking direction.

George walked away towards the Land Rover. He put the bottle back in the trunk, then stood there, one hand resting on the side of the tray.

Moyo raised her head, making a soft gruff noise. She looked down at her cubs, gathering them up in the sweep of her gaze, then bounded across to the Land Rover, leaping up over the bonnet and onto the roof without breaking her stride. She turned in a circle, sniffing the paintwork. She looked back towards Angel and the cubs, making the gruff noise again. Then she flopped down on the roof, looking instantly comfortable and relaxed.

One of the cubs ran towards her, then another followed. As the first of them reached the vehicle, George scooped it into his arms.

'If you climb up,' he called to Angel, 'I'll pass them to you.'

The third cub took a few steps towards the Land Rover, but then sat down, watching Angel with wide round eyes. The child hovered, looking torn. Emma stood very still, almost holding her breath. She was aware of Daniel beside her, doing the same.

Angel walked slowly towards George. As she reached the waiting cub, it stood up and began to follow her, sticking close to her ankles. At the Land Rover, she climbed up onto the tray, resting her bottom on the side and swinging her legs over. George handed the cubs to her one by one. They stood huddled together near the metal trunk, looking up into Moyo's face.

Angel sat down, cross-legged, resting her back against the outside of the cabin. She opened her arms to the cubs and they pressed in around her.

Emma walked quickly towards the Land Rover, Daniel following a little way behind. She wanted George to drive off straight away, in case Angel changed her mind – but as she reached the passenger side door, she faltered. One of Moyo's paws was draped over the top half of the window. Looking through to George's side, she saw that the tail was hanging down there: a thick rope of tan hide with a black tufted end. She watched George lift it out of the way before opening the door and climbing inside. She forced herself to act without thinking, picking up the heavy paw that hung close to her head. She felt the rough, dry pads, the thick fur that sprouted between them, the hardness of sheathed claws. Lifting it aside, she opened the door, then eased herself up onto her seat. As she slid across to the middle, Daniel climbed in beside her, manoeuvring the door closed, careful not to trap the paw.

Emma turned to him, their eyes meeting as they shared smiles of joy and relief.

'We found her,' she said quietly.

'And she is well,' Daniel added.

Emma felt a deep sense of satisfaction at what they'd done together.

'She speaks Maa as one who was born amongst us,' Daniel said, looking surprised and impressed. 'We have vowel sounds others cannot even hear, let alone say. I heard her use them.'

'She's an extraordinary little girl,' George said. 'She's got plenty of spirit, that's for sure.' He leaned to start the engine. 'Moyo's done a fine job, too. Keeping three cubs alive isn't easy in this kind of country. And she's had Angel as well.' As he accelerated away, he raised his voice over the noise of the engine. 'It's quite natural for lions to care for extra offspring, you know. The females of the pride synchronise their cycles so they give birth around the same time. They suckle one another's young.'

Emma opened her mouth, but took a moment to frame her question. 'You're saying you think she . . . fed Angel?' Even as the words came out, Emma knew the answer – the child looked so healthy, so cared for.

'Well, she hasn't been living on desert grass and berries,' George said. 'And you can see she's completely at home with them. She's one of the family.'

They sat in silence, each of them preoccupied with absorbing the meaning of what had taken place. Emma looked past Daniel, out of the side window. The big furry paw swung back and forth as the Land Rover jolted over the land.

After they'd been travelling for some time, she noticed they were climbing onto higher ground. In places, it was quite steep, the angle of the chassis tipping them back in their seats. Suddenly a beeping sound cut in over the engine. It took Emma a few seconds to realise it was her mobile, receiving a message.

Pulling the phone from her bag, she bent her head over the little screen.

Hope you are having a great safari. Have a sundowner for me! All fine in the lab. Mice still thriving. Moira.

Emma looked blankly at the message. In that moment, she could barely even picture the world from which it had been sent. Turning her eyes to the left-hand corner of the screen she counted the reception bars. There was a good signal. She could phone someone right now and let them know the missing child had been found. The police search party could be called in. The next of kin – whoever they were – could be informed.

Emma's hand tightened on the slim hard case of the phone. She remembered how Angel had reacted to their arrival at the den.

Go away. I want to stay here.

Clearly, she was not a child who was longing to be reunited with relatives. In fact, it seemed the only loved ones she wanted to see were the camels . . .

Still holding the phone in her hand, Emma twisted round to look through the rear window. She tensed with alarm. There was no sign of Angel, or the cubs. Half-standing, she craned her neck to look down, then breathed out with relief. Angel was there, curled up with the cubs, her limbs tangled with theirs. Her eyes were closed. She looked peaceful and comfortable, her body shaking gently with the movement of the Land Rover. The cabin cast a thin shadow over the girl and the cubs, cutting off the glare of the afternoon sun.

Emma switched off her phone and pushed it deep into her pocket.

TWELVE

It was nearly dusk by the time they reached the lion camp; mauve shadows smudged the sandy verges of the track, and the bright blue of the sky had faded to a milky wash. As the Land Rover neared the tall wire gates, Moyo's dangling paw disappeared from the side window and they could hear her shifting restlessly on the roof.

Inside the compound, smoke rose from a cooking fire beside one of the huts. An African man wearing a white Muslim cap squatted next to it, stirring a blackened pot. As George swung the Land Rover in through the entrance, the man jumped to his feet. He stared towards the roof of the cabin shaking his head in disbelief. Porridge dripped unnoticed from the wooden spoon that hung from his hand, white blobs spattering his full-length robe.

'That's Ndisi,' George said. 'He's my cook.'

Before the Land Rover had stopped, Moyo jumped from the roof. She ran straight to Ndisi and sat down in front of him. Something about her posture, the way her paws were arranged so neatly side by side, reminded Emma of the cubs – as if the return to her first home had prompted the lioness to throw off a mask of maturity.

Ndisi shook his spoon at her. 'No, no. Bad Moyo!'

George smiled, opening his door. Emma and Daniel climbed out the other side. Ndisi walked across to them, glancing back at Moyo as he came. He was unusually tall, with very dark skin. He beamed at Emma and Daniel. 'Welcome to Kampi ya Simba,' he said, waving his arm in a gesture that encompassed the whole of their surroundings. He might have been the proprietor of a luxury tourist lodge welcoming his guests.

When the greetings were complete, Ndisi turned to George. 'What has happened? Why have you brought that lioness back here? It took so long to make her go away!'

'Her pride has been killed by poachers,' George said.

Ndisi drew his breath in sharply.

'And she has cubs.' George pointed towards the Land Rover. 'Three of them.'

'Three!' Ndisi exclaimed. 'Are they healthy and strong?' Without waiting for an answer, he strode towards the rear of the vehicle, then came to a halt, his body stiffening with shock.

Angel's blonde head appeared over the cabin roof. She wiped her hair from her face, looking around her. Her gaze passed over Emma, Daniel and George and stopped on Moyo. As if drawing confidence from the sight of the lioness sitting calmly by the fire, she jumped down off the tray. She approached Ndisi. As she reached him she lifted her right hand towards him. In response, Ndisi bent his head.

'*Shikamu, baba,*' she said, touching him lightly on the crown of his brimless cap.

'*Marahaba,*' Ndisi replied.

Emma looked questioningly at Daniel.

'She said, "I kiss your feet, Father,"' he responded in an under-tone. 'And Ndisi replied, "Only a few times."' He nodded approvingly. 'It is the correct way for an African child to greet their elder.'

Ndisi turned to Emma. 'She is your child?'

The question took Emma by surprise, but then she realised it was a reasonable assumption: they had the same colour skin. She shook her head. 'No.'

Ndisi looked mystified. 'So where has she come from?'

'I will explain,' George said. 'Not now.'

Angel walked back to the Land Rover and stood by the cubs. All three were gathered at the edge of the tray, their paws resting up on the metal sides.

'They want to get down,' she said.

Daniel went to stand beside her. He picked up one of the cubs, handling it with the same gentle confidence Emma had seen him display with the lamb and then with the camels. He gave the cub to Angel, who placed it carefully on the ground. Then he picked up the other two in turn, passing them down to the girl.

The cubs ran over to Moyo, jostling one another as they each tried to take shelter between her front legs.

'Is there any meat, Ndisi?' George asked.

Ndisi was staring at Angel, transfixed by her. 'There is some,' he answered, tearing his gaze away.

George spoke to Angel. 'Let's give Moyo her dinner, shall we?'

He set off towards the rear of the camp. Moyo sprang to her feet and followed him, trailed by the cubs and Angel. Emma and Daniel came behind, while Ndisi returned to his place by the fire.

In the shade of a stooping acacia tree stood an old fridge connected to a large gas cylinder. The door was dented and rusty, patterned with smears of brown blood. George took an enamel bucket – white, with dark chips at the rim – from a hook mounted on the tree trunk. He handed the container to Angel.

'My lions come back and visit, quite often. They bring their families with them. Their mates, their young.' As George spoke, he tried to open the fridge, but the catch jammed. He grunted, wrenching the handle. 'I try to make sure I've always got something on hand to give them.'

The door creaked open revealing a plastic tub full of meat. The flesh had been roughly hacked into chunks, the hide still attached: patches of brown hair lined the slabs of red. Emma glimpsed a globe-shaped ear, and the tufted end of a tail.

George began grabbing pieces and putting them in the bucket. 'Tell me if it's too heavy.'

Angel clasped the bucket against her chest, her slender arms wrapped firmly around it. 'It won't be too heavy. I'm strong.'

Flies gathered, in spite of the late hour, quickly speckling the meat with black. One landed on Angel's cheek, but she took no notice of it.

Moyo gazed intently at the bucket. Emma watched her nervously. She couldn't help feeling that the sight of raw meat could make the lioness dangerous. She had to remind herself that Moyo must have been hunting animals and devouring them, skin and flesh, during the time Angel had been with her. And there was no hint, now, of aggression in the lioness. Rather, she seemed to be following some accepted etiquette. She stood well back from George and Angel, and made her cubs stay with her, growling when they strayed.

When the bucket was full, George closed the fridge. He took the load from Angel. 'Good girl.'

Angel breathed out heavily as she let her arms drop. Emma realised the bucket had been too heavy for her, but that she'd refused to admit it. Watching her standing there, solemn-eyed, ready to help again, Emma felt a twinge of pride – as though the child's strong spirit, her resilience, were somehow connected with her.

George carried the meat over to an armchair crudely built from pieces of limb-wood nailed together. Next to it was a wooden crate. On its sides, painted in black letters, faded and fragmented with age, were the words: *EAST AFRICAN AIRLINES. NAIROBI. WARNING – LIVE LION*. Resting the bucket on the top of the crate, George lowered himself into the chair. He looked tired, Emma noticed, the long day of driving over rough terrain having taken a toll. But there was a bright gleam in his grey eyes.

Angel went to stand on the other side of the crate.

Moyo's attention was still fixed on the bucket of meat. She pranced a little, clearly tempted to evade the constraints of correct behaviour.

George picked up a hunk of meat and held it out to her, waving it slightly. Only then did the lioness approach, head down. Carefully, almost tenderly, she took the meat from his hand, barely showing her teeth. Walking a few steps away, she dropped it in the dust. Turning her head on one side, she began chewing it. A low warning growl came from her throat, keeping the cubs at bay.

George threw a few smaller pieces of meat towards the cubs. They circled the food, pushing it cautiously with their noses, looking towards their mother for guidance. Then one of the cubs began licking and chewing. Soon all three were feeding hungrily.

When Moyo's portion was gone, she moved back to stand in front of George.

'Can I give her some?' Angel asked.

George gestured towards the bucket. Angel chose a large piece of meat with a segment of a dark curly mane running across the rectangle of hide. The lioness watched her with steady eyes, standing completely still, ears held forward, jaws slightly apart. Grasping her offering in both hands, Angel approached Moyo with slow steps. When they were almost face to face, she stopped. Moyo looked at her for a moment, then opened her mouth, revealing just the tips of her canine teeth. Putting out her tongue she licked the meat delicately, soft pink sweeping over red. Then she opened her jaws wider, grasping hold of the meat and carrying it away.

When Angel turned back, her eyes shone as if a light burned inside her. The glow was mirrored in the gaze of the old man.

Angel continued to hand out the meat, giving the big pieces to Moyo and dropping smaller scraps for the cubs. There was no sense of hurry. The meal was like a ceremony, requiring due time and care. The sun moved lower in the sky. It shone through the ends of Moyo's fur, fringing her body with gold. Angel's hair was a matching halo around her head.

When all the meat had been handed out, George carried the basin across to a water tank. Filling a small pot, he poured water over Angel's hands in short bursts. She rubbed her bloody hands quickly, expertly, under the thin stream. The water ran down into the basin, drumming against the enamel. When her hands were clean, she took the pot and poured water over George's. Washing like this, Emma realised, was probably more familiar to Angel than using taps and a sink.

'What kind of animal was that?' Angel asked.

'Camel,' George said.

Angel's head jerked up. Emma sent George a warning glance, but he didn't appear to notice.

'Sometimes I shoot impala or a gazelle, but mainly I buy unwanted livestock for the lions. Goats or camels, occasionally a donkey.'

Angel frowned. 'What do you mean – unwanted?'

'Ones that are too old to work,' George said. 'They can end up starving to death if no one wants them.'

Angel looked at him for a few seconds, then nodded, her face clearing, as though the arrangement made sense to her. 'Are we going to eat camel?'

George shook his head. He pointed towards a patch of ground a short distance away. At first, Emma couldn't see anything but bare sand and a few stones. But then, she picked out a scattering of grey feathers, some of them spotted with white – little curves with wispy ends – that matched the plumage of the guinea fowls she'd seen at the station.

'Do you like *kanga* stew?' George asked Angel.

She narrowed her eyes at him, as if the question could be a trick. 'I like any kind of food.'

*

A row of hurricane lanterns, hanging from long wire hooks attached to the roof, shed yellow light over the room. Emma stood near the dining table holding a cut-crystal glass of sherry. She took small sips, letting the sweet warmth slide across her tongue. Over by the sideboard, George and Daniel were examining a broken lantern, murmuring as they swapped opinions as to how it could be made to work. Angel was standing near the open front of the hut, her hair falling long over her back as she looked up at a row of photographs mounted on the ceiling. She'd already studied the rest of the gallery, going slowly from one image of a lion to the next. Not far away from her, Moyo sprawled on the Persian rug, the three cubs nestled close to her belly. Emma found her eyes being drawn back to the lioness again and again – lingering on the huge creamy gold shape set against the woven pattern of orange and red and black, settling on the paws that looked impossibly large, and on the wide clear eyes that gazed benignly across the room. Beyond Moyo lay the darkness outside – an inky purple sky, the moon yet to rise.

Moyo's head swung round towards the cubs. She began licking their faces, removing traces of blood left behind by the scraps of meat. The first two cubs sat meekly, quiet and still, but the third kept ducking her head out of reach. Emma smiled. The cub was behaving just like an uncooperative child.

Angel looked across to Emma. 'That's Girl. We can't manage her. She does whatever she wants.' She pointed to another of the cubs. 'That's her brother, Boy. The other cub is a male, too. I call him Mdogo.'

'Mdogo,' Emma repeated, stumbling over the name. 'Why did you choose that name?'

Angel looked puzzled. 'Because he's small.' She seemed about to speak again, when Ndisi came in, carrying the pot of corn meal porridge he'd been stirring on the fire. He put it down on the table, beside a steaming bowl of stew that had been brought out earlier.

'Let's eat, then,' said George.

Emma moved across to the table, taking her place on the safari chair closest to where she'd put down her shoulder bag. It was comforting to have her possessions nearby. At the station she'd become used to basic facilities, and had come to terms with eating food cooked over a fire in earthen pots. But here at the camp there was the presence of animals as well. Droppings left by birds and small animals were scattered here and there – George had a big tin of nuts on the end of the table that he said was for feeding his visitors. And there was a family of lions lounging on the carpet. If the station and the Salaam Cafe had been a challenge to her, this place was about as different from her spotless, minimalist apartment as it was possible to be.

Daniel sat down opposite her, with Ndisi at his side. George was at the head, seated on a wing-backed armchair. Emma had prepared a chair for Angel, with a cushion to give her more height. Angel took a few steps towards it but then stopped, halfway between Moyo and the table. She looked suddenly uneasy, almost afraid.

Emma felt her body tensing. So far, everything had gone smoothly, but their connection with Angel felt fragile – if anything went wrong Emma feared the child might take fright and run away. She tried to think how best to entice Angel to the table.

The next moment, Daniel pushed back his chair, standing up. 'Let's join Moyo,' he suggested, picking up the pot of porridge.

George reached for the stew. Ndisi watched, bewildered, as the two men took the food across to where Angel stood. As they set the meal down on the carpet, the cook raised his eyebrows.

'Now we are sharing our food with Moyo?' he asked.

'Hopefully not,' George said. He sat down, crossing his legs with an ease that was out of keeping with his white hair and lined face. Angel sat next to him, with Moyo looking over her shoulder. The cubs crowded around her, but she pushed them firmly away. Daniel joined them, along with Ndisi. Emma was the last to take her place on the floor. Daniel smiled at her reassuringly.

George motioned for his guests to begin eating. Emma eyed the two pots uncertainly. There were no plates, no spoons. It appeared that they were expected to eat with their fingers. She was glad she'd taken the precaution of putting anti-bacterial gel on her hands after washing them.

'You eat like this.' Daniel dipped his right hand into the porridge pot, picking up a white, doughy lump. Pushing his thumb into its middle, he formed a little bowl. Then he dipped it into the stew and carried it to his mouth.

George followed suit, and then Angel joined in, managing the porridge and stew with practised ease. She nodded appreciatively at Ndisi.

'*Vizuri sana,*' she said. '*Asante.*'

'*Si neno,*' he replied, smiling at her. He turned to Emma. 'Please, I am sure you must be very hungry.'

'I am.' Emma could smell the spicy steam that rose from the pot.

'Don't worry about dropping food on the rug,' George said, after finishing a mouthful. 'It'll come clean. These things were made by the Bedouin. They're the original safari tent floor.'

Emma took a ball of porridge in her hand. It was surprisingly easy to shape the little bowl and then scoop up the stew. As she tasted the meat she closed her eyes with pleasure. The guinea fowl was tender and moist, falling off the bone. The gravy was flavoured with green capsicums; they had a slightly bitter flavour, offsetting the richness of the spices.

'It's very good, Ndisi,' she said.

He bowed his head, accepting her praise.

'Excellent,' George smiled across the circle at Ndisi, then his gaze travelled around the circle of people and lions. He shook his head as though barely able to believe that they were all here, together. Then he looked back to Ndisi. 'Tell me, how are things at the village? Is Samu recovering?' He glanced around the circle. 'Samu is one of my helpers. He's been off work with malaria.'

'All is well,' Ndisi replied. 'He swallowed the *dawa* that you sent and he has nearly recovered.'

'Well, that's good,' George said. 'I must give you some nets for the children to sleep under.'

Emma paused, her hand hovering over the porridge pot. 'I heard that the people who worked here at the camp never became ill.' She regretted her words the moment they'd left her lips; she sounded as if she'd been naively taken in by something that could not be true.

'I know about that story,' George responded. 'It goes back to

2007 – the outbreak of Olambo fever. The toll in the local village was horrific. Whole families were wiped out. But my staff and their households came through completely unscathed. It was like that biblical story of the angel marking the lintels of the homes of the Israelites, and the plague passing over them.'

'It was just like that,' Ndisi said. 'Our neighbours were dying one by one – bleeding to death. And we all remained healthy.' A grimace of distress tightened his face.

Emma looked sideways at Daniel. He had stopped eating. His eyes were fixed on Ndisi, but he seemed to have nothing to say.

'Laura saw people with the bleeding sickness.' Angel's voice broke the quiet. Emma turned to her. Angel was looking down at her hands, clasped together in her lap. 'They came to the Sisters of Mercy. She helped look after them. I wasn't allowed to go with her because they were too sick. One day she came home with blood all over her clothes. She had to throw them away.'

Emma stared at Angel, trying to imagine how she had coped with seeing her mother in such a state. She felt a flash of outrage. What did Laura think she was doing – exposing her child to something so distressing? And why was she spending her time nursing victims of a lethal virus, when she had the welfare of her own small child to think of? Emma looked down at the carpet, watching her finger as it jabbed into the wool, forcing a path through the pile. She remembered how she used to stand by the school gates waiting for Mrs McDonald, overhearing her friends' parents swapping comments. Why was Susan Lindberg still doing fieldwork? Why would any mother want to take such risks? They never directly answered the questions, but they still managed to convey their opinions. Susan cared more about her work than she did about her little girl. She cared more about strangers than her own family. Her head still bent over the carpet, Emma dug her fingers deeper into the woollen pile, the lines of hard knots pressing into her skin. As a child she'd never wanted to hear anyone criticise Susan. If she had the chance she defended her mother. But now that she was sitting here, confronted with the pain on Angel's face, long-buried anger rose up, hot and sharp. Why hadn't Susan seen that her daughter needed her at home? That she needed her to stay alive . . .

Emma looked up at Angel. She felt the anger inside her give way to sympathy. The child was now staring straight ahead, her eyes wide, fearful. Over her shoulder, Emma could see Moyo's face reflecting the tension as well – her brow wrinkled, ears forward. She tried to think of something to say that would change the subject. She looked at Daniel, hoping he'd come to her assistance. But he was leaning towards George, his gaze intent.

'Why do you think your helpers were spared?' he asked.

The subject was too close to Daniel, Emma realised. He wouldn't want to let it go.

'They must have had some resistance that others didn't,' George said. 'I put it down to them having a better diet. My staff are the only people in the village with a steady wage.'

'Maybe,' Daniel said, 'but I have seen healthy young people killed by the virus.'

Ndisi nodded. His eyes looked haunted, as if he were reliving scenes of horror.

George seemed about to continue speaking when a black triangle nose, followed by a furry face, pushed in under his arm. Two paws crept up onto his leg. There was a mewing sound, loud and insistent. It drew everyone's attention. George smiled at the cub. 'Want some of our food, do you?' He offered a blob of porridge. The nose pushed eagerly into the dough, then pulled back. Bits of white clung to fur and whiskers. The cub shook its head, screwing up its face with clear disgust. Soft laughter broke out at the comic sight – laughter coloured with relief at the interruption. Angel picked up the cub and hugged it close to her.

As the tension eased, everyone began to eat again. Hands moved between the two pots, crossing over one another, almost meeting at times – fair-skinned and dark, big and small. From outside came the call of the night owl and the crooning of guinea hens sheltering in the trees. The silence was comfortable, painful memories banished for the while. As she ate, Emma scanned the gallery of photographs, running her gaze along the ranks of portraits – a pantheon of lions, looking down over them all.

George drained the last of his cup of tea. 'Time for bed, I think.'

Emma stifled a yawn. Though it was not late, she felt very tired – the day had begun early, and so much had happened. She glanced across at Angel, who was sitting with her head resting against Moyo's shoulder, her eyes half-closed. Emma turned to Daniel, wondering if he'd found out what the sleeping arrangements would be.

'We have sleeping bags and nets,' he said to George.

'You won't need nets here,' the old man said. 'It's too dry for mosquitoes.'

'I'd still like to use one,' Emma said hastily. Nets would keep out other things as well: scorpions, spiders, mice, perhaps even snakes.

'I always sleep outside during the dry season,' George continued, 'but if you prefer a roof over your head, my hut is free and there's a guest hut as well. Ndisi will find you some camp beds.'

He got up, stretching stiffness from his back and legs. Immediately, Moyo lifted her head. George nodded at her. 'You'll keep me company, won't you, old girl?' The man and lioness gazed into one another's eyes, as though sharing thoughts and memories. Then Moyo rose to her feet, disturbing the cubs, who raised their heads, confused. Angel stood up as well, one hand gripping the lioness's thick fur, as if afraid of being left behind.

George unhooked one of the lamps and led the way towards the entrance, followed by Angel and Moyo, the cubs trailing behind.

Emma watched them with a sense of disbelief. They were just heading outside to sleep as though it were a perfectly normal thing to do.

Ndisi shook his head and sighed. 'I hope Moyo will behave like a grown-up lioness and not climb on the bed.' He addressed Emma and Daniel. 'Where would you like to sleep? I myself sleep only inside my hut. But you may make your own choice. Whatever pleases you.' He sounded, again, like a hotelier, with a range of suites on offer.

'Where is the guest hut?' Emma asked. She certainly didn't want to sleep outside, but neither did she want to be too far away from Angel.

'It is there, next to the *bwana*'s hut.' He pointed outside, to where, in the glow of George's lamp, she could just see the shapes of two thatched roofs.

'That looks perfect.' Emma forced a smile to go with her words. The huts looked very basic. She wasn't sure they even had doors.

Ndisi turned to Daniel. 'Will you sleep together?' He looked embarrassed, as soon as he'd spoken. 'I mean—'

'I will join the others, outside,' Daniel said.

Ndisi nodded. 'I will get a camp bed for you.' He began collecting the cups and placing them on a tray with the teapot and milk jug. Emma stood up and went to offer her help.

'You will want to wash before bed,' Ndisi stated. 'I can heat water for a shower if you wish.'

'I don't need hot water.' Emma didn't want to be seen as a fussy foreign visitor. 'But I'd love to have a wash.' She wondered if there was a bath-hut, or perhaps a washstand in the guest hut.

Ndisi crossed to a cupboard near the fridge. He returned with two folded towels that were thin with wear and stained grey from being washed in dusty water. As he handed one to Emma, he tilted his head in the direction of the water tank where George and Angel had cleaned their hands. 'You will find soap out there, in a cup. There is a stone on top of it, to stop the rats taking it away. There is a basin to hold the water.' He gave Emma a stern look. 'This is not California. Please use only a little.'

'I'll be careful,' Emma assured him. She guessed he'd had to pull an American visitor into line at some stage. Although George had told them tourists were not allowed to enter the camp, it was apparent that invited guests did come here. A hut had been built for them, and amongst the photos of lions, Emma had seen a few that included people – there was Ndisi, of course, and George, but also some middle-aged, prosperous-looking foreigners. Emma guessed they were benefactors who funded the rehabilitation project. A young curly-haired woman appeared several times, as well. There were images of her feeding lion cubs, walking with a lioness, and also sitting here in the dining hut, using the old typewriter that still sat on an upturned tea chest in the corner.

Collecting her bag, Emma went outside. She stopped for a moment, watching Angel and George as they dragged a folded camp bed out through the door of his hut. Moyo was sniffing the ground, turning round and round, exploring the patch of the earth where she planned to settle down.

Emma washed quickly, using a dampened corner of the towel as a face washer. She unveiled her body bit by bit, not wanting to stand naked in the open air. There was no feeling of privacy out here, and no separation from the outside world. There was nothing between her and the wilderness beyond the camp but a chain wire fence. She took her clothes from her bag. She eyed her peach-toned silk pyjamas – the ones she'd chosen specially for the trip to Africa because they'd wash and dry easily and wouldn't need to be ironed. She decided not to put them on until she was inside the guest hut, dressing, for now, in her spare change of shirt and undies. She knew how the soft cloth of the pyjama jacket draped her breasts and how the trousers clung to her thighs. The thought roused in her mind the memory of Daniel stripped to the waist as he worked on Mama Kitu's foot. The sweat on his skin had the same silky sheen . . .

A sudden rustling above Emma's head made her freeze. Looking up, she saw the furry outline of some small animal running along the limb of a tree. It had the low-hung skulking shape of a rat. Quickly, Emma finished dressing, shoving her feet into her boots. She bundled up her dirty clothes and grabbed her bag. She only just remembered to replace the stone that covered the soap in its cup, before walking away at a fast pace.

A lantern, hanging from a tree-branch, cast a circle of light over the space in front of the dining hut, giving the scene the feel of a stage setting. Two canvas stretchers had been set up side by side. One was made up with faded striped sheets and had a pillow with a matching cover. On the other bed was a sleeping bag, unrolled, along with a folded *kitenge* that Emma recognised from the breakfast picnic.

Moyo crouched at the foot of George's bed like a guard on duty. Her head was raised, and her eyes fixed on the closest hut – the one Ndisi had told her belonged to George. When Emma came near she could hear the old man moving about inside. She glanced around and saw that Daniel was sitting over by Ndisi's cooking fire.

Angel was lying at Moyo's feet, with the cubs. They were asleep – eyes shut tight, hidden in their furry faces – but the child was still awake. Emma could see her alert, watching eyes.

Emma felt a painful rush of sympathy for her. She had an urge to bend down and touch her, maybe even kiss her goodnight. But

Angel was lying close to the three cubs and Emma remembered George's warning against touching cubs without an invitation. And anyway, Emma realised, it was probably not what Angel wanted. Emma remembered how it had felt to be caressed by women who somehow thought they could stand in for a mother who was lost.

'Good night, Angel,' Emma said softly.

'Good night,' Angel replied. She sounded polite, but reserved. She'd been like this ever since her arrival at the camp. Though she made sure she stayed close to Moyo, she didn't seem afraid. Rather, she appeared to be hanging back, watching, giving nothing away. Under Emma's gaze, the child curled up on her side, her back to the lioness, and closed her eyes.

George emerged from the hut, carrying a three-legged stool in one hand and a large plastic torch in the other. He had changed out of his shorts and safari vest, and was now wearing an African cloth wrapped around his waist. He set down the stool beside his stretcher, placing the torch on the wooden seat.

He turned to Emma, speaking in an undertone so as not to to disturb Angel. 'I hope you will be comfortable.' He repeated the anxious touching of his tongue to his upper lip that Emma had seen before. 'Things are rather simple here, I'm afraid.'

'I'll be fine,' Emma said firmly. She already liked this gentle, hospitable man. No matter how basic the hut was, she was determined not to complain in any way.

'Good night, then,' George said.

'Good night.'

Turning down his sheet, George climbed into bed, the canvas

creaking on its wooden frame. He lay on his back, face to the sky, as though he wanted to be able to see the stars, the moon, or the dawn light, the moment he opened his eyes. Moyo watched him until he was settled and still. Then she shifted her attention back to Angel, bending her huge head over the small body, nuzzling the wispy blonde hair.

Emma took a closer look at the child. She was breathing slowly and evenly; her body seemed relaxed. With the moon playing over her hair, picking up the roundness of her cheeks, she was like her namesake – a little angel, lost in her dreams. But then Emma noticed that her eyelids kept fluttering, showing she was not actually asleep. Perhaps she was over-tired, Emma thought. She'd heard parents use that phrase, on rare occasions when she and Simon had been invited to the home of people with children. The words would be delivered with a tone of desperation, as the wakeful children played and talked, disrupting the adult dinner party. Simon would be casting looks at Emma that said he was counting his blessings that they'd taken a different path.

Thinking of those pampered, carefree kids made Emma view at Angel with renewed admiration. She was so unlike them – but of course she was. She had an inner strength they had neither the need nor the opportunity to develop. Emma thought of herself at Angel's age. She'd been strong as well. No doubt Susan's regular disappearances had helped prepare her for the final abandonment, when it came. But after the crisis stage was over Emma had felt depleted, as if all her strength had been used up. Looking back now, she could see that she'd not only spent her life since then being drawn to people who would abandon her – she'd also chosen the ones who would take on the role of being strong.

She thought back to how she'd come to choose Simon, remembering the day they'd first met. They were at a conference about field safety training for scientists. Emma was only there because she was the first-aid officer for her lab, but Simon was one of the experts. He gave a talk about risk management in Antarctica, showing slides and then demonstrating equipment. Emma had been struck by the confident way he spoke of being able to win out against even the most extreme elements. In the projected images of him scaling an ice-cliff decked out in survival gear, he gave the impression of being almost superhuman. And after his talk, as he stood near the coffee machine dressed in his smart-casual clothes, the aura still lingered. Emma made an excuse to ask him about a laboratory safety procedure. She had to force herself to approach him, her step faltering as she saw that he was even more classically handsome close up than he'd looked on the podium. She asked her question and pretended to be interested in his answer. All the while, she was observing the way he stood, so at ease, and the way he faced the world with such a level gaze. Amazingly, he had seemed to be drawn to something in Emma, as well. After they'd been talking for a while, he'd asked her out for dinner. There was no hesitation in his voice, no fear of rejection on his face. She'd said yes straight away. In that moment, she'd wanted nothing more than to stay close to him.

That first date led to another and then another, and eventually to the prospect of a lasting relationship. During those months Emma made sure she did nothing that might cause Simon to doubt that she was the right partner for him. It wasn't too difficult – she already knew how to be decisive and authoritative in her work at the Institute; now she simply operated the same way in her personal life. Over time, Emma felt she was actually becoming like Simon – as if just by being near him she could absorb some of his certainty about his place in the world. But now, she could clearly see that she'd been fooling herself. The confidence and independence she displayed in Simon's presence was no more than a façade, like a dressing laid over a deepening wound.

Emma took a last look at Angel, running her eyes over the small curled body. The child must already be drawing on her reserves of resilience – she was being so brave and controlled. Did that mean that she, too, would end up spending her life searching for someone who could compensate for what she'd used up? Emma could only hope the little girl's life would not follow the same path as hers.

She turned away, heading over to join Daniel at the fire. She sat down beside him on a low wooden stool.

'Is she sleeping?' Daniel asked.

'Not yet,' Emma said. 'I hope she falls asleep soon. Tomorrow will be a big day for her.' She felt apprehensive as she tried to imagine what would take place.

Daniel nodded. 'George will have to radio the police and tell them we have found her.'

'What will happen then?'

'They will send someone to collect her. Or they may instruct us to drive her to Malangu. Perhaps we should offer to do that. Then we can stop at the station and she can see the camels. That would be good. We do not know what will happen once she is gone from us.'

Emma eyed him in silence. She wished they knew whom the next of kin was, where they lived. 'I hope it all works out well for her.'

'So do I.'

Emma frowned. 'I can't picture just handing her over and walking away. I know we'll have no say in anything. But I still feel like we should be able to make sure she's okay.'

'I do, too,' Daniel said. 'But it will not be in our hands.'

A heavy quiet fell between them. Then Daniel spoke again. 'And what will you do, now that we have found Angel?'

Emma sighed. 'I don't know. I don't think I want to join up with my tour group. It would be too strange, after all this . . .'

Daniel smiled. 'You would see lions surrounded by Land Cruisers and minibuses.'

'That's what I mean. But going home will be strange as well. This has been so . . .' Emma hunted for the right word, but gave up, her voice trailing off. She tried to picture her return to the real world. She imagined opening the door to her apartment. Breathing in the smells of spray-and-wipe polish and disinfectant left behind by the cleaning lady. She saw the heap of mail, collected by her neighbour and placed on the dining room table – some of it addressed to her, but most to Simon. She pictured the numbers on the digital clock in the kitchen flicking over and over. The creak of the heating system coming on, to warm an empty home, so that Simon's collection of maps would not get damp.

'Home seems so far away. It sounds weird, but all this seems more real.' She waved her hand to take in the surroundings of the camp, George, Angel and the lions. She turned to Daniel, searching his face in the firelight. 'You seem more real.' She shook her head slowly. 'I feel like someone else.'

Daniel's eyes were fixed on hers. 'I feel the same.'

THIRTEEN

Angel rested her head against Moyo's side, feeling the bony curve of her ribs beneath the soft covering of hair. She drank in the comforting smell of her – a warm milkiness, the metal tang of blood, and the musky fragrance that seemed to come from the lioness herself. On the ground next to Angel, the cubs were sleeping together in a heap, legs and tails entangled. Mdogo stirred, whimpering, and Angel leaned round to stroke his back. Moyo lifted her head briefly, then laid it back down again, as if satisfied that all was well.

Angel wriggled her hips, digging her bottom deeper into the bed of sand. A restless energy ran through her. She was not ready for sleep. She wanted to make a plan, so she'd be prepared for the morning. She sifted sand between her fingers. What she had to do first, she told herself, was to gather up all the facts – every little thing she'd found out since she'd arrived in this place – and lay them out in her mind. As she'd moved around with Laura she'd had plenty of practice in assessing new places and people. It was a vital skill that enabled her to make friends quickly and find a niche for herself in a new village.

She looked at the old man, sleeping on his stretcher. She wasn't quite sure of his name. The cook called him Bwana Lawrence, but the others referred to him as George. He was still resting on his back, his white hair draping the pillow. He lay straight-limbed, obviously well used to the narrow bed. If he had a wife or children, they didn't live here. The lions were his family. It was clear that he loved Moyo. And Moyo loved him. George-Lawrence was a good person, Angel thought. Someone you could trust.

Ndisi. Angel conjured his face in her mind. He had a line of little scars that ran across his forehead, just below the brim of his cap. She liked him as well. He made jokes about Moyo, but she could see he cared about her. And when the two baby cubs that lived here at the camp had cowered in fear as they watched the new lion family wandering through the compound, Ndisi had hurried into their enclosure to comfort them. When Girl had stood growling at the gate, he'd shooed her away.

Angel looked across to the couple sitting by the cooking fire – the Maasai man and the white lady. Glowing embers lit their faces. The man's was a dark shape broken by the flash of white teeth. His companion's face was like his in reverse – a white oval, marked with the darkness of brows, eyes, hair.

Angel couldn't hear what they were saying, their voices were too low. She did not think they were *wapenzi*, like the couples she and Zuri used to spy on, throwing dung balls and trying not to laugh. They didn't hold hands, or walk around arm in arm. But she could tell they liked one another. They probably worked together, she thought, at this place they called the 'station'. Maybe they lived there as well, like the nuns who had their own rooms at one end of the hospital.

Instinctively, she trusted the Maasai as much as she did the other two men. The moment he'd spoken to her in Maa, she'd felt comfortable with him. And he was the one who had operated on Mama Kitu's foot. There was something about the way he moved that reminded her of Moyo. He was a strong man, Angel thought, who would make a reliable friend.

She was not so sure about the white lady. Angel felt disconcerted by the way she looked at her – as if she was always trying to read her thoughts and feelings. What was her name? Angel mouthed the word. Em-mah. It could have been a Swahili name, the way it sounded. Not like Laura – Africans found that name too soft, shapeless. They said it did not suit the camel lady.

Angel closed her eyes as a memory swept over her. They were entering a village, she and Laura, riding high on Mama Kitu's back. All the mothers and fathers and children and old people were coming out of their huts, or in from their vegetable gardens, to welcome the camel lady. The people who knew her smiled and raised their arms towards her – some of them sang and danced. They called her *Malaika*, as though the name belonged to her, and not to her daughter. Angel felt tears burning behind her eyes. She could not afford to cry, she knew. She needed to stay strong. She grasped the painful thoughts, like handfuls of grass in her hands, and threw them aside.

She tried to focus on Emma instead. The woman was not at ease here at the camp; she must be used to being somewhere with concrete floors and mud brick walls. She kept looking where she was stepping, and peering up as well, wary of danger. And she needed to know exactly where her green bag was, all the time. She went to it for paper handkerchiefs, lip cream and special hand-wiping cloths that came out of a packet, already wet. She was not like a safari lady – she had no necklace, no sunglasses, no lipstick. But she was nothing like Laura, either. Angel thought back over what Emma had said, while they were all at the den – that she was there because of Mama Kitu and Matata. 'The camels found me,' she'd said. The way she spoke made it sound as if the camels had chosen her specially.

Thinking of the camels brought a wave of longing. The Maasai had told her they were at the station. They were safe, and she would see them very soon. Angel pictured how she would rub her cheek against Mama Kitu's nose, feeling the tickle of her whiskers . . . She caught herself up, again, reining in her thoughts. It was important to deal with things one at a time. Walaita had taught her this, during her long illness: that if you imagined the whole journey lying ahead of you, even the first step became impossible to take.

Angel sat up a bit, propping her head on Moyo's shoulder. What was the first step? The place to begin . . .

Moyo was bringing you here to the camp. She knew it was a good place. This is where you are meant to be.

Angel pictured herself helping Ndisi with his cooking, plucking the *kanga* for the stew, stacking the fridge with meat. She knew how to do tasks like this. She could be so useful here that George-Lawrence and Ndisi would soon wonder how they'd managed without her.

She would make sure she was always polite. She would not talk to them about Laura. She would never cry or even look sad. She had to show them how sensible and grown-up she was or they might not want to keep her. She'd nearly spoiled things during the meal, when they'd started talking about the fever. As she'd put words to the memory that had come to her – of Laura, holding her hands away from her bloodied clothes, tears running untouched down her cheeks – she'd felt her chest become tight. Her heart, squeezed inside, felt like it would burst. Tears ached behind her eyes. It was lucky Girl had chosen that moment to push her way onto George-Lawrence's lap. It was almost as if the cub had known that something had to happen, to catch people's attention, to break the spell of sadness and lighten the air.

Angel settled back down against Moyo. She tried to relax her body, limb by limb. She had not yet made a wrong move, she told herself. Everything was still possible. She let the plan evolve in her head. The camels could be brought here. Moyo and the cubs would have to be taught that Mama Kitu and Matata were part of the family, not prey, but she felt sure that would be possible. It could all work.

But there was a knot in her stomach. Her eyes refused to close; they kept searching the shadows as if something important to her was hidden there. Then it dawned on her. Her body tensed. The plan would not work. She could not stay here alone with George-Lawrence and Ndisi and the lions. Taking care of children was the job of women. The people from the village would soon find out she was here, and they'd want to know why she had no mother or auntie or grandmother. They'd say no one was caring for her properly.

Sooner or later, someone would report her to the police or a game ranger. Angel gazed blankly ahead. She was afraid that, if this happened, she would then be sent to England, to the uncle Laura had told her about. Angel had thrown the passport away, but that didn't mean no one would find out about him. Angel felt despair swoop over her like a bird descending on its prey.

She had to find a way to stay here. She had to. As the thought circled in her head, she shifted her eyes back to the cooking fire. At that moment, Emma lifted her face. The light of the rising moon played over her features. Angel stared at her as though seeing her for the first time. Suddenly it came to her: Emma was the one who could make the plan work. She could make Angel into her daughter. It took place all the time in the villages. If a wife had lots of children and her sister had too few, the auntie would choose the one she liked and begin feeding that child in her own hut. If everyone was happy with the arrangement, the child would become known as the boy or girl who belonged to that auntie. Emma could go on living at the station, along with the Maasai. All she had to do was visit the camp now and then, and let people from the village see them together. Or Angel could join Emma and the Maasai at the station. She could still visit Moyo, and the camels were already there. Either plan would work.

Angel looked across at Emma, studying her. She felt a twist of anxiety. The woman often had such a serious expression on her face. She didn't seem to be the kind of person who laughed easily. And she always appeared busy, even when she wasn't doing much. She might not have enough time to think about helping a child.

Another thought came to Angel then, settling cold inside her. What if Emma did not like children? What if she did not like Angel? Not all people were like the nuns, she reminded herself, who always liked everyone, all the time.

Angel eased herself away from Moyo, careful not to disturb her. She moved to a slightly different position, from which she could see Emma more directly. Then she curled up on her side, again, resting her cheek on her hands. She fixed her gaze on the pale circle of the woman's face. She replayed in her mind something Zuri had once told her.

'If you watch someone as you fall asleep,' he'd said, 'you take their face with you into your dreams. You can hold them inside you. And when they wake up, they will think of you straight away. They will want to be your friend.'

He'd spoken as surely and clearly as if he'd been reading the story of the night, written in the footprints outside his hut. Angel had no doubt that his words were true.

She lay still, watching Emma, forcing her tired eyes to take in every detail of the woman's face, her posture. She listened to the murmur of her voice. She drew all the impressions deep inside her. Only when she knew she could see them all in her head did she let her eyes slowly close.

FOURTEEN

Emma stood with Angel at the entrance to the enclosure that held the two orphan cubs, Bill and Ben. Peering through the wire mesh she scanned the bare ground with its patches of shade. A swing made from an old car tyre hung from the branch of a tree. Abandoned nearby was a tattered ball made of canvas sewn into a knot, and an old basket, chewed to shreds. And in the middle of the space, laying claim to it all, were the cubs. They were asleep in the gentle morning sun, curled up together so closely that they looked like one big furry animal.

Angel held two bottles of milk, resting against her chest. She had just had a wash, using what George called his 'bush shower' – a container with tiny holes in the bottom, that had been filled with hot water and hung from a tree. Her hair, hanging wet around her shoulders, looked darker and longer. She'd changed into the tunic and trousers Emma had brought from the station. They were similar to the ones she had been wearing before, but these were made from hand-dyed cloth in pastel rainbow colours. Emma was struck by how different Angel looked, draped in colour. Her eyes looked bluer, her skin fairer. When she'd emerged from the shower enclosure, her dirty clothes bundled into a ball in her hand, Moyo and the cubs had eyed her cautiously, as though they were no longer certain who she was.

Angel handed one bottle to Emma. 'You have to make sure you keep the bottle tipped up so they don't suck in air.'

Emma raised her eyebrows. 'You've done this before?'

'At the Sisters of Mercy. Sometimes I helped the nuns with the babies.'

Emma looked at her. A dozen questions sprang to her lips, but she forced herself to remain quiet. She didn't want to risk upsetting Angel by bringing up memories of her life with Laura. Since waking this morning, the child had been surprisingly friendly and relaxed, showing no anxiety about being with a group of people she didn't know. Rather, she'd seemed confident and independent, asking if she could have a wash, then insisting she needed no help with operating the bush shower. She'd asked for iodine and a bandage and then skilfully attended to a cut on her toe. And she'd been so eager to help prepare and serve breakfast and then clean up that she'd barely had time to eat any food herself.

'Are you ready?' Angel asked.

Emma eyed the cubs nervously. She'd suggested that Daniel help with this task – he was an expert, after all – but Angel had insisted on Emma. 'I want you to feed the cubs with me,' she'd said, looking straight into Emma's eyes. Emma had agreed immediately, her ambivalence outweighed by the pleasure she felt at being the chosen one.

'You open the gate,' Angel instructed. 'Please.'

At the sound of the wooden frame scraping over the hard-baked earth, two furry heads lifted. Four round dark eyes blinked slowly. Then there was a flurry of movement as the cubs untangled themselves, struggling to their feet. They were much smaller than Moyo's cubs, each about the size of a large cat. Their heads looked too heavy for their bodies and their paws too large for their legs; the light tan of their coats was speckled with big spots of darker fur.

The pair bounded up to Emma and Angel in unison, then stopped a short way away, looking uncertain about how to proceed. One of them jumped in alarm as the tufted end of its own tail flicked into view.

Angel laughed. 'They're still learning to be alive.'

Emma smiled. It was an apt description of the way they appeared to be only half at home in their bodies.

Angel crouched down, holding out her bottle. Both cubs raced towards her, stumbling over their feet.

'Show them you've got one, too,' Angel said to Emma.

Emma waved the other bottle in front of one of the cubs. 'Come on. Here you are.' Soon she had both cubs pawing at her shins. She watched them helplessly for a moment, then wedged the bottle into the front pocket of her jeans and bent down to scoop a cub into her arms. Her hands sunk into the soft fur, meeting the hard little body inside. She sat down on a section of tree trunk lying on its side, manoeuvred the cub onto her lap, and retrieved the bottle. After a few seconds of confusion, while she and the cub both tried to take charge of getting the teat into the right position, the cub began to drink.

'That's it,' Angel said. 'Good.' She came and sat down next to Emma with the other cub on her lap, the bottle angled against its mouth.

Both cubs gulped frantically for a while, then settled into regular sucking.

Emma looked sideways at Angel. Her face was bent over the cub's head, her hair draping its fur.

The cub on Emma's knee stirred, drawing her attention. He gazed up at her as he drank, making little sighing sounds between swallows. The front paws began kneading her lap. He reminded Emma of the cat that belonged to her neighbour in Melbourne. A big, tabby tomcat called Bruno. He would be missing her, Emma thought. After Simon had left on the ship, she'd begun offering Bruno titbits of food, tempting him to jump between the balconies of the two apartments. Then she'd let him come inside to sit with her on the couch while she read or worked, even though she knew Simon was allergic to cat fur and it took a long time to remove all traces of allergens from a room. She'd come to rely on Bruno's company. Since being with Simon she'd lost touch with her old friends. It didn't seem fair to contact them only when he was away, and when he was at home he and Emma did everything together. They didn't need anyone else. Emma sometimes saw their joint friends when she was alone, but she always felt like only half of the person they were expecting. So she usually just worked late at the Institute, or went to the gym, or stayed home on her own. She wanted to be self-sufficient like Simon was, but as the weeks turned into months, she'd become more lonely than she wished to admit. She'd even resorted to phoning her father a couple of times, telling herself she was just taking the opportunity to keep in contact, as a daughter should. The conversations had been unsatisfying, as usual, each of them trying to protect the other from anything that might cause an outburst of emotion. It was always like this, as if the pain they'd once endured together remained there between them, ready to rise up and tear them apart again. Both times, when she'd put down the phone she'd only felt more alone.

Emma glanced across to the cooking fire, where Ndisi and Daniel were cutting up firewood. George was looking on, his pipe in his hand. She realised that in the few days she'd been in Africa she'd not spent more than a few minutes by herself, unless she was sleeping. She'd gone from one extreme to the other. But it had not bothered her. In fact, she'd enjoyed the constant companionship. Her thoughts turned naturally to Daniel. He was so kind to her, so warm and open. He exuded a sense of inner strength, but Emma didn't have the feeling – as she did with Simon – that she had to measure up to his standards. She knew she could ask for help if she needed it. Last night, in the guest hut, she'd lain awake for a long time, listening to the rustlings in the thatch roof, and watching the wide crack under the door in case a snake slithered in. It was too hot to be inside the sleeping bag, so she'd stretched out on top of it, but she'd felt very vulnerable, with nothing covering her but the thin silk of her pyjamas. She'd checked, and then re-checked, that her net was tucked in all around. As she'd stared into the shadows, she'd begun to think she would stay awake all night. But then she'd tried lying still, relaxing her body and picturing Daniel resting on his camp bed only a few metres away. If a snake did come in, or some other unnamed danger materialised, she could call out to him.

And he would come to her straight away, she knew he would. The comforting thought had let her drift into sleep.

Emma lowered her face to the cub's head, letting the fur brush her chin. The animal smelled of warm dust and honey and something else, faintly fishy – cod liver oil. With her free hand she stroked its side. In response, the cub let the teat go, looking up at her with eyes that shone like melted chocolate. The tip of a pink tongue poked from between the black-edged lips. Emma smiled down at him. A few seconds passed, then she noticed milk trickling from the teat onto her forearm. Before she had the chance to wipe it away, the cub began licking her – the rough little tongue scraping rhythmically over her skin.

'His tongue tickles,' she said to Angel.

Looking sideways again she watched the girl holding the bottle to the other cub's mouth, carefully tilted and steady. Her face looked serious and intent.

Without shifting her gaze, Angel spoke. 'Don't tell anyone you've got me.'

The words jolted through Emma's body. She pretended to rearrange the cub on her lap as she hunted for a reply.

'We have to,' she said finally. 'We haven't any choice.'

Angel's head swung round. She looked towards the gate, and then along the track that led to the camp, as if she feared that someone could be about to arrive and take her away. 'When are they coming?'

'It's all right. We haven't told anyone yet,' Emma said. 'But people are worried about you. They could still be searching for you. We have to let someone know you're safe.'

'Not yet.' The flawless skin tightened into a pleading frown. 'Can't you wait – at least a day or two. Please?'

Emma felt a stab of pain as she heard the desperation in Angel's voice. Surely, she thought, a little time to rest and prepare for whatever was going to happen next was not a lot to ask. 'All right. But we can't wait too long. That would be wrong.'

Angel breathed out, her narrow shoulders dropping. She smiled down at the cub, looking relaxed and happy again. Emma grew uneasy. The pledge of a couple of days' reprieve seemed to hold more meaning than it should. She feared she'd spoken too soon. 'Angel, what about your father? Do you think he knows you're missing?'

Angel shook her head. 'He doesn't know anything about me. Nothing at all.' There was an airy tone to her voice; Emma had the impression she was delivering an answer she'd given many times before. 'Laura met Michael at a party in Nairobi. They were friends for a while, but then he went on with his travelling. We don't even know his second name.' She looked at Emma. 'I haven't got any brothers or sisters either. There was just me and Laura and the camels. Nobody else.'

Emma felt out of her depth. She didn't want to continue this conversation without Daniel and George. She pretended to be preoccupied, again, with the cub.

'Should I wake him up to keep drinking?' she asked Angel.

'Yes,' Angel replied. 'Otherwise it's a waste of milk.'

Emma jostled the cub gently and his eyes opened again. She teased his lips with the teat until he began suckling. When she looked up, she was relieved to see George approaching the gate.

He entered the enclosure and came to stand in front of Emma and Angel, watching as the cubs drained the last of their bottles.

'I've been very worried about these two,' he said. 'There's no suitable pride for them to join, around here. And I hate the thought of pushing them out on their own. But now Moyo's here we can blend the cubs with hers.' He looked at Angel. 'You'll be able to help with that. The older cubs look up to you. You can be the one to bring them all together. But it'll take some time to prepare them for it.'

Emma frowned at him, shaking her head slightly so that Angel wouldn't notice. He was speaking as though Angel were going to be here at the camp for some time, when surely he must know she wouldn't be. She glanced across the compound to where Ndisi was sitting near the cooking fire, shelling peanuts.

'Can you take the bottles to Ndisi?' she asked Angel. 'I'm sure he'd like some help with the peanuts.'

Angel nodded, as eagerly as if someone had just suggested a treat. As she left the enclosure, a bottle in each hand, Emma turned back to George.

'We need to talk.'

They had only just entered the dining hut when Daniel appeared. He'd been in George's hut, using the camp radio to contact Ndugu.

Emma eyed him expectantly as he joined them at the table. George put down his pipe, half-packed with tobacco and unlit.

'Ndugu has arrived at the station,' Daniel reported. 'The camels are fine. Mama Kitu's foot is healing well.' He gave Emma a brief smile. 'He stopped in Malangu on his way back from Arusha. Everyone was talking about the dead white woman and her child.'

'What did they say about Angel?' Emma asked.

'They said that no one was expecting to find any remains of the lost child. They told Ndugu that the woman's brother has come from England to collect her body.'

Emma stared mutely as she took in his words. So he was the next of kin. And he obviously cared enough about Laura – and presumably her daughter, his niece, as well – to make an urgent trip here from England.

'He'll take Angel back with him,' she said. There was a hollow in her stomach that felt almost like fear. She gazed out past the ragged palm fronds that edged the eaves. The sun was already hot, casting strong shadows. The air was warm, cloaking her skin. She pictured Laura's body being lowered into a cold grave in a rain-soaked churchyard. She pictured Angel standing alone in an asphalted schoolyard, bordered by concrete pavements, her camels lost to her, left behind in a faraway country. She wondered if the uncle had a wife or partner, whether Angel would have a stepmother. Maybe there were other children as well. Emma felt a cold sense of foreboding on Angel's behalf. Would she have to go through life, as Emma had, feeling like the leftover child that didn't really belong? But it didn't have to be like that, Emma reminded herself. Peoples' stories didn't necessarily follow the same path.

'We will have to radio the police,' Daniel said.

Emma turned to him. 'Angel asked me if we could wait a couple of days before we called anyone – and I said yes.'

'I should think so!' George said. 'She's only just come in from the bush. She shouldn't have to face the world yet. If she were one of my lions, I'd be keeping her here, undisturbed, for weeks.' He broke off, looking suddenly doubtful. 'But if her uncle is here, we have to let him know about her before he leaves the country.'

Emma picked at the tabletop with her fingernail. She knew the correct thing for them to do was to notify the authorities immediately. If they didn't, they could even be breaking the law. But she remembered the look on Angel's face. Emma had made a commitment to her. She knew, suddenly, that she was not going to let the child down. 'She *has* to have the two days.'

'I agree,' Daniel said. 'We will radio at the end of tomorrow, when it is nearly dark. They can inform the uncle. But it will be too late for anyone to come until the next day.'

Angel suddenly appeared at the entrance of the hut, her bare feet on the sand having given no warning of her approach. The three adults looked at her, saying nothing.

'Where's my knitting?' she asked Emma. Her bright face and voice broke the tension. 'I want to show Ndisi how to do it.'

Emma smiled at the thought of the cook puzzling over plain and purl stitches. She pointed towards the basket that was resting on the sideboard. 'It's in there.'

'Thank you.' Angel threw her a smile, then spun on her heels, running to the basket, grabbing the knitting. Then she was gone, the bundle of wool a red flash at her side.

*

The water in the basin was grey and gritty with desert dust. Emma twisted Angel's brown tunic in her hands, forcing water into the fabric then wringing it out. She was no expert at hand washing – at home, anything that couldn't go in the machine she sent to the dry cleaners – but after two rinses she had finally managed to get out most of the stains. She felt an odd satisfaction at what she'd achieved. Lifting the wet cloth from the basin, she walked over to the tree outside the dining hut. Hooking the arms of the tunic over some twigs, she left it to drip dry. Next, she turned to the trousers. When they, too, had been thoroughly washed, she shook them out, the legs unfurling, and draped them over a bush. Emma stood back from the two pieces of clothing. They looked so small, and fragile, somehow, as though they were made of something more delicate than homespun cotton. Even wet, they seemed to hold the shape of a small girl's body. The sight evoked a pang of regret. Emma knew she would never have a child of her own who would wear little clothes like this. It was not something she thought about very often. The decision had been made; it didn't have to be revisited again and again. But as she stood there, Angel's clothes laid out in front of her, she found herself going back over the reasons for the choice. The reality was that Emma had no room in her life for a baby. Her priorities had been set in train when she'd decided – at the age of just sixteen – to follow in Susan's footsteps. To achieve this had demanded an unerring focus on her studies at high school and then university, then postgraduate studies. Now, Emma was equally devoted to the work she was doing at the Institute. When she and Simon met, they'd recognised they had similar attitudes to their careers – it was one of the things that made them well suited. But as Emma had come to know Simon better, she'd realised it was more than a matter of professional commitment on his side. Simon didn't like children. He'd always felt like a nuisance to his parents and he believed a child would play the same role in his life. Emma knew he would never change. She'd always told herself it was just as well that the decision they'd made suited her, too. But now as she reached over to one of the trouser legs, spreading it more smoothly under the gaze of the sun, she felt a haunting sense of loss.

A shout of laughter came from the other end of the compound, where Daniel and Angel were playing hide and seek with the lions. Emma wiped her hands on the seat of her jeans as she walked over so that she could see them. Angel was chasing one of Moyo's cubs. Not far away, the dark outline of Daniel's head and shoulders was just visible behind a large bush. Moyo was stalking towards him, her body low-slung, eyes narrowed to slits. Soon, Emma knew, she would pounce. Then the two would play-fight until Daniel finally escaped, to stand by Angel panting for breath and laughing. At first, Emma had hardly been able to watch, but the game had been going on for nearly an hour, with Moyo never unsheathing her claws or curling back her lips to show her teeth, or letting her crushing weight rest in the wrong place.

Daniel was stripped to the waist, as he had been when operating on Mama Kitu. The sun glanced off his skin, highlighting the contours of his body. Beside him, Angel looked almost ethereal with her thin limbs and fair colouring.

Suddenly, Moyo leapt onto Daniel, pushing him sideways into

the dust. As they wrestled there, Angel laughed again. Emma moved closer, watching the child's face. No one would guess that, only days ago, she had buried her mother with her own hands. She looked like any carefree, happy little girl. Emma wrapped her arms across her chest as a shiver of pain ran through her. She remembered how it felt, that need to laugh – the urge to do something to balance the cold silence inside. When you gave in to it, people looked at you with questions in their eyes. How can you smile, laugh, have fun, when your mother is dead?

You split yourself in two. One of you ate and talked and got dressed and laughed. The other waited, silent, in the cold and dark. That one wished to be dead, as well, so that there would be no more moments of remembering, the weight of reality crowding in, bearing down. Susan was never coming back. The person called Mom was gone. Emma Lindberg had no mother. It was worst just after she woke up, making each morning a torture.

Then, there was her father. Emma's smiles, when she managed to produce them, had been like air to him. From the moment when the two men from the CDC had come to see him – talking in low voices in his study, then leaving him to emerge and tell the news to his daughter – it had been clear that what he needed, beyond anything, was to know that Emma was all right. If she cried, even softly, he broke down. And then, for her, grief slid into fear. He had always been a strong, quiet man. When he knelt on the floor, sobbing, she hardly knew who he was. She felt she'd lost her father, too.

The forced smiles, the acts of bright laughter, had served her well. Her father had returned to work. She had gone back to school.

n to treat her normally again. And in time, a new
rown up.

d her fingers against her lips, staring numbly at the
scene in front of her. She had never really cried about Susan – not
freely and openly. Over the years, when she'd had an excuse to cry
about something else, she'd felt a little of the pressure ease. But she
could still feel, inside her, the dull weight of all those captured tears.

'They're having fun.' George's voice came to her without warning. He appeared at her side.

Emma fought off her thoughts, turning to face him. She managed a smile. 'You'd think they'd be exhausted by now.'

George smiled back. He watched the scene for a while, then
pointed his pipe at Daniel. 'He's a handsome man. Strong, intelligent as well. And playful. That's why Moyo likes him.'

Emma felt her cheeks begin to warm. She had the idea that
George could tell how she felt about Daniel – how she wanted to
keep watching him, hearing his voice, being close to him. She forced
a casual tone. 'So, Moyo can recognise all that about Daniel?'

'Oh yes,' George said. 'A lioness will always show preference for
a handsome man with a sense of fun. And they admire a strong body,
of course. One to match their own.' He nodded towards Moyo. The
outlines of her muscles could be traced on her hide. They looked
rock-hard and tight.

'She looks so sleek and fit – so healthy,' Emma said.

'She's a fine lioness.' George spoke proudly. 'I could be biased,
but I consider lions to be the most impressive of all animals. They're
loyal, brave, intelligent. They have senses we've lost, you know.'

Emma raised one eyebrow questioningly.

'They can pick up our thoughts, I'm certain of it.'

'What do you mean?'

'I'll give you an example. A few times a year, I go to away to Arusha or Nairobi. The day I get back to camp – in the evening – at least one or two of my lions will turn up. Often I haven't seen them for some time; they weren't around to see that I was leaving. But they know when I'm coming back and they come to greet me.'

Emma said nothing. She didn't want to seem cynical.

'You're thinking they've seen me on the road, or heard something,' George continued. 'But it's not the case. Some of them have come from great distances. They've set out for the camp before I've even begun my journey home.'

George spoke with conviction, but his manner was not argumentative. Emma got the feeling he didn't mind whether she believed him or not. Strangely, the indifference added weight to his words.

'What other senses do they have, that we don't?' she asked. She had a flash image of her laboratory leader, shaking his head at her. Whatever this lion man had to say, it could most likely never be properly proved.

'As I said to you when you arrived, I don't like tourists dropping in. It confuses the lions, and I'm not running a zoo. But people write to me quite regularly, offering to come and help with my work. Most never arrive, but some do. Elizabeth was the last – a lovely American girl. She spent several months here, writing reports to the donors who support my work, bringing the accounts up to date. I was in quite a muddle with it all, but she sorted everything out.' There was a tender expression on George's face that reminded Emma of the way he responded to Moyo. She thought of the curly-headed young woman in the photos in the dining hut and guessed he was talking about her. 'There was something sad about Elizabeth. She seemed rather lost. When she left, she said the lions had healed her. I could see that it was true. And that's only one example.' He broke off, searching Emma's face. 'The lions draw people here. No one comes by chance.'

Emma felt exposed, as if he knew all about her and had determined that she, like Elizabeth, was damaged.

'Well, we're in a different category,' she said. 'Angel brought us here.'

'But Moyo brought Angel.'

George held Emma's gaze. As she looked into his faded blue eyes, she felt something begin to shift, deep inside her. It was like the sensation of the ground moving beneath your feet. Disorienting, unnerving. She fought an impulse to reach for the limb of a nearby tree to steady herself.

George gave her a small smile, then walked away. There was the scraping sound of the lid being twisted from a tin, then the honey-raisin fragrance of pipe tobacco drifted into the air.

Emma bent her head over the big lumpy sweet potato she held in her hand. She was using a peeler to slice off strips of the purple skin, revealing the white flesh inside. It was satisfying to watch the colour of the potato steadily change as her hands moved rhythmically. She made no attempt to hurry with her task – the relaxed mood of the camp had begun seeping into her. She was enjoying the feeling of the sun on her back and the sound of birds cooing gently in the bushes. From somewhere behind the dining hut came the crow of a rooster, a half-hearted sound, as if he were barely awake. Glancing up, she saw Moyo and the cubs still lounging in the shade. George, Daniel and Ndisi were over by the old Land Rover that they'd driven the day before; they had the bonnet up and were tinkering with something, but there was no urgency to their movements. Angel was sitting not far from Emma, adding to her knitting. The end of the scarf was now touching her knees.

Emma turned to look at her. She was sucking the end of a strand of her hair – it was stretched across her cheek, the end disappearing into the corner of her mouth. With a pang of nostalgia Emma remembered exactly how it felt to poke your tongue through the strand or run it across the spiky ends of the hairs.

Angel lifted her head, as if she could feel Emma's eyes on her. 'Thank you for washing my clothes, Emma. It was very kind of you.'

'You're welcome.' Emma was surprised by Angel's good manners; the image she had of Laura didn't suggest the kind of mother who would be too bothered with social niceties. But then, Emma reminded herself, Angel had grown up in Africa, where courtesy was constantly being displayed.

'I could have done it myself, you know,' Angel added. 'I can cook and clean. I can fix broken things. At the Sisters of Mercy, I helped sew vests for the sick babies.'

'The Sisters of Mercy,' Emma repeated. 'Is that a hospital?'

Angel nodded. 'It's in the fig-tree village. That's where I was born.'

'So you lived there?' Emma asked cautiously.

'No, we only visited the nuns when we needed more medicine. We didn't live anywhere. We travelled around visiting people who were dying from illnesses like cancer or AIDS. They lived in villages where there were no clinics or hospitals. They only had us.'

'So you helped your mother,' Emma said.

Angel nodded. 'I counted out their tablets. I held gourds up to their mouths so they could drink. I washed their faces and sang to them. We always made sure that they were never left alone. That was our job.'

Emma's lips parted in amazement. Angel hadn't just lived with a mother who worked in a remote part of Africa, she had been her colleague. Emma pictured Laura and her young daughter working side by side, helping people through the terminal stages of illness, and then staying with them as they faced their deaths. Emma's research had taken her into hospice wards now and then, and even with all that modern medicine could offer, she'd seen some very confronting scenes. She could hardly imagine what would take place in an African village hut.

'Weren't you afraid?' Emma studied Angel's face, as if there must surely be some mark left on her, from the suffering she had witnessed.

'Sometimes. But when that happens you just have to be brave. Anyway, Laura needed me. There was a lot to do. Sometimes we made our own medicines. Morphine causes constipation and we never had tablets for that. But you can dry out pawpaw seeds and grind them up. They work well. You can make medicine from the frangipani tree as well. And you can get special plants from the *laiboni*.'

Emma listened with a growing sense of disbelief. Angel spoke in such a matter-of-fact voice, casually using medical terms as though there was nothing unusual about what she'd been involved in. Emma felt, again, a desire to judge Laura for putting her work first when she was meant to be a mother. But then, when Emma considered the suffering Laura had worked to alleviate, her child at her side, the priorities seemed less clear. Emma remembered the look on Daniel's face as he'd sat beside her in the Land Rover, describing Lela's suffering. She pictured the tiny baby, grey and limp. She thought about how her own mother had devoted her life to trying to stop such tragedies taking place. In that, she had a lot in common with Laura. Should Susan have put Emma's wellbeing first? Should Laura have made the same choice for Angel? How many deaths was one child's happiness worth? Emma shook her head. It was a hard question to answer. And how was happiness to be judged anyway? Emma replayed in her mind the way Angel had said 'we' and 'our job', with such a clear note of pride in her voice. A deep sense of envy flooded through her. How extraordinary it must have been for mother and daughter to share such potent experiences – the joys and triumphs as well as tragedy. But most of all, how precious for them to have been always together. Emma felt an ache of longing. It occured to her that this was what could make Angel's future quite different from hers – the years of closeness, the intimate involvement in her mother's life that Emma had never known.

'Did you unpack the saddlebags?' Angel's words broke into her thoughts. 'To find these?' She gestured at her clothes, which were already smudged with dirt and speckled with gold-brown hairs.

'Matata unpacked the bags,' Emma said. 'He spread things all over the yard. Daniel gave him a good telling off.'

Angel giggled. 'He's always being naughty.' A tense look came onto her face. 'When can I see them?'

'Soon,' Emma said.

'You won't let them take me away without seeing them?'

Emma felt an ache of sympathy. Angel seemed to be accepting her situation so bravely. 'You will see them.' As the words came out she realised she'd made another promise. She hoped she'd be able to fulfil it.

'There were some really precious things in one of the saddlebags,' Angel said in an anxious voice. 'Did you see them? A bead necklace and a fly switch made from a lion's tail?'

'Don't worry, they're safe,' Emma said.

Angel breathed out with relief. 'They belonged to Walaita. When she was dying, we promised her we would take them to her brother's *manyata* at the foot of Ol Doinyo Lengai. That's where we were going, me and Laura – when she got bitten. We didn't even see the snake . . .' Her voice trembled, then died. She pressed her lips together.

Emma put a hand on Angel's shoulder. She could feel the bones, impossibly small and fragile. She didn't know whether to encourage the child to talk about what had happened, or try to divert her, but then Angel made her own decision.

'You've nearly finished that job,' she said. 'What can we do next?'

Emma noticed how Angel had included them both in the question – and felt, again, that warm sense of being chosen. 'We'll go and ask Ndisi,' she replied. She let her hand fall from Angel's shoulder.

'He likes having us here,' Angel said. 'He needs some helpers to run this camp.'

Emma watched her uncertainly. She had the impression Angel was trying to make a point with her remark, but she was not sure what it was.

Angel stood up. 'Come on.' She held out her hand, as if Emma were a child who needed to be jollied along.

Emma rose to her feet. As she took Angel's hand she felt a sudden sense of recognition. A memory came to her – one in which hers was the small hand, being held in the firm grip of the one that was bigger and stronger. She remembered clinging to it, wanting never to let go. The scene unfolded, playing out in her head like a fragment of a movie. Susan was peeling her fingers away, bending over her, speaking into her ear.

'Don't make a fuss, sweetheart. Mommy's got to go to work. But I'll come back soon.'

'What if you don't come back?' Emma heard her own child's voice, and remembered the unformed fear she'd had of that unknown place, 'overseas', where Susan kept going. She saw it as a dark, hidden place. If Susan got lost there, no one would be able to find her and bring her home.

Susan smiled. 'I always come back – you know I do.'

Emma shook off the memory. She had the feeling, again, that

by coming here to Tanzania she'd set in motion an upheaval over which she had no control. Thoughts and memories came to her as they chose, throwing up more questions than they answered. It was as if everything had been put under an electron microscope, but Emma was not in control of how deeply it scanned, or which viewing angle it chose to take. Her focus kept being dragged away from the mother she'd told herself she remembered. In place of the old Susan she saw a woman who had been so committed to her work that she'd excluded her only child from the true core of her life. And the example Susan had set, Emma could now see, had shaped all the key relationships in her daughter's life. Emma had chosen to be with people who were like Susan. She'd tried to be like Susan herself. She'd done this, because to do otherwise was to suggest that Susan was not the wise and perfect mother of Emma's dreams.

And now, there was a new element at play. Angel's physical presence was only going to add more layers to the puzzle. Emma sighed, trying to shed tension. She hoped this process would stop when she returned home – when she was back in her orderly life, with all the work that would have built up on her desk awaiting her. Then, with some distance, she might be able to make sense of it all. Perhaps, she told herself, that was what she would gain from this unexpected sidetrack to her journey. She tightened her hand around Angel's fingers as they walked together across the yard.

A small furry creature that looked like a grey squirrel sat in the middle of the dining table, using its tiny paws to scratch its ears.

Emma tried to ignore the thought that it might be harbouring lice. George opened his tin of nuts and shook out a few peanuts. The little animal raced across to him and stood up, dancing on its hind legs. It took the nut in its paws and began to nibble. Emma couldn't help smiling at its antics, even though she wished it was not playing on the dining table. She looked across to where Angel was sitting, to see if she was watching, but her blonde head was bent over her exercise book. Her hair fell forward, hiding her work, but it was clear she was drawing busily. She kept reaching for different coloured pencils and the movements of her elbow hinted at long, bold lines being made on the hidden page.

Emma turned back to the squirrel in time to see it finish off the nut and scurry away along the table, then hop onto George's arm, using it as a ramp to reach his chair. The next moment the animal had disappeared from view. Glancing back at the table, Emma saw that it had left behind several small brown droppings. George didn't appear to have noticed them. Emma reached into her bag and pulled out two wet wipes. She used one to scoop up the droppings, the second to dab the surface clean. It was just as well there seemed no likelihood, according to Daniel's careful research, that animals like this were hosts for the Olambo virus. She wondered about the lions – remembering he had not tested the large mammals yet – but then she recalled that people who lived at the lion camp had not suffered during the outbreak.

The sound of tearing paper made her look at Angel. 'This is for you.' The child slid her drawing across the table towards her.

Emma stared silently at an image of herself. It was immediately recognisable. Angel had drawn her with the same deft skill she'd used to depict Laura, the camels and herself in the picture she'd entitled 'My Family'. Emma's hair draped her shoulders, thick and dark. Her eyes were big, her mouth red. She was obviously meant to look beautiful. Angel had changed her clothes. The Emma in the drawing was wearing a tunic and trousers and wore bangles on her arms. She stood in the middle of the page, her head near the top, her feet at the bottom. There was something about her posture that made her look powerful and strong.

'Thank you,' Emma breathed. 'I love it. No one has ever drawn a picture of me before.'

A smile lit Angel's face. Then she looked curious. 'Never? In your whole life?'

'Never,' Emma confirmed.

Angel eyed Emma with a look of satisfaction. Then she signalled for Emma to return the drawing. 'I want to add something else.' She smiled again. 'Mama Kitu.'

At the end of the day, they sat on the floor again to eat their evening meal, as though observing an accepted tradition. Emma found herself sitting near Moyo, one of the big padded paws resting right by her knee. Now and then, when Emma glanced down at it, she felt a sense of shock. How could she be sitting there calmly within reach of those claws? But the feeling quickly passed, swept away by the aura of gentleness that surrounded the lioness.

They were using bowls and spoons tonight and there was the

sound of metal scraping against enamel as the five ate hungrily. The food was very basic – sweet potato and red beans cooked with tomato and a little salt. But as Emma ate she was struck by the way the simple combination allowed the flavours to come through cleanly. She didn't pause in her eating until her bowl was empty. Then she wiped her hands on her jeans, before pressing her palms against her cheeks. She'd forgotten to apply any sunscreen today and could feel the sting of sunburn. Aware of Daniel watching her, she smiled ruefully.

'I hope I don't shed my skin like that Dutchman you told me about.'

Daniel smiled. Emma wondered if he, like her, was remembering their very first conversation and thinking how much had happened since then.

'You might go brown,' Angel said. 'Then you'll be like me.'

'Not very much like you,' Emma responded. 'My hair is the wrong colour.'

'You know, my hair was once dark like yours,' George said, pointing his pipe at Emma.

Emma looked at his long white locks, swept back from his fine-boned face. He was the image of an ancient prophet from an illustration in a child's Bible. The look suited him so well it was virtually impossible to imagine him as a young man. 'Where were you born?' she asked him.

'Here in Tanzania. Of course, it was Tanganyika back then.' He smiled at Angel. 'I'm a white African, like you.'

He began to tell stories about his boyhood, spent on a coffee plantation in the foothills of Kilimanjaro. He'd been a keen trophy hunter until the day he decided never to kill an animal again, except to feed himself or his lions. He even told how he'd once been in love with a woman he'd met in Nairobi, but hadn't married her in the end, because he realised she didn't truly want to settle permanently in Africa. Ndisi listened avidly. It was obvious he'd not heard his boss talk like this before. Emma guessed that the presence of a child amongst them that had stirred up potent memories for George – just as it had done for her.

When all the food was gone, they sat there in the circle, sipping tea with honey. A peaceful mood settled over them. Soon it was time to begin preparing for bed.

'Why don't you sleep outside with us tonight?' Angel said to Emma. 'Then you won't be on your own.'

She spoke as it if were obvious that company was preferable to solitude. Emma considered how she would answer. She liked the idea of having a roof over her head, but after the intimacy that had formed during the evening, she didn't want to be cut off from the others. She looked across the circle to Daniel. She pictured her bed set up beside his – how they would lie there, not touching, but close to one another, for the whole long night.

'Okay,' Emma smiled. 'I will.'

Emma paused in the doorway of the guest hut. She was dressed in her pyjamas, but still had her boots on her feet. She looked across to her bed, now standing between the two that belonged to the men.

Ndisi had insisted on remaining in his hut, rolling his eyes over Emma's decision. Clearly he was unused to guests joining George in his eccentric behaviour.

George was already asleep, his body making a long low mound on his stretcher. Angel was in her place with Moyo and the cubs. Daniel had not yet returned from the shower enclosure.

Emma headed over to the beds. When she entered the pool of light cast by the lantern, the silk of her pyjamas glowed a pale apricot pink.

Angel's curious, wide-awake eyes travelled up and down Emma's body. 'You look beautiful,' she said. 'Like a princess.' Then a thoughtful look came over her face. 'Those clothes are exactly the same colour as a crocodile's tongue. You know, when you see them sitting on the river bank with their mouths open.' She shuddered. 'Flies sit on their tongues. They must swallow them.'

'You say some funny things.' Emma smiled at her. She found herself bending over the child, her hand smoothing the long soft hair. Angel didn't flinch from her touch. Instead, she closed her eyes, as though focusing on the caress. When Emma took her hand away, she uttered a tiny murmur of protest.

'Time for you to sleep,' Emma said gently. 'See you in the morning.'

'*Lala salama*,' Angel said in a dreamy voice.

'*Lala salama*,' Emma returned the night-time blessing, the words now falling smoothly from her tongue.

Emma climbed onto her bed and lay on top of the sleeping bag. She pulled down the sleeves and legs of the pyjamas to cover as much of her skin as possible. Without even a net to shield her, she felt very exposed. She pictured the land stretching away from her, beyond the edges of the camp, out into the boundless wilderness. She had to remind herself that the fences were high, and the gates had been locked at dusk, secured by a chain and a big old-fashioned padlock. And only a couple of metres away from her lay the huge shape of the lioness. The gentleness Moyo exuded was equally matched by an air of vigilance and power. She was like a guardian, looking over them all.

She barely heard Daniel approaching – his movements were almost silent. She watched him materalise, a dark shape emerging from the shadows, forming into a person. He moved around in the dining hut, extinguishing the lamps one by one. When there was just the one left, hanging from the tree outside, he came to stand by her bed. He wore only his *kitenge* wrapped around his hips. Drops of water still clung to his skin. Caught in the light, they were like diamonds, scattered across his chest and shoulders. She could smell the sandalwood perfume of the camp's homemade soap.

She lay still, watching his gaze travel over her, from her feet to her head. When his eyes met hers, they both smiled.

Daniel sat down on his stretcher. His expression became serious. 'Is she all right?' he asked in an undertone, nodding towards Angel.

'She fell asleep straight away, tonight,' Emma said. 'It's been a big day for her. She must be exhausted.'

'I am worried about her,' Daniel said. 'She seems too happy. She has not cried.'

'Perhaps she's not ready, yet. She might be afraid to break down. I remember how that felt.' Emma hoped it would not be too long before Angel found the right time and place to grieve properly. She knew only too well that tears held back turned hard and heavy as ice. She didn't want to think of Angel always having to carry that weight inside her, as she had done.

'I remember it, too,' Daniel said. 'It is good that she is very strong.' He shook his head admiringly. 'She has been so helpful, today. If she was my daughter, I would be very proud of her.'

Emma searched his face, wondering if was thinking of his baby girl. By now, she'd be three or four years old. If he was, it only brought a deeper warmth to his eyes.

He turned back to Emma. 'Are you comfortable?'

Emma nodded. The camp beds were firm but the sleeping bag underneath her provided some padding.

'I will turn off the light.' He stood up, reaching across to the lantern hanging in the tree. The whispering hiss slowly died away, taking with it the yellow glow. Then he lay down on his bed, the canvas creaking under the weight of his body.

Emma waited for him to say goodnight, but he didn't. She wondered if – like her – he didn't want to call an end to the day. They were both quiet and still. Emma could almost feel the heat of his body across the small gap between them. She strained her ears into the darkness, reaching for the sound of his breath. She imagined it, brushing her skin like the touch of the warm night air. Reaching in past the collar of her shirt to the fullness of her breasts. She pictured reaching over to him – just to touch him, to place her hand on his chest. There would be nothing more than that. They were not alone, after all – but that was not what kept them apart. Rather, it was that everything Emma knew about Daniel said he was not the kind of man who would want to begin something that had no future. And she felt the same. She did not want to risk having shame and regret come between them after all that they'd shared. Even so, she yearned for some small intimacy – something she could carry away with her and treasure in her mind, forever. But even a single touch seemed dangerous. She had to content herself with the knowledge that Daniel was right there, so close beside her.

She lay still, staring up at the sky. It looked velvety and soft, like a huge canopy spread over the world. The moon had risen, full and bright. It looked unfamiliar to Emma – the grey-mauve markings on the white were different from the ones she was used to seeing. She let her eyes wander over the patterns of the stars, constellations she could not name. She was struck by how far away she was from the part of the planet where she belonged. She lowered her gaze, peering across at Moyo – a silver lioness with a silver child at her side. The sight reminded her of the issues that awaited them in the morning. Someone would have to explain to Angel what was going to happen next. The police would have to be contacted. Emma would have to make plans for her departure. They'd all have to prepare themselves to say their last goodbyes.

She refused to let these thoughts crowd in on her. She wanted to lose herself in Daniel's strong, quiet presence, in the peace of the sleeping child, in George's gentle wisdom. She wanted to wrap herself in the warmth of shared comfort and rest.

She pictured the scene around her as if it had been preserved on canvas. She saw it painted in soft pastel tones. They would resemble some odd kind of family, sleeping close to one another like this. Lions and humans, young and old, friends and strangers – all drawn together, for this one night.

FIFTEEN

George poured whiskey into a tumbler, the golden liquid settling thickly in the bottom of the glass. Angel stood beside him holding an old-fashioned soda siphon. The mid-morning sun fell in a blur on the yellow frosted surface of the bottle.

'Shall I do it now?' she asked.

George nodded. 'Not too much,' he warned.

Angel frowned with concentration as she pressed the lever, then jumped in surprise as soda gushed into the glass.

'Well done, Angel,' George said. 'No one joining me?'

Emma shook her head, smiling. 'It's a bit early for me. I'm happy with a cup of tea.'

'Me, too,' Daniel agreed.

'I always have whiskey for elevenses,' George said. 'I believe it's what has kept me young and healthy!'

'It's not eleven o'clock though,' Angel said. 'It's *saa tano* – five o'clock.'

Emma looked questioningly at Daniel.

'It's Tanzanian time,' he explained. 'The day begins at dawn. That's six o'clock in English time. So seven o'clock is the first hour – *saa moja*.'

'The next is two o'clock, and it goes on until the sun goes down,' Angel added. 'Then the day is ended because everyone goes to bed.'

Listening to her, Emma glimpsed, again, the different world in which Angel had grown up. The child didn't know how to tell the time the way most of the rest of the world did, but she spoke three languages, apparently fluently, and knew how to make medicine from pawpaw seeds.

'Have Bill and Ben got water?' George asked Angel.

Her hand flew to cover her mouth. 'I forgot you asked me to.' Without hesitation she ran from the dining hut, veering off in the direction of the tank.

Emma turned to the task of pouring out mugs of tea. She was about to hand them around when a figure appeared at the entrance to the dining hut – an African man, carrying a cloth-wrapped bundle in his hand.

'Samu! *Karibu sana*,' George said, beckoning him inside. 'Welcome back.' He gestured towards the group seated around the table. 'These are our guests, Daniel, Emma and Angel.' He looked back to the newcomer. 'And this is my helper, Samu.'

Samu nodded at everyone in turn. Then he raised his eyebrows, looking concerned. 'That lioness has come back! With cubs! Our work is going backwards.'

'It's a long story,' George said. He waved Samu towards a chair and indicated to Emma that she should pour another mug of tea. 'Are you completely recovered, now?'

'Yes, I am. Your *dawa* worked very quickly. I would have asked for it at the beginning, but I thought it was just the *kampi* fever.'

'Well, if the quinine worked it was definitely malaria,' George said. 'It's an old-fashioned drug, but still a good one.'

Emma was stirring honey into the tea. Her spoon came to a halt as she looked up at Samu. 'What did you say? What was that about another fever?'

'We have a fever that comes to our village. At first it is the same as malaria, but then it goes away very quickly.'

'What did you call it?' Emma leaned forward, looking intently at Samu. The man shifted in his seat as though the attention made him uneasy.

'In English, it is "camp fever". We call it that because the people who get it are the ones who work at this camp, and their families as well. But do not be alarmed. It is not a bad illness like Olambo. A sick person will not miss more than one day of work.'

Emma turned to George. 'Do you know about this?'

He shrugged his shoulders, 'I've heard them speak of it, but I never paid much attention.' A wry smile came onto his face. 'I thought it was just another version of the rumour about the powers of the mad lion man.'

Emma stared blankly across at the wall of the hut with its collection of lion portraits. Her thoughts were racing. Snippets of ideas came to her. The people at the camp got one illness, but were protected from another. She remembered what George had said on her first night here. The words came back to her, delivered in his measured English accent. *It was like that biblical story . . . the plague passing over . . .*

Emma swung round to Daniel. 'How much do you know about

the victims of Olambo fever who survive? Do they acquire immunity to the virus?'

'Yes, they do. You can only get it once.'

'Well, I'm thinking . . .' Emma faltered over her words, the ideas behind them still being formed. 'There really could be a link between this camp and people being protected from Olambo.'

Daniel frowned at her. 'What do you mean?'

'You know the story of the smallpox vaccination?'

'We learned about it at primary school. All the Maasai kids liked this story because it was about cows. The milkmaids did not suffer from smallpox because they caught cowpox from their herds.'

'They had transferred immunity,' Emma finished for him.

There was a moment of quiet, broken by the sound of Angel over in the cubs' enclosure calling to Bill and Ben.

Daniel stared at Emma. 'Do you think . . . ?'

'It's just an idea,' Emma warned. But she could feel it growing stronger, deeper, inside her. 'If camp fever causes only a mild illness, no one would have noticed if lions had it as well.'

'The virus may not make them ill at all,' Daniel added. 'They might just be carriers.'

'That's right.' Emma stood up and began pacing between the table and the sideboard. Her racing thoughts made her limbs restless. 'I think it's worth investigating. All the people who spend time here should be tested. Their blood samples could be cross-matched for antibodies and then compared with tests on survivors of Olambo. The lions would need to be tested as well.'

On Daniel's face, excitement overlaid intense concentration.

He turned to George. 'Would you be able to take blood from the lions without tranquilising them? It may be possible because they do not fear you.'

The old man nodded vigorously. 'I'm sure I could. I've had to give an injection of antibiotics to the odd lion in the past. They don't even seem to feel the needle.' He gave a quick smile. 'Anyway they'd trade a small jab for a bowl of cod liver oil any day.' He looked at Emma. 'Are you saying my lions might hold the key to a cure for Olambo fever?'

'Not a cure, a vaccination.'

The squirrel dislodged a packet of tea from its place on a shelf. It fell onto the ground, but no one moved to pick it up.

'But we know vaccinations are too expensive to produce,' Daniel said.

'This is different. If it's similar to the cowpox–smallpox story it could be very simple – nothing like having to create a vaccine from scratch in the lab. Anyway, this work would be of interest to the entire medical research community. There could be implications for the treatment of other viruses. People would fall over themselves to fund it.'

Daniel rubbed his hands over his face, as if to make sure that he was awake.

George leaned forward. 'But it all relies on stopping the poachers.'

'We have to get the area protected,' Daniel agreed. 'Perhaps if the lions are involved in the fever research, it could help.'

'You'd be able to do some work here at the camp,' Emma said, 'and some at the station, but you'd need access to proper facilities as well.' She knew she was talking too fast, with too much excitement. She told herself to slow down, be more professional.

'There are suitable labs in Arusha,' Daniel confirmed, 'at the National Institute for Medical Research.'

'Good,' Emma said. 'You need to involve an organisation like that. You need to get hold of a really experienced medical research scientist.' Her voice broke off. Her words were left hanging in the air. She looked down at the carpet, staring at the intricate patterns of orange, red and black.

You need me.

She caught her breath. For a moment she let herself imagine a scenario in which she was the one who helped Daniel with the new research. She felt a shiver of excitement as she pictured them working side by side, bringing to a conclusion what Susan had begun all those years ago. She thought of how it would be, not having to go back to her own life. No more lonely evenings spent closed up in her small apartment. No more waiting for Simon to come home. And an escape from the competitive, inward-looking world of the Institute, where the focus of research got lost amid the need to get the next journal article published and to secure an invitation to speak at the next prestigious conference.

The idea of staying here in Africa rose before her, conjuring visions of open space, the luxury of having time to spend more slowly, the comfort of always being with people, animals.

And of being with Daniel.

But as quickly as the enticing vision rose in front of her, it began to crumble. What if she was wrong about the link between the fevers? She'd already seen on Daniel's face that he was daring to imagine an end to the nightmare of Olambo outbreaks. George was picturing a secure future for his lion family, and his hopes were mirrored in the faces of Ndisi and Samu. Emma didn't want to be the one who had raised hopes that proved to be false. And she couldn't turn her whole career – her whole life – upside down on the basis of what was just the seed of an idea. She tried to imagine herself walking away from her project at the Institute, giving up her research fellowship, losing her secure and comfortable lifestyle. Ending her relationship with Simon . . .

Slowly, she lifted her gaze. The link between herself and the need for a qualified researcher was so obvious that she was sure Daniel and George were thinking about it, too. Daniel avoided meeting her eyes. She guessed he didn't even want to look at her in case she thought he was trying to pressure her to stay. She felt a wave of bittersweet pain at the realisation that he wanted her to be completely free to make her own choice.

She swallowed on a dry throat. Anxiety sharpened inside her. It only began to ease as a decision formed in her head. She made herself look from Daniel to George and back. 'When I get home, I'll look into it. I can raise a research proposal at a team conference and see what people think.' She heard her voice as though from a distance. It sounded gruff and weak, both at the same time. 'There's a lot that would need to be worked out – funding, strategy. There's even the issue of patenting. Things must be set up properly. It's possible I can assist from Melbourne. It would be ideal to find an Institute with teams already set up to work in this region.

It would be worth looking at options in South Africa.' The words kept on coming. There were too many, Emma knew – it was as if she hoped to use them to build a protective barrier behind which she could take shelter.

Finally, Daniel spoke. His voice was firm but warm. 'I understand that you have to return to your own work and your own life. This is not your place.' He smiled. 'But you are here, now, at the beginning. The idea came from you. This work will always belong to you. And we will always be grateful to you.'

Emma smiled back at him, though her eyes ached with unshed tears. She felt a deep sense of loss as though something precious had just been given away.

Daniel stood up, moving a little apart from her. He gazed thoughtfully at the lion photographs, as if wondering which of them might have been the first to bring into the camp the virus that would save George and his workers from the threat of Olambo. Emma left him to his thoughts; she needed to let some time pass before they talked about the research again. She sat at the table, staring blankly down at a pool of pineapple juice left from breakfast. George began collecting the mugs of tea, the clinking of enamel breaking the quiet. Then an exchange began between Ndisi and Samu, carried out in fast-spoken Swahili. From the surprise in Samu's voice Emma guessed he was being given an explanation of the presence of these visitors, including an account of Angel's rescue by the lioness.

As if on cue, the child returned to the dining hut. She greeted Samu, lightly touching his head with her hand, while he eyed her with avid interest. After the exchange was complete, Angel came to join Emma at the table. As Angel stood there, pushing her finger into the pool of juice, George gave Emma a meaningful look. It took Emma a few moments to understand what he was trying to convey. Then she remembered – it had been agreed that after morning tea today would be the right time to talk to Angel about what was going to happen next. They'd all decided that Emma should be the one to do it, with Daniel and George looking on. Emma nodded faintly at George. After the conversation they'd just had, she felt drained, but she knew this next one couldn't be postponed.

'Sit down please, Angel,' Emma said. 'We need to talk to you.'

Angel pulled out her chair and climbed up onto the cushion. Then Daniel came over, taking his place at the table next to George. Emma braced herself to continue. The child sat upright, her hands clasped in front of her. She eyed Emma expectantly.

'Angel, your uncle has come from England,' Emma began. 'He is in Arusha.'

Angel stiffened visibly, but she said nothing.

'Do you know him?' Emma asked.

Angel shrugged. 'I know I have an uncle, but I haven't met him.' She was silent for a while, then words poured out of her. 'I don't want to go and live with him in England. I told Laura that. I don't care if he's got a big house by the seaside. I want to stay here.'

'Your mother talked to you about going to live in England?'

'She said if something happened to her, my uncle would take care of me. She wrote his name in her passport.' Angel's eyes sparked blue fire. 'I threw it away.'

'The police found it,' Daniel said. 'They showed it to us.'

Angel pushed her lips together in an obstinate line. 'I want to stay in Tanzania – so I can be with Moyo and the camels. I want to be able to see my friend Zuri and the nuns. And I have to go to Walaita's *manyata* like Laura promised we would.' She lifted her chin. 'I can't go to England.'

Emma glanced sideways at Daniel and George. Neither of them made any response; they were sticking to the agreement to leave the discussion in her hands. Emma cleared her throat. 'It sounds as if your mother made an arrangement for your uncle to be your official guardian.'

'I don't wish to have a guardian.'

'Angel, you must have a guardian. It's the law. Children have to have someone who is responsible for them.'

Angel smiled, as though she'd just won a point in a game. 'Then I want you to be my guardian.'

Emma could hardly believe she'd heard Angel correctly. But she could see, from the child's face, that Angel meant her words to be taken seriously.

'I could stay here at the camp and help George-Lawrence and Ndisi. You could visit now and then, and pretend to be my auntie,' Angel added eagerly. 'Or I could live at the station with you and Daniel and the camels. I don't mind, as long as I don't have to go to England.' She kept on talking as if afraid to leave room for a response. 'We could all go on safari together. I could take you to Walaita's *manyata* and the fig-tree village and the Sisters of Mercy.'

'Wait, stop,' Emma said. 'It's not possible for you to stay here, Angel – at the camp or the station.'

be really helpful. I can cook. I can wash pots. I can
⌐s.' A tremor crossed Angel's face. She seemed to
bec⌐⌐⌐⌐r, closed in on herself. She spoke in a low voice,
'Didn't you see? I showed you.'

Emma bit her lip. The girl's face was torn with disappointment,
backed by something that looked like fear. 'Angel, you are a very
good, helpful girl. You're amazing, in fact. But you don't understand.
I don't live at the station. I'm just a visitor.' Emma had the feeling
she was talking to Daniel, and to herself as well – as though the idea
of her staying on to work here in Tanzania had not yet been finally
dismissed. 'I'll be going home very soon. To Australia.'

Angel recoiled with shock. When she finally spoke, she sounded
angry with herself, as if she'd made a lapse of judgement. 'That's
why you couldn't say Mdogo's name properly. You didn't know what
it meant. You don't speak Swahili.'

'Even if I did live here, I wouldn't be able to be your guardian,'
Emma said gently. 'There are legal issues about custody. Relatives
usually look after orphans.' She broke off. The word 'orphan' sounded
out of place, evoking images of someone who was helpless; not this
girl, who had lived in the desert with lions and was more capable
than most adults. 'If there was no relative, someone else would
be found to look after you. But it wouldn't be someone like me. A
complete stranger. Not even married.'

Angel swung her gaze round to George, then Daniel, and Ndisi.
She eyed them hopelessly – obviously she already understood that
none of them would be allowed to take care of her.

Emma felt an impulse to take back all that she'd said. But she knew every word of it had been true. She pushed on, to finish the task. 'We will have to tell the police tomorrow. Your uncle needs to know you've been found. We will offer to take you to Malangu the day after that, but they may want to come here and collect you. Either way, we will make sure you can stop at the station on the way to see Mama Kitu and Matata.' Her voice faltered. She felt she was deliberately torturing Angel. She wanted to stop, but when she looked at Daniel and George they both nodded in support of what she was saying. She made herself continue. 'I'm really sorry. I know that doesn't give you much time here, or with the camels, but it's the best we can do.'

'But if you changed you mind and you didn't go back to Australia, if you said you would look after me . . .' Angel's hands gripped the edge of the table. 'They might listen to you. You don't know. You could try.'

Emma shook her head. She realised, suddenly, how young Angel really was. She just didn't see the magnitude of what she was asking – that Emma become a mother. Emma tried to make her tone understanding but firm. 'I can't do that. It would be completely impossible.' She spread her hands. 'Anyway, you don't even know me. I might be a horrible person for all you know. It makes no sense.'

Angel turned to Daniel, speaking in what Emma knew would be their private language, Maa.

Daniel screwed up his eyes with sympathy as he listened. Then he addressed Emma. 'She is asking me to tell you that I said you were a kind person. That you took good care of Mama Kitu as if she were your own camel. That Mama Kitu loves you.'

Emma looked from him to Angel. Again, she had a sense that her response was to them both. The child smiled encouragingly.

'No. No. You don't know how completely out of the question it would be for me to look after you, Angel, even if your relatives agreed to it, and the government – whoever decides these things – approved it. I can't move here. You would have to come back to Australia with me. I live in a small apartment in the middle of a city. I have important work to do that takes up all my time.'

Angel nodded slowly, measuring Emma's words. 'There is important work to do here as well.'

Emma couldn't help glancing across to Daniel. She saw Angel notice – and realised the child thought she was weakening.

'You could change,' Angel continued. 'Everything can be changed. Once, Laura was a safari lady, with lots of clothes and necklaces.' The way Angel spoke made it sound as if she were beginning a fairytale. 'She went on a safari bus to a village to see some dancing and singing. She saw a man sitting outside his hut. The sun was hot, but he was shivering. He was in pain and he had no medicine. Laura was a nurse and she knew she could help him. So she didn't get back on the bus. She stayed and took care of him. She never went back to England.' Angel spread her hands. 'She changed everything – her whole life – just like that.' She looked at Emma, waiting for her response. The air seemed taut. The squirrel pattered across the sideboard.

Emma tried to think what it would be like to do what Laura had done. To change everything – not just to take up the challenge of working here, but to agree to take care of this child, Angel. She thought of how strange and amazing it would be. She imagined saying yes. It was just one simple word. But she knew she would have to really mean it. She could not give Angel false hopes – that would be even worse than letting Daniel and George down. The way these two challenges had come to her, one after the other, made her feel she was being put to the test. She was suddenly afraid. The stakes were so high. She couldn't trust herself not to fail. When she searched inside herself for the courage that something so huge, so astonishing, would demand, she could not be sure that it was there.

Emma looked into Angel's face. The naked pleading in the blue eyes was like a knife cutting her heart. She tried to take a breath, but it caught in her chest. She had to force her words out. They sounded over-loud and harsh. 'I'm not like Laura. I'm sorry.'

Angel stood up. As she pushed back her chair, one leg snared on the rug and it tipped over behind her, scattering the piled cushions. She stepped carefully around them, then walked slowly from the room.

Emma turned to George and Daniel. They stared at one another, fraught with distress. Jumping to her feet, Emma went after Angel. She followed her out towards the place where they'd all spent the night. Moyo and the cubs were resting there in the shade. Moyo's head was held high, alert, as if she'd picked up the tension in the air.

Angel knelt amongst the cubs. They began making overtures of play, but the lioness batted them away with her paw. She bent her head over Angel, her chin touching the child's hair. They stayed in that pose as if frozen, like a statue of mother and child. Moyo stared across at Emma, her eyes blazing a deep burning gold.

*

The remains of the cooking fire were a red crumble of ash and coals. Night had fallen but the moon was yet to rise; the air was heavy with shadows. Emma sat beside Daniel, each of them on a low stool. It was not the heat that had drawn her here, but the rosy glow that came from the coals – its brightness seemed to be the only thing that stood against the gloomy mood that had fallen over the camp.

Picking up a stick, Emma shoved it into the coals. She thought back over the day with a bleak sense of dismay. The excitement they'd all felt about the connection she'd made between the two fevers had been quickly overshadowed by the question it inevitably raised about Emma's involvement. Though Daniel had neither said nor done anything to reproach her, she felt she had betrayed him. And she felt the same about Angel.

Emma looked across to where the child lay at Moyo's side. She had her face turned to the lioness, her back to the world. She had gone to sleep early. George had followed suit, as if he too couldn't wait to bring the day to an end. Emma felt, again, a deep admiration for Angel. She had made a brave effort to accept the situation. After retreating to Moyo for a time, she had resumed her role of camp helper. She'd worked for hours with Daniel, cleaning out Bill and Ben's enclosure. But as she'd carried out her tasks, her face had been solemn, her step dispirited. And she had kept her distance from Emma, gravitating instead to the men, and to Moyo and the cubs. The only time she'd come to Emma had been to hand her the green shoulder bag. She'd kept it hidden behind her back as she'd approached.

'Girl has done something bad,' she'd said anxiously. 'She found your bag.'

She brought it into view. There were teeth marks in the fine Italian leather, one pocket had been half torn off, the strap chewed through.

'All your things are still inside it, I checked.' Angel looked stricken. 'I'm really sorry. I know how important it is.'

'It's okay.' Emma found it hard to speak. Angel was so distressed on her behalf. Suddenly, the bag seemed of no worth at all. 'It really doesn't matter.'

Angel had smiled in relief, then walked away. Emma had gone back to her task of sweeping the rugs in the dining hut. She'd asked Ndisi to give her the job – any job – hoping to distract herself from the thoughts that plagued her. Instead, she just kept going over all the reasons why Angel's uncle was the one who should take responsibility for her. The fact that the man had been able to jump on a plane and come here to collect his sister's body meant he must be reasonably well off. He'd be able to offer Angel a good education. She would play sport, have music lessons and be taken on holidays like other English children. It wasn't easy for Emma to picture Angel belonging in such a world – or to see how these things would make up for the loss of the camels, the lions, her home. But she was a strong child. She would adapt. She would survive.

While she continued her sweeping, Emma had thought back to how she'd seriously considered, just for those few moments, the idea of staying here and trying to gain custody of Angel. She'd shaken her head in amazement. She knew that if she'd approached the proposal as she would any other that came her way – with logic and rigorous thought – she wouldn't have entertained it seriously even for a second. There were dozens of reasons why it was impossible. The same was true about the idea of her walking away from her own research project to join Daniel at his remote field station. She felt like someone who'd been poised to step into a dangerous current. It would have swept her away, but she'd pulled back just in time.

Now, sitting by the fire, she looked at Daniel from the corner of her eye. His shoulders were slumped and he was gazing silently into the coals. Emma could feel the rift between them. There was no rational reason for it – Daniel was not blaming her for her choices. But it was as if their relationship were an organism with a life of it own. It was responding to all that had happened in a way that could neither be controlled nor predicted. She searched for a way to break the silence.

'I saw you and George looking at a map,' she said. 'What were you discussing?'

'He was showing me the area that he had asked the government to consider making into a national park. It stretches from here to the other side of the mountain. There is a very big soda lake near Ol Doinyo Lengai. Flamingos breed there. They cover the water with pink. It is very beautiful. There is a waterfall where you can swim. The local people call it the "place of two waters". There is a hot stream that flows from the volcano and a cold one that comes from the plateau. You can stand in the middle and be washed by both at the same time.' As he spoke, the light returned to his eyes and the life to his voice. 'I think tourists would enjoy that experience very much. They could also climb the mountain. It is done at night, so that the air is cooler for the ascent. At dawn, you reach the top. You stand there, looking down over the *nyika*. All around you is the hardened lava. It is pure white. It would be an experience that a visitor would never forget.'

'It sounds amazing.' Emma bit back the words that came to her. *I'd love to go there . . .*

'A national park would be a good thing for this area. It brings many opportunities for the local people. And if we can develop a vaccine for Olambo, it could all happen.'

Emma frowned. 'What does Olambo fever have to do with it?'

'Even if there was a park here, no one would want to invest in building hotels and lodges while the threat of Olambo fever remained.'

'Surely, there would be a very small risk to tourists,' Emma protested. It was extremely rare for foreigners to become infected with viruses like Ebola or Lassa, and almost all who did were doctors, nurses or researchers like Susan.

'That is true, but tourists are very afraid of some things, and not of others. Everyone knows car accidents are the biggest danger in a country like ours – but that is not what tourists fear. They fear being mugged or getting ill.'

Emma nodded. She knew what he was saying was true. She thought back to her own preparations for her trip, how she'd stocked her shoulder bag with all those medical supplies. She'd told herself it was because she was a virologist, working with tropical diseases – she knew all the risks too well. But now she realised that it was the fear of what she didn't know that had made her so cautious. Car accidents happened in her own world; their horror was understood. What she'd feared was the sense of Africa as a wild and unknown place. She looked around her at the vague outlines of the huts, the fence, the land beyond. She was not afraid any more, she realised. Coming to know this place, even for such a short time, had changed her. She could already feel how much she would miss it when she was gone.

Daniel fell quiet for a time. When he spoke again, there was no real interest in his voice. Emma guessed he was trying to avoid letting the silence take over again. 'What will you be doing when you return to work?'

'I'm beginning some new research into diseases of the ageing brain. I've got mice waiting, ready for me. I need to get started with them. They've been bred with mutations; they don't live very long . . .' Emma's words petered out. Usually she had to stop herself from talking for way too long when she answered a question like this, but now, her head felt completely empty, her heart numb. She studied the fire, watching small puffs of smoke rising from the embers as pockets of air were unlocked by the heat. She imagined being back at the Institute, discussing Daniel's research with her laboratory leader, maybe even the Dean. There would be excitement about the possibility of cross-immunity and the interaction between the two fevers – and about the benefits to the Institute if it could find a way to stake a claim in the work. But in the end, they'd all be talking about the problem of Olambo fever in Tanzania in the same clinical way they discussed Dengue fever in Thailand or the

Ebola virus in Zaire. Emma knew she'd never be able to convey the special bond she now felt with this place – and with the veterinary researcher, Daniel Oldeani.

Emma turned to him. Words rose to her lips and she made no attempt to censor them. 'I'll never forget being here. It's been the most amazing experience of my life. I'll treasure my memories forever.' She looked into Daniel's eyes. 'I'll never forget you.'

Daniel smiled. He seemed torn between sadness and pleasure at hearing her words. 'I will never forget you either.'

Emma thought of saying that she might end up coming back here in some professional role to help set up the research or to report on its development. But she knew that the moment she returned to her own world, the spell binding them together would be broken. What they shared now would have no more substance than a dream.

Daniel picked up the stick Emma had been playing with earlier and fed it to the fire. The two sat without speaking, watching as the flames chewed at the bark, then ate into the wood.

Finally the stick broke in half, collapsing into the ashes.

SIXTEEN

Slowly and carefully Angel lifted the bulging sack out of the empty fuel drum. The earthy smell of hessian, mixed with old diesel, rose up to her as she hoisted the load onto her back. The moon was high in the sky, throwing a harsh silver light over her as she turned to walk to the gate. She bumped against a stack of dried palm fronds and the leaves rustled loudly. She froze, darting a look back towards the three camp beds. No one seemed to have been disturbed. She checked the cubs, from whose midst she'd eased herself only a few minutes before. They were motionless as well. Breathing out with relief, she turned to Moyo. The lioness's eyes shone in the moonlight. She followed Angel towards the gate, moving silently on velvet-padded feet.

Angel tightened her hand on the key, the metal shape pressing into her skin. She knew that if she dropped the dull brass key it would be hard to find amongst the shadows cast by the trees. She thought uneasily about the fact that she wouldn't be able to return the key to the hook where she'd seen Ndisi hang it, after she'd helped him with the task of padlocking the gates at nightfall. The best she'd be able to do was to leave it in the lock for someone to find in the morning.

Her breath quickened. By morning, she would be well away from the camp. The daylight would find her gone, just like the night animals who rustled and whispered in the darkness, then vanished without leaving a trace.

It took a long time to unlock the gate, removing the padlock and hanging it back on the chain, making sure not to let the metal chink. The gates were tall and heavy. Leaning all her weight against one of them, Angel only just managed to scrape the wooden frame over the earth. When she'd made an opening wide enough to squeeze through, she laid down the sack, then turned to face Moyo.

She wrapped both arms around the lioness's neck.

'Goodbye,' she whispered, her lips brushing Moyo's fur. 'I'll find you again. I promise.'

She clung to Moyo, wanting to draw into her own small body the warmth of the lioness's blood, the power of her muscles. Then she straightened up. As she pulled away, her fingers trailed through Moyo's fur, reluctant to let go of the last touch of softness.

Moyo let out a high sad cry, like the wind singing over the plains. Stepping forward, she put her body between Angel and the open gate. She swung her head from side to side, as though undecided about whether or not to let Angel go. But eventually she stepped back, leaving the way clear.

Angel looked quickly into Moyo's golden eyes, then turned her gaze respectfully away. She took one last look at the three sleeping figures stretched out on their beds. Then she peered towards the cuddled mass of the cubs.

Goodbye, Boy. Girl. Goodbye, Mdogo.

Her body tensed as she saw the outline of a small head lifting up. Moments later, one of the cubs was bounding towards her. A shaft of pain tore through her as she recognised Mdogo. She longed to crouch down, opening her arms to him. She could almost feel the tickle of his whiskers against her cheek, the rough kiss of his tongue.

Quickly she shouldered the sack and pushed forward through the opening. She shoved the gate shut behind her, forcing it roughly over the ground. If Mdogo reached her, she knew, she simply would not be able to make herself leave.

She walked away. She refused to look back. But she could feel Moyo and Mdogo watching her go. The cub began whining. The plaintive sound reached out after her like desperate hands, begging her to come back.

The moonlight glittered off the angled planes of the stones, and painted inky shadows on the sand. The bright unearthly light made everything more detailed, and yet, somehow flatter, both at the same time. Angel walked at a good pace, the sack rubbing against her back with each stride. She could feel the hard shape of the clay cooking pot at the bottom, and the outline of the two water gourds. As she moved there was a faint sloshing sound, and a rattle of matches that reminded her of the patter of mice footsteps. She pictured the cotton sack of rice that she'd packed, and the cloth-wrapped bundle of dried beans. She'd wanted to bring some bananas, but had decided they were too heavy. The only luxury she'd allowed herself was a single sweet potato. Even so, the load was heavy. Along with the food and water, she'd brought her sandals and a framed photo of Moyo as a young lion, which she'd taken from the dining room wall. She was only borrowing it, she told herself. And George-Lawrence would still have the real Moyo to look at.

She pictured the people at the camp, waking up. Their urgent voices, anxious faces. They'd want to follow her, she knew, but when she'd left the camp she'd headed straight for a nearby outcrop of rocks so that she would leave them no trail. She felt a pang of guilt. They'd all been so kind to her. Their faces came to her one by one: George-Lawrence, who looked like someone's grandfather with his white hair and pipe; the Maasai, Daniel, who had joined in her games with Moyo and the cubs, chatting to her in Maa, making her feel at home. Ndisi, who couldn't yet knit without her talking him through the steps.

And Emma.

When she thought of Emma, the guilt leached away. It was her fault that Angel had to leave. She remembered the blunt way Emma had said the words: *I'm not like Laura. I'm sorry.*

Fixing her eyes on the hillside ahead, Angel quickened her pace, resolve setting hard inside her. Emma had refused to help. But Angel would look after herself. She ran back over the information she'd gleaned from Ndisi. When she'd asked him where Daniel's station was, casually, as if she didn't really care whether he answered her or not, he'd pointed beyond the slope that rose behind the camp, towards a rounded hilltop. It was long and low; the shape of a lion crouching on the horizon.

'It is on the other side of that second hill. The road is long – it goes right around it. But if you could fly like a bird, it is not very far.'

Angel frowned. She was not a bird, but a small girl, carrying a heavy load. She shifted the sack to her other shoulder, and struggled on. She looked around her, at the smudges of shrubs, the spattering of grass. There was no movement amongst them, no sign of animals on the prowl. She was not afraid of walking in the night by herself – living with the lions, she'd lost much of her fear of wild animals. But without the cubs clamouring around her ankles, and without the sight of Moyo in front of her – the rolling movement of her haunches, the swing of her tail – she felt very alone.

Soon, she told herself, she would be with Mama Kitu again. She pictured herself riding comfortably along, properly packed saddlebags mounted behind her, Matata following behind. There would be no danger, then, of hunger or thirst or loneliness. As she headed into the desert there would be, again, the gift of sweet milk, always there for the taking.

The weight of the sack ground into her shoulder as though it would wear away her bones. The other shoulder was already sore. Angel tried balancing the load on her head, but the bag was not full enough and the edges flopped down, hiding her eyes. She felt she'd been walking for ages, but she was only now nearing the top of the first hill.

When she finally struggled over the brow, she stopped with a sigh of relief. Wiping the sweat from her face, she looked into the distance towards the lion-shaped hill. Her mouth fell open in dismay. A wide plain stretched away below her, a flat collage of silver and grey that went on and on. The hill was much further away than it had looked from the camp. Angel stared numbly ahead. She thought of turning back. If she hurried, no one would even know she'd tried to escape. But she knew she had only this one chance.

You are a stubborn girl, she reminded herself. It was true. Laura had told her that many times. Angel searched inside for that strong feeling her Mama was talking about. She pictured it growing, like a fire fed by breath. The nuns used to say she was stubborn as well – that once she got an idea in her head, she would never let it go. As Angel walked on, she held their words inside her, like a charm to keep her on her way.

Never let it go. Never.

SEVENTEEN

Emma stared up at the sky, a pool of dark blue embracing a big yellow moon. She listened into the night, wondering what it was that had woken her. Beyond the soft regular noise of George snoring nearby, there was a deep quiet. Then she heard it – an eerie sound, like a mad wild laugh, coming from somewhere outside the camp. A hyena, she thought. People said they made a noise like a laugh. Emma glanced across at Daniel and George. They were both still sleeping peacefully. She turned her head to check on Angel. She sat up, instantly awake. In the place where Angel had been sleeping, she could see just two cubs, curled tightly together. There was no sign of Angel, Moyo or the third cub. She checked her watch. It was after three in the morning. There was no need to raise an alarm; she knew the camp was secure. She climbed off the stretcher, trying not to make any noise. Then she shoved her feet into her boots and tied the laces.

She walked quickly over the moon-washed ground, the silk of her pyjamas whispering as the trouser legs brushed together. She darted glances all around her. Before long she saw, over by the gates, the big solid shape of the lioness. Moyo was sitting close to the wire, her head lifted as she stared out through the barrier. The cub sat beside her, mirroring the same watchful posture. But Angel was not there.

As Emma half-ran across to them, she tried to see what it was that held Moyo's attention. Her gaze seemed to be focused on the top of the hill that rose behind the camp.

Finding herself at Moyo's side, Emma stopped short, a shiver of fear tightening her skin. In the moonlight, the lioness looked unfamiliar and daunting. Her gaze, still trained on the hillside, seemed fierce, her bulk threatening. Emma was about to back carefully away when Moyo swung her head round. She pushed at Emma's shoulder with her muzzle – a gesture that felt urgent, impatient. A groan came from deep in her throat. Emma realised that Moyo was worried. She was relieved that Emma had come.

Emma looked tentatively into the big shiny eyes, green-gold in the moonlight. The lioness didn't seem to mind. Their eyes locked together. It came to Emma, then, that it was not the cry of a hyena that had entered her sleep. Moyo had called to her. And Emma had heard. Shock travelled up her spine. For a long moment, she stared at the lioness. Then Moyo nudged her again.

Emma shook herself out of the daze. Turning towards the gate, she saw that the chain was no longer locked in place and a key was sticking out of the padlock. Then she saw Angel's footprints in the loose sand by the gate. They led away from the camp, but quickly disappeared on hard ground.

'Where is she?' Emma whispered.

She strained her eyes into the distance, where Moyo had been looking before. There, just visible against the grey-black sky, she saw a thin column of smoke. It rose straight up in the still night air, from behind the brow of the hill.

Emma stared at the smoke. The fire was hidden from view, but she pictured Angel sitting there, alone in the night, little hands feeding twigs to the flames. Questions chased through her head, but she didn't let them settle. Instead, she went back to her bed to retrieve her clothes. Part of her thought she should wake the others, that it was reckless to head off alone. But she was conscious that Moyo had chosen her. The lioness could easily have woken George if she'd wanted to.

She was still buttoning her shirt as she reached Moyo's side. She pushed open one of the gates, then paused, waiting to see if the lioness would come with her. Moyo backed away, indicating she was staying with her cubs, but she made a soft encouraging sound. Emma closed the gate behind her and set off towards the hill.

She walked quickly, finding it easy to pick her way in the strong moonlight. She was very fit, after all her visits to the gym. Angel was no doubt fit as well, but her legs were shorter; Emma guessed she must have set off at least a couple of hours earlier. She wondered why Moyo had waited so long to send Emma after her. Perhaps she'd been torn over whether or not to intervene in Angel's plan. Perhaps it had been the appearance of smoke that had alarmed her. But Moyo was only an animal, Emma reminded herself. She was not capable of this kind of thought. And yet the reality of what Emma had seen with her own eyes contradicted this accepted view. Moyo definitely *was* able to think abstractly and visualise the future. In fact, it now seemed to Emma that George was right: the lioness had the benefit of a sixth sense – one that humans had either never possessed, or that they'd lost somewhere on their journey of evolution.

Emma moved with an even rhythm, looking ahead at the plume of smoke. When the brow of the hill was not far away, she paused to catch her breath and let her heart slow. She could smell the fragrant wood smoke, now, and see red sparks spiralling in the heat draft.

She felt a clutch of tension inside her. She had no plan for what she was going to say or do. Was she meant to talk sense into the child and entice her back to the camp? Would she drag her there if necessary? She really didn't know why she had come. She felt she had nothing useful to offer. She only knew that she had to be here – that *she* had to be here.

Finally she reached the stony top of the rise. She paused, looking down at the fire, a short distance away. Angel was kneeling beside it, her face lit pink by the flames. In the moonlight, her fair hair seemed to throw out a glow of its own.

As if sensing Emma's presence there, Angel lifted her face. She looked at Emma, saying nothing. The sparkle in her blue eyes was gone.

Emma walked over to the fire.

'My pot broke.' Angel's voice, too, was dull. She waved towards a pile of broken pottery – curved shards that looked like strange sharp-edged petals. 'I can't go, now. I won't be able to cook rice, or beans.'

Near the remains of the pot, Emma saw an old sack, split open at the bottom. The large tear revealed a water gourd and something wrapped in cloth.

'The sack was not strong,' Angel said. 'It was old. I didn't look at it properly.' She was frowning into the fire.

'Can I sit with you?' Emma asked.

Angel shrugged. 'If you like.'

Emma found a large smooth stone and moved it next to Angel, then sat down, crossing her legs in front of her. She watched the child from the corner of her eye.

Angel used a stick to poke at a blackened lump that was lying in the coals, deftly turning it over.

'Do they have sweet potatoes in England?' she asked. There was no hint of curiosity in her voice, just resignation.

'I think so. We eat them in Australia. But they're orange, not the same as the ones here.'

Angel nodded, suggesting her suspicions had been confirmed. She tidied up the fire, edging stray twigs back into place. The fire had been very neatly laid, Emma noticed, made from a pyramid of sticks. As she watched Angel pushing coals up over the potato, Emma understood what was happening. This was a last meal, for Angel – a ritual. She was saying goodbye to her life in Africa.

The two sat side by side, watching the fire. The quiet seemed dense with unshared thoughts.

Then Emma spoke, her voice gentle. 'Where were you planning to go?'

Angel turned towards the long rounded hill in the distance. 'Over there, to the station. I was going to get Mama Kitu and Matata. Then I was going to ride to Walaita's *manyata*.' Angel pointed in the direction of the Mountain of God. 'Her uncle is the chief. He is a very important man. He could stop them sending me away. I was with his sister when she died. I helped Mama nurse her.' Angel looked back to Emma; fire flared briefly in her eyes. 'He would help me. I know he would.'

Emma was silenced by the thought of the courage it would have taken to set out alone on such a venture, even as an adult.

'But the sack tore and the pot broke,' Angel said, with a quaver in her voice. 'And anyway, the station is too far away.'

Emma watched the slumped shoulders, the fallen face. She reached a hand towards her, then let it drop. Pain swelled inside her. When she spoke, the words came straight from her heart. 'Oh, Angel, you're only a little girl. You don't have be so brave all the time – so strong.'

Angel swung round. 'Yes. I do. I have to be brave because Laura is dead.' Her words were forceful, loud. 'I'm on my own. I have no mother any more.' Then her voice died, as if strangled in her throat. Emma could barely catch her next words. 'You don't know what it's like.'

Angel pulled up her knees, clutching them to her chest, burying her face against them.

'I do.' Emma said softly. 'I do know what it's like.'

Angel's shoulders stiffened with surprise. Slowly she raised her head, fixing her gaze on Emma, questions in her eyes.

'I was the same age as you when my mother died. Her name was Susan. She was working at the Olambo Fever Research Station. She caught the virus.'

Angel stared at her. 'Were you there with her?'

Emma shook her head. 'I was back in America. I was waiting for her to come home so that we could have my birthday party. Some men from her office came to tell my father what had happened. For a long time, I didn't really believe she was dead. I thought that if I could just come here – to Tanzania – and search for her, I'd find her. But in the end I just had to accept that she was never coming back.'

Emma listened to herself speak. She was amazed that her manner was so calm.

'Did you miss her?' Angel's voice cracked. Tears brimmed in her eyes. 'I miss Laura. I miss her so much.'

She began to cry quietly, making a low mewling sound, like one of the cubs. Gradually the sound grew higher and louder, building into a wail. Tears streamed down her face, shiny in the moonlight; she let them fall untouched, splashing onto her knees. Her next words seemed wrung from her by force. 'I need my mama. I want her back.'

Emma gasped, her breath snagging in her lungs. Tears sprang to her own eyes, hot and sharp. 'I know. I know you do.' As she watched Angel weep, and heard her cry, something broke open inside her. She was a child again, devastated and afraid. Pain rose up, pushing out of her in long shuddering cries. 'I still miss my mum. I still want her back.' The flames were a crimson blur before her eyes. There was nothing but sorrow and abandonment, enveloping her, holding her in its grasp.

A hand came to rest on her arm. Emma turned to look at it, a small pale shape. Her own hand moved to cover it, holding it tight.

She reached for Angel then, drawing the child towards her. The little body, still shaking with sobs, fell into her arms. Emma pressed her tear-swollen lips into the silky hair. Her own halting breath matched the heaving of the narrow shoulders.

They cried together, grief flowing back and forth between them. As time passed – a long time, measured by the gradual sinking of the moon towards the horizon, the dying of the fire – they both became quiet.

Angel wiped her eyes and nose on her sleeve and leaned to pick up her stick.

'Are you hungry, Emma?' she asked. As if a storm had raged through her and passed on, she seemed suddenly calm.

'No – yes.' Emma smiled. 'I don't know.'

Angel cocked her head. 'You'll like it.'

Reaching for the pouch at her hip, Angel removed her penknife. Frowning with concentration she opened the blade and wiped it clean on her tunic. Emma had the feeling Angel was turning instinctively to everyday words and actions, to provide landmarks in a journey that had led her far beyond the edges of any map. Emma felt lost, as well, unsure where they had travelled. She, too, wanted to feel the steadying touch of normality. 'Okay. Yes. I'd like some.'

Angel raked the potato from the ashes, then cut the black shape in half, exposing white flesh inside a coating of charcoal.

'Don't burn your tongue,' Angel warned as she handed a piece to Emma.

'I won't. Thank you.'

'*Asante,*' Angel corrected her. 'You know, you should learn a bit of Swahili – even if you won't be in Tanzania for long.'

'*Asante,*' Emma repeated.

'And now I have to say something back to you, to be polite. *Si neno.*'

'What does that mean?'

'It means, in Swahili, "no words". It's a way of saying you don't have to thank me.' She smiled. 'But, of course, you must, if you want to be polite.' She pointed towards the potato in Emma's hand. 'Try some.'

Emma dug out a hunk of white flesh with her finger and lifted it to her mouth. It was firm and sweet and smoky. 'It's delicious. Perfectly cooked.'

Angel nodded proudly. Then she began chewing her piece of potato, her lips becoming blackened with charcoal.

Behind her, the strength of the moon was fading, overtaken by a lightening sky.

EIGHTEEN

Emma and Angel walked side by side down the hill. Their footfalls made a mismatched beat, the woman's stride much longer than the child's. They had emptied the water bottles and scattered the rice and beans for the animals; the sack was just a small bundle under Emma's arm.

The sky was tinged with pink, the first rays of sun already breaking over the horizon.

As they wound their way between rocks and bushes, Emma looked down at the camp laid out below them, tracing the outlines of the huts, enclosures and the perimeter fence. The place appeared small, the structures flimsy. She felt like a giant in comparison. But it was not just a matter of physical perspective, she realised. During the hours spent by the fireside with Angel, a weight had been lifted from her. She felt she could stand taller, breathe more deeply. She felt stronger and more free.

Angel reached for her hand, holding it lightly. They moved at a leisurely pace. Whenever something caught the child's eye – a tiny pink flower, nestled under a rock; a beetle rolling a fragment of dung over a rock; a wispy grey feather – she stopped to look at it. Occasionally, she met Emma's gaze and smiled. She seemed unburdened, as if she'd finally given up trying to control her future. But there was no sign on her face of the desolation Emma had seen when she arrived at the fireside. Emma took a few moments to identify what had taken its place. Then she knew. It was trust. Angel had decided to leave the things that were too hard for her to face in the hands of others. She had gone back to being a child.

Emma's step faltered as the meaning of this dawned on her. Someone else now had to take up the role that Angel had relinquished. Just as the cubs needed their lioness, Angel needed someone to protect her and love her and guide her. Emma felt the warmth of the small hand resting in hers. The realisation grew from deep inside her, then launched into her consciousness. Emma was the one. Whether she'd been chosen by Angel, by Moyo, or by some age-old force at work in the heart of Africa, or just through some chance combination of circumstances, the outcome was the same.

You can change everything.

She walked on down the hillside, her feet automatically choosing the best path, while her thoughts raced ahead, stumbling over obstacles, one after another. She reminded herself of what she'd said to Angel about custody. There was nothing to indicate that Emma was in a position to make any choices at all about Angel's future. And what about Daniel? What if she lost Angel, and what if the research idea came to nothing – would she still want to stay here, just to be with him? She barely knew him. He seemed so perfect, yet he had to have at least some of the usual human faults. She didn't know what would emerge when they spent more time together, or how they would react to conflict when it arose. Anyway, she didn't even know how exactly Daniel felt about her. She believed he was attracted to her and enjoyed her company, but that didn't mean he wanted to spend his life with her. Emma felt a pit opening in her stomach. There were no answers to these questions. Her thoughts and emotions were all bound up with each other. They couldn't be broken into bits, each measured against the other, and lined up in order.

Her pace slowed as she raised her eyes to the horizon, where the sun was now a round golden ball. Thorn trees made a sketchy pattern against the sky. As Emma pictured how the sun would rise inexorably through the day, she had a sense that this was how the next part of her journey would unfold. She could not plan or control what was going to happen next. Her future was in the hands of the same forces that had brought her here – the ones that had determined she would be standing on this hilltop with another woman's child at her side, instead of sitting in the dining room of Serengeti Lodge, finishing off her three-course breakfast in time for a dawn game drive.

Emma came to a standstill.

Angel stopped as well. 'What's wrong?'

'Nothing's wrong,' Emma said. She crouched down to Angel's level. Her own eyes felt hot and gritty from crying, but the child's were clear and bright. Emma reached out her hand and smoothed Angel's cheek with her fingers. 'Angel,' she said slowly. 'I know I told you I couldn't stay here in Africa. But I've changed my mind.'

Angel's eyes widened as she took in Emma's words.

'I've decided to ask the government to let me look after you. I don't know if they will agree. But I am going to ask.'

Angel caught her breath. Emma could see thoughts passing over her face like ripples on water as she replayed what had been said. 'Does that mean you like me?'

Emma felt the sting of fresh tears in her eyes. 'Yes, Angel, I do like you. I like you very much.'

Angel smiled broadly. 'I like you, too.'

Emma found she could not speak. She just pushed her trembling lips together and smiled back.

They walked on together, the rising sun warming their faces.

When they were near the camp, Angel pointed ahead. 'There's Daniel. And Moyo.' She looked up at Emma. 'Can you see them?'

'Yes, I can,' Emma said. The man and the lioness were standing at the gate.

Angel ran ahead, pausing to greet Daniel, before hugging Moyo. Then she headed into the compound as if eager to be reunited with the cubs.

Daniel stood beside Moyo, one hand on her shoulder. His face was strained with anxiety. As Emma reached him, he looked at her with questioning eyes.

'She ran away,' Emma said. 'I went after her.'

Daniel nodded slowly. He searched her face. Then his expression cleared, as if he could see past her tear-reddened eyes and was able to tell that something extraordinary had taken place in her. Emma felt no need, right now, to explain all that had happened.

'I want to stay here,' she said simply. 'Angel needs me. And I want to take care of her. I don't want to lose her.' She paused, taking a breath. 'I don't want to lose you, either.'

Daniel stared at her. A long moment passed, then he smiled, his eyes shining. He pulled her into his arms, holding her close. She pressed her face into the soft skin of his neck and felt his strong shoulders under her hands. She breathed his smell of wood smoke and honey. Her eyes closed as she let joy wash through her, sweeping all her doubts away.

NINETEEN

Emma sat at the dining table, her head bent over the green shoulder bag, mending the damage that had been inflicted by Girl. The leather was soft, but the needle Ndisi had provided was thick and blunt. Nevertheless, Emma had managed to rejoin the two sections of the strap. Now she turned to the torn side pocket. She tried to lose herself in the repetitive nature of the task, but her thoughts kept returning to the uncertainty surrounding Angel's future. As she forced the needle through the leather, drawing the cotton after it, she replayed the events of the previous afternoon when Daniel had made contact with his politician friend, Joshua. He hadn't wanted to use the radio because the transmission could be picked up by others, so he and Emma had headed back up the hillside to get reception for the mobile phone. By the time there were enough bars displayed on the screen they'd reached the site of Angel's fire, marked by a circle of ashes and the broken pottery shards scattered nearby. Daniel dialled a number he'd located in a notebook.

'Joshua, my friend,' Daniel greeted the Minister of Home Affairs. Then he switched to what Emma could now recognise as their mother tongue, Maa. Daniel paced around as he talked, but kept his gaze fixed on the distant pyramid of the volcano, as if he were directing his words to the Maasai god whose home it was. When he ended the call he handed Emma the phone.

'He understands everything about Angel and about you,' he said. 'And I told him of the new work we plan to do together. Joshua said he will make some enquiries. He will also inform the Chief of Police that Angel is here and let him know of his personal interest in this case.'

'When will we know what's going to happen?'

'We have arranged to speak again tomorrow at this same time.'

'So we just have to wait? There's nothing else we can do?' Emma felt herself reaching for the old patterns of behaviour.

'I trust Joshua. He will make wise choices and he will do all that he can to help.'

Offering Emma his hand, Daniel had set off on the downward slope. Together they'd returned to the camp.

Emma knew he was right – there was no one better placed to handle this situation than his childhood friend. But it was hard to be patient. Putting down the bag, she stuck the needle into the ball of cotton for safekeeping. Then, pushing back her chair, she wandered outside.

She found Angel and Daniel sitting on the two stools by the cooking fire. Smoke drifted around them in a faint mauve cloud. The sun had climbed halfway up the sky and the shadows cast by their bodies were already dark and sharp-edged. They were sharing the iPod headphones, each listening to one earpiece. Emma could almost see the music moving through their bodies. The rhythm seemed to flow naturally, as if they were responding to the recorded beat with something that had been born inside them.

There must have been a break in the music; the two bodies became still. Then, Angel began wrinkling up her nose and shaking her head at Daniel, rejecting his next choice of song. Daniel frowned at her, pretending to be offended, but quickly moved to adjust the iPod. Watching them, Emma felt an ache of mixed pleasure and pain. It was such a normal, happy scene. Angel looked so secure and at ease. It was unimaginable that she should be sent away to England. Emma found herself creating pictures in her mind – more scenes like this one, so ordinary yet so special. She wanted to believe that by evoking these images she might be able to shape the future. Her anxiety ebbed slowly away as she brought the scenes to life, letting them play out over the days and months that were to come.

Emma held the two empty milk bottles against her chest as she headed back to the dining hut. Angel followed at her heels. They had left George behind at the gate to the cubs' enclosure, smoking his pipe and watching Bill and Ben play. Just after they had been fed, he and Angel had spent some time introducing them to Mdogo – the first step towards blending them into Moyo's family. Emma had looked on, with Moyo at her side keeping a watchful eye on her cub. The experiment had not gone well at first – there had been a lot of hissing and spitting, and Angel had been scratched on the cheek. But eventually the three cubs had calmed down. Mdogo even showed signs of wanting to play.

'That's a good start,' George had said. 'Soon, they'll be one happy family.'

Emma walked past the sleeping area – the earth swept clean, the bed packed tidily away for the daytime. Then she stopped, turning her head. She could hear a faint throbbing sound in the distance.

Angel looked up at Emma. 'What is it?'

'I think it's a helicopter.'

Angel was instantly tense. 'Is it the police?'

Emma felt alarm spike through her, but she shook her head. 'It's a very expensive way to travel. It's more likely to be tourists, or people from the mining company.'

Before long the helicopter came into view. At first it was just a small shape in the sky, but it drew quickly nearer, travelling with an even, steady movement that made it look as if it were growing bigger rather than coming closer.

Emma exchanged glances with Angel. The helicopter was definitely approaching the camp. She saw George and Daniel looking up at it, their hands held to their faces, cutting the glare of the afternoon sun. Ndisi was luring Moyo's cubs into the enclosure next door to Bill and Ben's, and locking them safely away.

The sound became louder and louder until it filled the air. Birds broke from the bushes, flying off in the opposite direction. The helicopter wheeled in a large circle above the open space outside the gates, then lowered itself to the ground. The rotor slowed, the blur of the blades transforming into separate long shapes.

'Come on,' Emma said to Angel, keeping her tone light. 'Let's see who they are.'

She took Angel's hand and together they walked over to the gates. The helicopter squatted there like an over-sized crab. Emma guessed it was privately owned, or had been chartered from a commercial company – it didn't look like a police or military helicopter, or one that belonged to some other government department.

She led Angel over to join Daniel, George, Ndisi and Samu, who were standing as a group in the entrance to the camp, like guards. Moyo prowled in their midst, her head lifted, sniffing the air, tail beating from side to side.

The pilot's door swung open and a man in a white shirt and sunglasses jumped out onto the ground. He strode round to open the passenger door. As he flung it back, Emma strained to see into the interior. She glimpsed flashes of colour, then people began climbing out. A thickly built African came first, wearing what Emma recognised as a police uniform. She felt Angel shrink behind her and she tightened her grip on her hand. A second African followed. He was tall and wore a pale blue suit with a Mao collar. He searched the group waiting at the gate and a smile of recognition broke over his face. He raised his hand in a salute to Daniel.

'I think that's Joshua,' Emma told Angel, feeling a rush of relief. 'Daniel's friend.' She willed him to be bringing good news.

Movement in the doorway to the cabin drew her eyes away. Her body stiffened. A white-skinned man appeared there, stepping carefully down onto the dust. He looked out of place in smart city clothes. But this was not what held Emma's gaze. It was his white-blonde hair. It was the same colour as Angel's – and identical to the hair Emma had revealed as she'd removed the stones from Laura's grave. She had no doubt he was Angel's uncle.

Emma heard Angel draw in her breath, reaching the same conclusion. She rubbed the child's hand soothingly. She wanted to tell her not worry, that everything would be all right. But she was afraid herself.

Moyo walked towards the man, eyeing him curiously as if she, too, had discerned his link with Angel. He backed away, casting nervous looks at the policeman. The officer's hand moved towards a pistol at his hip. The pilot kept his distance, staying close to his aircraft.

'Don't worry about Moyo,' George called. 'She won't hurt you. Just stand still. And don't stare at her.'

The officer and Angel's uncle looked unconvinced, but they followed George's instructions. Their eyes were fixed ahead, their arms rigid at their sides as she moved slowly around them, sniffing their bodies. Joshua complied as well, but instead of fear on his face there was a look almost of reverence. When Moyo retreated to her place beside Angel, Joshua seemed to have to tear his eyes away from her.

He came forward to greet Daniel and the two men shook hands, clasping their left hands together, and placing their right hands on their own left forearms. Daniel had told Emma it was done this way to show that the strong right arm was not holding a weapon. When the handshake was complete, they threw their arms around one another. Their delight in the reunion was obvious. Then Joshua gathered himself, remembering his formal role.

He approached George, greeting him with a brief European handshake.

'Welcome to Kampi ya Simba,' George said courteously.

'I am sorry to arrive without warning,' Joshua said. 'But Mr Kelly—' he gestured towards the blonde-haired man, '—was just about to depart for London when I gave him the news about Angel. As you may have guessed, he is her next of kin, the brother of her mother. He was keen to charter a helicopter and come here straight away.'

As he spoke, Emma looked at the Englishman. In his pressed white shirt and well-cut jacket, he would have been at home in a boardroom or a smart restaurant. Emma glanced down at her crumpled shirt, stained with milk from the cub's bottle and spotted with blobs of Daniel's Stockholm tar; her jeans ingrained with sweat; her boots caked in dust. She knew Angel's clothes were equally scruffy and dirty. She felt a sense of satisfaction that even though she had the wrong accent and hair, she and Angel matched one another in this way. But the feeling was quickly replaced by misgiving. Emma's appearance might create the impression she was not the kind of person who could be trusted to care for a child. Aside from her clothes, her face and arms were quite badly sunburned, her hair dusty. And Angel's own appearance could easily suggest she'd been neglected these last few days. Her face was smeared with charcoal and the scratch on her cheek was still bloody.

When Emma looked up she found Angel's uncle studying her

with a frank gaze. She wondered what – if anything – Joshua had told him about her. She felt a shiver of fear. Maybe everything had already been worked out in a way that did not include her. Maybe Angel was about to be taken away forever.

Emma became aware that Joshua was about to greet her. She turned to him, smiling politely, hiding her fear that he might have let his old friend down. When she looked into his face she felt like she was seeing Daniel's brother or cousin. Joshua had the same high cheekbones and finely moulded lips. He had the same graceful bearing as well. Emma realised that while she was observing him, Joshua was searching her face. She wished she knew exactly what Daniel had said about her – about them – up on the hillside. To hear him tell one of his friends that she was going to stay here in Tanzania and work with him, live with him – be with him – would have made it all seem more real.

Joshua smiled at her, before turning to the police officer. 'This is Mr Malindi, Chief of Police, Arusha area.' The heavily built man bowed his head. There was a sense of restrained power about him that was almost palpable.

Finally, Joshua swung his arm round towards the uncle. 'And this is Mr James Kelly from England.'

James was staring at Angel as though he couldn't quite believe she was real. He only wrenched his gaze away to offer hasty greetings to the adults. He moved round until he could see her face, peering out from behind Emma. 'Hello, Angel. I am your Uncle James.'

'Hello, Uncle,' Angel said politely, then she looked down at the ground.

James spoke to Emma in an undertone. 'How is she?'

Emma hunted for a reply. 'She is fine.'

'She was found – what, two days ago? She's made an amazing recovery.'

'No, she was well when we found her. Moyo took good care of her.'

James eyed her doubtfully. 'You're saying the lioness . . .'

Moyo shook her head, suddenly; a fly buzzed away from her eye. James jumped back in alarm.

'It's all right, Uncle, she won't hurt you,' Angel said. 'She's very gentle.'

James turned back to her, staring even more intently, captivated by her voice. He crouched down to match her height. Emma saw that his eyes were the same shade of blue as Angel's. Watching their two blonde heads so close together, Emma felt a spike of jealousy. They looked like father and daughter.

'I'm so pleased to meet you, Angel.' James had a nice smile, Emma noticed, warm and kind. 'Do you understand who I am? Your mummy's brother?'

Angel nodded.

He seemed about to say something else, but then looked at her without speaking, his eyes moving over her hair, her face, her body. 'Oh, God, you look just like Laura, when we were little.' He bent his head, pushing his lips into a line. 'I'm sorry . . .' When he had composed himself, he looked up again.

As he met her gaze, Angel spoke. 'I don't want to come and live with you.'

James flinched, but then nodded slowly. 'I know. Mr Lelendola has told me.' He looked at Emma. 'You want to live with . . . her.'

'Yes,' Angel said.

Emma cleared her throat. 'I wish to apply to become her legal guardian.'

James frowned at her; he seemed to be fighting to control his emotions. 'And you've thought all this through? I mean, I know you helped find her. Understandably you've formed a bond. But that doesn't mean she should now stay with you. Frankly, it's . . . absurd.'

Emma found it hard to respond – she was aware that only a short while ago the proposal had looked that way to her as well. 'I have thought about it very carefully,' she said eventually. 'I think it would be the best plan for Angel – and for me, too.'

James forced a smile. 'The thing is, ah – Emma – I made a promise to my sister. I want to honour it. It's the right thing to do. My wife supports me, of course.' He took a photograph from his pocket and showed to Angel. 'This is your Auntie Louise.'

Angel took a quick look at her and turned her face away. Emma glimpsed a tall woman in jodhpurs and a neat shirt. She had a charming smile.

'I understand your situation, Mr Kelly,' Joshua's voice broke in. 'A promise should always be kept. And when the one to whom it was made has died, it becomes a sacred duty.'

'Absolutely,' James agreed. Emma's chest tightened. She threw a glance at Daniel. He looked as tense as she was.

'But the living matter more than the dead,' Joshua continued.

'And the welfare of this child must come first, even before your duties and wishes are considered.'

A flicker of impatience crossed James's face. 'Look, I'd have thought it was all pretty straightforward. I am the next of kin. There is no father involved. I have a legal right to take her back to England.'

'Actually, you do not,' Joshua explained. 'The decision about who should care for this orphaned child belongs to the Tanzanian government since she is here in our country.'

Angel eased herself from behind Emma, until she was standing at her side. Emma put her arm around her, holding her close. Angel looked up, her face pale with fear. Emma gave her a reassuring smile, but her stomach churned. She fixed her eyes on Moyo, who was now sitting rock-still on Angel's other side. She tried to draw a sense of calm from her presence.

James took a step towards Joshua. 'I'm sure that's true, technically, Minister. But it would be very unusual . . . One would expect . . .' He fell silent. He seemed to be having trouble grasping the reality of what was happening.

'So the question we have to answer,' Joshua continued, 'is this. Who will love and care for this little girl in the best way?'

James gave a confident grin. 'Well, let me put it this way. We have a lovely home by the sea. There is a big garden with a heated swimming pool. Angel will attend Louise's old school, St Mary's College. She'll have riding lessons, ballet classes, piano. There will be overseas holidays . . .' His words petered out, his gaze travelling over Angel as if he were struggling to match his vision with the reality of the child standing there. But he finished in a firm voice. 'She will have everything.'

'It is easy for wealthy people to provide these things,' Joshua said. 'But what about love, care, companionship?'

'That goes without saying,' James said. 'She is my sister's child. And in due course Louise and I plan to have children of our own. Angel will be part of a proper family.'

Joshua nodded. 'You have a great deal to offer your niece.'

Emma's heart pounded. As she felt Angel shrink trustingly against her side, a fierce protectiveness flared within her. She wished she could rise up, as though she were herself a lioness, and fight for her child. But she knew she had to force herself to stand still, and listen.

'Mr Kelly,' Joshua said, 'I must tell you that you will need to prove this commitment before the child can be taken from the country. Under Tanzanian law, a child cannot be adopted by a foreigner unless that person or people live here with the child for a minimum of two years. During that time, the foreigner can be the foster parent.'

James let out a disbelieving laugh. 'That's ridiculous. I can understand if there's no next of kin, but surely—'

'It would be very different if you had a close relationship with the child. However, during the flight you told me that you have not met each other before this moment?'

'But she's my niece!'

'Blood is not everything, Mr Kelly.' Joshua turned to Emma with a piercing look. 'Emma, are you willing to make this commitment to Angel?'

James broke in. 'Just a minute, you can't seriously be suggesting that Louise and I should move to live here for two years! We both have careers. For me to come here now, just for a few days, was almost impossible to arrange.'

The Minister raised his eyebrows. Then he looked back at Emma. 'And what about you? I ask again and I beg you to answer thoughtfully – are you in a position to make this kind of commitment?'

Emma felt Angel's body growing still, her breath held in her chest. 'Yes, I am.'

'And do you truly want to?'

She smiled down at Angel. 'I want it more than anything.'

Angel let out her breath, resting her head against Emma's side.

'And so,' Joshua continued, addressing Emma, 'you are planning to move here to Tanzania? That is a big change.'

'Yes, it is,' Emma said, 'but I can do it. I know I can.' As she spoke she was struck by how certain she not only sounded, but felt.

'I understand you plan to join Daniel in his work on Olambo fever? He has told me you are a very experienced medical researcher.'

Emma looked across to Daniel. He gave her an encouraging nod. 'We want to begin a new research project. We believe we may have found the link that will make the development of a vaccine possible.'

James cleared his throat, wanting to bring the conversation back on track, but Joshua appeared not to notice. He was quiet for a moment, looking away into the distance. When he turned back to Emma she saw a shadow of pain in his eyes. 'This matter is very close to my heart. I lost my only son to the bleeding fever.'

Daniel said something, then, in Maa, that brought a sad smile to Joshua's face. Then Daniel switched back to English. 'But our research will rely on the lion camp remaining here and on the poachers being driven out of the area.'

'George's lions are the key,' Emma said. 'They live in both worlds – animal and human. They are unique. They must be protected.' She was aware of George's grateful eyes resting on her as she spoke.

Joshua waved his hand towards the police officer. 'That is why I brought my friend Mr Malindi here today. He is going to investigate why the application Mr Lawrence made to have a national park declared has been ignored. I wanted Mr Malindi to come here and meet Mr Lawrence and see the camp, the lions – everything – before he begins his enquiry.'

George's face was tight with anxiety. 'But what does that mean? Time will go by and the poachers are killing animals all the time . . .'

Joshua smiled. 'You will see a temporary ranger's post established here within two weeks. As soon as the legislation has been passed the park will be declared.' He looked into George's eyes. 'Do not worry. It will happen. When I return to Dar es Salaam I will discuss this new research with the Minister for Health. He, too, will be supporting it. If necessary we will go together to speak to the President.'

George's mouth hung open. He seemed stunned with amazement and joy.

The Minister shifted his attention back to Angel. He didn't crouch to her level – he just looked down at her like someone who was well used to being taller than his companions. 'Now I would like to ask you a few questions, Angel. Where were you born?'

'In the fig-tree *manyata*.'

'The one by the story hill? I know it well. Did you live there long?'

'We didn't really live there. We didn't live anywhere. We just travelled around with our camels, stopping in places where people needed our help. When we ran out of medicine we went back to the Sisters of Mercy to get more. When we had no money, we went to a town and found a bank.' She nodded wisely. 'Mama had lots of money, but we never wasted it.'

'Laura had a trust fund from our father,' James said. 'I didn't realise she was working like that. We lost touch years ago. Our lives were so different. She was always wild, headstrong, getting involved in mad schemes. I assumed she was just . . . having fun.'

'We did have fun!' Angel said. 'We did everything we wanted to.'

Emma heard the faint crack in her voice, and stroked her shoulder. Through the thin cloth of the tunic, she felt the warmth of her skin.

'So you liked living in that way?' Joshua asked. 'Just you and your mama.'

'And Mama Kitu and Matata,' Angel added.

'Who are they?'

'Our camels. Mama Kitu is a very good camel. She sent Emma to look for me.'

Joshua smiled gently. 'So, what would you like to happen now?'

'She's just a child!' James protested.

Joshua shook his head. 'She has buried her mother with her own hands. She has lived with a lion. She is not "just" anything.' He turned back to Angel. When he spoke again, Emma immediately recognised the distinctive cadences of Maa. He talked for some time. His last sentence ended with his voice rising questioningly.

'I want to stay with Emma and Daniel,' Angel responded in a

firm voice. 'I want to be able to see Moyo and the cubs, and George-Lawrence and Ndisi. I want to get my camels back.' As she talked, James moved closer as if drawn physically by her words. 'I want to visit my friend Zuri. And the nuns. There's another thing – I have to go to the *manyata* at the foot of Ol Doinyo Lengai. I have something for the chief. And I'm teaching Ndisi how to knit.'

James looked as if he were seeing Angel properly for the first time. Admiration and fascination mingled on his face, along with the shadow of disappointment and loss. Joshua was watching his reaction; when Angel fell quiet, he spoke to her uncle in a kind tone. 'You can see for yourself – she is an African child. She belongs here.' His gaze was soft with compassion. 'This is a difficult time for you. You are grieving for your sister. I am sorry for your sadness. But I must listen to Angel.'

James stared at him for a second, then looked down at the ground. He wiped his nose with the back of his hand, and rubbed at his eyes. Then he lifted his face. 'To be honest, I think it's what Laura would have wanted.' He turned to Emma. 'I think she would have liked you.'

Emma smiled at him through a film of tears. 'Thank you.'

Angel stepped forward then, approaching James. Emma felt a twinge of anxiety. She wanted to pull Angel back and hold her tight.

'Uncle James?' Angel said. 'I'm really sorry you can't have me. I didn't mean to be rude.'

James reached out his hand and ruffled her hair. 'Maybe we can be friends. Write letters. One day you might visit.' He wiped a tear from his face and gave her a grin.

Joshua gave him a respectful look, then shifted his attention to

Emma. 'You will have to come to Arusha and have a formal interview with a social worker. Documents will have to be drawn up. Her schooling will also have to be discussed.'

'There is a school in the village near the station,' Daniel said. 'The teacher is a friend of mine – a Maasai.'

Angel turned to him eagerly. 'Can I have a uniform?'

'Of course,' Daniel said, 'you must wear a uniform like all the other children.'

Angel's eyes lit up as she looked around at Moyo to share her excitement.

Joshua watched her for a moment, before addressing Emma again. 'There are many plans to be made. But it can all wait a few weeks. This child needs time to recover from her loss, that is the most important thing.' He paused, as if running through some last thoughts. The quiet seemed to lengthen, stretching thin. Emma held her breath. Finally he nodded slowly. 'I am officially leaving her in your care. If all goes well, I see no reason why this arrangement should ever have to change.'

Emma closed her eyes for a second, unable to speak.

'Of course,' Joshua added, 'if you were to marry, your future husband would have to be assessed as well.' He gave Daniel a cheeky look. 'The Department would have to be confident that he was the kind of man who would make a good father.' Joshua's face turned serious as he said in a low voice to Emma, 'I am glad to see my old friend happy again.'

Emma smiled. 'I am happy as well.'

George's voice broke in over hers. 'I think we've stood out here for long enough. Everyone should come inside for a cup of tea. Or better still, an early sundowner.' There were murmurs of agreement. George put his hand on James's arm. 'You should spend some time with Angel before you go. She can introduce you to the cubs.' He shepherded James away towards the gate.

Dimly, Emma was aware of Joshua joining George and James. Mr Malindi followed them, accompanied by Ndisi, Samu and the pilot. Emma and Daniel stayed with Angel and Moyo.

Emma knelt on the ground in front of Angel. 'You're going to stay here with us. You really are! We don't have to worry any more.'

Angel's blue eyes were awash with tears. '*Asante*,' she said. '*Asante sana*.'

Emma pulled her close, hugging her tight. She breathed wood smoke, soap and a hint of Moyo's lion smell. The Swahili phrase Angel had taught her came back to her. *Si neno*. No words. She pressed her lips into Angel's hair.

There are no words.

She felt Daniel's hand brush her head, then come to rest on her shoulder. She looked up into his smiling face. As she rose to her feet, she took his hand, folding her fingers around his. Angel held her other hand. Moyo led the way back into the camp. Her powerful tawny body walked ahead of them, paws padding over the sand, throwing up swirls of grey dust. On the smooth ground her distinctive tracks could be clearly seen, the three undamaged feet and the one with the injured pad. Within moments they were joined by three more sets of prints – those of a man, a woman and one small child, moving forward together, making a new pattern of their own.

AUTHOR'S NOTE

The character of George-Lawrence was inspired by the original 'lion man', George Adamson, of *Born Free* and *Christian the Lion* fame. My interest in George Adamson arose while I was researching the making of the film version of *Born Free* for my novel, *The Hunter's Wife*. (Adamson was the lion handler for the production and later rehabilitated some of the lions used in the film.) George Adamson's autobiography, *Bwana Game*, gives a fascinating picture of his life, as does Sandy Gall's book and documentary film, both titled *Lord of the Lions*. Tragically, George Adamson was murdered by bandits – possibly poachers – at his isolated camp in Kora, Kenya, in 1989, when he was eighty-three years old.

Olambo fever is a fictitious disease modelled on haemorrhagic fevers such as Lassa and Ebola. These two diseases have not, historically, been a threat in Tanzania. However, countries all over the world are potentially at risk of outbreaks of deadly viral diseases. The dangerous but crucial work carried out by virus hunters from the Centre for Disease Control in Atlanta, USA, is well documented in the book, *Level 4 Virus Hunters of the CDC* by Joseph McCormick and Susan Fisher-Hoch.

Since ancient times there have been stories of children being raised by animals. Legend has it that the founders of the city of Rome, Romulus and Remus, were reared by wolves, and there are more recent, well-documented cases of children being kept alive by a range of foster-parents including apes, dogs, wolves, sheep and goats. There is even an account of a 'gazelle boy' living in the Sahara. Children who spend substantial periods of time being solely nurtured by animals can't usually re-adapt to a conventional lifestyle and their stories are inevitably tragic. But there are intriguing cases where animals have brought babies or children into their families for short periods of time, before rescuers have arrived and returned the humans to their normal world. Far from being tragic, these stories are both uplifting and challenging. As an example, while researching *Lioness* I came across a news report about a teenage girl in Ethiopia, who had been abducted from her village by a group of men. Her cries of distress were heard by a pride of lions who surrounded her, driving off her attackers. She was later found by police, unharmed and still in the company of the pride.

The setting of *Lioness* was inspired by my visit to the Lake Natron region in northern Tanzania. The soda lake – which is a breeding ground for flamingos – is not far from Ol Doinyo Lengai. Ash scattered by the volcano during its frequent eruptions has created the hauntingly beautiful yet desolate plains that surround both the lake and the volcano.

Though the musician Nasango is a fictitious character, there is a vibrant hip-hop culture in Tanzania. The Arusha-based Maasai group 'X Plastaz' is known for blending traditional chanting with

Swahili rap. One of their video clips was filmed partly on the summit of Ol Doinyo Lengai and includes images of the unusual white lava.

ACKNOWLEDGEMENTS

I would like to express my appreciation to everyone at Penguin Australia – it has been such a privilege to work with you again. Ali Watts and Belinda Byrne, your contributions have been both invaluable and enjoyable. My thanks to all at Curtis Brown Australia, especially Fiona Inglis, and to Kate Cooper in London. I am very grateful to Dr Alan Champion for providing vital assistance with medical science research and to Clare, Elizabeth, Hilary and Robin Smith and Kate Bendall for reading the manuscript and offering helpful advice. A big thank you to my trusty Tanzania safari companions, Elizabeth, Robin and Andrew 'Fujo' Smith, and to the wonderful Vanessa Smith for making an amazing journey possible. Thank you also to Jonny and Linden Scholes and Hamish Maxwell-Stewart for your encouraging company on the long journey of this book, and to my ever-supportive dear friends and relatives, including – as always – the Curry Girls. Most of all I want to acknowledge the involvement of Roger Scholes, who shares my passion for the themes of this story, and without whose tireless help and inspiration *Lioness* could not have been written.

THE STONE ANGEL

One summer changed Stella Boyd forever.
It was 1975. And his name was Zeph.

Fifteen years later, Stella's life is full of excitement and danger as she travels the world writing magazine articles about women. But then one day she receives an urgent message that changes everything. Her father is missing at sea.

Stella heads home to Halfmoon Bay, the Tasmanian fishing village where she grew up. She desperately doesn't want to face the painful memories that await her. But as she takes part in the search for her father, the life of her old home draws in around her. She finds herself taken back to that extraordinary summer when she met a young man who was sailing the world alone. A time of devastating tragedy, but also of first love . . .

Like the sea itself, the past rises up, refusing to be ignored. There are dark secrets to be unearthed, lost dreams recovered. Only then can hearts be healed, and an unexpected reward be claimed.

'Full of passion . . . Wonderful stuff.'
AUSTRALIAN WOMEN'S WEEKLY

'A beautifully descriptive read and a soul-searching take on human relationships.'
NEW IDEA

'A truly absorbing book filled with secrets and conflicts.'
WOMAN'S DAY